Praise for Susan Grace's GOLDEN FIRE

"Golden Fire is a seductive and rich historical saga with a tempestuous romance. I loved it!"
—Bertrice Small, NY Times–bestselling author

"Susan Grace dishes up a passionate and suspenseful historical adventure, a magical story tinted with the true colors of exotic India and England."
—*Romantic Times*

"Golden Fire is a sensational reading experience from a new author destined to be a bestseller!"
—Virginia Henley, NY Times–bestselling author

"Susan Grace has woven a wonderful tale that captures the reader from page one. A rich story told with compassion, and the passion in it is sizzling. Five stars!"
—*Affaire de Coeur*

"A treasure to add to anyone's collection of keepers! Full of suspense, danger, and one of the most passionate romances I have read in a long time! Five stars!"
—*Huntress Reviews*

TO TRAP A MURDERER . . .

"I offered you freedom, but you decided to stay and help me. Why?" Miles asked.

Avoiding his gaze, Catherine shrugged and sat on the sofa. "Because you needed me."

Miles sat beside her. "So you cut your hair and agreed to go through with this plan to trap Edward Damien just for me?"

"Being smug doesn't become you, English. I'm going through with this charade for you *and* Victoria."

"But you don't know Victoria," Miles pointed out, trying to mask his disappointment.

"As I listened to you talk about her, I came to admire Victoria Carlisle. I can't let the man responsible for her disappearance go unpunished."

Miles took her hand. "And what have you learned about me, Cat?"

Catherine gazed into his eyes. "You may be a titled lord, but your spirit yearns to be free. I pray you won't sacrifice your soul for someone else's dreams."

DESTINY'S LADY

Susan Grace

Zebra Books
Kensington Publishing Corp.

http://www.zebrabooks.com

I dedicate this book to six extraordinary people:

To Katherine Kelly Lang and Ronn Moss, who inspired me with their passion and performances to create Cat and Miles and the story that became DESTINY'S LADY.

To the late Kay McMahon, a wonderful author and friend who told me to learn patience and to have faith in my work no matter what.

To Bertrice Small, for her support and friendship, and for being the very best "big sister" I could ever have.

To Kathryn Falk, who told me years ago that I was going to "do it" and didn't lose confidence in me.

And to my husband, John, who loves me and never stopped believing in me or my dream of becoming an author.

ZEBRA BOOKS are published by

Kensington Publishing Corp.
850 Third Avenue
New York, NY 10022

First Printing: May, 2000
10 9 8 7 6 5 4 3 2 1

Printed in the United States of America

Prologue

Fellsmere Manor
Eastern coast of Ireland
October 18, 1783

"Drop that knife, woman, or by all that's holy, I shall use the damned blade on you!" Geoffrey Carlisle was horrified to discover the midwife cutting the hand of his newborn child.

"But, Your Grace," the woman stammered, "I had no choice. Your daughters are exactly alike. A heritage scar is necessary to prove who was firstborn and your heir. If you ne'er have a son, this babe will carry your title."

Geoffrey's ancestor Jonathan Carlisle, the third Duke of Chatham, had been a loyal supporter of Elizabeth Tudor. To show her gratitude, the young queen asked what he would desire as his reward.

Though a duke with great wealth, Jonathan lacked a male heir. He had six daughters, but without a son his title and estates would revert to the crown on his death.

Elizabeth granted him a special boon. If a son wasn't born into the Carlisle family, the oldest girl would inherit all. After marriage, she would retain the Carlisle name and pass it and the title on to her son. The queen's edict was perpetual, assuring a true descendant of Jonathan Carlisle would always hold the title and rights to Chatham.

"The wee lass didn't suffer overly from the cut, and it will heal quickly, Your Grace."

The midwife prattled on as Geoffrey looked at the two naked babies on the bed. The tiny girls were identical, right down to the birthmark every child born into the Carlisle family for more than ten generations had carried—a unique crescent-shaped mark over the heart.

Kneeling beside the bed, he kissed his daughter's bleeding palm and silently apologized for the injury. Geoffrey regretted the need to prove his heir, but it was his responsibility.

Responsibility was something Geoffrey had mastered early in life. He'd been eighteen when his father died, leaving him little more than a title. Malcolm Carlisle's wife died birthing their only child, and he had never recovered from the loss. Abandoning Geoffrey to the care of servants, Malcolm spent his remaining years drinking and gambling away the family's vast fortune.

When Geoffrey discovered the sorry state of his inheritance, he pledged to restore his family's financial status. Over the next nine years, his entire life had revolved around those goals, making him one of the wealthiest men in Europe. His success in business earned him the nickname of Lord Midas. But, like his mythical namesake, the ambitious young duke eventually learned wealth wasn't enough. He fell in love.

"Geoffrey? Are the babies all right? They seem awfully quiet for newborns."

The sound of his wife's voice shook Geoffrey from his reverie. Smiling at his beloved Evangeline, he swaddled

the babies in their blankets and gently lifted them for her
to see. "Our daughters are fine, my sweet. Enjoy the peace
while you can, for I believe these two will soon prove to
be quite a handful."

As if on cue, one of the babies began crying, and no
amount of cooing could stop the high-pitched wails. Taking the child from her husband, Evangeline held it to her
breast.

"Geoffrey, we agreed to name our first daughter Catherine Elizabeth for your mother. Since there are two, I'd like
to name the other in memory of my own mother, Victoria
Roxanne. Could we do that?"

The duke smiled into her sparkling blue eyes and
stroked back the lock of golden hair that had dipped onto
her forehead. "Catherine and Victoria are fine names, my
sweet, but which is which?"

Evangeline gazed at the tiny girl suckling at her breast.
As the babe drew on the nipple, her little fist opened to
reveal the cut. "This one is Catherine," she replied sadly.

Sensing his wife's distress. Geoffrey decided on another
way of telling their daughters apart. He hired a local jeweler
to make a gold heart-shaped pendant for each, the polished center to be engraved with the daughter's initial.

He put the fine gold pendants on his daughters and
ordered that they were not to be removed.

Geoffrey swore he would never look at the accursed scar
again.

The Price of Envy
Ireland & England
December, 1784

Chapter 1

Fellsmere Manor

"Catherine Elizabeth, you're a precious jewel of a child, but when are you going to sleep through the night like your sister? 'Tis well past midnight and you're wide awake," the old woman scolded as she wrapped the baby in a pink blanket.

Having raised and nurtured three generations of Carlisles, eighty-year-old Ella McKay from Dublin was more of a family member than a servant. She refused to let her advanced age stop her from caring for the twins.

Victoria and Catherine had their mother's blond hair and dainty features. But their eyes, though blue at birth, were now emerald green. Ella loved both children, yet the temperament of this twin intrigued her. A little over a year old, Catherine was always climbing on furniture and exploring the house. She was curious and vocal.

Careful not to disturb anyone else, Ella carried the child

down to the kitchen pantry. Holding the baby in her arms, Ella poured milk into a cup.

She suddenly heard men's voices coming toward the kitchen. She recognized the voices of Dicky and Billets, two men recently hired to work around the manor. Not wanting to be seen in her bedclothes, she closed the pantry door.

"Why's it gotta be t'night, Dicky? Thar's a storm comin'."

"You bloody fool, tha's why it's gotta be now! No one's gonna be out in this kind o' squall, and tha' means no witnesses!"

"I wonder what 'e got against these folks, Dicky. They seems like a nice lot t' me."

"Well, 'is lordship wants 'em dead. He won't get 'is heritance if we don't kill 'em all."

Ella pressed her ear to the door as she listened. Their thick accents made it difficult, but the words she made out caused her heart to skip a beat.

"Billets, grab dem candles 'n fetch me tha' jug o' lamp oil. This place is gonna burn like a tinderbox if we does it right."

"But, Dicky, killin' babes ain't right," Billets whined. "We's gonna rot in 'ell for this, you know. An' if we gets caught, our necks won't be worf a bloomin' farthing."

"You should'a thought o' that afore this, you bloody dolt. Cross Edward Damien now, and 'es likely to kill you 'isself! Now remember, if anyone gets in the way, use your gun and shoot 'em. Let's light the fire and get outta 'ere."

The horror of what she'd overheard sank into Ella's mind. "Oh, Edward, your envy of Geoffrey has gone too far this time. After all your brother's done for you, how could you arrange such a foul deed?"

Ellie eased open the door and peeked out into the kitchen. *Dear God, what can I do? Those men have gone toward the stairs! I cannot get past them to alert everyone else.*

Feeling a tug on her hair, Ella looked down to see

Catherine staring at her. The baby started banging her hand on the door. "Saints above, Catherine, I've got to get you out of here. Don't make a sound. Ella will keep you safe, I promise."

When she stepped out of the pantry, the air was thick with the noxious fumes of lamp oil. She heard the men coming back toward the kitchen, and she smelled smoke. Wrapping the blanket around Catherine, Ella rushed to the alcove where her wool cape hung. She grabbed it, threw it over her shoulders, and escaped through the rear door into the blustery night.

The only time she looked back, flames burned brightly in the windows of the first floor. The glass panes began blowing out, and the flames flared higher. Even from a distance, she recognized Billets and Dicky when they ran from the front of the house. Covering the baby with her cloak, she started running again. In her desperation, she didn't realize she was heading toward the sea.

Sleet fell in torrents. Ella was soon wet and cold. Her sodden slippers offered little protection from the hard ground, but still she continued to run. With the babe pressed hard against her beneath the damp cape, Ella found herself wandering along the rocky shore.

The sleet stopped, and the full moon peeked out from behind the clouds. In the distance, torches flickered in the wind. She instinctively rushed toward them.

Ship's captain Sean O'Banyon set his crew of Irish smugglers to delivering a load of cargo. Then, as if God had guided his eyes, he saw the old woman stumbling toward them and called his first mate, Padraic. Before they reached her, she fell to the ground. Sean knelt beside the gasping woman and tried to help her sit up.

"Mother, be patient with you now. Let my mate and me carry you to our fire."

Obviously in pain, the woman shook her head and struggled to talk. "Too late for me. You must take her away. Her family was murdered ... meant to kill her, too ... but ... I fooled them ... told her I'd save her."

Her voice was so low, Sean had to lean over her mouth to hear what she said. "Who are you talking about, Mother? Have you left someone down the beach who needs help?" Before she could reply, a curly blond head peeked out from the folds of her cape.

The baby looked up at him and smiled. Her hand reached over to touch his fuzzy cheek. As he stared at the pretty child, she yanked on his thick red beard.

"Ouch, that hurts!" Sean pulled her hand from his whiskers. Instead of cringing in fear, the tiny girl giggled. The sound of her laughter brought a smile to his lips.

"Her name is Catherine. Please don't let them harm her," Ella pleaded.

"But who does the wee lass belong to, Mother? Has she no relatives to take her in?"

The old woman shook her head. "No one is left. She's alone now. Promise me you'll keep her safe and find her a good home."

"I swear I'll protect the wee lass and see she's well cared for," he assured her. "You've naught to fear, good woman. Sean O'Banyon, the Irish Hawk, always keeps his word."

"See that you do, O'Banyon, or I pledge to return and haunt you myself." Ella touched the baby's cheek with her finger as a sharp pain wrenched her heart. "You be good, Catherine, and know your Ella is still watching over you." A look of peace settled on her features as she closed her eyes and died.

Sean lifted the baby in his large, calloused hands. Wrapping his cloak around her, he instructed Padraic to get some of the men to bury Ella. Then he walked down the beach toward his anchored ship.

Leaning her head on his shoulder, Catherine stroked

his beard. In the moonlight, Sean was captivated by her trusting smile. He would never give this child away.

"Well, little lady, it appears destiny has brought us together, and that's where you're gonna stay. You'll be my daughter. My wife Erin is always telling me how she wants more children, so I'm sure she'll be quite pleased to have you in the family."

Padraic watched his friend walk away with the little girl, and Sean's words carried back to him on the wind.

". . . your new brothers, Colin and Roderick. But don't you ever be callin' Roderick by his given name. Though he's but a lad of five, he won't answer to anything but Rory. Damned stubborn lad he is! Can't imagine where he gets that foul trait."

Chapter 2

Carlisle House
London
December 10, 1784

"Of all the luck, mine must be the most damned!"

Edward Damien's mood was as dark as his onyx eyes and brown hair. After all the planning and expense, his ambitious scheme had failed. He scowled at his brother's portrait, which hung over the mantel in the study.

"Damn you to hell, Geoffrey. Our father, Malcolm, may have been lacking as a parent, but at least he gave you the title and the noble Carlisle name. I was the bastard he hid in an orphanage until you found me twelve years ago." Edward raked his fingers through his tousled hair. "You have it all, Geoffrey, even the woman I love. Bloody hell! Evangeline should have been mine."

Evangeline was the only child of Sir Thomas Westlake, one of Geoffrey's business partners, who had died two years earlier. Westlake's will named the Duke of Chatham his daughter's guardian. After discussing it with Edward, Geoffrey agreed to bring the child to live at their family estate as his ward.

But Evangeline, almost nineteen years old, was the most beautiful young woman either brother had ever seen.

Edward had welcomed Evangeline into their home. For the first time in his life, he was in love. While Geoffrey was away on business, Edward took her to church and escorted her to social events. Friendly and charming, Evangeline seemed to return his affection. He'd never been so happy. After he completed his final term at Oxford and took on the position Geoffrey had offered him at Carlisle Enterprises, he planned on asking Evangeline to be his wife.

"You ruined that for me, Geoffrey!" Edward snarled at the painting. "While I was at university, you abandoned your work to romance my Evangeline and propose to her yourself. I went home and begged her to marry me instead, but she turned me down and claimed she was in love with you. All she could offer me was friendship!"

Weighed down by his memories, Edward sat in the chair beside the hearth and drained the brandy from his glass. The pain of Evangeline's rejection had set in motion circumstances that drastically changed his life. He'd angrily accused her of using him and leading him on with false hope. Of course she'd want Geoffrey, he'd shouted. His brother had the wealth and the title, while he was born a bastard with nothing—and the moment she told Geoffrey about Edward's rage over their upcoming marriage, he'd lose his brother, too.

His accusations may have had some validity, because Evangeline didn't defend herself or tell Geoffrey of their confrontation. Hoping to add to her guilt, Edward didn't return to Oxford. He remained at home and taunted her with his presence. He stared at her during meals. When she passed him in the halls, he turned to watch her. He never spoke to her unless Geoffrey was present. His silence and watchful eyes made her miserable.

Geoffrey faulted himself for her distress. Evangeline had lived a very simple life on her father's rural estate in Sussex. He feared his zeal to show off his lovely country girl to society and the grand plans he'd made for their wedding were plaguing her. Rather than subject her to any further pressures, the duke made some decisions that surprised Edward.

The elaborate wedding was canceled and a small informal ceremony was arranged. After the wedding, Geoffrey would take his wife to his mother's family estate in Ireland, a lovely rustic area on the coast he was sure would please Evangeline.

But the duke's plans for him stunned Edward the most. During his absence, Geoffrey asked Edward to run Carlisle Enterprises. When Edward pointed out he was hardly qualified for the position, the duke refused to hear it. They were family, and he wanted his brother to be a part of his business. Touched by his brother's sentiments, Edward accepted the offer, hoping hard work and time apart would cure him of his infatuation with Evangeline.

As agreed, Edward took over Geoffrey's position at Carlisle Enterprises. For his services, he received a generous salary and a portion of the profits. He did extremely well the first year. Every month, he and Geoffrey exchanged letters. Although the messages were cordial, they always pertained to business.

But the letter Geoffrey sent the previous October had been different. Instead of questions on market stability, it was an announcement of good news—Evangeline had given birth to a pair of beautiful girls. The love in the duke's words tore into Edward, whose buried feelings of jealousy rushed to the surface.

"Damn you, Geoffrey! If not for you, Evangeline and I would have been together and those babes would be mine.

You're happy, but all I do is work." Edward tossed the letter aside. "The bishop is right! Starting today, I'm going to live for me."

Bishop Chamberlain had been Edward's confidant since meeting him at Oxford two years before. The highly respected church leader had known and despised Malcolm Carlisle. Through the elderly cleric, Edward learned how Malcolm forced his mother to abandon him. The bishop tried to convince Edward to seek revenge against Geoffrey because of his bastard status, but he had refused to until now.

He sought out his old friends from school and was soon caught up in their social circle. He became a well-known player at London's private clubs. Gambling challenged him, but his luck soured. He went through his own funds and signed notes to cover his debts. When his markers were no longer accepted, he took funds from Geoffrey's holdings. In desperation, he forged his brother's signature on a note, using the Westlake stables and the estate Evangeline had inherited from her father as collateral.

A few days later, Edward received a letter from Geoffrey regarding the Westlake property. In the missive, the duke told him of his plans to visit the breeding farm when he returned to England with his family for Christmas.

It was only a matter of time before Geoffrey discovered his crime. The thought of going to prison inflamed the anger he had stored up. It was all Geoffrey's fault, he decided. His brother had everything: the money, the title, and the woman Edward loved. He despised Geoffrey and Evangeline. He wanted them to suffer. They had to die.

After making inquiries, Edward hired two men and sent them to destroy the house in Fellsmere. If Geoffrey and his family were killed, he'd be the sole surviving heir. As a bastard, he couldn't inherit the title, but all of his brother's wealth would belong to him. It was a perfect plan.

Or so Edward had thought.

Today he'd gotten word from the authorities in Ireland that Geoffrey's home had suffered a terrible fire. Local rebels were suspected of starting the blaze, but thanks to a change in the wind, only the servants' wing, kitchen, and nursery had been destroyed. The housekeeper and one of the Carlisle babies were killed in the blaze, their bodies burned to ashes by the intense flames.

The constable reported the duke and his wife had taken Victoria into their room when she woke up crying during the night. Geoffrey and the baby were fine, but Evangeline had been injured when she tried to rescue the other child. As soon as the duchess was up to traveling, the family planned on returning to England. The doctor was confident the trip could be made in six weeks. Geoffrey would contact him with the details.

Refilling his glass with brandy, Edward paced the study. "Six weeks, six months, even six years! Where in the hell can I get thirty thousand pounds? My friends have disappeared from sight, and because of my damnable debts, I can't get into White's or the other clubs to look for them. The bishop is too ill to help me. The only place I'm welcome is Sedwick Manor . . ."

Edward smiled. The Countess of Sedwick, Lorelei St. James, was a beautiful widow and one of the wealthiest women in England. While others treated him with disdain, she offered him an open invitation to her palatial home and grand parties. Edward was sure he could rely on their friendship to secure the funds he needed.

He would send word and pay a visit to her today. Lorelei would help him.

Lorelei St. James shook out the skirt of her lavender silk gown and preened before her mirror. "Do you think Edward will approve of my gown, Rosalie?"

Her maid laughed with familiarity. "The man would

have to be blind not to, my lady. The gown flatters that
fine figure of yours and the color matches your eyes. He'll
be dazzled."

Lorelei sat at her dressing table to brush her thick sable
hair. "Dazzled is a fine start, Rosalie, but I mean to have
Edward Damien for my own."

"A lusty lad like him will certainly keep your bed warm."

"I want more than my bed warmed, Rosalie. Edward will
be my husband." Lorelei waved her brush at her maid.
"And if you say one word about my robbing the nursery
by marrying such a young man, I'll throw your worthless
self from the balcony."

Chuckling, Rosalie took the brush from her mistress's
hand. "You'll do no such thing, my lady. I've been with
you since you were a girl, and no one knows you like me.
If marrying this fellow makes you happy, then I'm all for
it. Now let me finish your hair so you'll be ready when he
arrives."

Lorelei stared pensively into the mirror. "Men take
younger spouses all the time. Why, I was barely seventeen
when I married Vincent, and he was forty-nine."

"And what a scandal that caused," the maid chortled.
"I couldn't blame you for marrying a handsome widower
with the wealth of a king and no kin. He loved you."

"Vincent St. James was a weakling," Lorelei countered.
"When his peers treated him like a pariah for marrying a
merchant's daughter, he refused to fight back. He put on
a brave front, but I knew the ostracization of the *ton* caused
Vincent a great deal of pain." She scowled. "Those con-
temptuous prigs pushed him into drinking. Within two
years, he was dead."

"Aye, but you had your revenge on them all, my lady."

Lorelei smiled at the memory. Using her wealth, she
had declared war against the *ton*. She'd made friends with
others who had been shunned or cast aside by the social
elite of London. The Countess of Sedwick became queen

of the rakehells, defender of the outcasts, and champion of the abandoned mistresses of the nobility. At her home, she hosted parties for her friends. Besides serving good food and liquor, there was music for dancing and a salon set up for gambling.

Years had passed, and her parties were still well known. That was how she'd met Edward Damien. From the first time she saw him, Lorelei was drawn to the handsome young man. Once she knew of his background, she began making plans.

Even though Edward was bastard born, he was a Carlisle. Being married to the half brother of a powerful duke might help her gain the acceptance of polite society. After eighteen years, Lorelei was being ignored by the *ton*. As Edward's wife, new possibilities would be open to her.

When she learned of his gambling debts, she had her solicitors buy up all his markers, as well as the note on the Sussex property. Edward owed *her,* and he was desperate. His visit this day would make her task easier. When her butler came to her suite and announced her visitor was waiting in the drawing room, Lorelei stood up and moved toward the door.

"Good luck, my lady," Rosalie called out.

Lorelei laughed triumphantly. "Luck has little to do with it, Rosalie. Success will be mine."

"Edward, darling, I'm so pleased to see you." Lorelei smiled as he kissed her hand. "Would you care for some tea? My chef, Henri, has quite a way with meringue tarts."

Edward shook his head. "No thank you, my lady. As tempting as they sound, I haven't much of an appetite this afternoon."

"Poor dear," she crooned, "it's obvious something is troubling you. Sit down and tell me all about it."

The image of heartfelt concern, Lorelei patted Edward's hand while he explained his need for a loan. When he was through, she sighed. "We're good friends, Edward, and if it were a few hundred pounds, I wouldn't think twice about it. But what can you offer as collateral for the exorbitant sum of thirty thousand pounds?"

He shrugged. "Only my promise to repay the debt with interest. I'd work day and night to see it done."

"I believe your sincerity, but I can't loan you the money."

Dejected, Edward got up to leave. "Well, thank you for listening to me, Countess."

"One moment, Edward. I won't lend you the money, but I *would* give it to you."

"Why would you do that?"

"As a wedding present, darling. You're everything I want in a husband. Besides wealth and a home, I can give you a title. Marry me, and you become the new Earl of Sedwick."

"Me, an earl? But that's impossible!"

Lorelei smiled. "With my money and the friends I've acquired over the years, nothing is impossible. Many owe me favors, including the Crown Prince. I introduced him to his beloved, Mrs. FitzHerbert. Prinny has already had the documents delivered to me regarding your confirmation as the new Earl of Sedwick. Say yes and it will be yours."

In less than a moment, Edward nodded. "All right, Lorelei. I'll marry you. But I need to have the money as soon as possible so I can redeem a mortgage on some property in Sussex."

"Don't trouble yourself with that, darling. My solicitor will take care of that repayment when he draws up our marriage contract. He'll see to it all your debts are paid. You'll also receive a very large allowance, and your living expenses will be taken care of. You'll have the title, the use of the house, and everything that goes with being the

Earl of Sedwick, but I will control my fortune. Do we have a deal?"

Edward smiled. "Yes, my lady. We have a deal."

He swept Lorelei into his arms and closed their transaction with a kiss.

Destiny's Lady
Catherine O'Banyon
Ireland
1784–1802

Chapter 3

The morning after Ella's death, Sean O'Banyon docked his ship in Corbin's Cove. With the baby the old woman had entrusted to him sleeping in his arms, he made his way home. During his walk to his house nestled on a hill overlooking the village, Sean wondered what his wife's reaction would be.

He and Erin had been happily married for ten years. They had wanted a large family, but had been blessed with only two sons. The older boy, Rory, had red hair and a fiery temper like his sire. Two-year-old Colin resembled Erin, with dark hair, blue eyes, and a gentle disposition.

Sean quietly entered the house and found his wife busy at the stove stirring a large pot of soup. As if sensing his presence, Erin turned to face him. She put down the ladle and rushed to give him a proper welcome. When she spied the blanket-wrapped bundle in his arms, she stopped and looked up at him.

"Sean O'Banyon, don't tell me you brought the boys another pet. I'm at me wits end with the two dogs and

three kittens you brought back from your other voyages."
Erin sighed. "Just tell me, is it a pup or a wee cat you've
graced me with this time?"

"Neither, my love. You see, I—"

At that moment, Catherine pushed the cover off her
head and blinked. Seeing Erin staring at her, she smiled
and held out her arms.

Erin took the baby from Sean. "You poor sweet darlin'.
Where did Hawk find you?" Sitting in her chair beside the
hearth, she held the little girl on her lap. Though the
child's nightdress was dirty, it was made of fine lawn fabric.
She noticed the gold chain around the child's neck and
pulled a heart-shaped pendant from beneath the gown.

"Sean O'Banyon, tell me where you got this babe. I'll
not be havin' any rich gentry tearin' down my door to
fetch their child back. Who is she and how did you come
to be having her?"

Kneeling beside her, Sean told Erin what happened the
night before on the deserted beach. "I promised the old
lady before she died that I'd care for the babe and protect
her from harm. Destiny's brought us the daughter you've
always wanted, Erin. I was hopin' you could find room in
your heart for this precious wee lass."

Erin's eyes sparkled with tears as she kissed the baby's
cheek. "Oh, Sean, how could you doubt me wanting this
angel? I've worn me knees raw in church beggin' God to
grant us another babe. It must have been His will. Can we
really keep her?"

Sean nodded. "The old woman said all her kin were
dead. The babe's name is Catherine. She can be Catherine
O'Banyon now. It has a pleasant sound, don't you agree?"

"Aye, Sean, 'tis a fine name indeed. Let's see about
gettin' this waif cleaned up and into warm clothes. Go to
our room and fetch me some of Colin's old baby things
from the chest."

* * *

From then on, Catherine was an O'Banyon. Rory and Colin were too young to ask questions and readily accepted her as their sister. Sean didn't know her date of birth, but she appeared to be a year old. The day she came to their family, December first, was thereafter celebrated as her birthday.

The years were good for the O'Banyons. Sean had great success in his pirating and smuggling jaunts. While he was away, Erin took loving care of their home and children.

Much to their delight, Catherine was a very bright child. When she was five, they asked the priest who taught school to allow her to attend classes with her brothers at the church. Father William thought educating girls was a waste of time, but, not wanting to infuriate Hawk, he grudgingly agreed.

Catherine proved the priest wrong and was an excellent pupil. Like Colin, she was adept at reading, writing, Latin, and arithmetic. Rory was sorely bored with school, though he enjoyed history. Catherine shared his enthusiasm for the subject and listened intently as the priest taught them about the explorers, wars, ancient civilizations, and countries that comprised the history of the world. She especially enjoyed the lessons about the Vikings and their long boats.

"Vikings were fierce warriors," Father William explained. "They believed the only honorable way to die was in battle, sword in hand. According to their beliefs, when a man was killed, one of the maidens of Odin, called a Valkyrie, would seek out those who died bravely and conduct them into Valhalla, the Viking heaven."

"Did a Valkyrie look like an angel?" Catherine asked.

The elderly priest smiled at the curious eleven-year-old. "She looked more like a warrior than the sort of angel Christians would expect to see." He opened the large book on his desk and held it up. "This is a drawing of a Valkyrie."

The illustration was of a tall woman with a horned helmet and long, plaited gold hair. She wore heavy armor across her chest and held a broadsword and shield.

Leaning over, Colin pulled on the end of Catherine's blond braid, "She's got hair just like yours, little sister."

Catherine shook with excitement. She was fascinated with the idea that a woman could be a warrior. The old priest had no idea what his lesson had evoked that day.

Between voyages, Sean spent most of his time with the children. Erin was concerned with their education, while he worried about their safety. He encouraged the boys to learn respect for weapons and how to use them. Rory and Colin were tutored in the use of swords and guns. Ireland was filled with civil unrest, and he wanted his sons ready to fight if the need ever arose.

"Da, when are you going to teach me how to use swords and guns?" Catherine asked him one day after he'd practiced swordplay with his sons in the barn.

Sean scowled at her. "Reading and writing are fine pursuits for young ladies, little girl. Fighting is men's work."

Catherine wouldn't be daunted by her father's refusal. When Sean and Colin went up to the house, leaving Rory practicing with his sword, she sought his help.

"You're very good with that sword, Rory. You'll be good as Da someday. Colin's not half as capable as you," she cooed. "You're so skilled, I bet you could teach anyone to fight."

"I am good, but I'll not be wastin' me time teachin' the likes o' you. You're naught but a lass, and you don't need to fight with swords," Rory snorted as he walked away from her.

"What's the matter, Roderick? Afraid you'll be a failure as a teacher? Did you hear me, Roderick? Don't think you're up to the task, Roderick?"

Catherine's use of his given name caused Rory to spin

around. "A body could get hurt for tormentin' me with
that name. Do yourself a favor, lass, and leave off!"

Catherine's smile wilted into a frown. "Oh, Rory, I'm
sorry, but I am desperate. I must learn to fight. What will
happen when you and Colin go off with Da? I'll be home
with Mam, and we'll be defenseless. I won't have my big
brother here to protect me. Whatever shall I do, Rory?"
Turning her teary eyes to his brought the results she
wanted.

"Oh, all right, Cat. I'll see what I can teach you. Just
remember, 'tis hard work. Rapiers are heavy and lasses are
not up to strenuous swordplay, so don't be ashamed if
you're not able to do it." He chuckled. "Now come on.
Let's begin your first lesson."

Much to Rory's surprise, Catherine learned well and
quickly. With their daily practice in the barn, she honed
her skills and endurance. Rory stopped laughing at his
sister. His amusement was replaced by respect, and he was
proud of how much she learned.

One day during a lesson. neither was aware of their
father's presence in the barn. Sean could hardly believe
his eyes. His golden-haired little girl was wielding a rapier
with poise and confidence. At first he was going to stop
the swordplay, but found himself intrigued by the vision
before him. Catherine was very good. She could anticipate
Rory's next move and was always a step ahead of him.
The match came to an abrupt conclusion when Catherine
caught his rapier at the hilt with her blade and flung his
weapon into a nearby pile of hay.

Instead of being angry, Rory cheered her feat. He
grabbed her up into his arms and spun her around. Soon
they fell into a haystack, laughing. Their laughter ceased
when Sean stood over them. Rory jumped to his feet,
avoiding his father's knowing stare. Catherine stood up,
brushed the hay from her clothes. Smiling, she boldly
looked Hawk in the eye.

"What's the matter, Da? Have you never heard of the Viking warrior maidens, the Valkyrie? They could handle a sword, and so can I."

Rory groaned. "Cat, 'tis not the time to anger Da with such tales."

Sean laughed and put his arms around them both. "I'd ne'er thought it possible, but Rory proved me wrong. A lass *can* learn how to fight. From here on, Cat, I will see to your training. We'll have the devil of a time getting your Mam to agree to it, but don't worry. Just leave her to me."

He was correct about Erin's acceptance of Catherine's need for such lessons. He begged, cajoled, and pleaded, but she would not defer. It was Catherine who got her to change her mind.

"Mam, remember when Father William said teaching girls was a waste of time? Now the old priest boasts I'm the best pupil he's ever had. Why don't you let me try these lessons for a time? If I don't do well, I'll stop."

As usual, Catherine got her way. After that, there were confrontations about her wearing britches, handling fire-arms, and riding horses astride. The worst one occurred when Catherine decided she wanted to go on a voyage.

She was fourteen years old and, much to her mother's chagrin, Catherine could outride any man in the parish, could outshoot anyone with a gun, and, with the exception of her father, no one could match her expertise with a rapier. Her brothers had been sailing with Sean for several years, and now she wanted to do that, too.

But nothing could convince Erin or Sean that she was capable of joining the crew of the *Cat's Cradle*. Catherine had always been able to talk her way in or out of anything she set her mind to. She refused to consider defeat. When the ship named for her set sail for its next voyage, she was determined to be on it.

First, Catherine assured her parents she'd accepted their refusal. She applied her time to reading. They failed to notice her choice of books all pertained to ships, sailing, and navigation.

Next, she "allowed" Colin to give her a tour of the ship. As he explained the workings of the *Cat's Cradle*, Catherine made mental notes on the location of the cabins, the hold, and anyplace else she might be able to hide. Her brother spoke of sails and riggings, never realizing what his sister was really doing.

Catherine gathered the items she needed for the voyage. Since she'd be hiding in cramped quarters, she could take only the bare essentials. In a canvas bag she packed a hairbrush, a shirt, britches, some undergarments, and a towel. Before the ship sailed, she added a small wheel of cheese, strips of dried meat, apples, and a cask of water. By rationing carefully, she'd be able to make her supplies last several days.

Everything was ready by the night the family gathered for their farewell dinner. As was their tradition, Padraic Flynn joined the O'Banyons for the special meal.

Padraic had been Sean's friend and first mate for many years. He was a large man with a craggy face. His thick mustache and dark hair were peppered with silver. His fierce gray eyes would frighten the devil himself, but never Catherine. As her Uncle Paddy, he usually knew her better than anyone else.

The food was good, but the cheerful mood of the gathering was restrained. Catherine's disappointment at not going with her father and brothers was felt by everyone.

Sean hugged her. "Cat, I pray you're not angry with me for saying no to this voyage. You could be in danger if you came with us, and I'll not take the chance of seeing you hurt."

"I know your reasons, Da. Someday you might even understand mine. I'm going to turn in. Since I don't want to embarrass you and myself by crying at the dock, I'll say farewell now."

Catherine kissed her parents and brothers. She hugged Padraic and kissed his ruddy cheek. She moved quickly away from him, but not before he saw the tears shining on her face.

After the boys and Erin went to bed, Padraic stayed a few minutes to talk to Sean. "Cat's never failed at anything she set her mind to. Mayhap you're wrong to refuse her this voyage."

Unhappily, Hawk shook his head. "She'll only get on that ship when I'm too old and feeble to stop her. Cat is a young woman. Women don't belong on pirating ships, and that's that."

Padraic smirked. " 'Tis a task easier said than done, Sean. I've a feelin' Cat will have her voyage sooner than you think."

When her family had retired for the night, Catherine dressed in black britches and a black shirt with long sleeves that she'd taken from Colin's closet. Checking her appearance in the mirror, she was amazed by what she saw.

Catherine hadn't realized how much she had grown. Not long ago, the clothes she borrowed from her brothers hung loose on her tall, lean frame. Now the britches hugged her hips, while the shirt pulled tight across her bosom.

Scowling at her reflection, Catherine brushed her blond hair. She never allowed her mother to do more than trim the ends of her hip-length tresses. Dividing it into three sections, she plaited it and secured the end with a leather thong. After pulling on her stockings and knee-high boots, Catherine secured her rapier to her waist with its belt and sheath. She tucked the jewel-handled dagger Rory had given her the previous Christmas into the top of her right boot.

After donning a dark blue cape with a hood that covered her hair, Catherine grabbed her seabag and climbed out the window. Her bedroom door was locked. Her mother expected her to be upset about the ship's departure, and Catherine knew Erin wouldn't check on her until noon. When her mother got into the room, she'd find a letter of explanation on the pillow.

In the note, Catherine had apologized for the deception. All of her life, a part of herself seemed to be missing. She hoped the voyage would help fill that void.

Keeping to the shadows, Catherine made her way through the village to the dock where the ship was anchored. Everyone in Corbin's Cove were friends or family to the O'Banyons. No one would steal from the Hawk, so a guard wasn't posted.

On board the *Cat's Cradle*, Catherine went to the empty hold. There was no cargo, so she would have privacy for a few days. If she were discovered after that, they'd be too far away to return home.

She'd spotted a large storage closet during her tour of the ship with Colin. It had a sturdy door with a small lattice window near the top that let air into the tiny room. Putting her bag on the floor, she scouted the deserted ship and soon had an old pillow, blankets, a flint, some candles, several books, and a bucket of water to use as a necessary. Securing the door to her hiding place, Catherine stretched out on her makeshift bed and fell into a deep, dream-filled sleep.

Catherine always had unusual dreams. In them, she wore beautiful clothes made of silks and lace. Sometimes she'd be dancing, sometimes eating food on fine china and sparkling crystal. Once in a while, she saw herself in a fabulous library filled with leather-bound books. One time she saw herself speaking to people in a strange foreign language.

But one dream had truly frightened her. She saw herself riding sidesaddle on a magnificent black stallion. The exhilaration she felt distracted her attention and the horse caught his hoof in a rut in the path. She screamed as she was thrown to the ground. In her dream, the pain in her leg was blinding in its intensity.

Ironically, the next morning Catherine had discovered she couldn't walk. Her leg throbbed and wouldn't support her weight. Later that day, as she related the events of her dream to Colin, she realized the leg she'd injured in her vision was the one giving her pain. Colin was the only person she ever told about her dreams. As her closest friend, he never teased her about her fancy musings.

Sean's voice shouting orders to his crew and the rocking caused by rough seas jolted Catherine from her sleep that first morning. Listening to the hull of the frigate gently groaning as it crashed through the waves, she laughed out loud at her victory.

"I did it! The *Cat's Cradle* has set sail and I'm on board. In a few days, when we're well away from home, I'll finally get to go up on deck. Dear God, I hope I can wait that long!"

During the next two days, Catherine passed some of the long hours alone exercising. Using the rapier her father had made for her, she practiced her fencing drills. The hilt was fitted to her smaller hand and allowed her to use the weapon with ease.

On the third day, Catherine was sitting on the floor of her sanctuary brushing her hair when the ship suddenly lurched to change course. She heard the commotion on deck as the orders to prepare for battle were given. Within moments, the sound of cannon fire drowned out all else. The acrid smell of gunpowder hung heavily in the air.

"This isn't fair," she declared, getting to her feet. "I didn't stow away on my father's ship so I could hide during a skirmish. If I'm careful, I can sneak up on deck and view the action topside."

Strapping her rapier to her waist and easing her dagger

into the top of her boot, she ran through the passageway. By the time she reached the deck, the *Cat's Cradle* had overtaken the slower merchant vessel.

The order to board the other ship rang out. In a flash, Hawk's men swung over the side on ropes and landed on the deck of the besieged ship.

From her position behind the passageway door, Catherine watched Rory take on and easily defeat a tall thin officer on the other ship. When she craned her neck to see where her father and Colin were, she unwittingly called attention to herself. A group of sailors from the captured vessel had boarded the *Cat's Cradle*, and the biggest among them spotted her.

"Well, well, what 'ave we 'ere? 'Tis a bit of a girl! Don't ya wanna come out to play wif' us, lit'le darlin'?"

His ugly face leered at her, but Catherine didn't flinch. She waited for the huge hulking man to close the gap between them. When she unsheathed her rapier, he started laughing.

"Lit'le girls ought not to play wif' sharp toys. Ya can get 'urt that way, y'know."

"No, I don't know. Why don't you show me?" she replied.

"Yer a pesky bitch who needs a good tamin'." He lewdly rubbed his hand against his crotch. "Once I gets done wif' dis lesson, I'm gonna teach ya things I enjoys even more."

The burly seaman started the attack, but within moments Catherine had taken the offensive. By watching his shifting eyes, she anticipated his actions. Her blade sliced a gash in his jowled cheek with an ease that made her unworthy adversary even more anxious. His lack of skill was evident. He threw too much of his weight into his next lunge and lost his footing.

Catherine took the opportunity to bring the duel to an end. She didn't hesitate to guide her sword to its mark.

Pulling the rapier from his body, she surveyed the battle around her.

On the bridge, Colin and her father were fighting with six enemy seamen. Though badly outnumbered on the raised platform, Hawk never lost his composure. His rapier swung through the air with precision and eliminated their opponents.

A noise at her left alerted Catherine that she was going to be attacked. Assuming her stance, she wounded another foe in a matter of minutes. Two more men challenged her and lost.

Catherine had no idea what an impression she was making on the men of both ships. With her golden hair swinging free in the wind as she fought, she was the picture of danger and beauty. She lunged and parried with thrusts that were calculated and strong. The daughter of the Irish Hawk was born on the deck of the *Cat's Cradle* that day.

By some miracle, her father and brothers never saw her during the siege. If they had, their distraction could have cost them their lives. Catherine suddenly realized this. Fearing for their safety, she returned to the passageway.

The crew of the English merchant ship was soundly defeated. The survivors surrendered to the captain they knew as the Irish Hawk. Hawk was reputed to be a man of honor because he allowed men who surrendered to keep their lives. They were gathered on the deck of the *Cat's Cradle* as their fate was determined by him. While the captured booty was being removed from the beaten vessel, Catherine decided to make her presence known to her father. Members of his crew had seen her, and she knew it would be wiser to face him on her own.

Leaving the passageway, she walked toward the bridge to meet her fate. Sean had his back to her as she climbed the stairs. All talking among the crew ceased. Padraic shook his head in silent humor and waited for his old friend's reaction to their uninvited guest.

Sean was speaking to Colin when Catherine came up behind him and touched his shoulder. He turned toward her, and a wealth of emotions passed over his face. Surprise, joy, and then anger flared in his eyes. Without saying a word, Sean conveyed to his daughter that she was in trouble.

For the first time, Catherine was too ashamed to face her father. She turned from him and caught a sudden movement among the prisoners. A gun was aimed at her father's chest!

Quickly, she made her move. Taking the dagger from her boot, she threw it, striking the offending seaman in the arm just as he fired. It deflected the man's aim, but not enough. The shot tore a bloody hole in Sean's right shoulder and brought him down.

As Padraic and several men pounced on the would-be assassin, Catherine knelt beside Sean and cradled his head in her lap. "Oh, Da, I'm sorry. 'Tis all my fault. Please forgive me."

When Sean groaned and lost consciousness, Catherine turned to Colin. "Don't stand there! Go fetch the ship's surgeon."

At that moment, Rory got to the bridge. "Sorry, Cat, but Doc was hit in the cross fire. Let's get Da below and we'll see about getting that piece of lead out of him."

"But, Rory, his wound is bad," Catherine warned as her brothers and two crewmen lifted Sean. "Da could lose the use of his arm."

"Excuse me, miss. May I speak to you?"

Looking up, Catherine saw one of the captives beckoning her to his side. "What do you want?" she snapped.

"My name is Justin Prescott. I'm a physician, and I'd like to help your captain," the light-haired young man offered.

Catherine walked up to him and put the point of her rapier to his throat. "Give me a reason why I should trust a bloody Englishman with my father's life. You're the enemy."

"I'm an American who was a passenger on that ship. As a doctor, I have no politics. If you want my help, we'd better get moving. Your father is losing a lot of blood."

Catherine admired the man's courage. Instinctively, she knew he could be trusted. She lowered her sword and led him to the captain's cabin.

Over the next few hours, Catherine assisted Dr. Prescott while he treated her father's wound. The lead ball was removed and his broken shoulder was set. They worked on Sean until he was sleeping peacefully in his oversized bunk.

Catherine was fascinated by the American doctor. Justin Prescott was tall and well built. His light brown hair was streaked blond by the sun. He was a handsome man, yet the most riveting thing about his looks were his eyes. They were the gold of topaz.

Justin pulled the blanket over Sean's chest, then turned to face her. "Your father's doing fine, Mistress Catherine. Thank you for assisting me."

"Thank me? I held a blade to your throat! No, I'm the one who's indebted to you. I'll be forever grateful for what you've done for my da, Dr. Prescott."

"Grateful enough to address me by my given name?"

Catherine blushed. "If that'll please you . . . Justin."

Dimples creased Justin's cheeks as he smiled. "You're quite incredible, Lady Cat."

"Lady Cat?" she asked.

"After seeing you in battle today, it seems an appropriate title for you. I was tending the wounded on the other ship when I looked over and saw you engaged in combat with a man twice your size. Wherever did you learn to fight like that?"

Catherine turned toward the bed. "First Rory and then Da trained me. Our homeland is fraught with danger from the English, and I wanted to be able to protect myself." Tears welled in her eyes when she looked up at Justin. "And today I learned the price of protecting myself could cost a man his life."

Justin stroked her cheek. "Don't cry, Catherine. You shouldn't feel remorse for dispatching that man in an act of self-preservation. If you hadn't stopped him, that brute would have killed you. And that would have been a tragedy."

"But, Justin, I never—"

Catherine's words were interrupted as her brothers came in with fresh water and a tray of food. She moved away from Justin when Rory set the tray on the desk and came toward the bunk.

"So, Dr. Prescott, how is Da faring?"

"Your father is doing well. My main concern now is the possibility of his developing a fever. If he begins thrashing about in a feverish state, I'm afraid he'll tear his stitches and cause further damage to his shoulder. That's why I'll stay with him throughout the night."

Colin put his arm around Catherine's shoulder. "We appreciate all you've done for our father, Dr. Prescott."

Rory gave Catherine her dagger. "We removed this from that sailor's arm. Thought you'd like to have it back, Cat."

"Does he require my attention?" Justin asked.

Colin shook his head. "No. We bandaged his arm and threw him in the brig. We'll set him adrift with the others."

"You were too kind to that animal!" Catherine groused. "I hope his arm rots off."

Colin hugged her. "I know, Cat, but Da would have wanted it that way. That man will be punished by the rest of his crew for breaking the truce and putting their lives in danger." He kissed Catherine's brow. "Come along, little sister. You can use my cabin while I aid the doctor tonight."

Catherine nodded toward Justin. "Good night, Dr. Prescott. I'll be back in the morning to sit with Da."

As the two brothers walked out with Catherine between them, Justin didn't doubt they'd do anything to protect their sister. Who could blame them? She was beautiful and unlike any woman he'd ever encountered. He looked forward to knowing the mysterious woman he'd dubbed Lady Cat.

During that next week, Justin learned Catherine had a quick mind that absorbed knowledge like dry kindling caught a flame. When he brought out his prized chess set and taught her how to play, she grasped the concept and beat him soundly by the third game. Though she spoke with a brogue like her family and crew, she was well read and only used poor grammar when she was angry or upset.

When Sean was well enough to sit up and eat solid food, Justin and Catherine began taking long walks on deck. During these outings, he asked questions and she told him about her home, family, and interests. One evening as they stood watching the moon rise, Catherine turned the tables on him.

"Justin, it would please me greatly if you would tell me about yourself."

Bracing his hands on the railing, Justin looked out over the water. "I'm the eldest son of a Virginia planter—and his biggest disappointment. My father owns the largest plantation and stud farm in the state. He threatened to disown me when I refused to take my place in the family business and became a doctor instead."

"But that's terrible. What did you do?"

"I wrote to my grandmother in England and asked her advice in dealing with my father. Knowing how stubborn her son is, Grandmama sent me the funds I needed for school. Her father had been a physician, and she wanted me to follow in his footsteps.

"Grandmama believed in me. I was going to visit her once my practice was established, but three months ago I received word from her solicitor that she had died." His voice was taut with emotion. "She always said I was like her father. I hope I can live up to her expectations."

"You're a wonderful doctor. She'd be very proud of you," Catherine said. "Is that how your story ends?"

"No. Grandmama named me as her heir, but in order to inherit her wealth and holdings, I must practice medicine in her hometown of Windell for the next five years. I'll have use of her home and receive an annual stipend of ten thousand pounds. If I refuse, her estate will be used to establish a clinic for the residents of the town."

In the solicitor's packet, Justin had found a bank draft for five thousand pounds and a personal note from his grandmother. She requested he use the money for his traveling expenses or keep it as his only inheritance. The decision would be his.

"I never had to think twice about it. Within a week, I gave up my house, transferred my patients to another doctor, and began packing. By month's end, I boarded the ship headed for England." Justin smiled at Catherine. "And during that voyage I was captured by the most beautiful lady pirate."

"I'll not be taking all the credit for your capture, sir! Da never wanted me to be involved in his business."

"Your family may have captured my body, but you're the one who's stolen my heart, Lady Cat." Justin stepped closer to her.

Catherine turned to laugh with him. When she saw his face bending toward hers, her smile quickly faded.

Justin drew her into his arms, closed his eyes, and touched his lips to hers in a tender kiss. It felt so right he did it again. He held her against him as her lips responded to his. Reluctantly pulling back from her soft pliant mouth, he watched for her reaction from beneath hooded lids. He was shocked to see her eyes wide open, looking at him.

Hugging her, he laughed. "Do you always kiss a man with your eyes open?"

"I don't rightly know," she answered with a sigh. "I've never been kissed before."

"Surely you're—or have your brothers been threatening all your suitors?"

"There were no threats. I've never had any suitors."

She answered with such ease that Justin had to look her in the eye. "Don't you like men, Catherine? A beautiful young woman like you should be married, with children and a fine home. Perhaps you're just afraid of men."

"I'm not afraid of anyone. As far as marriage, I can wait a few more years."

"People will start calling you a spinster if you wait too long," Justin chided her.

"That's silly! Whoever heard of a fourteen-year-old spinster?" Catherine laughed as his mouth fell open.

"Did you say fourteen? Please tell me you're only teasing."

She shook her head. " 'Tis the truth. I'm fourteen years and six months old. Please don't be angry with me."

Justin dropped his arms. "I'm not angry. Disappointed, but not angry." He kissed the tip of her nose. "Maybe when you grow up, you can come to England and see this old man."

"You're not old!"

"At this moment, Cat, I am feeling every one of my twenty-six years. Compared to you, I'm ancient."

"Don't you be saying that, Justin Prescott. The difference between fourteen and twenty-six may seem far apart, but the span between nineteen and thirty-one sounds just right! Can you wait for me? I promise to grow up as fast as I can!"

Her face was radiant in the moonlight and her smile melted the icy disappointment in his heart. Justin laughed and kissed the back of her hand as he bent into a courtly bow.

"My dearest Lady Cat if you're still interested in this old man in five years, you know where I'll be."

"Oh, Justin, you are such a dear man. Don't worry. I'll find you."

Copying her brogue, Justin replied, "And you, me dear Lady Cat, are truly wise beyond your years."

Chapter 4

"Well, at long last you've returned," Sean complained as Catherine and Justin entered his cabin. "A body could go daft spending so much time alone."

"Now, Da, quit the tirade!" Catherine went to the bed and kissed his whiskered cheek. "We just needed a bit of fresh air, and you were napping when we left."

"I'm tired of nappin' and lying about! If I can't go topside soon, I'll likely go mad!" Sean threatened.

"You can take a walk on deck in the morning," Justin advised him. "Your shoulder was severely damaged, and it will take time to mend properly. I've given Lady Cat orders regarding exercises that will help you restore the strength in your arm."

Sean raised a skeptical brow at his daughter. "Lady Cat, is it? Since when have you been dubbed a title, little girl?"

" 'Tis a pet name Justin gave me, and I rather fancy it. If you can be the Irish Hawk, I see no reason why I can't be Lady Cat." She smiled at Justin.

Sean's attention turned to the man standing beside his

daughter. "By the way, Prescott, I've made arrangements
for your departure. Originally, your destination was Bristol.
Because of my, ah, reputation, the *Cat's Cradle* can't sail
into any English ports. The best we can do is land you and
your belongings in a cove we use near Bristol. You should
be able to get assistance and complete your journey from
there."

"Thank you, Captain. That will be fine." Justin reached
over and shook Sean's left hand.

"You've got that wrong. I'll not forget what you've done
for me, Dr. Prescott. If you're ever in need of my help,
send word through Hal, the owner of the Laughing Dog
Tavern in Bristol. He knows how to contact me." Looking
at Catherine's expectant face, he added, "You can also
send letters to us through Hal. I have a strong suspicion
my girl might be interested in knowing how you're faring
in your new home."

Justin smiled at Catherine. "Aye, sir. I'll do that."

Scratching his bearded chin, Sean watched them.
"Padraic said we'll arrive at the cove shortly before dawn,
so you'd better gather your things and get some rest. You'll
be having a busy day tomorrow. Good night, Dr. Prescott."

"Thank you and good night, sir." Justin turned to escort
Catherine out of the cabin.

"One moment, if you please," Sean called out. "Cat,
I'd have a word with you before you turn in."

Catherine bid Justin good night and watched helplessly
as he went out the door. Biting her lip, she turned toward
the bed. "Da, maybe we can talk in the morning . . ."

"Catherine O'Banyon, come here this minute."

Sean studied Catherine as she straightened her spine,
lifted her chin, and sat in the chair beside his bed. His
precious little girl had grown up to be a beautiful golden-
haired young woman. Her tall thin figure had filled out
with soft feminine curves. When had she changed? Why
hadn't he noticed?

"You've no idea how angry you made me, lass. The deception was bad enough, but you risked your life by stowing away on this ship. You're stubborn, spoiled, and quick tempered. But I've only myself to blame. I've always doted on you. Even when I tried saying no, you'd show me the error of my ways and I'd say yes."

Sean leaned back on his pillow. "I'll ne'er forget the day I came upon you and Rory fencing in the barn. I was amazed by your skill and had to admit I'd been wrong not to have given you a chance. Can you forgive me for being wrong again?"

Catherine shook her head in disbelief. "What was that you said about being wrong, Da?"

"I said I was wrong. You wanted to come on this voyage, and I should have given you the chance you deserved. I'm sorry, Cat, but I did it out of love. Smuggling and raiding ships are dangerous. I didn't want you involved in this business."

"But it's our family's business," she reminded him. "I'm as much a part of this family as Rory and Colin, am I not?"

After a moment, Sean nodded. "Um . . . aye, to be sure. What I mean to say is you're a girl and this is a man's business."

"Since when has my being a girl ever stopped me from doing what I really wanted to do?" Catherine sputtered. "I know I'm young and have much to learn, but during the skirmish with that other ship, I did what I had to do and I survived. Can't you see that, Da?"

"Aye, Cat, and if it wasn't for you, I'd likely be dead by now. 'Tis why I've decided to keep you on board. But I'll be having your promise to do everything I say. Do you agree?"

Catherine regarded him warily. "Before I accept, Hawk, I'll be hearing your terms."

"First, Lady Cat, you'll be moving into Padraic's cabin next door. Then you'll learn all there is to know about this ship. I'll not have you hurt due to your ignorance. In the coming weeks, you'll stay as close to me as my shadow. And when we find ourselves engaged in another battle, you'll fight at my back."

"Da, you needn't worry about me. I can defend myself."

Smiling, Sean cocked his brow. "I was rather hoping you'd be there to help defend me."

With that remark, they began laughing. Catherine sat on the bed and hugged him. "I swear, Da, I'll work hard and make you proud of me. If I don't like it, I promise to return home and never ask to go to sea again."

Holding her with his good arm, Sean smiled and kissed her brow. He knew this last promise would never be kept.

Before the morning dawned, the ship arrived at the cove. Justin went to Catherine's cabin and gave her his chess set.

"Now you can remember me every time you play, Lady Cat."

"But, Justin, I don't have a gift for you," she protested.

"You can kiss me good-bye and I'll keep the memory locked in my heart forever." Justin pulled her into his arms and kissed her until she was gasping for air.

When he finally released her, Catherine laughed softly. "Not forever, Justin. Only five years, I promise!"

Hand in hand, they walked up to the deck. After promising to keep in touch, Justin loaded his belongings into a small boat. Hawk stood beside his daughter and watched until they saw the doctor waving safely from the shore.

Suddenly, Catherine turned to Sean, her green eyes bright with mischief. "Now, Captain, teach me how to sail this ship. I've only five years to spare!"

Sean O'Banyon didn't understand her cryptic remark and had little time to question it. As he promised, he taught her all about the ship he had named for her. Catherine never complained about the long hours on deck nor the calluses on her hands from handling the ropes and canvas sails.

Catherine learned about all the parts of the ship and worked at every task until she understood the job each seaman did. She had no fear of heights and seemed to fly up the tall riggings.

Padraic taught her how to navigate by instruments, charts, and the stars. He seemed to understand her inquisitive nature, and his patience was boundless. In a short time, she could plot out a course, monitor the navigation, and steer the ship all on her own.

Much to her father's chagrin, she learned how to be a good pirate, as well. Catherine could spot a rich prize of a ship and maneuver the *Cat's Cradle* into overtaking it in record time.

News of the beautiful Irish outlaw Lady Cat quickly spread far and wide. Songs were sung about her. Lady Cat with the gold hair and the face of an angel had become a legend.

The following year, Sean gave Rory a ship of his own, *Erin's Pride*. Some of the *Cat's* crew left to sail with him. Padraic refused to go, saying he was too old to make changes. His real reason for not going was his concern for Catherine.

But Padraic was worrying for nothing. Catherine's uncanny instincts made her unbeatable. Whether it was a British naval ship that tried to capture them or a terrible storm that would threaten their safety, she always knew how to handle them.

More and more, Sean allowed her to run the ship. Rory was on his own and Colin wanted no part of being a captain. Hawk was tired. His right shoulder pained him every morning and caused him continual irritation in the winter.

On Catherine's seventeenth birthday, Sean officially gave her the *Cat's Cradle*. Leaving Padraic as first mate, he was free to go home to enjoy his well-earned retirement with his wife.

Two more years quickly passed. Lady Cat's victories as a privateer put the highest bounty on her head. Damned by the British, she was heralded by the Irish as a heroine. When she traveled to Paris to arrange arms purchases for the rebels in Ireland, Sean went along to aid in the negotiations.

Returning from France with a hold filled with ammunition and guns, Sean stood on the deck of the *Cat's Cradle* and watched Catherine. She was dressed in doeskin britches, boots, and a white wool shirt. Her vest and gloves were soft black suede. The sun glinted on her plaited hair as she stood at the wheel issuing orders to a crewman.

"Look alive, Emmet! I'll not be having that topsail coming down on our heads 'cause you can't tie a proper knot. If you can't do it, let me know and I'll climb the rigging and show you how. Did you hear what I said, Emmet?"

"Yes, ma'am ... I mean, Captain. I'll secure it proper, I will," the young sailor shouted as he climbed up the rigging.

"Good lad." Catherine turned to Padraic, who was standing beside her. "Have you checked our heading this morning?"

"Aye, Captain. We'll be home before nightfall tomorrow."

She smiled. "We've been away three months. Mam was worried we wouldn't be back in time for my birthday on the first, but we're going to get home with more than a week to spare."

Looking up, she frowned. "Emmet, are you having no luck securing that line? You best be careful. I'll not be wanting your death on me conscience if you fall."

Once the sail was secured, she praised the seaman for his efforts. "You did a fine job, Emmet. I knew you could do it."

Emmet blushed to the roots of his copper red hair.

"Thank ye for havin' faith in me, Captain. I'll do better next time."

"Very good, Emmet. You can return to your post now." Catherine turned her attention back to the wheel.

Sean couldn't help but smile. Catherine was a fine captain. She handled her crew and the ship with a tempered hand and a just heart. He was very proud of his daughter.

"My daughter?" Sean mused, turning his gaze toward the sea. "Destiny brought the two of us together, little girl. I've always wondered what your life would have been like had I not been on the beach that night. I know my own existence would have been sorely lacking without you. But who are you really, my precious girl?"

Turning around, he found the beloved object of his musings standing next to him.

"Excuse me, sir. Do you think you might give your captain a big hug and kiss this morning?" she asked with a wink.

"Aye, Captain! If you don't mind me bein' an old sea dog."

She shook her head. "No, Da, I'll not mind at all. I'll just keep loving you anyway!" Catherine smiled up at him.

A memory flashed in Sean O'Banyon's mind and warmed his soul. This was the same enchanting smile that had captured his heart on a lonely stretch of beach one cold December night almost eighteen years before. Kissing her brow, he pulled Catherine into his arms and held her close.

Cat may have grown up to be destiny's lady and an outlaw of renown, but she'll always be my little girl. I'll thank God Almighty for the rest of my days for the gift of my most precious daughter.

Lady Victoria Carlisle
England
1784–1802

Chapter 5

After the fire, Geoffrey and his family returned to England. Recovering from her injuries, Evangeline needed the tranquillity their estate in Chatham offered.

They agreed never to talk about Catherine. It was a twist of fate that Victoria had lived, while her twin was lost in the blaze. The Carlisles wouldn't allow their surviving child to be burdened by their tragedy.

Victoria grew into a beautiful, sweet-tempered child. She was bright and inquisitive. By the time she was four, she could print letters and was learning to read and work with numbers.

Recognizing her intelligence, Geoffrey hired the best tutors for her. Victoria had an uncanny talent for learning languages. Well before she reached her teens, she was fluent in French, Italian, German, and Spanish.

But Victoria was hardly a bluestocking. From her mother, she learned to love horses and often spent her afternoons riding. As a present for her tenth birthday, Geoffrey let her choose any horse she wanted from the Westlake stables.

"All right, Victoria, you've looked at all the stock. Which one have you selected?" Geoffrey asked as they stood in the large, well-kept barn. "That lively bay mare has exceptional lines—or has the dappled Arabian captured your fancy?"

Victoria shook her head. "Neither, Papa. I want him."

Geoffrey was stunned when she pointed to the stall that held the pride of his breeding farm. The powerful black stallion, aptly named Nightshadow, stood more than fifteen hands high.

"But, sweetheart, you're just a little girl. I don't believe you can handle a horse as large and fast as Nightshadow."

"Papa, Nightshadow is the most beautiful horse I have ever seen. He's the one I want. You and Mama taught me to be a good rider. If you let me have him, I promise I'll be careful."

Victoria had never been a demanding child, but she was adamant about wanting the stallion. Geoffrey finally relented, and Nightshadow was taken home to Chatham Hall.

Every day, Victoria rode the countryside on Nightshadow. During one ride, she was distracted by her thoughts and failed to see a pothole in the path. Nightshadow lost his footing, and she was thrown from his back. Sharp pains shot up her right leg when she hit the ground, and she was unable to stand on her own.

The horse was grazing nearby, but came quickly when Victoria called him. Using his foreleg for support, she pulled herself off the ground and, with a great deal of effort, dragged herself onto the saddle.

Geoffrey was standing at the library window when he saw Victoria and Nightshadow coming slowly toward the house. From the pale, pained look on her face and her disheveled appearance, he knew something was wrong. Ordering a footman to go for the doctor, Geoffrey ran outside and caught her in his arms as she slid off the saddle.

"Papa, please don't blame Nightshadow," she begged while he carried her into the house. "It was all my fault."

Geoffrey shook his head. "No, honey the fault is mine. I never should have given you that brute of a horse. You could have been killed."

"Please, Papa, I'm responsible for the fall. He didn't—"

"We'll discuss this later, Victoria. But if I had any sense, I would send that black devil back to Sussex."

The physician set Victoria's broken leg and confined her to bed. For the next three days, she suffered considerable pain and accepted the doctor's orders and her mother's gentle care. But by the fourth day, the need to see her horse outweighed the discomfort she felt.

Pleading for sunshine and fresh air, Victoria convinced her father to carry her downstairs to the veranda that overlooked the gardens. After setting her on a chaise with a blanket and a pillow under her injured leg, Geoffrey returned to his library to work on correspondence.

Once she was alone, Victoria called to the caretaker's son, who was working in the garden. "Liam, could you help me?"

The smiling, freckle-faced boy hurried over and yanked the cap from his head. "O' course, milady. What can I do for you?"

In a matter of moments, Victoria convinced him to aide her. Knowing it would be difficult to move her, with her splinted leg, she sent Liam for the wheelbarrow. He placed the pillow under her and carefully rolled her to the stables.

Geoffrey was shocked and annoyed when he found her sitting in the wheelbarrow in Nightshadow's stall. The unhappiness on Victoria's face cooled his ire, but her words as she stroked the nose of the mighty stallion nearly broke his heart.

"Papa wants to send you away, Nightshadow. It was my fault you stepped in that hole. I was daydreaming, and now Papa might punish you for my stupidity. He refuses to listen to me."

Victoria was surprised when her father knelt beside her. He assured her Nightshadow wouldn't be sent away and he promised in the future to take the time to listen to her.

An hour later, Evangeline entered the stable to find her husband sitting in a dirt-encrusted wheelbarrow with Victoria on his lap. He smiled and beckoned her to join them.

"Evangeline, I was just telling Victoria about the day we met. Come sit with us and make sure I don't leave anything out."

She sat on a bale of hay as he continued his tale.

"As I was saying, the solicitor told me I'd been named guardian to Sir Thomas's orphaned child. After talking to your Uncle Edward, I went off to Sussex, expecting to meet a little girl. To my surprise, I discovered the most beautiful lady in the whole world . . ."

The mention of Edward's name distracted Evangeline for a moment. Recalling his actions in the past, she still found it difficult to trust him. She scoffed at her silly misgivings and turned her attention back to Geoffrey and Victoria.

Content with country life, the Carlisle family shunned the hectic pace of London. Though far from the city, they never hungered for guests. Many of Geoffrey's business associates and friends were invited for weekend visits. The best-loved guests were Mark and Vanessa Grayson and their two sons.

Their eldest son, Adam, was Viscount Ryland. He was a serious young man who had been groomed all his life to be the next Earl of Foxwood. When he came to Chatham with his family, he ignored Victoria, who was twelve years his junior, but she never minded the slight.

Victoria's best friend was his younger brother, Miles. Miles was eight years older than she, but he always had time for her. They spent countless afternoons in the library of Chatham Hall, talking about their dreams and hopes for the future.

"Someday, Torie, I'm going to sail my own ship around the world." His blue eyes shone with excitement. "I'll visit all those exciting places I've read about in books. By working hard and taking on cargo, I will buy other vessels and have my own shipping company."

Victoria smiled in awe at her dark-haired friend. "I know you're going to succeed, Miles. You're not afraid of work, and you enjoy challenges. I'm only sorry I won't be able to visit those exotic ports, too. Perhaps you could write to me once in a while and tell me about your daring exploits."

The someday Miles envisioned came on his twenty-first birthday, when he inherited a large sum of money from his maternal grandfather's estate. Although not a fortune, it was enough to secure a ship and crew. Before he set sail, he visited Victoria at Chatham Hall.

"You must be so excited, Miles. Not only will it be a great adventure, but your dreams of having your own company might actually come true."

Miles laughed. "It's going to take many voyages to do that, Torie. Lots of time, effort, and an incredible amount of luck will bring it all to fruition. I pray I'm up to the task."

"You are, Miles. I know it. In just a few years, you'll have the largest shipping company in England."

"I appreciate your faith in me. Thank you." Miles kissed her forehead and gave her an affectionate hug. "I'm going to miss you, but I'll write every chance I get."

Moments later, he bid her farewell.

Victoria was saddened by his departure, but understood his need to succeed. Doing well in this endeavor would gain Miles the status and respect he felt was missing in his life.

She knew something was missing from her own life. Unable to find the source of her discontent, Victoria kept herself busy with her studies, her family, and her horses. Perhaps the missing part of the puzzle would fall into place someday.

Evangeline sensed her daughter's loneliness. One night as she lay in bed, she shared her thoughts with Geoffrey. "I think Victoria misses the company of other children. I feel I've cheated her by not having brothers and sisters for her to share her life with."

"You mustn't feel that way, sweetheart. Both of us were raised without siblings, and we've turned out all right. Because Victoria's our only child, she is more special to us. Close your eyes and try to get some rest." He kissed her and held her close until she fell asleep.

Geoffrey knew Evangeline felt bad about not giving him more children. After the twins were born, they had talked about having a son, but the injuries Evangeline sustained in the fire at Fellsmere had ended those plans. Her broken pelvis and internal injuries made childbearing impossible. There would be too much stress on her body to carry to term. If she became pregnant, she and the baby had little chance of surviving.

He loved Evangeline too much to risk her life. Victoria would have to be enough for them. The price of another child was too great. From the first time he was able to make love to her again, Geoffrey was careful never to spill his seed inside her. There'd be no son, no other babies, and he had no regrets.

But Evangeline was haunted by demons of her own. His wife often sought the solitude of the duchess's bedchamber in the master suite. She made this room her private salon, where she kept the secret of their lost daughter safe from the world.

The fire at Fellsmere hadn't destroyed everything. Among the rooms that escaped the carnage was Geoffrey's study, where a very special portrait hung on the wall.

When the twins were almost a year old, he had commissioned an artist from Dublin to do a portrait of his wife and daughters. It was a beautiful painting. Evangeline was sitting on the grass with the two babies gathered on her lap. She wore a gown of royal blue. The girls were dressed in matching pale blue gowns and the heart pendants engraved with their initials. Upon seeing the completed work, Geoffrey named the portrait the Carlisle Jewels. He claimed it depicted the most valuable things he had in his life.

Now the Carlisle Jewels were hidden in Evangeline's salon, along with a locked box that contained Catherine's baptismal certificate. Every October eighteenth and December first, the dates of Catherine's birth and death, Evangeline spent hours sitting in her rocking chair, staring at the painting. Afterward, she would be her usual cheerful self, never letting anyone know of the sad anniversary she'd celebrated.

Geoffrey protected her tender feelings and let her keep her private sanctuary.

That following November was Geoffrey and Evangeline's fifteenth wedding anniversary. Hoping to brighten his wife's spirits, the duke planned a weekend party with their friends and a gala ball on Saturday night to celebrate the occasion.

Edward and Lorelei received the coveted invitation. Though the countess abhorred the dull three-hour trip by coach to Chatham, she agreed to go to the gala event.

At fifty, Lorelei, still beautiful, was obsessed with the fear of growing old. She kept her figure trim and never left her rooms without her hair and her makeup perfectly done. Custom-made lotions and herbal pastes were constantly being tried on her skin. A color rinse concealed the gray in her hair.

The morning they were to leave for Chatham, Lorelei told Edward she had an excruciating headache. She begged him to go without her and promised to join him the following day.

Edward agreed and set out in his coach with a driver and footman. An hour into the journey, he remembered the rare porcelain vase he'd purchased for Evangeline and Geoffrey was still at home. He ordered his driver to return home.

As he entered the house, he was greeted by his elderly butler, Wilson. "Ah . . . you've returned, my lord. Is something amiss?"

"I forgot the present I purchased for my brother." Picking up the wrapped package from the foyer table, Edward handed it to Wilson. "Take this out to my coach while I see how my lady wife is faring."

Wilson's shaking hands nearly dropped the box. "But, my lord, the countess issued orders she w-was not to be disturbed."

Edward patted the old man's arm and turned to the staircase. "Don't worry, Wilson. I know how to deal with my lady's temper when she's not well. If she's asleep, I won't wake her."

When Edward reached the bedroom door, he was startled to hear Lorelei laughing. The sound of a man's laughter joined hers. Edward ducked into the closet across the hall and waited to see who came out of his room.

A dapper young man with flaxen hair emerged from the master suite. Lorelei, provocative in a red silk robe, stood at his side. He kissed her passionately before closing the door. Whistling a lively tune, he cantered down the stairs.

Edward kicked open the master bedroom door and

found Lorelei sitting at her dressing table brushing her hair. "You heartless bitch!" he snarled. "You demand my fidelity, but you don't seem to have the same rules."

She turned to face him. "I'm not the one who promised never-ending fidelity. You did. If you want a divorce, get one. According to our nuptial contract, you'll get nothing if you do. I don't see why you're complaining. You have money, a home, and you are Earl of Sedwick. Before you married me, you were nothing! So before you make any more rash threats, I suggest you take the next few days at your brother's home to get your priorities in order."

Lorelei waved her brush at him. "If you decide to remain my husband, I expect you to live up to our original bargain. Should you betray me, I'll not hesitate to be rid of you. Now leave. My bath water is being brought up, and I won't be delayed further by you."

Edward didn't move as Lorelei turned back to her mirror. He stared at her, angered by her vehement dismissal. Only the sound of the servants coming down the hall enabled him to gain control of his temper and leave the room.

With fury burning through him like acid, Edward set out on his journey to Chatham Hall.

Chapter 6

The duke's guests were gathering in the drawing room before dinner when Edward arrived. He recognized several friends and returned their greetings as he accepted a glass of wine from a servant. Across the crowded room, he saw Evangeline talking to Geoffrey and the Graysons.

She is so beautiful, Edward thought. *How different my life would have been if she had married me instead of Geoffrey.*

A hand touched his arm, and he turned to discover a pair of emerald eyes watching him.

"Good evening, Uncle Edward. Where's Aunt Lorelei?"

Edward had never been comfortable around Victoria. His niece was a pretty girl, but far too clever for his liking. He sometimes felt she was trying to read his thoughts.

"Good evening, Victoria." He kissed her cheek. "Your Aunt Lorelei wasn't well, so I came without her. I was hoping you'd be my dinner companion this evening." Tucking her hand in the crook of his arm, he led her toward the dining room. As they followed the other guests, Edward studied Victoria. *I'll have to be careful around this*

*little minx. Perhaps if I encourage her attention, she'll grow weary
of the game and leave me alone.*

When they entered the dining room, Geoffrey walked
over and shook his brother's hand. "Welcome, Edward.
Where's Lorelei?"

"My wife was taken ill and regrettably couldn't make
the trip. Victoria has consented to be my companion this
evening, and I'm grateful for her company." Smiling,
Edward escorted Victoria to her chair.

Evangeline was seated at the other end of the long table.
Seeing Edward and Geoffrey speaking warmly to each
other did not dispel the foreboding that haunted her. She
was so distracted she never heard Mark talking to her.

Mark touched her hand. "You look pale, Evangeline.
Are you feeling ill?"

Her smile tentative, Evangeline shook her head. "Forgive me, Mark. Preparing for this weekend has taken more
out of me than I thought. Perhaps I'll retire early tonight."

As dinner was served, Evangeline scolded herself. *After
all this time, I should be accustomed to Edward's presence. If I
don't rid myself of these silly suspicions, I'll never be able to enjoy
the celebration.* Armed with her new resolve, she smiled and
began chatting with the guests at her end of the table.

After dinner, the ladies retired to the parlor for tea while
the men stayed in the dining room for cigars and port.
Victoria and Evangeline sat together on the settee to talk.

"I noticed your Uncle Edward came alone. Will Lorelei
be joining him tomorrow?"

Victoria shrugged. "I don't know, Mama. He told me
she was too sick to make the trip. He said he felt dreadful
about leaving her home, but she insisted he not miss the
celebration."

"Thank you for keeping Edward company at dinner.
With all of our guests, I've been very busy." Evangeline
yawned and blushed in embarrassment.

"Mama, why don't you retire now? I'll make your excuses

to Papa and see to our guests. Tomorrow is going to be a big day, and you could use the rest."

Victoria sensed her mother's relief. Apologizing to the ladies, Evangeline bid them good night and went up to bed.

A few moments later, the men came into the parlor. Victoria was quick to see a look of disappointment flash across Edward's face when she told her father about her mother's need to retire early. A second later, his expression changed and, once again, he was charming and attentive toward her.

"Victoria, my dear, your father tells me you have a lovely singing voice. Do you suppose you could honor your old uncle with a song or two?"

The remainder of the evening, Victoria was kept busy being hostess in her mother's stead. Edward offered his assistance whenever possible. He was cordial and complimentary.

After he escorted her to her suite, Edward kissed her forehead and bid her good night. As he walked toward his room, Victoria shook her head and watched him with a jaundiced eye.

"What are you really up to, dear Uncle Edward?"

The guests met for an early breakfast before heading out for a morning ride across the autumn countryside. When Edward mentioned the old Norman church in the village had remarkable stained glass windows, the group divided into two. Some would go with the duke down to the village; the others would ride cross-country with Victoria.

As they prepared to leave, Edward noticed Evangeline was not among the riders. He wanted to speak to her alone, and this might be his only opportunity. Carefully, so no one would see him, he loosened the cinch of his saddle.

The riders departed, with Edward accompanying Geoffrey's group. A mile down the road, he told his brother something was wrong with his saddle and he'd have to go back to the stable and have it repaired. He promised to catch up with the group at the church.

Edward returned to Chatham Hall and sought out Mrs. Oliver, the housekeeper. "Where's the duchess? Is she entertaining some of the ladies here at the house?"

"Her Grace is in her salon in the master suite," the dark-haired woman told him. "All the guests are out this morning."

"Evidently my sister-in-law is resting for tonight's festivities. Keep everyone away from her suite and see to it she's not disturbed."

Mrs. Oliver nodded. "As you wish, my lord."

The upstairs was quiet as Edward made his way down the hall. Leaning his ear to the door of the salon, he detected muffled footsteps and straightened up just as the door opened.

Edward lost the ability to speak for a moment. Evangeline stood in the doorway. The sunshine behind her appeared like a halo around her golden hair. "I'm sorry, Evangeline, if I startled you. I need to speak to you for a few minutes. May I come in, please?"

After a moment's hesitation, she invited him inside.

Edward looked around the feminine pink and white room. There was a loveseat and chair covered in a pale floral fabric. In front of the white marble fireplace was a carved rocker with velvet cushions. On the table beside the rocker was a small wooden chest. An Oriental rug adorned the polished floor. The only thing that didn't seem to fit in with the pretty decor was a large framed painting, covered with a sheet, that leaned against the wall near the fireplace.

When he walked toward the painting, Evangeline closed the door and called to him. "Why don't you sit down? I'll send for tea, if you like."

"Please don't bother. I just needed to talk to you." He sat on the loveseat and waited for her to join him. When he saw her moving toward the chair, he looked away and let a sob catch in his throat.

Evangeline sat beside him and touched his arm. "Edward, are you all right?"

Edward took her hand and gazed into her trusting face. "I don't know what to do. I'm too embarrassed to admit something like this to Geoffrey."

"You can talk to me. Please let me help you."

"It's Lorelei," he admitted, his voice husky with emotion. "I've been the best husband I can be for her. My wife means the world to me, but yesterday I made a dreadful discovery about her, and I . . . I—" He shook his head and closed his eyes.

Patting his hand, she encouraged him to continue. "Go on. I'm listening."

"There's no delicate way to say this. My wife has been unfaithful to me. I found her with a lover." Edward dropped his face into his hands.

Always a compassionate person, Evangeline soothed him and stroked the hair on the nape of his neck, as one would an injured child. "Calm yourself, Edward. Things may still work out for the two of you. Lorelei is beautiful, but women like her need to feel men are still attracted to them. Don't blame yourself for her lack of self-esteem."

"Perhaps it *is* my fault. Although I care for Lorelei, she knows I've never been in love with her. Maybe she needs my love to feel complete, but I don't love her and I never will."

Edward sat up and looked into Evangeline's eyes. "You're the only woman I have ever loved. There's never

been anyone to take your place in my heart. Please don't
send me away. I cannot accept your rejection any longer."

Clasping her tightly in his arms, his lips took hers in a
bruising kiss. Evangeline opened her mouth to protest and
he took swift advantage. His tongue swept into her mouth.
She struggled to push him away. When she was finally able
to free her mouth from his, she was gasping for breath.

"Have you lost your mind? You must release me!"

"No, my darling, I cannot let you go. I love you, and
no one will keep you from me any longer."

Terror filled Evangeline as he began to caress her body.
He caught her scream by covering her mouth with his own.
She struck him with her fists, but she was no match for
his strength. When he started nuzzling the side of her
neck, she tried to talk him out of his intent.

"Edward, don't do this. If I scream, someone will come
to help me."

Edward shook his head. "I won't be stopped. If anyone
comes in, I'll kill them. You should have been mine years
ago, and now I mean to have you or die trying!"

He stroked her hair, coaxing it from the pins that held
it in place, while his voice droned on in a disquieting
confession. "I never wanted to hurt you, but Geoffrey wrote
to me, boasting how happy you were. I was so miserable,
so alone. It made me do crazy things. I was desperate, and
it seemed the only way out. Thank God you survived it
all."

Some of Edward's words garnered her attention. What
had he said about hurting her? What crazy things had he
done?

Evangeline continued to strike him, but he was so intent
he didn't feel the blows. Realizing the futility of her attacks,
she tried another ploy. If she could convince him she was
a willing participant, perhaps she could divert him long
enough to escape.

"All right, Edward. You can have me if it pleases you,

but we can't do this here. Geoffrey could walk in at any moment, and he would kill you."

A feral gleam sparkled in his eyes. "No, my brother doesn't possess the killer instinct I have. Geoffrey is the one with something to fear. I never make the same mistake twice."

The malevolent expression on his face spurred Evangeline into fighting back. With a sudden burst of energy, she tore free of his hold and raked her nails across his face. He fell back and gingerly ran his fingers over the bloody furrows on his cheeks. While he was momentarily stunned, she tried to get away.

Before she reached the door, Edward pounced on her. Picking her up in his arms, he carried her struggling body back to the loveseat. He set her on the floor and wrapped his arms around her. His embrace was so tight she could hardly breathe.

"You lied," he snarled. "You're no better than that bitch wife of mine. Perhaps I should treat you all like the whores you really are!" He grabbed the bodice of her gown and savagely jerked it down, exposing her silk camisole.

Emitting a strangled cry, Evangeline slapped his face. Enraged, he struck her, catching her jaw with the back of his fist. She crumpled to the floor from the blow.

Evangeline was too dazed to move as Edward loosened the ribbons on her camisole. He kissed and suckled her breasts, whispering of their beauty, while he explored her body. Within minutes, he worked her skirts up to her hips and parted her thighs. Holding her hands over her head, he used his greater weight to pin her to the floor as he opened his britches. His manhood soon throbbed against her.

When she felt his staff pressing inside her, Evangeline came to her senses. She wriggled and pushed him, but it was of little use. Tears of frustration coursed down her cheeks. "Please, Edward, don't do this. You don't know what will happen."

She repeated these words over and over again like a litany, but Edward was too caught up in his ardor to hear. His heart thundered against her naked breasts until he shuddered in the quake of his release.

As the birds chirped outside the salon window, a totally sated Edward fell back on the floor. Basking in the glow of his spent passion, he closed his eyes to relish the feeling.

Suddenly, the awful truth of what he had done hit him. Sitting up, he quickly adjusted his clothes and cautiously looked over at Evangeline.

She was lying on the rug beside him, silently gazing into space. Her clothes were torn and her hair framed her face like a golden cloud. Her cheeks were wet with tears, her eyes red and swollen.

"Oh, my love, I am so sorry. Please, Evangeline, you must forgive me. I have loved you for so long that I lost control of myself." As he rambled on with apologies, he tried to repair her torn bodice and pull down her skirts. "Please say something to me. Scream at me, tell me you hate me, but please say something! Your silence is scaring me."

A few moments later, Evangeline spoke in a low, solemn voice. "What would you have me say? What would it change? Words cannot alter the fact you raped me. You curse Lorelei for what she did, but your sin is far worse."

Edward moved away from her. "What can I do to prove my apology is sincere and my remorse is truly from my heart?"

Evangeline came slowly to her feet. The frigid glare from her blue eyes sent a winter-like chill to Edward's soul.

"You will leave this house immediately and never return. I'll not have your venom poisoning my home. If this was an example of your love," she continued, "then I would rather live with your hate. Should you ever come near me again, I will kill you. Have I made myself perfectly clear?''

She turned her back on him in dismissal, and he went out the door. Tears filled his eyes as he stood in the corridor and listened to Evangeline sobbing inside the salon.

During the next few weeks, Evangeline put on a facade of smiles and gaiety to benefit her family and friends. She fooled everyone, but it wasn't long before she realized her worst nightmare had come true.

She was with child, and Edward was responsible.

Evangeline had no one to confide in. Her friend Vanessa didn't know Edward very well and knew nothing about his effect on her life. Victoria was too young to understand the situation.

But she needed to tell someone what was in her heart. Sitting in her salon, looking at the portrait of herself with the twins, she found an answer to her dilemma. She would tell Catherine.

Taking pen to paper, Evangeline wrote a long letter to her daughter and purged her soul of all the pain Edward had inflicted on her. She told Catherine about the things he'd said when he attacked her. She shared her fear of being pregnant and its ultimate outcome.

She wrote of her decision not to tell Geoffrey what Edward had done to her. It would destroy the kinship between the brothers, but, more importantly, she feared some of the guilt was hers. She knew Edward cared for her, but she had never realized he was still in love with her. Had he misinterpreted her concern for him as love? Had she inadvertently misled him? Had she invited his attack that day? She voiced all these questions in her letter.

After ridding herself of this poison, Evangeline wrote of her love and concern for Geoffrey and Victoria. She might not live to deliver the child she carried, but her anxiety was for them and how they would be hurt by her death.

Finally, Evangeline told Catherine how much she'd loved her and how cheated she felt by losing her on that tragic night in Ireland. She wrote of how she commemorated the anniversary of her birth and death to soothe the aching in her heart.

At the end of the missive, she confided her wish that God was benevolent and would someday allow Catherine's soul to return to earth so she could have a life filled with happiness. She signed the letter with love, and placed it in the box with Catherine's baptismal record.

Writing the letter brought a great change in Evangeline. She decided to live each day to its fullest. If she had to depart this life, she would leave Geoffrey and Victoria with wonderful memories of their last months together.

During the following weeks, the three of them spent every available hour together. They played games, read to each other, and sang songs in the music room.

Evangeline carefully hid her condition. When Geoffrey was away on business, she visited the village doctor. Dr. Louden's prognosis was grim. There was little chance she or the baby would survive. She promised the physician she'd take care of herself and would send word if she needed him.

In March, she began having pains. Though only in her fourth month, her body was already feeling the stress of the pregnancy. She refused to let her discomfort keep her from her family and friends.

She and Geoffrey hosted an anniversary party for Mark and Vanessa in late March. The celebration was under way when the contractions started. As the orchestra began playing, she led Geoffrey to the dance floor to waltz with her.

"Do you remember when we danced at our engagement

party, Geoffrey? It was like a fairy tale. I was the princess in the tower and you were the prince who rescued me."

Geoffrey shook his head. "No, my dearest, you rescued me. Before you, my life was empty. I was a shell of a man, caught up in business. You made me complete." He felt her tremble in his arms. "If you're tired, sweetheart, we can sit down."

"Certainly not, Geoffrey. There's no place I'd rather be than here dancing with you. Do you think it would shock our friends if you kissed me in the middle of the ballroom?" she asked, looking adoringly into his eyes.

"If it bothers them, then let them be hanged!" With that declaration, Geoffrey gave her a kiss filled with love. When he eased back to look at her, he saw her grimace. A second later, her knees buckled and she fell to the floor.

Geoffrey lifted her into his arms. Shouting orders to Mrs. Oliver to send for the doctor, he carried Evangeline out of the ballroom and up the stairs. Mark and Vanessa followed close behind.

When they arrived in the master bedroom, Vanessa loosened Evangeline's clothes. "My word," she remarked. "This corset is much too tight. It's a wonder she can breathe at all."

Geoffrey was much too distracted to hear Vanessa's words. Suddenly, the door opened and Victoria came rushing in. "Papa, is Mama ill? Is there anything I can do to help?"

His daughter's concerned voice brought Geoffrey back to reality. "Yes, love. See to our guests. As soon as we know something about your mother's condition, I'll come for you." After kissing her cheek, he sent her downstairs.

Evangeline stirred on the bed, and he went to her side. Her eyes opened slowly as he sat beside her. "Evangeline, what happened? I kissed you, and the next thing I knew, you were falling to the floor."

She smiled weakly. "Your kisses were always potent. You

made me swoon." The smile vanished as her body tensed in pain. "Geoffrey, send for Dr. Louden. I think I'm running out of time," she whispered hoarsely.

"What are you talking about? Please, Evangeline, tell me what's wrong," he pleaded as she winced again.

Shaking her head, tears filled her eyes. "It's too soon. I need more time. Just a little more time." A scream of pain escaped her lips.

"God Almighty, what's happening to her? Evangeline, tell me where it hurts. Please, I want to help you." Mark forcibly pulled him from the bed and Geoffrey tried to fight him off. "Damn it all, Mark, I can't stand here while she's suffering like this. She's in so much pain."

When Dr. Louden arrived a few minutes later, he asked the men to leave so he could examine Evangeline. Geoffrey refused to go until Mark convinced him he was delaying the doctor from his task and took him out to the hall. Vanessa remained behind to assist the physician.

Out in the corridor, Geoffrey paced back and forth. He begged God to take the pain from Evangeline and give it to him. After what seemed like an eternity, Vanessa came out and sent him inside. As the door closed, she rushed into her husband's arms and cried.

The death of Lady Evangeline Carlisle, the Duchess of Chatham, shocked everyone, but no one more than Edward Damien.

The morning after she died, Edward received a note from his brother telling him of Evangeline's passing and asking him to come to Chatham. After reading the missive, a cold numbness encompassed Edward's heart. His pain was genuine, his grief unbearable.

This must be a cruel hoax to drive me mad. I'll not believe it until I see her for myself.

Within minutes, Edward's coach was on the road to

Chatham Hall. When he arrived, black bunting hung over the front of his childhood home, notifying visitors that the family was in mourning.

Edward instructed Mrs. Oliver not to announce his arrival. He went into the front parlor and closed the doors behind him. Slowly, he turned to face the truth. The draperies were drawn over the windows. Scores of candles flickered in silver candelabras, illuminating the sole inhabitant of the room.

Evangeline was lying in repose, wearing a gown of sapphire blue. Her hair was brushed free and flowing. She looked like Sleeping Beauty, but there would be no happy ending.

Stepping up to her, he stroked her hair. "My Evangeline, I have missed you so. You were right to hate me. My only excuse was that I loved you too much. I will never stop loving you." He bent down and pressed a kiss to her cold, lifeless mouth.

Edward sat at her side, his tears rushing down his cheeks. That was how Geoffrey found him several hours later.

The duke put his hand on Edward's shoulder and spoke softly to him. "It's inconceivable to think she is gone. For nearly sixteen years, Evangeline was my life. I don't know how I will live without her."

"Tell me what happened. I need to know."

Geoffrey sat in a chair beside his brother and told him about Evangeline's old injuries, her inability to have more children, and her brave attempt to bear another child. He also told him of the doctors' warnings and the precautions he'd taken to prevent her pregnancies.

"So you see, Edward, I blame myself for her being with child. Had I abstained from making love to my wife, she would still be alive."

Still staring at Evangeline's porcelain-like features, Edward asked one more question. "How far along was she?"

"She was nearly five months gone. Evangeline never told

me about the baby. She hid her condition because she didn't want me to worry. Now I've lost her and my son."

As the day came to an end, the two brothers sat in the darkened parlor, each suffering the loss of the woman he loved, each mourning a son he thought was his own.

Chapter 7

A month after the funeral, Victoria realized her father was having a difficult time accepting her mother's death. He sat silent and brooding for hours. His business correspondence went unanswered. He'd even locked the doors to her mother's salon in the master suite and refused to let anyone inside. His actions, though understandable, frightened her. Somehow she had to help him deal with his grief and make him get on with his life. The first step she took was convincing him to leave Chatham Hall, which was filled with many wonderful memories, but also a great deal of sorrow.

"Papa, why don't we move to the London house for a while? With the opera, museums, and galleries, there will be plenty to do," she suggested.

The duke shrugged. "Moving to London isn't a very good idea, Victoria. Carlisle House is fine for short visits, but it's far too austere to suit our needs."

"A home is what you make of it. Together we could pick

out new furniture and draperies. We can have all the rooms painted. I rather fancy a sunny yellow for the walls—"

"Victoria, I refuse to live in a house of yellow rooms."

She laughed. "Oh, Papa, I wouldn't do that to you. I want yellow for the walls in *my* room! What colors do you like?"

Arrangements were quickly made and Geoffrey and Victoria took up residence in the family's spacious town home. They selected new furniture, wall coverings, window treatments, and works of art. No expense was spared to make Carlisle House a showplace.

Once the house was completed, Victoria began getting her father involved with his business again. Over breakfast one day, she asked him to tell her about his company.

"I want to learn all about your work, Papa. You own one of the most successful investment firms in England, and I've never seen your offices."

Geoffrey patted her hand. "I don't think you'd like it, sweetheart. The paperwork is tedious and confusing. An office isn't a place for most young ladies."

Victoria scowled. "I am not most young ladies. I may be only fourteen, but I'm fluent in five languages. My penmanship is impeccable, my mathematics flawless. Because of my gender, I can't go to Oxford or any great university. So what am I to do with my life, Papa?"

"All right. I'll take you to Carlisle Enterprises and show you what we do. If you don't like it, I'm sure we can find another venue for your talents."

Victoria was amazed to find her father's company was quite large and employed many people. Each division had its own staff of clerks, accountants, and counselors. There was even a solicitor who handled nothing but her father's business affairs.

Victoria decided she'd found her niche in life. Within four years, she planned on knowing her father's business inside and out.

But it didn't take that long. By the end of two years, she was fully ensconced in Geoffrey's company, working right at his side.

When it came to investment ideas, she also proved to be her father's child. Like Geoffrey, who'd been called Lord Midas by his friends and associates years before, anything Victoria touched turned to gold.

As Victoria approached her eighteenth birthday, Vanessa Grayson convinced Geoffrey that his daughter had to make her debut into society. She was too young and lovely to spend her life behind a desk. Most girls her age were married or betrothed. Victoria wasn't even receiving suitors.

Geoffrey began to wonder if he had taken up too much of his daughter's life. She was so much like him, he was stunned by the comparison. Burdened with guilt, he allowed Vanessa to sponsor a ball for Victoria. He hoped his daughter would be pleased.

"Papa, how could you do this to me? I'm not interested in parties or impressing the *ton*. I like my life the way it is," she said, after learning about Vanessa's plans.

Her anger shocked Geoffrey. "Victoria, it's only a party. What are you really upset about?"

"I refuse to be a docile little debutante, Papa," she told him, sighing. "The *ton* dictates young ladies wear white during their first Season. I look dreadful in white, and I won't do it. Coming out usually means one is looking for a husband, and I am not! The average man wants a lady to adorn his table, his arm, and his bed without question or pause. I will be no man's empty-headed puppet."

Geoffrey hugged her. "Victoria, you could never be anyone's puppet. You are too intelligent for that. The man who falls in love with you will accept you as you are or not at all. Never change, sweetheart. Be yourself and let the rest follow you."

"All right, Papa. I'll make my debut in society, but on my terms," Victoria conceded. "I'll choose the fabrics, styles, and colors that please me. I just pray I don't get too bored at my own birthday celebration. Perhaps I should take a book along to pass the time."

The ball went as planned, with the cream of society in attendance. Even the Graysons' son Adam condescended to come.

"Mother, I know it would be poor manners not to attend a party you were hosting, but don't expect me to remain till the end. I promised to meet Drew at White's later on."

"You may change your mind after you see Victoria," Vanessa assured her son. "Besides being a very lovely young woman, she is intelligent and well read. You couldn't find a better candidate for your viscountess, my son."

"Please, no matchmaking, Mother. I'm only thirty, and I have no intention of getting married anytime soon. In fact . . ." Adam's voice faded as he saw a woman dressed in gold silk at the top of the stairs that led to the ballroom. Her blond hair was swept up and long curls dipped over her shoulder. Wispy tendrils framed her perfect face. "By God, she is exquisite. Who is she?"

Vanessa gave him a wry smile. "Victoria Carlisle. Now, what were you saying about leaving early?"

Adam was stunned. The skinny child he had known was gone. In her place stood a tall, shapely young woman who exuded confidence and poise. He watched as Geoffrey led his beautiful daughter down the stairs. After Victoria was presented to his parents, she curtsied before him. Taking her hand, Adam gazed into her eyes. "It's been a long time, Lady Victoria."

"Good evening, my lord. I trust you weren't coerced too harshly into attending this celebration."

Adam smiled at her low, melodious voice and was instantly intrigued by her. "It's true I seldom get involved in balls and parties, but I'm rather pleased I came tonight." He lifted her hand to his lips and kissed it. "May I request the first dance?"

During that dance, Adam Grayson decided to make Victoria Carlisle his wife.

Victoria's debut was a grand success. Dubbed the Golden Girl by the leaders of the *ton,* she was invited to every ball, tea, and soiree sponsored by the nobility and gentry. When she attended any of these functions, Adam saw to it he was her escort.

Rumors were rampant that Viscount Ryland had discouraged all other men from trying to pay court to Victoria. He'd called out a rather aggressive young swain, Robin Greely, faced him in a duel, and sent him home to Surrey with a gunshot wound in his arm.

Their betrothal announcement surprised no one. They set February first as their wedding date. The couple's respective families were thrilled with the match, and the duke gave them a party to celebrate their engagement.

"Adam, can we please stop dancing for a while?" Victoria pleaded, smiling up into her fiancé's handsome face. "I need to catch my breath."

"I thought I was the only one getting tired. Come with me, Goddess, before someone blocks our escape!" Laughing, he grabbed her hand and pulled her out the door and into the garden.

"This is silly. We have to run away from our family and friends just so we can sit down for a bit," Victoria said as Adam led her to the gazebo in the far corner of the garden.

In spite of the chill in the air, they were both warm from

their hasty retreat. Sitting on the gazebo's carved bench, Victoria waved a black lace fan in front of her flushed face.

Adam's brow rose. "Where did you purchase that fancy thing?"

"I didn't. Miles sent it with a letter I received last week."

Rage entered Adam's voice. "We're to be married soon. I won't have you accepting gifts from my brother or anyone else!"

"Oh, Adam, don't take on so. I've exchanged letters with Miles since he left. Every month I send him a missive with all the latest news, and he writes about the ports he's been to. Occasionally he sends me a token of the area. He sent the fan from Spain."

Adam frowned. "I don't think you should continue writing to Miles. If the gossips discover you're corresponding with my brother, they'd be setting odds as to when you'd run off to sea to join him."

Victoria patted his cheek. "For an intelligent man, Adam Grayson, you can be so foolish. Perhaps I should set your mind to rest on a few things. First, I love you very much. Second, I would never run off to sea with Miles—or anyone. I get seasick at the slightest provocation. Papa took me across the channel once, and I spent the entire voyage hanging over the rail."

Adam laughed at her comments. Seeing him relax, Victoria continued talking. "If you find that amusing, I should tell you about the outrageous dreams I've had all my life. In the past few years, I've dreamed about sailing on a big ship as a lady captain. I saw myself wearing tight britches, standing at the ship's wheel issuing orders to the crew. When I was younger, my dreams weren't any better. I saw myself fighting with a rapier and a jeweled dagger."

Adam kissed her and held her in his arms. "Maybe you're a lady pirate at heart, Goddess. Lord knows I'd gladly walk the plank for you!"

Resting against his shoulder, Victoria recalled a dream

she could never tell her very jealous fiancé about. In that vision, she'd been kissing a handsome man who had fascinating gold eyes.

In early December, Victoria received a letter from Miles telling her his ship had cargo to deliver in London right after the new year. On January first, she hired a runner to stay at the docks and let her know when his ship, the *Foxfire,* was sighted. Two days later, she received word the ship would dock that afternoon. After sending a messenger to alert the Graysons, she and Geoffrey went to the harbor.

It was past two when the *Foxfire* moored at its berth. The docks were swarming with people as Miles ordered the gangplank lowered. Hearing a woman's voice calling his name, he scanned the area for its source. His eyes fell on a pretty young woman dressed in a green cloak. She waved at him and her hood fell back, revealing bright golden curls. He couldn't fathom who she was until he noticed Geoffrey standing beside her.

"Torie!" he shouted. Pushing everyone aside, Miles ran down the gangplank and across the dock to reach her. He scooped her up into his arms and eagerly kissed her soft lips.

Geoffrey cleared his throat. "Ah, Miles, I hate to intrude, but Adam and your parents are coming this way."

Miles released Victoria and turned to greet his family. Adam shook his hand. "Welcome home, Miles. You're certainly looking well. Traveling the world seems to have agreed with you."

Vanessa patted Miles on the shoulder. "Did you develop these muscles by loading that ship all on your own?" She shook her head. "You'll have to see your father's tailor right away if you want to have a new coat made before the wedding."

"Wedding?" Miles asked. "Who's getting married?"

Adam smiled. "Victoria and I are getting married next month. We'd be honored if you'd be the best man."

"Please say you'll do it, Miles," Victoria implored him.

Miles had always known Victoria would never be his. She was going to be a duchess someday and had to marry a man of equal station to her own. But he'd never imagined that man would be his pompous brother, Adam. Hiding his disappointment, he nodded and forced a smile to his lips.

Over the next few weeks, many parties were given to honor the betrothed couple. Adam and Victoria invited Miles to attend the celebrations with them. Victoria enjoyed her friend's company, while Adam quelled his jealousy and hoped his brother would meet a lady of his own.

Two days before the wedding, Adam was walking through his club when a strange man stood up and blocked his path.

"Good afternoon, Grayson. I'm Richard Greely. We've never met, but you're acquainted with my younger brother, Robin."

Adam nodded. "Oh, yes, Robin Greely from Surrey. How is your brother? Has he recovered from his wound?"

"Not really. The wound festered and the doctor had to remove his arm to save his life."

"I regret what happened, but surely you realize Robin brought it on himself. He cast dispersions on a certain lady and refused to apologize. The challenge was issued and accepted. There are witnesses who can attest to this, if you doubt my word."

Greely shrugged off his comment. "I've heard congratulations are in order, my lord. Lady Victoria is going to be your wife soon."

"Yes, the wedding is Saturday."

"It amazes me you allow your brother to share your fiancée's company. Perhaps he's sharing more than her company, Grayson. Maybe he's more of a man than you are and the lady knows it."

At the last remark, Adam lost control and punched Greely on the jaw, knocking him to the floor. Standing over his prone opponent, Adam issued the challenge.

"Dawn tomorrow at Belmore Greens. Bring your second, Greely. The choice of weapons is yours."

Greely wiped the blood from his mouth with his hand. "Pistols at twenty paces, my lord. Same as when you met Robin—except you'll be facing a man this time, not a green lad."

That evening the Grayson and Carlisle families went to the opera. Adam told no one of his dawn appointment with Greely. He'd participated in many duels and always won. He wouldn't let Victoria or his family worry needlessly.

Friday morning, the sun was shining, the birds were singing, and Victoria was humming to herself as she came down the stairs. She'd just reached the foyer when the footman opened the door and admitted Miles.

"Good morning, Miles. I wasn't expecting to see you today."

"Victoria, where is your father? I need to see you both," Miles replied guardedly.

"Papa had a meeting with his solicitor. Miles, what is wrong? I can tell by your face something's happened."

Miles led her into the drawing room and placed her on the settee. Taking her hands, he sat beside her and searched for words that refused to come.

Suddenly, Victoria knew. "It's about Adam, isn't it? Tell me what's happened to Adam."

Miles nodded and told her about Adam's confrontation with Richard Greely. "I don't know what Greely said, but Adam hit him and challenged him to a duel at dawn. Adam's second, Drew Harper, said all was going well this morning. But as they stood back to back with the loaded pistols, Greely taunted my brother about never really being sure. The count began, they paced, turned, and fired. Adam was struck in the chest. Greely received a flesh wound. Drew said my brother had been distracted by Greely's words, and that was his undoing.''

"Where is he now? Where is Adam?" she asked tearfully.

"Drew and the doctor brought him home. The shot severed an artery. Everything was done to stop the bleeding, but within minutes, Adam was dead. I'm sorry, Victoria, that I was the one to tell you this.'' With tears in his eyes, Miles put his arms around her.

"Please hold me, Miles. I need you to . . .'' Victoria buried her face against his shoulder and cried.

Two weeks after Adam's funeral, Victoria returned to work at Carlisle Enterprises. She was making notes in the acquisition journal her first morning back when the new clerk rushed in and announced a gentleman named Grayson was asking to see her.

"That must be Uncle Mark, checking on his mining investments. Show him in while I look up the figures.''

Miles walked into the office a few moments later and watched Victoria working at the large mahogany desk that dominated the center of the room. She was adding up columns of numbers in an open ledger book.

Without looking up, she directed him to a chair in front of the desk. "Have a seat, Uncle Mark, while I check these totals.''

Miles smiled at her error and took the opportunity to study Victoria. Dressed in dove gray silk, she wore her hair swept up in a neat coil, with fine wisps around her face. Her only jewelry was small gold earrings and her heart pendant.

"Well, Uncle Mark, I think you'll be pleased . . .'' Victoria looked up and discovered Miles smiling at her. "Oh, Miles! Forgive me. My clerk said Grayson, and I assumed it was your father."

"Don't be flustered, Torie. It's my own fault for not having an appointment. I need some business advice. If you're too busy, I can come back another time."

Victoria frowned. "Don't be silly. I'd never be too busy for you. What can I do for you this morning?"

"My trading and cargo business during the past six years has been very successful. I've accumulated enough funds to purchase and outfit two new ships. The first, *Torie's Treasure,* leaves next week on her maiden voyage with a full hold."

"You named your new ship after me?"

Miles smiled and nodded. "Of course. You were the only one who believed in what I was doing. You're my good luck charm."

Victoria blushed. "I am honored you think so, but it was your hard work and determination that brought you success."

"Be that as it may, now I have the responsibility of being Viscount Ryland and my father's heir. I won't be able to continue working as I have. With proper planning, I think I can fulfill my obligations to the family and still see my dreams become a reality." Miles explained how he could set up his base of operations in London. By hiring suitable captains and crews, he could remain in England and expand his company even more.

"There are offices available here in our building," Victoria suggested. "This location is convenient to the harbor as well as the business district."

"Not to mention it would keep me close to my investment advisor." Miles reached over and touched her hand. "Will you help me? Going from being a sea captain to being a titled businessman is going to be difficult. Your assistance would make it much easier."

"You know, Miles, I'd enjoy the challenge of starting a new company with you. I'd even be willing to invest some of my own capital. Would you be interested in forming a partnership? I'd be content with twenty-five percent."

Miles accepted Victoria's offer. During the next six months, they worked hard building up their company, Ryland Shipping. With his experience in sailing, ship construction, and ports, and her ability to make profitable investments and purchases, they were an unbeatable team.

One evening, Miles went to Carlisle House for dinner. Since her father was away, Victoria arranged to have their meal served in the morning room. After the dishes were cleared away, she reached across the table and held out a ring to him, a large, square-cut emerald surrounded with small round diamonds. "This is the Ryland betrothal ring. The day Adam died, I took it off and put it away. It belongs to you now."

Not saying a word, Miles shook his head.

"But this ring should be given to the woman you'll marry."

Miles took her hand and closed her fingers around the ring. "She has it already."

Victoria looked at her closed hand and then at his impassive face. "I don't understand."

"For a woman who speaks five languages, I didn't think I had to translate. I want you to be my wife, Torie."

Victoria was shocked. "You've always been my best friend, and I care for you a great deal, but I'm not in love with you. I'm still trying to deal with losing Adam. Is friendship enough to build a marriage on?"

"I know we'd do well together. Someday you might even learn to love me."

"But what about the company? Could you live with the same person you work with? And what about our families? Will they understand? Oh, Miles, I'm so confused. What should I do?"

Miles kissed her closed hand. "Be my friend, be my partner—be my wife."

"It would mean having me around twenty-four hours a day."

Standing up, Miles drew her into his arms and kissed her. He took the ring from her hand and placed it on her finger. "All day, all night, all of my life. I want to be with you, Victoria."

Victoria sighed. "If you give me the time I need to adjust, I'll marry you. We won't make a formal announcement just yet, but our families should be told immediately. Of course, we'll have to be careful about the way we conduct ourselves in public. It wouldn't do to start rumors now. Miles, stop grinning and say something. Have you heard one word I've said?"

He nodded happily. "Yes. You said you'd marry me."

"But I meant what I said about needing time. When we marry, I don't want ghosts, gossip, or anything else to shadow our relationship. I want to be the best wife I can be."

Miles kissed her forehead. "All right, Torie. I've waited this long to get what I wanted. I can afford to be patient a while longer."

Chapter 8

"Papa, don't fight me on this. The doctor said you need rest, so I'm taking you home to Chatham."

"Victoria, this is ludicrous!" Geoffrey declared. "I'm only forty-seven years old. I never smoke tobacco, nor do I indulge heavily in food or liquor. A man half my age couldn't look more fit than I."

Victoria placed a hand on her father's shoulder and forced him to remain in bed. "Looks can be deceiving, Papa. I know you've been experiencing bouts of breathlessness and chest pains. This afternoon, you collapsed at your desk. I'm going to see you follow the doctor's orders."

"Doctor's orders," the duke scoffed. "You mean his *no* doctrine—no work, no stress, no spirits, no rich foods, no nothing! I have a business to run and estates to oversee. How can I do that if I follow his bloody dictates?"

"You're not. I'm going to take care of everything from Chatham. Your solicitor will send me daily missives about Carlisle Enterprises. The stewards at your estates will do the same. I've already sent word to Mrs. Oliver to have the house prepared for our arrival."

"But what about Ryland Shipping? Doesn't Miles need you?"

Victoria shook her head. "Miles can take care of things while I'm away. Right now you're my only concern."

The following day, they returned to Chatham. The duke's anger over being coddled disappeared when he realized this would be his last chance to spend time alone with his daughter. Victoria was engaged to marry Miles. Although the betrothal wouldn't be announced until New Year's Eve, their wedding was set for February fourteenth. During the next six months, Geoffrey knew he had to prepare for her departure from his life. Until then, he'd make the most of their time together.

The two of them read books, played games, took carriage rides, and spent a lot of time talking. Geoffrey told her of his sad childhood and his absent father. He also told her how Edward had come into his life.

When the duke spoke of his younger brother, Victoria could hear the love in his voice. But the dark-haired waif with tattered clothes and haunted eyes her father described bore little resemblance to the Edward Damien she knew.

Victoria had never trusted Edward. Now she wondered if her misgivings were caused by the fact she really didn't know her uncle. Knowing it would please her father, she decided to contact Edward and invite him to visit Chatham.

Edward and his wife were avid travelers. In the past four years, they'd visited various countries in Europe and were seldom home. Occasionally, Geoffrey received letters from him, but Edward hadn't been to Chatham since Evangeline's funeral.

Victoria sent letters to friends and business contacts inquiring if they knew of her uncle's whereabouts. Investigators were hired to aid in the search. Within two weeks, Edward was located in Wales. She wrote to him, explaining

that Geoffrey hadn't been well, and asked him to come
for a visit.

Ten days later, a large traveling coach with the Sedwick
crest emblazoned on the doors pulled up to Chatham Hall.
Mrs. Oliver hurried to greet the arrivals. Edward was talking
to the housekeeper in the foyer when Victoria came down
the stairs.

"Edward, can it really be you?"

Turning around, Edward was stunned by her appearance. His breath caught in his throat and he couldn't
speak.

Victoria ran to him and kissed his cheek. "Uncle Edward,
I'm really glad you came. Papa will be so happy to see
you."

Hearing her words brought Edward to his senses. "Victoria, you look so much like your mother. You startled me."
He smiled and studied her face. "Don't see much Carlisle
in you now."

"Papa says the only things I got from that side of the
family were my green eyes, my height, and my birthmark."

Edward laughed. "I've got the birthmark, too. On a lady,
it might be provocative, but a crescent mark on a man's
chest is a dreadful bother. At school, the lads teased me—"

"Victoria, whose coach is that?" Geoffrey walked out of
the library and saw Edward. "By God, this is a surprise.
It's good having you home, Edward."

"I've been away entirely too long," Edward replied as
his brother hugged him. "Can you abide my company for
a few days?"

"Not days, weeks! We've a lot of catching up to do,
brother. Come to the library and tell me of your travels."

Before following Geoffrey, Edward kissed Victoria's
cheek. "Don't worry, my sweet. I'll stay as long as you need
me."

Victoria stood at the library door and thought about her
uncle. Edward hadn't changed much in the passing years.

The only noticeable thing was the gray hair at his temples, but that didn't detract from his rakish good looks. In fact, she thought the silver wings of hair added a rather devilish touch to his handsome appearance.

At dinner that night, Edward told them Lorelei had gone directly to London. Since they'd been away so long, she was anxious to reopen the house and get things in order. He spoke with such love for his wife that Victoria felt a little envious of her. She hoped her own marriage would be as strong as theirs.

A week after Edward's arrival, Victoria received a dispatch from London. A major problem had developed at Ryland Shipping and Miles needed her back immediately. The following morning she left, promising to return in a few days.

Edward watched her departure from the gallery window on the second floor. Wonderful! Victoria was going away. He couldn't have planned it better. Just one more detail to see to, and then he'd be ready to deal with Lorelei. Soon he'd be a free man.

As she'd gotten older, Lorelei had grown desperate to retain her beauty, visiting mineral springs in Bavaria, a chemist in France whose mixtures promised to eliminate wrinkles, and mud baths in Italy. One crazy scheme followed another. She spent years searching for a fountain of youth that didn't exist.

With every failure, Lorelei became more vicious and angry. Making love didn't please her. Where sex had once been a thrilling experience with her, now it was perverted. She derived pleasure from pain and domination. Edward refused to play her games, so she sought others who would. He knew she had lovers, but he didn't care. She'd become a sick animal, rather like a mad dog. The only way to cure a mad dog was to kill it.

He would cure Lorelei.

Victoria's invitation had given Edward an opportunity. By showing just the right amount of affection for his brother and niece, there'd be no doubt of his tender feelings for his family.

The final piece of Edward's plot came together the afternoon of Victoria's departure, when Geoffrey took him to the horse barn to show him the newest arrival from the Westlake stables.

"This young stallion is Black Magic. He was sired by my daughter's Nightshadow, but he's faster than his father," the duke boasted, rubbing the big black's neck. "Besides speed, this fellow's been bred for endurance. Isn't he a fine animal?"

"He certainly is," Edward agreed, taking note of the horse's stall. *I'll do it tonight,* he decided as Geoffrey secured the stall. *With Victoria away, I'll have no problem carrying out my plan.*

That evening, the two brothers were playing chess in the library when Mrs. Oliver brought in their tea and dessert. Edward stopped her from pouring the tea. "Don't trouble yourself with that, Mrs. Oliver. We'll serve ourselves when we're ready. Good night."

The housekeeper left the room and closed the door. A few minutes later, the game was over. Geoffrey was the winner.

"Since I lost, I'll pay my forfeit by playing parlor maid," Edward teased as he poured the tea. "Cream and one sugar, my lord." He bowed, handing Geoffrey the cup and saucer.

"The next time I need to hire a maid, I'll keep you in mind, young man." Geoffrey chuckled.

Edward raised his cup in salute. *"Touché!"*

Taking a sip, Geoffrey frowned. "This isn't our regular tea—or has my taste been ruined by my ailment, as well?"

"Perhaps Mrs. Oliver is trying a new blend. Don't you like it?" Edward watched as Geoffrey drank more from his cup.

"It's not bad, but I prefer the tea we usually have. This is bitter." Geoffrey started to yawn. "I beg your pardon. I must be more tired than I thought." Finishing his tea, he leaned back in his chair. Moments later, he was asleep.

Edward took the cup from Geoffrey's hand and set it on the table. Looking at the clock on the mantel, he noted it was almost eleven. With no time to spare, Edward went to his room and changed clothes. Dressed in black, he stealthily crossed the grounds to the stables.

He saddled Black Magic and within minutes was on his way to Sedwick Manor on the outskirts of London. The trip by coach took three hours. By riding cross-country on the superior mount, Edward made the trip in little more than an hour.

When he arrived at his home, everyone had retired for the night. Gaining entrance through the French doors in his study, Edward made his way up the stairs to the master bedroom. Three tapers burned in the candelabrum on the bedside table. The golden light showed Lorelei asleep on the bed. A glass nearby held a few drops of the red wine with a mild sleeping draught in it that she drank every night.

Lorelei was resting peacefully on her stomach. Her pink nightgown had worked its way up, revealing her pale thighs. The quilts were pushed completely off the bed. Edward removed several silk scarves from her bureau drawer. Going to the large four-poster bed in the center of the room, he tied one scarf securely around the carved post. The other end he knotted around Lorelei's wrist. He repeated the procedure until she was lying spread-eagle on the bed, her hands and ankles tied to the corner posts.

Edward sat beside her on the bed. "Wake up, Lorelei. You must see the lovely surprise I have for you," he cajoled her.

Lorelei struggled to open her eyes. "Edward? Why are you here? Supposed to be in Chatham. Go away and let me sleep."

As her eyes closed again, Edward leaned over her. "Wake up and see your surprise!" He yanked hard on her hair. When she tried to scream, he stuffed a scarf into her mouth. Lorelei glared angrily at him. The scarves on her wrists and ankles tightened as she fought to free herself.

He laughed. "A sailor taught me that knot when I was a lad. The harder you pull, the more taut they become." Getting up, he walked to her chiffonnier next to the bed.

"During the past five years, Lorelei, you've enjoyed playing sick games. When I refused to participate, you found lovers to take my place. You had such fun I wondered if perhaps you were right about this kind of amusement. So I've come home to play your game—except this time, the roles will be reversed."

Opening the bottom drawer, he extracted two of her toys, a dagger and a cat-o'-nine-tails, a whip with nine knotted straps attached to a tooled handle. He slapped it against the bed, and Lorelei's eyes widened in fear.

"What's the matter, pet? Not up to the game?" Using the tip of the sharp dagger, he slit open the back of her gown. "Sorry about the nightrail, puss. I don't want a single thing to interfere with your enjoyment . . . or mine."

Edward put down the dagger and whip and removed his clothes. Unconcerned with his nudity, he picked up the whip. Lorelei's eyes followed his movements, and she flinched when the leather straps slapped the mattress beside her face. Her obvious terror made him smile.

"Is that fear or anticipation I see on your face, my dear? You've always enjoyed doling out punishment. Perhaps you'll relish receiving it, as well."

With cool deliberation, Edwards inflicted dozens of blows to Lorelei's back. Her screams were barely muffled by the wadded silk in her mouth. His muscles flexed as he whipped Lorelei into submission. Instead of being fatigued by his actions, a surge of power pounded through his veins.

"Oh, Lorelei, now I see why you love to wield the whip. I'm in control, all powerful!" Throwing the whip down, he tangled his fingers in her hair and jerked her head back. "It evokes a sexual hunger I've never experienced before—and you, my pet, shall sate me. Like the bitch you are, I shall rut you until I find my release."

He knelt between Lorelei's parted legs and pulled her hips up from the bed. Swiftly, without preamble, he pushed his manhood deeply inside her. Lorelei tried to escape his attack, but he was relentless. He pounded her without mercy, pressing her face to the bedding. The gag slipped unnoticed from her mouth.

When Edward felt the force of his satisfaction flooding inside her, he was amazed by its intensity. No sexual peak had ever been as great for him. Drained, but wonderfully sated, he pulled himself away from Lorelei. He staggered from the bed and sat on the bench in front of the dressing table.

Edward surveyed her beaten form and shook his head. "You didn't heed my warning, Lorelei. I told you not to hit me. No one ever struck me and lived to talk about it. *He* whipped me because he said I was bad. You did it because you wanted fun. That one time you beat me, I told you I would get even, but you laughed. Now I'm the victor. I have won!"

A gasping voice spoke from the bed. "You're a fool, Edward. You've won nothing. I'll have the last word yet."

Edward rushed to the bed. "You can go to hell, Lorelei."

She lifted her head to leer at him. "And when I get there, you'll join me. I won't have long to wait."

Grabbing the dagger from the night table, Edward

plunged it into her back over and over again. He let the knife fall from his hand. "Hell was at your side these past years, Lorelei. Nothing Satan could devise would be able to touch the evil in you."

Edward dressed and quickly fled to the grove of trees where Black Magic was hidden. Taking the same route he had used earlier, he returned to Chatham Hall.

After replacing the horse in its stall, Edward went to his room and changed into the clothes he'd worn at dinner. Running downstairs, he reset the hall clock from four o'clock to half past one. He entered the library and changed the time on the mantel clock as well. Taking the seat across from Geoffrey, he dropped a cup and saucer to the floor. Edward leaned back in his chair, feigning sleep as the crash woke the duke.

Rubbing his eyes, Geoffrey looked at the clock and nudged Edward. "Wake up, Edward. It's half past one. We must be getting old, sleeping in our cups—of tea, no less. Come on, let's go to bed." The duke stood up and swayed slightly. "By God, I'm so groggy I may never find my room."

Yawning, Edward got to his feet and put his arm around Geoffrey's shoulder. "Have no fear, big brother. I'll lead the way. You can count on me to help you get to bed."

The two brothers were laughing as they left the library and climbed the stairs.

Chapter 9

When Victoria arrived at Ryland Shipping, her office looked like the headquarters of an army under siege. Maps hung on the walls. Papers were strewn across her desk. Miles and two men were quarreling over a chart laid out on the table next to the window.

Miles slapped his hand on the table top. "I'm going to find that damned O'Banyon and make him pay for this!"

Curiosity made Victoria ask, "Who's O'Banyon?"

The men turned to face the doorway where she was standing. Miles's angry scowl was replaced by a warm smile as he walked to her side.

Kissing her cheek, he put his arm around her. "My friends, may I present my fiancée and business partner, Victoria Carlisle. Torie, this is Jamie Campbell, captain of the *Foxfire,* and this tall rogue is Captain Garret Morgan of *Torie's Treasure.*"

Garret stood several inches taller than Miles. He was a handsome man of thirty, with hazel eyes, dark hair, and an elegant beard and mustache. Jamie Campbell, though born in Scotland, looked like a Norseman with his flaxen hair, pale blue eyes, and muscular build.

Garret stepped forward and kissed her hand. "It is a great pleasure to meet you, my lady, and my biggest regret that I did not meet you first. Had you met me earlier, this scamp never would have stood a chance at winning your heart."

He shot Miles a quick grin. "Congratulations, old chum. I offer you both my best wishes."

Jamie took her hand. "I'm not the golden-tongued dandy Garret is, but my wishes are just as sincere, my lady."

"I'm delighted to meet you both. Miles has told me so much about you. I feel I've known you for years. Now tell me, who is this O'Banyon you were discussing when I came in?"

Miles frowned. "Rory O'Banyon is a renegade Irish pirate who attacked *Torie's Treasure* on her return from America. Thanks to Garret's quick thinking and a Royal Navy ship's coming upon them, our losses were minimal, but that damned cutthroat got away!" Regaining his composure, he continued, "I refuse to wait for the Admiralty to find him. I'm going after him myself."

"But, Miles, you're Viscount Ryland, a member of one of the most prestigious families in England. How can you expect to find an Irish outlaw like O'Banyon?" Victoria asked.

A smile curved his lips. "Long before I became a viscount, I was known as Miles Trelane, the Fox. For six years, I sailed on the *Foxfire* and had my share of privateering, honest trading, and sea battles. I can become the Fox again. In my old guise, I will trap O'Banyon and bring him to England to face charges."

Victoria tugged nervously on her heart-shaped pendant as she spoke. "Miles, this could be very dangerous. You cannot do this alone."

"He won't have to," Garret informed her. "I was trying

to offer my services in his stead before you arrived. When I met O'Banyon, I had no beard and my attire was befitting a captain. With the right costume, my beard, and longer hair, I believe I'd make a wonderful pirate."

"This isn't a theatrical performance, Garret," Miles snapped. "Those bastards could kill us if we're not careful."

Jamie interrupted them. "But Garret has seen Rory O'Banyon, and you haven't."

"And the damage inflicted by O'Banyon's attack on my ship is going to take at least eight weeks to repair," Garret stated. "If I don't go with you, the inactivity will drive me insane."

Miles held up his hands in surrender. "All right! We leave on the morning tide."

"Gentlemen, may I make some suggestions? I may be a lady, but I'm involved in this project, too." Victoria approached the map of Ireland spread out on the table. "Where will you start looking for O'Banyon? The coast is full of small ports. If the man's a real pirate, I doubt he'd frequent the larger harbors or cities."

She began to pace. "And not using your whole name isn't going to be enough, Miles. All three of you must unpolish your speech and manners when you go ashore. Adapt their brogue, if you can. Select a crew from the combined forces of the *Treasure* and the *Foxfire*. Take only the best. Also, I would—"

Victoria turned to find the men staring at her. Miles was grinning, but Garret and Jamie looked stunned. Miles laughed. "Now you see why this lady is so important to me. Beauty and brains—what more could a man ask for?"

They spent the rest of the day making plans. The *Foxfire* would dock in Bristol between trips to Ireland. Garret's family had an estate close to the port town that would serve as a base for the operation. Supplies would be stored there for the voyages and a courier would be sent once a week to pick up and deliver reports regarding the business and their search.

Victoria would remain in London to take care of Ryland Shipping. No one, with the exception of Mark Grayson, would know where Miles really was. If asked, people would be told he was visiting his estate in Sheringham.

After midnight, Miles escorted Victoria back to Carlisle house. "I wish you'd reconsider and stay with my parents while I'm away."

"I'll be fine here, Miles. With all my work, I won't have time to be lonely. On weekends, I'll go home to see Papa."

Miles hugged her. "Are you going to miss me, Victoria?"

"Of course I am," she assured him. "Just be careful and come back as soon as you can. I don't think I could stand losing you, too, Miles. Please take care of yourself."

"Don't worry, Torie. I'll be back sooner than you think, and we can get on with our lives together."

Victoria was working at the Carlisle offices the following morning when the magistrate, Sir Nigel Bradford, came looking for Edward Damien.

"May I ask why you're looking for my uncle?" she asked.

Bradford was a nervous little man, with gray hair and spectacles. "My lady, I regret to inform you that Lorelei Damien, Countess Sedwick, has been murdered. We must contact the earl regarding her death."

His announcement caused Victoria to fall back in her seat. "He's been staying with my father in Chatham. The duke has been ill, and Uncle Edward was kind enough to stay with him so I could come to London on business. This news will come as a great shock to my uncle. I'm leaving immediately for Chatham. You may follow in your own coach, sir."

The inspector bowed. "As you wish, my lady."

Three hours later, Victoria arrived home with the officer.

Mrs. Oliver told her the duke and Edward were in the library having tea.

"Victoria, this is a surprise!" Geoffrey exclaimed when she entered the library. "See, Edward, she couldn't stay away from us." As he stood up and hugged her, he noticed Bradford standing near the door. "And who is this gentleman, my dear?"

"Papa, Uncle Edward, this is Sir Nigel Bradford. Sir Nigel, may I present my father, His Grace Geoffrey Carlisle, Duke of Chatham, and my uncle, Edward Damien, Earl of Sedwick."

With the introductions completed, Victoria directed everyone to be seated. Bradford and Geoffrey used the leather armchairs, while she sat on the sofa with Edward. "Sir Nigel is a magistrate. He has some grave news."

Bradford turned toward Edward. "My lord, it grieves me to inform you that your wife died last night at Sedwick House."

Tears glittered in Edward's eyes. "How did it happen? Was there an accident?"

The gray haired man shook his head. "No, my lord. She was murdered. If Lady Victoria will excuse us, I would tell you—"

"Don't expect me to leave," Victoria interrupted, taking hold of Edward's hand. "I will not let my uncle go through this without me. Go on, sir. Tell him what happened to his wife."

After Bradford described the gruesome crime, Edward's chin trembled. "What kind of animal would want to kill my Lorelei? She was such a warm, loving woman. My poor Lorelei, the pain she must have endured." He turned to Victoria. "How can I live without her?"

Victoria embraced him. He cried against her shoulder as Geoffrey motioned for Bradford to follow him out of the room. "I'm so alone, Victoria," Edward moaned softly.

"No, Uncle Edward. You have us. We'll be here for you," she assured him.

While he regained his composure, Victoria went to the liquor cabinet across the room and filled a glass with brandy, then gave it to Edward and encouraged him to drink it.

Edward finished his brandy and stared into the empty glass. "I don't know how I'll ever be able to face Sedwick Manor again. Just knowing what happened to Lorelei . . ." His voice faded to a hushed whisper.

She patted his hand. "You are welcome to stay here as long as you like, Uncle Edward. If you prefer living in town, you can stay at Carlisle House. Papa deeded it to me last year for my birthday, but with my own business and overseeing Carlisle Enterprises, I'm rarely there. You would have free run of the house and all the privacy you require."

Edward got up and walked to the window. For a few moments he stood there staring out at the gardens. "This morning I was a happy man. Then I learned that I've lost my Lorelei, and I'm suddenly alone. But your love and concern gives me hope and courage to face the future." Victoria joined him at the window and he hugged her.

"Thank you for caring about me, Victoria. I've never had children of my own, and many times I was a bit envious of your father. Even when he lost your mama, he still had you."

"You can depend on me, Uncle Edward."

With her head against his shoulder as they embraced, Victoria never saw the sinister smile that curved Edward's lips.

Late that night, after Sir Nigel returned to London and Edward had gone to bed, Geoffrey and Victoria sat on the sofa in the library and watched the flames flickering in the hearth.

"Victoria, did you know Bradford believed Edward was responsible for Lorelei's murder? For the love of God, my brother was totally devoted to his wife. Well, I'm sure the statement I gave that fool inspector will clear Edward of any further suspicions."

"What did you tell him, Papa?"

"Nothing out of the ordinary. Edward and I retired here to the library last night to play chess. We drank tea, talked, and enjoyed a very quiet evening. As a matter of fact, we both dozed off for a bit in front of the fire. Around one-thirty, we went to bed."

"You spoke to Sir Nigel. Do they have any clues?"

"He said Edward's housekeeper had gotten up around two in the morning to get a glass of water. While she was in the kitchen, she looked out the window and saw a dark figure running across the grounds to a nearby copse of trees. Thinking the man a prowler, she checked the doors and windows, and found them locked. Several hours later, the maid went to Lorelei's room and found her dead. Bradford's convinced the prowler and the murderer are one and the same."

Victoria snuggled closer to her father. "What would drive a person to commit such a horrible crime?"

Kissing her forehead, Geoffrey cuddled her gently. "Don't waste your time worrying over this tragic event. Bradford and his department can deal with it. We have enough to do helping Edward and seeing to the funeral arrangements. Come on, sweetheart. Let's go to bed."

Lorelei Damien, Countess of Sedwick, was laid to rest on a lovely October afternoon. Her family and friends mourned her passing, shed tears, and comforted each other for their loss. But within a week, the funeral was forgotten, the friends were gone, and the family was left to carry on with their lives. Geoffrey and Victoria returned to Chatham; Edward moved into Carlisle House.

Edward had never liked Sedwick Manor. The cavernous old mansion, filled with portraits of the former earl and members of the St. James family, always reminded him he was an interloper. Once Lorelei's estate was settled, he intended to buy a new home, one that would be his alone. A residence like Chatham Hall would please him.

He knew Geoffrey had included him in his will. After Evangeline's death, Edward had paid a hefty bribe to secure a copy of his brother's last will and testament. According to the document, Geoffrey was leaving him forty percent of Carlisle Enterprises and a large trust fund. The balance of the company and all the estates and properties would go to Victoria. Because of the old royal edict, the title would pass to her, as well.

Lorelei's attorney, Mr. Farnsworth, set up the reading of her will at his offices on November first. Edward was shown to a chair near the large walnut desk. The room quickly filled with assorted servants, a select group of friends, and various members of his dead wife's family.

Though Edward appeared to be listening intently as Mr. Farnsworth commenced the reading, he was actually contemplating what he would do with his newfound wealth. Occasionally he heard mention of someone receiving a pension; others received a piece of Lorelei's jewelry.

When the solicitor began announcing charities that were to receive endowments, Edward started to listen. He had never known his late wife to be so civic minded. Large cash bequests were named for various children's homes, schools, and six different churches. As the names and amounts were read, Edward lost track of how much money was involved.

When he heard his own name, Edward gave Mr. Farnsworth his full attention.

"And lastly, to my husband, Edward Damien, I bequeath

the sum of twenty-five thousand pounds, to be divided into five yearly payments of five thousand pounds each. To give him more would be an insult to the wealth he has shared with me all these years. His influence directed me to dispense my wealth to those less fortunate than ourselves. For couples like us, it is truly more blessed to give than to receive."

Before Edward could speak, Mr. Farnsworth handed him a sealed letter. "The countess asked that I give this to you." Within moments, Edward was alone in the office, staring at the familiar handwriting. Carefully, he opened the parchment and read her final message to him.

> *Edward,*
>
> *After Evangeline's funeral, you hid in the study and drank for days. I went to you and tried to get you to stop. In your drunken state, you implored me to forgive you. I was amazed when you told me you loved me, but I was more shocked when you called me Evangeline. You begged to be forgiven for raping her and wept because she died while carrying your son.*
>
> *At that moment, I dedicated myself to making your life hell. I did it all for my revenge on you. My will is legal and binding. I could not withhold the ownership of Sedwick Manor; it comes with the title. I mortgaged it. The balance is due one year after my death. The amount of the note is one hundred thousand pounds.*
>
> *Not wanting you to starve, I provided the trust fund. Now you can eat and perhaps buy a new cravat every year. Either way, I hope you choke!*
>
> *Lorelei*
> *Countess of Sedwick*

Rage filled Edward's entire being. "That bloody bitch robbed me of my youth and self-respect. I will not allow her to destroy the rest of my existence!"

* * *

Late that night, Edward paced his bedroom at Carlisle House as he reviewed his life. If he hadn't gotten into debt gambling years ago, he would have continued working for his brother and not been forced to marry Lorelei. He'd enjoyed the work at Geoffrey's company and had done a fine job while he was there. Maybe he could do it again.

"Tomorrow I'll go see Geoffrey and ask him for a position with his firm. Victoria could use the help, and God knows I need the money."

Edward went to bed smiling, confident he had made the right decision.

Chapter 10

On the same day, the two brothers received letters from their dead wives. Edward Damien got his from a solicitor. Geoffrey Carlisle found his by mistake.

Geoffrey and Victoria had returned to Chatham after Lorelei's burial. The trip was quiet and uneventful. After dealing with the funeral and helping Edward where they could, the Carlisles looked forward to the solitude of their country estate.

But shortly after they arrived home, Victoria received a message from London. Additional work was needed on *Torie's Treasure,* and she had to approve the expenditures. Early the next morning, she returned to town.

Following her departure, the duke was enveloped by loneliness. He roamed the grounds, visited the stables, and took refuge in his library. While catching up on his journal entries, he noticed the date.

It was the first of November. Twenty years ago that day, he and Evangeline had been married.

Tears filled in his eyes as the pain of losing her came

rushing back. He needed to feel close to her again. Opening the top desk drawer, he removed a hidden brass key.

Geoffrey walked silently through the house and stood at the entrance of the salon adjacent to the master suite. This place had been special to Evangeline. No one had been inside since her death. He unlocked the door and stepped inside.

The room was dark, the air was thick with dust. He went to the windows, threw back the draperies, and lifted the sash. Sunlight and a brisk wind swept through the room. Geoffrey removed the covers from the furniture, then piled them in the hall and closed the door. A smile came to his lips when he looked around the salon.

"Evangeline, my dear, even after all this time, I still feel your presence in this room."

Picking up the portrait that stood in the corner, he hung it over the mantel. As he stepped back to look at the painting, he bumped into the table beside the rocking chair. The carved box on the table fell to the floor and he bent to retrieve it.

The latch had sprung. Lifting the lid, he saw folded parchment. He carefully removed the pages and began to read them aloud. "To my darling daughter, Catherine . . ."

Geoffrey was still in the pink salon when his brother came to Chatham Hall the next day. Edward arrived just before noon and was admitted by the new maid, Lucy Harper.

Lucy's auburn curls peeked out from beneath her mobcap as she shook her head. "I'm sorry, my lord, but His Grace has not come down this morning. Would you like to leave your card and come back later in the day?"

"That won't be necessary, my child. I'm Edward Damien, Earl of Sedwick, the duke's brother," he informed her with a patient smile. "Just go up and tell him I wish to see him."

At twenty-eight, Lucy was hardly the child Edward credited her to be. The eldest daughter of the village schoolteacher, she could read and write and was very intelligent. During the past two days, she'd witnessed the duke's strange behavior and knew something was troubling him. Reluctantly, she went to the salon.

Geoffrey stood at the window and gazed outside for a few minutes before he replied to her announcement. "Show him up here, and please see to it personally that we're not disturbed. No one else is to be allowed near this room, Lucy."

Lucy escorted the earl to the salon. As he went in and shut the door, she returned to polishing the fixtures in the hall while she guarded her employer's privacy.

In the salon, Edward was assailed by pain as he recalled the last time he'd come to this room. Nothing had changed in five years. The only thing missing was Evangeline.

"This was my wife's favorite room," Geoffrey explained, standing at the window with his back to Edward. "Yesterday would have been our twentieth anniversary. I decided to spend the day up here and celebrate the occasion with my memories of her. I must be getting old. I found myself speaking to her as if she were still here."

Edward sat on the loveseat. "Don't deride yourself, Geoffrey. Sometimes it helps to speak to the dead."

Geoffrey continued to gaze out of the window. "Yes, I spoke to Evangeline—and she answered me. It wasn't a voice from the air like those in ghost stories, but she definitely had something to say. Since her death, no one has entered this room. I could never bring myself to come in here. The pain of losing her was too great. But yesterday, I was mysteriously drawn here. I found a letter she wrote shortly before she died.''

Edward cringed. He wanted to flee, but he couldn't. He had to know about the letter.

"Evangeline wrote a long missive when she discovered she was pregnant," Geoffrey went on. "She was a gentle creature who never wanted to burden anyone with her woes. I suppose it gave her peace when she put her thoughts to paper. But it wasn't all sad. No, she celebrated the joy of our life together and the love we shared. Evangeline wrote about our Victoria and her hope that our daughter would find happiness in marriage just as we had.''

He grazed the window pane with his fingertips. "My Evangeline also wrote of regret. She missed the daughter fate had stolen from us that cursed night in Fellsmere. My wife was haunted by the death of our baby. She would come in here and sit for hours. Let me show you what kept her company in this lonely room.''

Moving to the corner, Geoffrey took the sheet from the painting and placed it on the mantle. "I call this painting my Carlisle Jewels. Isn't it lovely?''

Edward's eyes were transfixed on Evangeline's smiling face. He never noticed his brother inching toward him.

"Evangeline was so beautiful and loving," Geoffrey continued in a soft, modulated voice. "She would sacrifice herself rather than hurt someone she loved. That's exactly what she did. Rather than hurt me, she never told me what happened to her and kept the pain and worry to herself. She died before letting me know the truth—the truth of what *you* did to her!''

By this time, Geoffrey's voice was loud, filled with rage. Edward didn't move or reply. "You are despicable, Edward! You said you loved her, but you raped her! Your vicious attack made her pregnant. You're guilty of murdering my wife as surely as if you held a gun to her head and pulled the trigger! How can you live with yourself knowing you killed her?''

When Geoffrey shoved him off the loveseat and onto the floor, Edward glowered up at him. ''How can I live with myself, you ask? I don't. I exist in a hell of my own making! My conscience has eaten away at my soul till there is nothing left. I'm sorry I hurt her, but I'll never regret why I did it. From the moment I saw Evangeline, I loved her. No one will ever take her place in my heart. When she died, a large part of me died with her. Can't you understand that?''

Geoffrey seized Edward by the front of his coat and yanked him to his feet. ''I understand that you wanted something that didn't belong to you, so you took it! You're a spiteful, vindictive animal, and I can't bear the sight of you. But before you go, explain what you said to Evangeline the day you attacked her. You said I had something to fear and boasted you wouldn't make the same mistake twice. What was your first mistake? Bloody hell! Tell me before I toss your worthless carcass from this window and break your foul neck!''

Edward pushed away his brother's grasping hands. ''I have no intention of telling you a thing. Not knowing will frustrate you all the more. So go to hell, brother dear. I'm leaving.''

As he turned toward the door, Geoffrey charged after him. He spun Edward around and punched him squarely in the face. Edward fell to the floor, and Geoffrey continued pummeling him with his fists.

''It was Fellsmere, wasn't it? You tried to kill me and murdered my daughter instead. You injured my wife and nearly destroyed everything I loved that night. Damn you to hell, admit it! You ordered the fire at Fellsmere!''

''Yes!'' Edward shouted, struggling to free himself. ''You had everything I wanted, and I hated you for it. You were so bloody happy, I despised you!''

His brother's confession stunned Geoffrey. He loosened his hold on Edward and staggered to the mantel. "Get out of this house and never come near me or Victoria again. If you do, I'll kill you with my own hands."

Edward got to his feet and stumbled out the door.

As Geoffrey took the portrait down and recovered it with the sheet, tears flowed from his eyes. A knifelike pain suddenly coursed through his head, and he collapsed on the floor.

Chapter 11

"Good grief! It's already the second of November. At this rate Miles will never get home," Victoria complained to Mark Grayson as she dropped a folded sheet of parchment on her desk. "According to his letter, they still haven't found Rory O'Banyon. Your son is off playing pirate while I'm expected to wait here like a good little girl."

Mark reached over and patted her hand. "I'm sure Miles will be back soon. I've never owned a shipping company, but I do have other business experience. I'd be honored if you'd allow me to help you."

"I may have to accept your offer," Victoria sighed. "With Papa in Chatham, I have to keep my eye on the Carlisle offices, too. As it is, I had to leave Papa alone, and I can't help but worry about him. If he finds out Miles is gone, I'll have to tie him to his bed."

"What you need is an assistant, someone who will oversee your father's business and answer directly to you."

Victoria suddenly smiled. "Uncle Edward would be perfect. He worked for my father before. I can offer him a good salary and make him a part of the company again. He went out of town this morning, but as soon as he returns, I'll ask him."

"That's a capital idea, my dear." Mark rose and moved toward the door. "While you're handling things here, I'll see how the work is progressing on *Torie's Treasure*. That will save you a trip to the docks and give me something to do. I'll report my findings to you in the morning."

By the time Victoria returned to Carlisle House that night, she was exhausted. As she was finishing dinner, her butler, Cosgrove, entered the dining room with Billy Fletcher, a servant from Chatham Hall, close at his heels.

"I beg your pardon, my lady," Cosgrove began, "but the lad—"

"My lady, you've got to come straightaway," Billy blurted out in a panic. "The duke's real bad and the doctor sent for you. Once we change the horses, we can leave immediately."

Victoria held back her own anxiety and spoke calmly to the young man. "Thank you, Billy. While I'm gathering my things, Cosgrove will get you and the driver something to eat. You'll need it for the trip back."

After eleven, Victoria entered her father's bedroom and found the doctor leaning over Geoffrey's motionless form. She quickly approached the bed.

"Dr. Louden, how is my father? What happened to him?"

The doctor turned to her. "His Grace suffered a brain seizure and is now in a coma. He was found unconscious this afternoon on the floor in the room next to this one."

Victoria frowned. "That's strange. Papa hasn't entered that room since my mother died. Why would he go in there today?"

"I don't know, but there's nothing more we can do for

His Grace at this time. We'll just have to keep an eye on him and see to his needs."

"Dr. Louden, my father's recovery is uppermost in my mind. No matter the cost, I want it done. I'm also requesting his condition be kept secret. His Grace wouldn't want news of his illness to reach his business associates or competitors. Have I made myself clear?"

The doctor nodded. "As you wish, my lady. If you'll excuse me, I'm going to send for the woman who assists me with my patients. Miss Foster has vast experience and will take excellent care of the duke."

Alone in the room with her father, Victoria sat on the bed and held his hand. Tears filled her eyes as she prayed. "Dear God, why must I always lose the ones that I love? First Mama, then Adam. Am I some kind of jinx? I'm afraid to love anyone. Please don't let me lose Papa. Please, God, don't do this to me again. Please, not again . . ."

Early the next morning, Victoria assembled the household staff and questioned everyone about the previous day. Had the duke been ill? Had he had any visitors?

No one admitted seeing anything out of the ordinary. Mrs. Oliver watched as Victoria interviewed each member of the staff. The only one who seemed overly upset was the newest maid, Lucy Harper.

After dismissing the others, Victoria asked Lucy to come up to the pink salon with her. Once they were inside, Victoria locked the door and had the maid sit beside her on the sofa.

"Lucy, you know something about my father, don't you?"

"But Mrs. Oliver said I shouldn't . . ." Lucy looked at the floor, unable to face Victoria.

"In spite of what Mrs. Oliver thinks, I run this house. If she's threatened you in any way, I'll deal with her. Now tell me what you know about what happened to my father yesterday."

Lucy nodded. "After you left, His Grace appeared to be quite sad. He wandered aimlessly around the estate. Two days ago, as I was waxing the banisters at the top of the stairs, he passed me and entered this room. A few moments later, he put a pile of dust covers in the hall and went back inside. When I went to retrieve the sheets, I heard him talking to himself. I couldn't make out everything he said, though I did hear words like happy, love, and anniversary."

"My goodness, how could I have forgotten? The day before yesterday was my parents' anniversary." Victoria sighed. "Go on, Lucy. What happened next?"

"I took the sheets to the laundress. When I returned to polishing the woodwork, the duke came out of the salon and asked me to step inside." Lucy smiled. "I was frightened I'd done something wrong, but he was nice and asked me my name. Then he gave me a key and sent me to the library to fetch the inkwell, pen, and paper from his desk. Once I did that, he sent me for his dinner and a pot of tea. He told me to bring enough for two.

"When I returned with the food, he'd moved the table and had it sitting between the rocker and the straight-back chair. He set aside the papers he was working on, told me to put the tray on the table, and asked me to sit down and eat with him."

As she smiled at the memory, Lucy's cheeks glowed. "I saw how lonely he was and agreed. His Grace talked about you and his late wife. He even asked about my family. When he heard I had ten brothers and sisters, he said I was lucky to come from a household so full of love. He laughed when I told him the house was also filled with far too many people. We had a lovely time. As I cleaned up the dishes, he told me to find another servant who could write his name and bring him back here to the salon."

She returned with Billy Fletcher, and the duke asked

them to witness his signing of the documents he had prepared. Then he had Lucy and Billy sign their names where he directed. After dismissing Billy, the duke had Lucy wait while he folded the papers into two separate packets.

"His Grace placed one in his pocket and addressed the other to Mark Grayson, Earl of Foxwood. He told me to put that one in his desk and be sure I locked the library door. He handed me the key and packet and bid me good night. I carried out his orders and went to bed."

Lucy sighed. "The next morning I brought up his breakfast and discovered he'd spent the entire night in the salon. His Grace looked so forlorn. Your father agreed to eat only if I stayed and kept him company. When he finished, I picked up the tray and went about my duties." Her smile suddenly vanished. "Just before noon, the earl came and asked to see the duke."

Victoria interrupted her. "An earl? Who was he?"

"I don't recall his name, but he was dark and handsome, with silver streaks in his hair. Said he was the duke's brother."

"That was my uncle, Edward Damien, Earl of Sedwick. But I'm confused. How did he visit without anyone else seeing him?"

Lucy shrugged. "The footmen were being fitted for their new livery and Mrs. Oliver was busy in the kitchens. I let the earl into the house. Your father asked me to bring him to the salon and ordered me to keep everyone away from the room while the earl was here." A shiver rushed through her. "I was cleaning the fixtures in the hall a few minutes later when the fight started and the shouting began."

"Who was shouting?" Victoria asked.

"At first it was your father. He sounded so angry. I ran when the earl screamed, 'Yes, I did it, and I hated you.' The duke ordered him to leave the house, threatening to kill the earl if he ever returned. I was standing in the alcove across the hall, but the earl didn't see me when he hurried out of the room and down the stairs. Within a moment or two, his coach pulled away from the house.''

Lucy clenched her hands in her lap. ''I knocked several times, but His Grace didn't answer. When I peeked in and saw him lying unconscious on the floor near the corner, I went for help. Then I returned to the salon, covered him with a quilt, and waited till the doctor came.''

The implications of what might have come between the two brothers filled Victoria with suspicion and renewed her old doubts about Edward. She had to find out what happened.

The maid's ardent voice garnered her attention. ''I'm sorry I didn't tell you of this sooner, but after I told Mrs. Oliver about the earl's visit and what I'd overheard, she insisted I was wrong and threatened to discharge me without reference if I mentioned it to you. Please believe me, I was only worried about your father. I pray you won't turn me out for this.''

Victoria placed her hand on Lucy's shoulder. ''I appreciate your honesty, and I have no intention of letting you go. In fact, you'll be getting a promotion. I'm putting you in charge of my father's care. Dr. Louden and the nurse will see to his medical needs, and the guards I'll bring from London will protect him from harm, but you will oversee them all. I have to go see my uncle. While I am away, no one else will be permitted in the master suite, not even Papa's valet, Quigley. Do you understand?''

''Even Mrs. Oliver?''

''Especially Mrs. Oliver. Until I know why she wanted to keep Edward's visit a secret from me, I can't trust her. The only person you have to answer to, Lucy, is me.''

''When will I start my new duties?'' Lucy eagerly asked.

Victoria smiled. ''Is now too soon?''

''Oh, no, my lady. It will be an honor to serve His Grace. I promise not to disappoint you.'' Lucy dipped into a quick curtsy and hurried out the door.

Alone in the salon, Victoria considered the questions she needed answers to. Why had Mrs. Oliver stopped Lucy from telling about Edward's visit? What had her father and uncle argued about? Most intriguing of all, what had Edward done that caused her father to threaten his brother's life?

Victoria went to her father's room an hour later and found Lucy sitting in a chair beside the bed talking to him. The nurse was seated in the corner reading a book.

Lucy stood to greet her. "It may seem silly, talking to a man who isn't responding, but I believe he's listening and just can't tell us. I'm glad you're here, my lady. This is the packet your father put in his coat pocket. As you can see, your name is on it. The other one is in the library."

Using her key, Victoria entered the library and went to her father's desk. She searched for the packet meant for Mark Grayson and wasn't surprised to find it missing. Sitting down, she opened the one addressed to her.

It was a codicil to her father's will. In it, he directed that all sections of his current will regarding Edward Damien were to be deleted entirely. His brother was to receive nothing from the estate. Edward had been totally disinherited.

Victoria had known of her father's plans to leave Edward a portion of the firm and a trust fund. Again she wondered what Edward had done to gain her father's wrath. But before she could leave to confront her uncle, there were a few things to attend to at home. She summoned the housekeeper to the library.

An attractive widow in her fifties, Jessica Oliver soon stood before Victoria, dressed in one of her customary gray gowns. Her dark hair was neatly pinned up in a coronet on her head.

"Mrs. Oliver, before I leave for town, I have a few matters to discuss with you. First, Lucy Harper has been assigned to a new position. She will be a liaison between the medical help and the household. No one other than the small group that I'm bringing in will be allowed in my father's suite during his recovery. Anyone defying my orders will be discharged immediately. Please pass this on to the rest of the staff."

Mrs. Oliver nodded. "As you wish, my lady, though I'd hoped I might help with His Grace's care."

"Your concern is appreciated, but I count on you to keep the household running as well as you always do." Giving the woman an encouraging smile, Victoria continued. "Has anyone been in the library this morning?"

"No, my lady. The maids aren't due to clean this room until tomorrow. I personally oversee their work, and the door is always kept locked as per His Grace's orders."

"Fine, Mrs. Oliver. Please see that these practices are continued," Victoria replied, not missing the touch of color on the older woman's cheeks. "By the by, no one is to be told of my father's illness. I don't want word of this to reach the Graysons or my uncle Edward. It would alarm them. I'll be the one to break the news to them, and no one else."

The housekeeper nodded. "Yes, my lady. Will there be anything else?"

"I want to thank Billy for getting me back here so quickly last night. Please have him sent to me at once."

"But, I, ah, sent him on an errand this morning. He won't be back for some time." Mrs. Oliver's left eye twitched slightly. "I'll be more than happy to convey your thanks to him when he returns, my lady."

"Very well. That will be all, Mrs. Oliver."

As soon as the housekeeper left, Victoria went to her room. She dressed in a green wool riding habit, pinned up her hair in a neat chignon, and paid a visit to her father's room.

"Lucy, I'm leaving for London now, but I should be back by tomorrow evening. Mrs. Oliver knows of your new position and won't interfere with your duties."

"Don't worry, Lady Victoria. I'll follow your orders to the letter and see to your father's care. You can depend on me."

Victoria surprised Lucy by giving her a quick hug. "Thank you. I'll never forget your loyalty."

"God speed, my lady, and please be careful."

Victoria rushed to the stables and had a groom prepare Black Magic for the long ride to London. Not knowing whom to trust, she decided to travel cross-country on horseback alone. With a pair of loaded pistols hidden beneath her cloak, she mounted the large black stallion and raced off in search of the truth.

With nowhere else to go, Edward returned to Sedwick Manor. He spent the night in his study drinking brandy and fell asleep in a chair beside the fireplace. His butler woke him early the next day to announce the arrival of a messenger. Billy Fletcher entered the study and handed Edward a leather pouch before returning to the foyer to await his reply.

Ignoring his throbbing head, Edward opened the pouch and read its contents. According to the note, Geoffrey had suffered a brain seizure minutes after his departure and was lying in a coma. His brother's prognosis was poor; it was unlikely the duke would survive. Victoria had rushed home, but knew nothing of the circumstances regarding her father's ailment or Edward's presence at Chatham Hall that day.

The missive went on to say that the enclosed document had been intercepted before it could be delivered. Edward read the codicil that would have disinherited him, and his liquor-induced headache was forgotten.

He chuckled out loud. This could work to his advantage. The codicil hadn't been delivered to Mark Grayson, so Geoffrey's original will remained in effect. If his brother was truly near death, it wouldn't be long before Edward's financial problems were solved.

Edward's high spirits were instantly dashed when he recalled something Geoffrey had said to him. His brother might not survive to condemn him, but that letter from Evangeline could seal his fate. Bloody hell! That letter had to be destroyed before Victoria found it.

He wrote a brief reply and gave it to Billy, sending him on his way. In his note, he asked to be kept informed of the duke's condition and ordered the salon searched for Evangeline's letter.

Edward's decision was made. No one was going to get in his way this time. He'd do whatever was necessary to gain his inheritance.

Victoria arrived in London to learn that Edward had sent for his things and returned to his own home. After informing Cosgrove about her father's condition, she told him there would be three for dinner and asked that her carriage be brought around front. Before setting out for Sedwick Manor, she sealed the codicil to her father's will in a packet with a hastily written note and instructed Cosgrove to deliver it to Mack Grayson.

Victoria knew Mrs. Oliver would send a warning to Edward, and she was determined to intercept the woman's missive before it could be delivered. She had her driver stop at the gate of Edward's home and waited. Within minutes, she recognized the weary-looking rider coming toward the house. She leaned from her window and called to him.

"Billy Fletcher, is that you? Are you all right?"

Caught in a yawn, the servant smiled with embarrassment as he guided his horse toward her and doffed his hat. "I'm fine, my lady—just a mite tired. Two trips t' town in one day surely drains a body." His cheeks flushed. "Mind you,

I'm not complaining. Mrs. Oliver said you wanted me to bring another missive to the earl, and I was glad to help."

"I appreciate your efforts, but after your departure, I decided to visit my uncle instead."

Billy frowned. "And you got here ahead of me. Did I fall asleep in the saddle? Mrs. Oliver is going to have my neck for this."

"Don't worry, Billy. You have every right to be tired. Give me my note and go back to Carlisle House for the night. When you return to Chatham in the morning, just tell Mrs. Oliver you delivered the letter and spent the night in town to rest your horse."

Happily, Billy pulled the letter from his coat and handed it to her. "Thank you, my lady. I'll never let you down again, I promise." With a quick bow, he turned his horse around and headed towards Carlisle House.

As her carriage went down the drive, Victoria broke the seal on the parchment. Although it wasn't signed, she recognized Mrs. Oliver's bold script. The note told Edward that his brother's illness was to be kept secret. She also told him the duke's suite was kept locked and only a select few were allowed inside. The missive closed with a word of caution: *You don't want to lose it all again, Edward, so be careful.*

Ripping the note to shreds, Victoria hid the pieces inside her reticule and removed the pins that held up her hair. It would take a bit of acting to pull it off, but she was confident her portrayal of a nervous young woman fraught with worry would gain Edward's sympathy and draw him into her trap.

Wilson stood in the open doorway to Edward's study. "My lord, you have a visitor waiting to see you in the parlor."

"Who can that be? No one knows I'm here."

Before the old retainer could reply, Edward hurried past him to the ornate drawing room. He saw a lone figure standing before the hearth. Her unbound hair and bedraggled appearance caused him to gasp when she turned to face him.

"Victoria? What's happened? Why are you here?"

With tears cascading down her cheeks, Victoria ran into his arms and sobbed. "Uncle Edward, Papa may be dying, and I'm so frightened!"

Guarding his words, Edward led her to the sofa and sat beside her. "Calm yourself, dear. Tell me everything. Is your father all right?"

"Last night I was summoned to Chatham," she explained, twisting her necklace with her fingers. "Papa had a brain seizure, and Dr. Louden doubts if he will survive. I just could not face it all on my own. You're the only family I have, so I had Black Magic saddled and rode to town by myself to see you."

"By God, Victoria, it's not safe for a young lady to travel alone! You could have been set upon by villains or killed."

Victoria nodded and looked up at him. "I know, Uncle Edward, but don't worry, I won't do it again. My coach is waiting outside. Would you please come to Carlisle House and have dinner with me tonight so we can talk?"

A surge of hope made Edward smile. Perhaps things would work out after all. "Of course I'll come to dinner. We can ride back to your house together. You shouldn't be alone at a time like this."

Victoria hugged him. "Thank you. I knew I could count on you."

A short time later, they arrived at Carlisle House. As Edward handed his greatcoat to Cosgrove, Victoria found a note waiting for her on the foyer table. She barely had time to shove it in her pocket when Edward came up behind her and placed a hand on her shoulder.

"You've had a dreadful day, my girl. Why don't you go up and have a long, leisurely bath before dinner?"

"What a wonderful idea! If you don't mind being alone for a bit, I'll do just that."

The tub was soon filled with steaming water. Once the maids put out the soap and draped the towels over the back of her privacy screen, Victoria dismissed them. Soaking in a hot tub was a daily ritual she enjoyed. It was the one part of the day when no one was talking to her or demanding her attention about business or anything else.

In spite of the comforting water and solitude, peace eluded her. Her mind dwelled on the man waiting downstairs. How much did she really know about Edward Damien?

During the past year, her father had told her a great deal about his half brother and the sad circumstances of his birth. Setting aside her misgivings, she'd allowed herself to trust him and had welcomed him into their home. But no longer. There was a deadly conflict between her father and Edward. She had discovered treachery in her household and now her father's life was in great danger. Something had to be done before it was too late.

Victoria completed her toilette and dressed for dinner. The note she had taken from the foyer table was from Mark. He had read her plan and agreed to help. Between them, they'd keep Edward busy until her father recovered from his seizure or she could discern the truth about what he'd done to cause the rift with his brother.

As she came downstairs, she heard Mark talking to Edward in the drawing room.

"I'm very concerned with Victoria's well being, Edward. She's far too young to handle such strife and responsibility. With the added problem of Geoffrey's failing condition, she needs someone to assist her at Carlisle Enterprises."

Victoria smiled. Her accomplice was doing a fine job of setting the trap. It was up to her to snare their prey.

Breathlessly, she hurried into the room. "I'm sorry for taking so long. I was more tired than I thought, and I nearly fell asleep in my bath."

Mark stepped forward and kissed her cheek. "No need to apologize, my dear. We understand, don't we, Edward?"

"Of course. Mark and I have been talking. Perhaps I may have a solution to your tiring problems. Let's go in to dinner and we'll speak of it there." Edward offered his arm to lead Victoria into the dining room.

When she glanced back over her shoulder, Mark saluted and shot her a smile of victory.

By noon the following day, Victoria was on her way back to Chatham. The new nurse sat in the coach with her, while two burly, well-armed guards rode on horseback behind them.

The nurse had been a doctor's assistant in London. The gray-haired matron came highly recommended, with excellent references. The two guards, Tom White and John Sexton, were actually members of the *Foxfire's* crew. Their loyalty was outshone only by their fighting skills. When Victoria asked for their help, she didn't have to ask twice. They promised her the duke would be safe under their protection.

Victoria was pleased. Everything was falling into place. At dinner the previous night, it was decided she would return to Chatham to be with her father while Mark took care of Ryland Shipping and Edward oversaw Carlisle Enterprises in her stead.

Before leaving London, she'd given Mr. Lawrence, her father's solicitor, instructions regarding Edward's position with the firm. He was to be a figurehead—no real decisions were to go through him. He'd have access to only the generous salary he was to be paid weekly. He could negotiate terms, prices, and contracts, but couldn't sign them. But Edward would be kept too busy to notice.

Mark would stop and see him every day. They would become good friends. Mark would invite him to his club and introduce him around the business community.

Yes, Edward Damien would be a very busy man, indeed.

Mrs. Oliver was in the foyer when Victoria led her three new employees into Chatham Hall. "My lady, is there anything I can do to help these, ah, staff members with settling in?" the housekeeper called out as the two rough-looking men who had just arrived ignored the footmen and carried their trunks and baggage up the stairs.

Not bothering to stop, Victoria shook her head. "That won't be necessary, Mrs. Oliver. I'll see to the arrangements myself. Just advise Cook we'll need supper in an hour."

Lucy unlocked the door and admitted Victoria and the others into the duke's room. Victoria went directly to her father's side. "How is Papa? Any change in his condition?"

"Dr. Louden left an hour ago," Lucy informed her. "He said the duke's color is good and there's no sign of a fever. But until His Grace regains consciousness, we have no idea if he's suffered any permanent damage."

"Yes, I know." Victoria leaned down to kiss her father's cheek before she turned to address Lucy and the others. After the introductions were completed, she gave them their orders. "Other than yourselves and Dr. Louden, no one else is to be admitted into this suite. One of you men must be in this room at all times. Trust no one in the household and suspect everyone. The life and well-being of the duke depend on it.

"Furthermore, none of you will be staying in the servants' wing. John and Tom will share the room across the hall, and the nurses will use the chamber next to this suite.

Lucy will share my room. All your meals will be brought up here."

Victoria's eyes moved to each of them in turn. "The final thing I must emphasize is the importance of keeping my father's condition a secret from everyone outside of this room. I don't care if he gets up and does a jig. No one is to know."

As she thanked them and moved toward the door, Lucy stopped her. "Lady Victoria, I can stay in my place in the attic. You don't have to share your fine room with me."

"I want you to. With Papa so ill and my fiancée away, I have no one to talk to. I was hoping we might even become friends."

Lucy gasped. "But, my lady, I'm a servant. I'm not good enough to be your friend."

"Why, Lucy Harper, you're a snob!"

"I am not a snob," she retorted.

"Prove it!" Victoria challenged. "First, call me by my given name. Titles make me sound ancient. Would it be so difficult to be my friend?"

Lucy nervously returned her smile. "Not at all, my la . . . I mean, Victoria."

"Fine!" Victoria took her arm. "Come, my friend. Let me show you to our room."

While they were getting ready for bed that night, Victoria told Lucy about the arrangements she'd made regarding her uncle.

Lucy sat on the bed and watched her pace the room. "Now that you've seen to your father's protection and found a way to keep the earl busy, what will you do next?"

"In the morning I'm going to search my father's files and papers in the library. Edward must have done something vile to make Papa threaten his life. Before their fight in the salon, they were very close. Since Papa hasn't had any visitors lately, it stands to reason he must have gotten a written message about his brother. The proof must be here in this house, and I intend to find it.''

"What will you do if you find the proof?"

"I'll take it to the authorities and see Edward never touches my father's money nor has the chance to harm him. Whatever he did, whomever he hurt, Edward will pay for it.''

A sound in the hall drew Victoria to the door. She quickly opened it. After finding the corridor deserted, she moved back into her room and shook her head. "All of this intrigue is taking a toll on me. Now I'm hearing things that aren't there."

Lucy put her head on the pillow and pulled up the quilt. "You're just tired. Come to bed and get some sleep. You have a great deal to do tomorrow."

"You're probably right. I feel like I haven't slept in days." Blowing out the candle on the table, Victoria climbed into bed. "Good night, Lucy."

"Pleasant dreams, Victoria."

A lone figure stepped out of the guest room across the hall from Victoria's suite. "Edward must know of this immediately."

Chapter 12

Damn! That contemptible minx couldn't keep out of it. What was he going to do about her now?

Edward was vexed. Sitting behind his desk at Carlisle Enterprises, he reviewed the message he'd received early that morning.

Thanks to Victoria's efforts, Geoffrey's suite was a veritable fortress. No one other than the staff hired to care for him was allowed inside. The pink salon and the library were also kept locked. Victoria had taken the keys to these rooms and several bedrooms from the housekeeper.

According to the conversation Mrs. Oliver had overheard the night before, Victoria knew about the fight in the salon and blamed Edward for Geoffrey's seizure. She was sure he'd done something to provoke the altercation with his brother. If she found any proof, she intended to use it against him.

If she found Evangeline's letter, his life wouldn't be worth a penny. Even if Victoria didn't connect him with the fire at Fellsmere, his part in Evangeline's death would force her hand. With his niece's social contacts, she could have Lorelei's murder investigation reopened, as well.

Edward tossed the letter into the blazing hearth and made a decision. "I cannot let Victoria destroy me. Whatever it takes, I must stop her."

After telling the clerk he had an appointment across town, Edward began searching the seedy pubs along the waterfront, where only the dregs of humanity were found. Money could buy anything there. It wasn't long before he found a likely candidate to help him deal with his niece.

The man's name was Clive Walters. A thief and assassin, he specialized in abductions. Clive was an ugly brute of a man, with crooked teeth and a drooping lower lip.

"Now, lemme get this right, milord. You wants me ta pinch this bird and get rid of her. Then I'm ta bring you somethin' of hers ta prove I did her in. That's when you'll be givin' me the rest of me money." Clive swilled down his ale and wiped his mouth on the sleeve of his dirty coat.

Edward cast a wary eye on his companion. "I want the deed carried out immediately, Walters, and don't think to cross me. Others have tried and have paid for their mistakes."

"You'll not be havin' a lick o' trouble outta me, milord. Who knows? You might be needin' me services again. I'll get me 'alfwit cousin, Andy, to lend a hand, and we'll nick the bird by weeks' end," Clive assured him with a lopsided grin.

"Fine." Edward shoved a pouch over the table. "Here's five hundred pounds and a map to Chatham Hall. I've already given you a description of Victoria Carlisle. Once you've completed the task, bring the proof to me at Sedwick Manor. The balance of the money will be paid to you at that time."

As Edward left the tavern, Clive chuckled to himself. He'd been involved in abductions many times, but not for ransoms or rewards. He was a supplier of sorts for a captain who sailed out of Bristol. What he supplied was beautiful young white women who could be sold at the slave markets in faraway ports like Istanbul.

"If this bird is as comely as 'is lordship sez, I'll be makin' a double fee for me work," Clive snickered. "Even if she ain't pretty, maybe I'll be takin' a turn at her first, afore I finishes me job."

Victoria spent the day searching the library while Lucy carried on a similar hunt through the duke's bedroom. Every book was opened, all the drawers were emptied. Cabinets and closets were scoured from top to bottom. Even the furniture was examined for hiding places. But nothing was found.

Instead of being frustrated by failure, Victoria became more determined to succeed.

While eating breakfast the following day, Victoria realized a courier would be arriving by noon to bring her packet of correspondence from London. Deciding this would be an excellent opportunity to send word to Miles, she wrote him a long detailed letter about everything that had transpired in the past week. She also told him about Lucy and what a good friend this woman had become to her. As Victoria closed the missive, she wished him well. She prayed he was safe and would be home soon.

The courier arrived just as she sealed the parchment. Leaving her a large leather pouch of documents, he took her letter and made his way back to London. Among the reports Victoria found a message from Vanessa Grayson, saying she and Mark were coming to visit the next week.

Setting her work aside, Victoria went up to see her father. She sat on the bed beside him and talked to him, just as Lucy had done. She didn't know if he could hear her, but it made her feel better to think he could.

"I want to be strong for you, but I depend on you, too.

You must get well and come back to me." She kissed his cheek, then sat back to look at him.

Staring back at her were the most beautiful green eyes she had ever seen. "Papa, you're looking at me. Your eyes are open. Lucy, come quick! Papa's awake!"

Excitement surged through the room. Victoria sent for Dr. Louden. Within the hour, the trusted physician was at Geoffrey's side, completing his examination.

"Papa's getting better, isn't he, Dr. Louden?"

The elderly man nodded. "Apparently so, my lady. Your father is awake and alert. He still can't speak or move on his own, but with time and proper care, I'm confident His Grace will regain some of these functions, as well." He patted Victoria's hand. "I will give the nurses their instructions and be back in the morning. Good day, my lady."

Victoria sat beside her father and looked into his eyes. "You can hear me, can't you, Papa?" Slowly, his lids closed and opened again. "Are you in any pain?" This time he blinked twice. Comprehension made her smile. "One blink means yes and two means no. Am I right?"

He blinked once.

She gave him a quick hug. "Oh, I'm so pleased that you're getting better. I don't want to tire you, but I must know what caused the fight you had with Edward. Did you get a letter or message about something he had done?" Geoffrey blinked once.

"When you confronted Edward about it that day, did he deny it?"

His response was no.

"Then it must have been something truly awful for you to become so angry. I've already searched the library and it wasn't there, so you've probably hidden it. I want to see the letter."

His negative reply sparked her ire.

"But why? If Edward is guilty of some vile deed, I have a right to know what it was."

His answer was another no.

Lucy touched her shoulder. "Victoria, calm down. I think your father is simply worried about your safety and doesn't want you to be hurt. Is that not correct, my lord?"

Geoffrey looked from Lucy to his daughter and blinked once.

Victoria could see the obvious concern in her father's weary eyes and was assailed with regret. "Forgive me, Papa. I never meant to upset you. We can talk about this after you're fully recovered." She kissed his cheek. "I have some correspondence to take care of downstairs. I'll be back later."

Fraught with confusion, Victoria tugged on the chain of her necklace and slowly walked along the corridor. Her father's wish to protect her was understandable, but he wasn't aware of the real possibility that Mrs. Oliver was involved in a conspiracy with Edward against them. What should she do now?

Victoria looked up and saw she was standing at the door to the pink salon, her mother's special place. Occasionally, Evangeline would bring her here and they would read, embroider, or have little tea parties together. Some of her fondest memories of her mother were connected with this room.

Taking the ring of keys from her pocket, she unlocked the door and stepped inside.

A feeling of peace engulfed Victoria as she walked around the familiar surroundings. She felt as if time had turned around and she was a child who had come to this lovely room to spend time with her mother.

"Oh, Mama, when I was little, I could come to you with my questions and you always had the answers. I wish you could answer me now. What did Edward do that caused Papa to get so angry?" Her eyes brimmed with tears.

As she dabbed her face with her handkerchief, Victoria noticed a painting covered with a sheet standing in the corner. "Where did that come from?"

She removed the cloth and saw an oil portrait of her mother and two baby girls. Her mother was very young and lovely. The babies appeared to be twins, with blond curls and green eyes. They wore matching blue dresses and golden heart pendants.

Victoria sat on the floor to study the picture. The baby on the right had the letter "V" engraved on her pendant, while the one on the left had the letter "C."

"That's my pendant," she gasped. "Could this baby be me? And what became of the other child? Did I have a sister? Was she my twin?"

For a long time, Victoria was too stunned to move. Myriad questions ran through her mind. If she had a sister, why hadn't she been told about her? What happened to her? Did she die? What was her name? Christine? Cassie? Caroline? She couldn't believe her parents had kept something this important from her.

In need of answers, she locked up the salon and rushed to her father's bedroom. When Lucy told her he was asleep, Victoria decided on another course of action. "Lucy, please go tell Billy and Gerald to get my coach ready. I want to be on the road before dark."

"Did you find the proof you were looking for?" Lucy asked.

"What? Oh, you mean about my uncle. No, this is a different matter entirely. Something has come up, and I won't rest easy until I talk to Mark Grayson. He's Papa's closest friend. I'm counting on him to tell me what I need to know."

Victoria placed her ring of keys in Lucy's hand. "While I'm gone, I don't want anyone in the pink salon. Keep the door from the hall and the one from Papa's bedroom locked."

"No one will go in the salon, Victoria, I promise. Please be careful and hurry home to us."

Victoria gave her friend a hug. "Don't worry, Lucy. I'll be back before you know it."

Victoria was on the front portico waiting for her carriage a half hour later, unaware she was being observed by two pairs of greedy eyes.

"See, Andy, me instincts is never wrong," Clive cackled to his cousin, who was crouched with him behind the garden hedge. "I knew if we watched long enuff, she'd be comin' out to us."

Andy's homely face creased in an awed smile. "Ain't she pretty? I never seen the like."

Clive ignored Andy and nodded with satisfaction as the horses and carriage bearing the ducal seal of Chatham pulled to a halt at the entrance of the mansion. "Only one coachman for us to worry about. That's gonna make things a mite easier." He tugged on Andy's sleeve. "Let's get going. If we 'urry, we can cut 'em off 'fore they gets to the post road."

"Sorry I took so long, Lady Victoria," Billy called out as he leaped off the coach and opened the door for her. "Your driver, Gerald, is feeling poorly, so I hitched the horses all by myself. Are we heading to Carlisle House?"

"No. Take me directly to the Grayson's home in town—"

A burst of lightning flashed across the dark, swirling clouds. Thunder clapped and rain began to fall.

Victoria frowned. "I'm sorry to drag you out on a night like this, Billy, but it's imperative I get to London."

"Don't fash yourself, my lady. I've a slicker to keep me dry," he replied, helping her into the coach. "Rest assured, I'll get you to town as soon as I can."

Settled into her seat, Victoria rocked with the movement of the coach and thought about the questions she'd pose to Mark when she saw him. As the rain poured down, she became lost in her musings. A few minutes later, the coach pulled to a halt.

Billy opened the door. "A tree's fallen across the road. Shouldn't take but a minute to move it, my lady." She nodded and he was gone.

A moment later, a gunshot rang out. Victoria swung the door open and stepped onto the muddy road. "Billy, are you all right? I thought I heard gunfire."

"Ain't nothin' wrong with your hearin', ducks."

Victoria spun toward the sound of the crude voice. In the next flash of lightning, she saw a big, ugly brigand carrying a pair of pistols coming toward her. She turned to run, but her way was blocked by a tall, thin man.

"Sorry, me lady," he said, "but you ain't goin' nowhere."

She screamed as the other man came up behind her and caught her around the waist with his muscular arms. She kicked at him, but her legs did little damage. He lifted her off the ground and carried her back to the coach.

"Stop your bloody caterwaulin' or I'll knock you out!" He threw her into the coach and tied her hands with a leather thong. When she continued to scream, he backhanded her across the face several times. "I told you to shut your mouth."

Victoria lay dazed against the seat while her attacker stuffed a gag in her mouth. He yanked the gold chain from her neck and held up the heart-shaped pendant. "Well, well. 'Is lordship wants proof we got you. I'm sure he's gonna recognize this lit'le bauble."

He turned to his accomplice. "Andy, toss the bloke's body in the coach and tie our horses to the back of the rig. I'll ride inside with 'er ladyship while you drive."

The sight of Billy's bloody corpse on the floor beside

her feet was more than Victoria's tattered control could deal with. Tears ran down her face and her body trembled. She prayed that this was just a horrible nightmare. The reality was too gruesome to accept.

Revenge,
Regrets,
and Reunion

Chapter 13

The cold November winds were blowing harshly as three old friends shared a bottle of wine after dinner. Miles got to his feet and began to move about his cabin.

"We're finally going to get O'Banyon. By this time next week, he'll be in prison and I can go home to Victoria. Her father is extremely ill, and she thinks her uncle has committed a crime against her family. I'm afraid she's going to take it upon herself to prove Edward's guilt and endanger her own safety."

Jamie set his glass on the table. "She wrote that letter four weeks ago. Didn't she say your father was helping her? He wouldn't allow her to take unnecessary risks."

Garret sighed. "Stop worrying. We'll be back in London soon, and the three of us can help Victoria with these problems." He looked at Miles and laughed. "Before you see Victoria, you'd better make some changes, my friend."

Miles walked to the mirror to look at his reflection. For his guise of Trelane the Fox, he'd grown a beard and his black hair was long and tied at the nape. From his fine lawn shirt to the high boots that hugged his legs, he was clad in a deep midnight blue. A heavy medallion depicting the snarling face of a fox hung suspended from a gold chain around his neck. A gold loop pierced his right ear.

"I guess you're right. Looking like this, I almost scare myself." Miles scratched his beard and looked at Garret. "I can't wait to rid myself of this. How can you stand wearing one all the time?"

"I like my beard. It gives me a rather rakish appearance," Garret boasted. "Besides, I love it when the ladies stroke it and ask if it would tickle their faces if I kissed them. I show them that I can tickle their faces, their necks, their—"

"That's enough bragging from you tonight." Miles sat at the table and turned to Jamie. "Did McNab and the others from the crew bring back any more information from town?"

"Our informant was correct in sending us here to Youghal Bay. Rory O'Banyon spends a great deal of time at the Sheep's Head Pub trying to romance the tavern owner's daughter when he's not out at sea. He would have been there tonight, but he had to be home for some kind of family celebration."

Garret sat up in his seat. "Too bad we don't know where the O'Banyon stronghold is. There's been a hefty bounty on his father, the Irish Hawk, for over twenty years. It would be quite a feat if we could bring them both in."

Miles shook his head. "I'm not after the Hawk. Let someone else play the hero and capture him. I want that hotheaded son of his. Rory attacked my ship, and I mean to have him hanged for it. I'll do whatever it takes to get him."

Not far down the coast in Corbin's Cove, a beautiful young woman sat in front of her vanity mirror scolding herself.

"Catherine O'Banyon, you're a lucky woman! You have a wonderful family, good friends, a devoted crew, and one of the finest ships around. Why are your spirits so low?"

During the past four and a half years, Catherine had become a legend. Her exploits as Lady Cat had made her infamous. Her courage and success were well known. Eighteen months before, she and her crew had stopped attacking ships and become gunrunners.

The French government wanted to aid the Irish in their never-ending struggle against England. Their help took the form of guns and ammunition. The Irish rebels knew Napoleon and his generals wanted to undermine the English cause for their own purposes, but they didn't care.

The profits weren't as great for Catherine and her men, but the patriotic fervor was beyond any wealth imaginable. They were proclaimed heroes among their countrymen. The O'Banyons also sent food and medical supplies to many stricken areas of Ireland. Payment for these items came from their personal coffers, and they never regretted the cost.

"Maybe I'm just tired," she decided with a sigh.

For several weeks she'd been plagued with nightmares. She saw herself dirty and cold, imprisoned in a dilapidated hut where a big, ugly man came to torment her. Her hands were bound tightly together with straps. Catherine often woke up with her wrists cramped and throbbing. Her dread of the visions had affected her ability to sleep through the night.

Today, her family had gathered to celebrate her nineteenth birthday. Even Rory and Colin had come home to be with her. A special dinner had been planned by her mother. So why was she depressed?

Catherine scowled at her reflection. "Admit it, Catherine O'Banyon. Family, friends, and work aren't enough. You're out of sorts because you're lonely. You want a man in your life, a special man to love you. Could that man be Justin Prescott?''

Though they hadn't seen each other in over four years, she and the handsome doctor had exchanged letters every few months. She looked forward to receiving his missives. Justin told her about his patients and the village of Windell. He'd even told her of the silly songs being sung about her in the English pubs. He closed every letter with love and reminded her how much time they had left before the five years was up and she'd return to him.

It had started out like a game. She'd been a silly fourteen year old, flirting for the first time in her life, but she no longer thought of it as a game. Did she really have a chance of finding happiness with Justin?

Catherine sniffed at her doubts. "And why not? I may captain a ship, but that doesn't mean I can't be a lady, too. After all the hours I spent studying with Neville, how could I be anything less?''

Following his retirement from the sea, her father had rebuilt the cottage into a large two-story house befitting a man of his wealth. But fancy new furnishings were not enough. Despite his wife's objections, Sean employed a married English couple, Neville and Sharon Stimpson, to be their servants.

Neville was a sixth-generation butler who brought dignity and polish to the expanded household. He also proved to be an excellent tutor for Catherine. His diction was perfect, and it wasn't long before he had her speaking in cultured tones. Her brogue surfaced only when she was angry. But their tutelage went beyond grammar.

Catherine still preferred snug britches and loose-fitting blouses when she was aboard ship. But with Sharon's advice and her mother's encouragement, she also had an extensive feminine wardrobe. Lovely dresses, petticoats, lacy undergarments, and fashionable slippers filled a large cabinet in her room.

Toying with the heart pendant she always wore, Catherine felt her confidence waning. "What if Justin doesn't find me attractive anymore? I doubt if he's changed at all during these past four years, but I certainly have."

Walking to the pier glass in the corner of her room, she turned to study her reflection. She hadn't grown taller, but her figure had filled out too much for her liking. The fitted bodice of her forest green gown emphasized her trim waist and the full, womanly curves of her bosom.

"There's naught I can do," she sighed. "I only hope he doesn't fault my hair. I have no intention of changing it for anyone, not even Justin Prescott."

Catherine hated the current styles with masses of short curls and ringlets. She favored wearing it down, with the sides pinned away from her face. While at sea, she wore it in a thick braid that hung to her hips.

She was tying a ribbon around the hair she had gathered at the nape of her neck when someone knocked on her door. Opening it, Catherine smiled at the man waiting there.

"Happy birthday, little girl. Can you spare a kiss for your old da?"

She hugged him and kissed his whiskered cheek. "I've plenty to share, Da. There's no one else clamoring for my attention."

Sean shook his head. "You're a lovely lass, daughter mine. By the saints, I can't fathom why there aren't armies of suitors hanging about trying to win your hand."

Catherine arched her brow. "I believe it has something to do with intimidation. Even if a man has nerve enough to approach me, he has to contend with my two brothers, my guardian angel Padraic, and my overly protective father."

"Overly protective? But I never . . . at least I don't think . . ."

Taking pity on him, she laughed. "I was only teasing,

Da. Besides, the only man I might be interested in is already waiting for me in England."

"So you're still thinking about young Prescott? I guess a doctor would make a good husband for you, Cat."

"Slow down, Da. I've not said we're getting married. After Christmas, I'm going to visit Justin in England for a few days. We've not seen each other in a long time, and I've changed quite a bit. Perhaps he won't like the way I look now."

Sean chuckled. "Justin will be well pleased with you, little girl. Just promise me one thing. If you decide to marry Prescott, bring him home for the wedding. The way your Mam despises traveling on a ship, I doubt if she'd be willing to make the voyage to England for the ceremony."

"Of course I'd come home to be married, Da. I'd want my whole family to share my happiness." Catherine suddenly laughed. "Listen to us! I've not set eyes on the man in years and we've already got him marrying me!"

Sean gave her a quick hug. "Come along, Cat. After all the effort your Mam and Sharon put into this to-do, we shouldn't be late." Bowing at the waist, he snapped himself up and offered her his arm. "May I escort you, Lady Cat?"

"An honor, Hawk." She took his arm, and they went down the stairs. She leaned towards him and whispered, "I love you, Da."

"I know," he replied. "I love you, too, little girl."

Dinner was a tasty array of Catherine's favorites—roast beef, green peas, new potatoes, crusty rolls, and a three-layered spice cake with vanilla icing. A rich red wine accompanied the meal and brandy followed the dessert.

Colin looked at Catherine's half-filled wine glass. "Cat, I brought the wine especially for you. Didn't you like it?"

"I'm sorry, Colin. I rarely drink spirits. When I do have a dram, I much prefer Da's favorite, *uisge beatha.*"

Neville picked up the coffee tray from the table. "What, pray tell, is *uisge beatha,* Mistress Catherine?"

"Uisge beatha is Gaelic and means 'the breath of life.' It's what we call Irish whiskey. It warms your insides as it goes down," Catherine informed him.

Rory snorted. "Aren't you the little authority? Is there anything you don't know about?"

"Brother dear, what's put the burr under your tail? You've been moody all evening." Catherine reached over and touched his hand. "What's the matter?"

Shaking his head, Rory silently drank his brandy.

Colin chuckled. "Rumor has it Mistress O'Hara at the Sheep's Head Pub has turned down his proposal again."

Rory stood up and grabbed Colin off his chair. "Keep your nose out of me business, little brother, or I'll bloody it for you."

Erin slapped down her napkin. "Roderick O'Banyon, you will sit down and remember to act like a gentleman at my table! If you can't refrain from acting like a beast—"

"Then I'll have to take my meals in the barn with the other animals," Rory finished for her. "Forgive me, Mam. I didn't mean to let my temper get the best of me."

Padraic leaned back in his seat. "That's not your only problem, lad. Word's out you made an enemy of some English lordling. That ship you attacked two months back was owned by a viscount who didn't take kindly to your attempt."

"He'll have to find me first!" Rory boasted. "Damned *Sassenach* doesn't worry me at all."

"It shouldn't take him long to find you," Padraic countered. "According to my source, this viscount knows your name and is willing to pay a hefty sum of gold to capture you."

Sean's attention flew to his son. "How in the hell did he get your name, Rory? What happened to hand signals and giving orders in Gaelic? I was in the business twenty years before my real name was known. By God, how could you be so careless?"

"Careless wasn't the way of it," Colin taunted. "Rory introduced himself to the captain when he ordered the hold searched. If the Royal Navy hadn't come upon us, perhaps he was expecting an invitation to tea."

"What were you thinking of? Telling the captain your name was inviting trouble," Sean declared angrily.

"But what about Catherine, Da? She's so damned famous, the bloody English are singing songs about the daring Lady Cat," Rory fumed bitterly. "It gets me sick."

Sean snorted. "Sick with jealousy. As for your sister, they know her as Lady Cat, not Catherine O'Banyon. They don't connect her with our family or this village. That's why we avoid using our names." Sean sighed. "Promise me you'll be careful, son. If Padraic is correct, 'tis just a matter of time before that *Sassenach* finds you."

His anger deflated, Rory nodded. "I will, Da. I'm sorry for acting like a fool. 'Tis not easy being the brother of a legend." He winked at Catherine. "Sorry, Cat."

Erin stood up. "For now, can we stop worrying and adjourn to the parlor. The musicians will be here soon, and some friends are going to be stopping by, as well. This is Catherine's party. I won't have it spoiled."

Before she proceeded toward the parlor, Erin turned and glared at the surprised occupants of the dining room. "We're going to have fun tonight, and that's an order!" she firmly stated.

"Da, I think Mam missed her calling," Rory exclaimed. "Too bad she's not fond of sailing. Our family could always use another captain."

Everyone laughed and began moving to the parlor.

The following evening, Miles and his crew were in their places in and around the Sheep's Head Pub. The capture of Rory O'Banyon would have to be as quick and quiet as possible. The *Foxfire* and her crew were in a rebel stronghold pretending to be outlaws and gunrunners. If their true plan was discovered, the entire town would be upon them.

Several crew members were sitting around tables in the pub. Jamie was stationed behind the building with three men. Miles sat at the table farthest from the door, facing the entrance, as Garret tried to change his mind about the plan.

"Miles, use me instead of yourself as bait."

"I can't risk Rory's recognizing you. I'm counting on you to have the ship ready to sail as soon as I get O'Banyon on board. Just point him out when he arrives, and I'll try to distract him while you go out the back way."

Garret looked at Miles and laughed. "Distracting him shouldn't be a problem. I don't know another captain who wears a bull whip on his belt."

"This whip has come in handy many times. It gives me the advantage of keeping my distance from an attacker. A Turkish trader taught me how to handle it properly." Miles touched the leather handle resting at his hip. "I can flick this around a person's body and not leave a mark. Whenever I travel on my ship, Baby is always with me."

Garret chuckled. "Baby is a strange name for such a fine weapon. I think you should have named it—" A commotion at the front of the pub ended his statement and drew his attention.

A petite, dark-haired beauty stood in the opened doorway, shouting at someone outside the tavern. "You can't go off and leave me for months and expect me to sit by and wait for you!"

"Meg, darlin', you don't mean that," the unseen man implored her. "Your da and I discussed it. O'Hara knows I've been away making me fortune so we could be married."

She shook her head and tied an apron around her trim waist. "I don't care if you've the Pope's blessing. I've no intention of marrying you, and that's that, Rory O'Banyon."

Hearing the man's name, Miles looked at Garret and nodded toward the back door of the establishment. As Garret left, Miles caught sight of his prey.

Rory O'Banyon was a muscular young man with red hair, a neatly trimmed goatee, and a determined glint in his eye as he smiled and moved toward the pretty woman.

"Don't take on so, Meg. You know you want to marry me. All I need is one more good deal to build that fine house for you."

"Then I'll hear naught of it until you've completed the task," Meg declared, picking up a tray from the bar. "My da is home with the gout and I've customers to tend to."

Miles couldn't believe his luck when Meg O'Hara turned away from Rory and walked directly toward his table. At last his quarry would be within his reach.

"Good eve'nin to you, sir. Can I bring you another ale?"

Miles grinned at the pretty woman standing beside him. "Only if you'll keep me company."

Meg's pale cheeks flushed under his scrutiny as she smiled and reached to pick up his empty tankard. "I wish I could, sir, but I've duties . . . customers to serve."

He touched her hand, his fingers lightly grazing hers. "But I'm a customer, too—a visitor here with no one to speak to. Your beauty lightens my heart and my loneliness. Have you no sympathy for a weary traveler, my fair *colleen*?"

Without warning, Rory came up behind Meg and pulled her away from Miles. "Some of my men have arrived and they need ale. You best be seein' to the lads before they get rowdy."

Meg yanked herself free of his hold. " 'Tis your jealousy, naught concern for me Da's tavern or your men that brings you here. Why don't you go to the devil and let me be?"

As she angrily walked away with the empty tankard,

Rory's attention fixed on Miles. He pulled out a chair and sat down uninvited across from him. "The name's Rory O'Banyon, captain of *Erin's Pride*," he stated arrogantly. "Who might you be?"

Miles looked directly into his eyes. "Captain Trelane of the *Foxfire*."

"With your fine clothes and that whip, 'tis obvious you're not from these parts, Trelane. May I ask why such a worldly man such as yourself has come to Ireland?"

Miles shrugged. "I'm a trader, come to do some business."

"Business, you say? This wee village is far from bein' a commercial port," Rory pointed out, his grin wry. "Could your business be more aptly described as smuggling?"

Cocking his brow, Miles sighed. "To admit that could be dangerous for me, O'Banyon."

Rory chuckled. "To be sure, you've nothin' to fear from me, Trelane. I'm a purveyor by dubious means of weapons and certain valuable wares meself. If you've a need to market such goods, my connections might be of help to you."

"And afford you a bit of profit as well?" At Rory's frown, Miles grinned. "I heard you talking to the lass and I know you're looking to make money. But my cargo is very valuable to me and to a certain group of your countrymen."

" 'Tis arms you're talkin' about. I know it," Rory boasted. Leaning forward, he whispered, "How large a shipment do you have?"

"Enough to wipe out an entire regiment."

Rory didn't conceal his enthusiasm. "I can help you sell the entire lot by week's end. When can I see the goods?"

"Why should I trust you, O'Banyon? You might be setting a trap for me."

"If it's a need for trust, I'll offer you mine. Take me to your ship and present your cargo. I'll go alone, without my men. We can talk price and such, perhaps strike a deal that will benefit all concerned. What say you to that, Trelane?''

Miles nodded and stood up. "Come along, then, O'Banyon. We'll look over the goods and have a few drinks in my cabin while we discuss terms.''

As Miles and Rory walked toward the docks, the crew members of the *Foxfire* left the pub. Jamie and his men fell in behind them. They were so intent on getting back to the ship they never saw the rough-looking stranger following them.

With a bounty of gold being offered for information about Rory's whereabouts, Padraic was convinced young O'Banyon was in danger. He kept to the shadows and followed the strange procession down to the harbor.

Padraic hid behind some crates as Rory and the other man walked up the gangplank of an impressive ship. The night was clear and the breeze carried their voices along the water.

Rory laughed and made polite conversation. " 'Tis a splendid ship, Trelane. How many cannons have you?''

"Enough." Miles smiled.

"You're a man of few words, Trelane, so I know you can't be Irish." Rory laughed at his own humor.

Garret joined them on the deck and handed Miles a pistol. "Good evening, Captain. All is as you ordered, sir.''

Looking at Garret, Rory frowned. "I know you, don't I? Where did we meet?" Surprise lit his eyes. "The *Sassenach* captain! What in the hell goes on here, Trelane?''

Miles aimed the pistol at Rory. "My name is Miles Trelane Grayson, Viscount Ryland. You attacked one of my ships, and now you're going to pay for your crime." When Rory tried to move, he poked him in the chest with the gun barrel. "Just give me an excuse, O'Banyon, and I'll save the hangman the task.''

* * *

Padraic heard parts of the conversation and knew he was too badly outnumbered to rescue Rory. The young man was led away and orders to set sail for Bristol were given out. Running back to the inn, he retrieved his horse and raced toward Corbin's Cove.

When Padraic entered the O'Banyon household an hour later, Catherine greeted him at the door with a hug. "You missed dinner, but if you're hungry, I can fetch you something from the kitchen. Then you can play chess with me. I've just beaten Da, and Colin won't . . ." She stepped back and looked at his face. "What's wrong, Padraic?"

"Rory's been captured. That bloody Englishman got him and they're takin' him to Bristol. They set sail from Youghal an hour ago, on a ship named the *Foxfire*."

Plans were made and immediately set into action. Since the *Cat's Cradle* could be ready to sail within a half hour, Catherine and Padraic would gather their men and try to catch the English ship. Sean and Colin would get the crew of *Erin's Pride* and follow as soon as they were able.

As Catherine was preparing to leave, Sean told her to take Colin with her. When she asked why, he shrugged. "I don't rightly know, but I've a feeling it would be best if your brother went with you. Anyway, you might be needing some extra help in rescuing Rory. But I'll be right behind you." He hugged her close. "Take care, little girl. Remember, I love you."

Catherine kissed his cheek. "I love you, too, Da." When she eased away from him, the fine chain on her necklace caught on the button of his coat and broke, sending her heart pendant to the floor. "Oh, no. I've broken another chain."

He knelt down and retrieved the gold charm. "Yer mam

can take this to the goldsmith in the morning. Don't worry, lass. It'll be good as new by the time you get back."

Sean watched her kiss Erin, and a feeling of loss suddenly pervaded him. He never liked saying good-bye to Catherine, but this was different. This was a fear he'd never felt before, a gut-wrenching fear of losing his precious child forever.

"Little girl, maybe I should go with you." His voice didn't betray his misgivings. "You might be needing another strong arm when you meet up with that *Sassenach*."

Catherine frowned. "And what happens if my ship gets captured, as well? It wouldn't be wise having all the O'Banyons on one ship. You need to bring along the *Pride* and her crew in case we run into trouble, Da."

Rubbing the gold pendant with his fingers, Sean watched Catherine and Colin mount their horses for the ride to the dock. He prayed she'd live up to her legendary reputation as being unbeatable and that his intuition was wrong.

Chapter 14

Two nights later, the *Foxfire* docked in Bristol. Thanks to good weather and strong tail winds, the crossing was quick and uneventful. Miles and his crew had no idea the *Cat's Cradle* was close behind them.

The *Foxfire* was navigated into her berth as Catherine's ship sailed past. A dinghy was lowered over the side so she, Colin, and Emmet could get to shore. Since they'd been unable to overtake the English ship at sea, a rescue would be attempted on dry land. Catherine sent Padraic and her ship to a nearby cove to wait while she and the others scoured the harbor area for information about Rory's captor and his transfer to prison.

Dressed in black, they made their way to the Laughing Dog Tavern. Being involved in smuggling meant sneaking around at night, and Catherine was accustomed to her unusual black costume. Besides the snug britches and loose-fitting blouse, she had a tricorn hat and a silk mask that covered her hair and face. The thin fabric allowed

her to breathe, and slits were cut for her eyes. A long cape
and thigh-high boots completed the outfit.

Donovan, the proprietor of the pub, led Catherine and
the others into the back room of his establishment to talk.
"The *Foxfire* docks here between voyages. Messengers meet
the ship each time it arrives. The owner's said to be a titled
lord, but I ain't seen the toff," Donovan said, rubbing his
balding pate. "The crew ain't friendly with anyone outside
their own, so gatherin' news about 'em is difficult."

Catherine impatiently slapped her hat against her thigh.
"You're a curious sort, Donovan. Surely you've heard something."

The man nodded. "Well, there's been a courier waitin'
over a week for that ship to return. Over a few mugs of
ale, the lad told me he had to deliver his pouch the moment
the *Foxfire* docked. There's a family crisis and the captain's
been ordered back to London straightaway."

Catherine realized the importance of this news.
"Emmet, take one of Donovan's horses and ride to the
cove. Tell Padraic what's happening. We haven't a moment
to spare if we're to rescue Rory before he's transported to
London."

"Shall I bring back the others to help, Captain?"

"No. Colin and I will sneak aboard that ship and get
Rory. I won't risk anyone else in this plan. Tell Padraic I
want my ship to remain hidden in the cove. My brothers
and I will be there by morning."

"What in the hell has happened to Torie?"

For more than an hour, Miles had raved over the letter
that had been waiting for him when they returned to Bristol. Garret and Jamie sat quietly in his cabin as he ranted
on.

"According to my father, Victoria's been missing since

the sixth of November. That was four weeks ago. The authorities have no clues as to her disappearance."

Garret frowned. "Didn't Victoria tell you in her last letter she suspected her uncle of committing some kind of crime? Maybe he abducted her."

"That was my father's first thought. The ironic thing was, on the very night she vanished, my parents had dinner with her uncle, Edward Damien. When her disappearance was reported, his show of concern was monumental. He's offered a large reward for the return of his niece or information about those who may have done her harm." Miles ran his fingers through his hair. "Torie once said her uncle was a brilliant but deceptive man. I wonder how truly devious he is."

Jamie was perplexed. "What would he gain if he did away with Victoria? Her father controls the family's holdings."

"Since his seizure, the duke is totally helpless. Torie had Edward put in an advisory position at Carlisle Enterprises while she gathered evidence against him. He has no real power. My father believes that's why Edward has called for a stockholders' meeting on January fifteenth. He'll probably demand the partners and shareholders put him in charge because his brother is too ill and his niece is missing and presumed dead."

He went to his cabinet and removed a bottle of whiskey. Pouring some in a glass, he drank it in one swallow. "I know that bastard's responsible for Torie's disappearance, but I can't prove it." Miles threw his glass, shattering it against the wall. "Damn him to hell! If I could get my hands on Edward Damien, I'd kill him!"

Garret stood up and grabbed Miles by his shoulders. "That won't bring Victoria back. If you kill him, you'll hang for it. Can't you seek your revenge in another way?"

Jamie picked up the broken glass. "Is there a chance the duke will recover in time for the meeting, Miles?"

"That's another problem. Before Torie vanished, her

father regained consciousness. He was alert and answering questions with eye signals. The doctor was hoping for a full recovery, but all that's changed. Although they haven't told Geoffrey Torie is missing, he seems to know something's wrong. He won't respond to the doctor and appears to be giving up."

Garret sighed. "So Edward wins anyway. If Geoffrey dies, he'll inherit everything."

"Oh, no, he won't," Miles said with a rueful smile. "The day before his seizure, Geoffrey wrote a codicil to his will. He drew up a duplicate and had both of them signed and witnessed. One was hand delivered to Torie. The other was intercepted by the housekeeper and probably sent to Edward. Torie gave her copy to my father when she discovered her servant's betrayal.

"The codicil cuts Edward out of his brother's will, leaving everything to Torie. Because we were betrothed, I was named as the co-inheritor. In other words, it will all be mine."

"If Edward discovers the codicil still exists, he may come after you," Jamie warned him.

"Then let him! I won't cower from that bastard." Miles punched one hand against the other. "If I could get some evidence on Edward, I'd make him pay!"

"Too bad you don't know a ghost or two to haunt that son of a bitch," Garret suggested as he stood up and stretched. "Between making arrangements for our prisoner and leaving for London, we're going to have a busy day tomorrow. Most of the crew are spending the night on shore or have turned in already. I'm off to bed myself. See you in the morning."

James placed a reassuring hand on Miles' shoulder. "You'll find a way to stop this man. It may take time, but you'll succeed. Good night, Miles."

"I pray you're right, Jamie. I pray to God you're right."

* * *

"This could be our chance, Colin—no sentry, few lights, and many of the crew are going ashore."

Colin grabbed Catherine's arm and pulled her down beside him. "This is too dangerous. We don't even know where they're holding Rory. That's a very large ship."

"I know, but think. These people won't be concerned with Rory's comfort, so that eliminates the cabins. A ship this size should have a room in the hold for locking up valuables or perhaps a prison cell or a brig. That's where I'll find him."

Colin yanked her closer. "If you think I'm going to allow you to go in there alone, you're crazy!"

Catherine smiled, then pulled the silk mask over her face. "I appreciate your concern, big brother, but I'm not a little girl. I have a dagger in my boot and a rapier to defend myself with, and I certainly know how to use them. I'm going aboard that ship while you keep watch. If my plan goes awry, get to the *Cradle* and head back to Ireland."

"But, Cat, what if something—" Before Colin could finish his statement, Catherine was across the dock and hurrying up the deserted gangplank.

It was after midnight, and Miles couldn't sleep. Abandoning his bed, he pulled on his boots and clothes and settled for a walk on deck. As he opened his cabin door, he spotted a figure in black running silently down the passage. Grabbing his whip from the peg beside the door, he followed the lone intruder toward the hold.

While he watched, the intruder crept up to the crewman who was guarding the prisoner and struck him on the head with the handle of a rapier, rendering the sentry unconscious. The assailant took the keys from the seaman's belt and approached the cell door.

Miles was momentarily startled when he heard a feminine voice calling out in a husky whisper to his prisoner.

"Rory, are you in here?" the woman asked, looking into the dark cell. A rustling sound and a sleepy groan was her only reply. "Damn you, Rory O'Banyon, answer me!"

"Cat . . . Cat, is that you?"

As she put the key into the lock, Miles flicked his whip and wrapped it around her body. With a pull of his arm, she was flung away from the cell door. The keys and her sword fell to the floor. Tugging on the whip, he soon had the woman in his arms. When he threw her over his shoulder, she began screaming at him.

"Put me down, you overgrown, self-indulgent libertine! I'm not a bag of coal to be tossed around like this. Let me down!" She swore in Gaelic while she tried to wriggle from his grasp.

"Trelane, or whatever your damned name is, you better not hurt her," Rory shouted from behind the bars of his cell door. "If you hurt Cat, I'll find you and tear your bloody heart out."

Miles slapped the struggling woman across the buttocks. "Stop your screeching, you damned hellcat! I'm taking you to my cabin and you're going to answer some questions for me."

When he got her to his cabin and closed the door, Miles lowered the masked woman to the floor. While he unwound the whip from around her body, she kicked his right shin with the toe of her leather boot. Miles lost his temper and clipped her jaw with his fist. As she crumpled toward the floor, he caught her up in his arms and placed her limp form on his bed.

Jamie burst into the cabin. "Miles, what's going on? Did I hear a woman screaming in the passageway?"

Garret was right behind him. "If that wasn't a woman, then I was having the most realistic dream of my life."

"There's no time to worry about screaming women,"

Miles explained. "Someone just tried to release O'Banyon. Wake the crew and search this ship for other intruders immediately."

After Jamie and Garret left to carry out his orders, Miles locked the door and put the key in his pocket. He walked to the bed and sat beside the black-clothed figure lying there. Anxious to see what his mysterious guest looked like, he removed her hat and lifted the mask from her face.

"This can't be." Miles shook his head in confusion and ran his fingers over her face. The same lovely nose, chin, and lips haunted his thoughts. "Victoria, it must be you." He took hold of her shoulders and lifted her slightly from the bed. "My God, Torie, what have they done to you?"

At that moment, the woman's eyes opened and focused on him. Pushing his hands away, she sat up. "Don't touch me, you arrogant, egotistical *Sassenach*! They call me Cat. Leave off, or I'll show you just how well I take after me namesake!"

Miles couldn't believe she wasn't Victoria. The face was identical, her eyes the same emerald green. Her voice was similar, but had a decisive Irish lilt to it. Before he'd be convinced, he needed to see the rest.

He reached over and pushed the silk scarf completely off her head. The pins that held her hair were loose. He plucked them out, releasing her golden hair. It hung full and straight to her hips. Miles couldn't resist stroking the silky tresses as he recalled Victoria's short blond curls.

Although he hadn't seen Victoria in several months, she couldn't have grown this much hair. But how could two women look so much alike?

Catherine stopped struggling and found herself mystified by the man who was staring at her, stroking her hair. Despite his beard, he was very handsome. His eyes were a rich blue and his black hair fell below his shoulders in thick waves. A second later, she shook herself. This man was her enemy.

With renewed vigor, Catherine shoved him away and got to her feet. She was nearly to the door when his whip shot out and snaked around her waist.

"You're not going anywhere," he taunted, pulling her toward him. "Sit down. We can have a little talk."

"Why in the hell would I want to chat with the likes of you? Talk to yourself, for all I care. You'll get naught from me," she grumbled as she dropped into the chair beside the desk.

"All right, Miss, how many others are with you? Surely you didn't try to rescue Rory all on your own."

When he sat on the desk next to her, she turned from his scrutiny and faced the wall.

"Who'd be foolish enough to send a mere girl to do a man's job? Everyone knows females are the weaker of the species, not to mention their lack of superior intelligence."

Catherine folded her arms over her chest and refused to be goaded by his taunts.

"Perhaps no one sent you," he continued. "Maybe you tried to rescue Rory all by yourself because you're his mistress. Were you afraid you wouldn't be able to survive without him if he were sent to Newgate? I've got it! You're carrying his child!"

Catherine's hair furled around her when she turned to confront the Englishman. "Of all the contemptible, pompous fools, you are the lowest! How dare you assume such things? Rory is my brother. Moreover, I might be a female, but if I had a sword, I'd show you how weak I am not."

"Would you know how to use a sword if you had one?"

"You're damned right I would! I'm Lady Cat. My conquests and victories are many. I can outsail any captain on the seas, including you and this oversized, barnacle-covered tub of yours."

Catherine moved away from her tormentor to walk the floor. "Some man you are! You don't even fight fairly. You use that silly animal whip instead of a rapier. Well, I'm not afraid of you or any man. I'd gladly match my wits to yours any day."

As his eyes followed her movements, Miles recalled the stories he'd heard about the outlaw she claimed to be. She fit the description of the beautiful Irish pirate who captained her own ship and reportedly could wield a sword with incomparable grace and expertise. With the bounty currently being offered for the capture of Lady Cat, she'd have to be insane to admit to her identity if it wasn't true.

And this woman wasn't insane or helpless. She possessed male arrogance, though there was no mistaking the shapely female form emphasized by the britches that hugged her hips. Suddenly, there wasn't a doubt in his mind that this young woman was Lady Cat.

She was also a near perfect copy of Victoria Carlisle. He contemplated a way of making use of this amazing coincidence. Surely providence must have led to their meeting.

At that moment, Catherine came toward him and spewed new threats. "When the Hawk finds you've imprisoned me, he'll track you down and tear you apart! O'Banyons take care of their own. My father won't rest until he sees you dead."

"I don't doubt your family loyalty, Cat. Why else would you try single-handedly to rescue your brother? Or perhaps you weren't alone," he suggested, grinning. "For now, I want you to sit down by the desk and stay put."

Catherine stood motionless, her hands on her hips.

Getting to his feet, Miles loomed over her. "Make another attempt to escape, and I'll have your brother punished for it. You can scream like a banshee, but you'll stay where I tell you, you Irish hellcat! Now sit down, or I'll tie you to the chair."

She returned to her seat. When Jamie came to the door and reported no other intruders had been found, she sighed with relief. Noting her reaction, Miles made a hasty decision.

"Jamie, find Garret and come back here in five minutes," Miles called through the door. "I have a surprise to show you."

After Jamie left, Miles sat on the edge of the desk beside Catherine. "You appear to be an intelligent woman, Lady Cat, and very loyal to your brother. I wonder what you would do to keep him out of prison. Would you be willing to bargain with me in order to secure his freedom and your own?"

Catherine looked up at him. "What do you have in mind, English?"

"Someone dear to me is missing, and you look exactly like her," he replied. "I need you to impersonate this young woman so I can trap the man responsible for her disappearance. I will teach you to act like her, dress like her, and talk like her. For all intents and purposes, you will become Lady Victoria Carlisle, daughter of the Duke of Chatham."

Catherine couldn't contain her laughter. "You must be daft, English! It wouldn't work. Maybe I resemble her slightly, but no one could look as much alike as you're suggesting."

Miles studied her face. "I'm telling you the truth. When I removed your mask, I thought you were her. With tutoring, I think you could convince anyone you're Victoria Carlisle."

She smiled sadly. "For years, I dreamed I was a member of the nobility. In my dreams I wore fancy clothes, lived in big houses, and attended grand parties. But they were only the musings of a silly Irish lass. I'm not a titled lady. I couldn't carry off such a charade."

"I think you're wrong, Cat. You are very bright. Aside

from an occasional show of temper, your vocabulary reveals that you're educated. If you help me expose this man, I'll return you and Rory to Ireland and give you five thousand pounds for your efforts."

Catherine raised a cynical brow. "And what happens if this man isn't fooled by my portrayal of Victoria Carlisle? Will you ship the two of us off to Newgate?"

"No. If you make an honest effort to carry off this charade, you have my word you'll receive the reward, as well as the passage home I offered. I'll even allow you to send a message to your family so they won't worry about the two of you. The decision is yours, Lady Cat."

Gazing down at her hands, Catherine contemplated her dilemma. If she said no, she and Rory would be turned over to the authorities. With the charges against them, they'd be tried and executed. If she agreed to this scheme, perhaps she would be able to come up with a plan of her own and escape later on.

She turned to Miles. "As much as I want to accept, English, I still doubt anyone will believe I'm Lady Victoria. No matter how well I walk, talk, and act, I look like *me*."

"If I can prove you look exactly like Victoria, will you agree to my plan?"

"I suppose. But how can you do that?"

"My two friends will be joining us soon. The blond is Jamie Campbell and the tall gent is Garret Morgan. When they come in, don't say a word. Allow them to do the talking."

Catherine shrugged. It seemed simple enough, so she remained in her seat and awaited their arrival. Within minutes, there was a knock at the door. Miles turned the key in the lock and opened the door.

"Come in, my friends. My prayers have been answered, and I want to share my good news with you." Miles stepped aside and gave them a clear view of Catherine.

Garret rushed in and began scolding her. "Victoria, have

you any idea how you scared us? Miles was ready to kill your uncle. Where were you?"

Jamie scowled at Garret. "Watch your manners. Lady Victoria doesn't need to explain herself to you." He bowed to Catherine and smiled. " 'Tis good to see you again, my lady."

"Forgive me, Victoria." Garret took her hand and kissed it. "My only excuse is that I was worried about you."

Affecting her most cultured tones, Catherine smiled and replied, "Thank you, Garret. The concern you and Jamie have shown on my behalf is appreciated, and I am indebted to you both."

Jamie shook his head. "You owe us nothing, Lady Victoria. We're pleased to see you're all right."

Catherine looked over at Miles and smiled. "It appears we have a deal, English. Would you care to join me in a drink to our success?"

"Whatever you say, Cat," Miles answered with a grin.

"My name is Lady Victoria Carlisle—and don't you forget it, English."

Spurred by their triumph and their combined relief, Miles and Catherine started laughing.

Garret looked quizzically at the two of them. "English? Cat? What's all the laughing about? I hate it when I don't understand a joke. Miles, tell me what's so funny. Torie, would you please stop giggling long enough to let me in on the jest? Or am I the brunt of your humor?"

Miles shook his head and clapped Garret on the back. "Calm down, Garret. We're not laughing at you or Jamie. But when I tell you about my little plan, you'll see the joke will be on Edward Damien. Sit down, have some whiskey, and listen to a fairy tale that's about to come true. It's all about a selfish ogre, a clever fox, and a beautiful cat from Ireland . . ."

Chapter 15

The deserted cottage was an hour's ride from Bristol. Its main room had a fireplace, a battered table, and one chair. The sleeping chamber was little more than a closet. Dampness from the tiny window permeated the old bed with a foul musty odor. Only a moth-eaten blanket covered the filthy mattress.

In this dank, miserable hovel, Victoria Carlisle had been imprisoned for nearly a month.

After hours of traveling on dark roads, her abductors had stopped to bury Billy. She'd sat gagged and bound at the window of her coach, watched them work, and listened to them talk about her.

Clive had tossed kindling into the small fire they had built for light. "When I get you and the tart hidden out o' sight in the woods, I'm off to see his lordship." He dangled the heart pendant from his stubby fingers. "This wee piece'll get me the other five hundred pounds 'e owes me. Then we go to Bristol and get on to the real business."

Andy stopped digging and leaned on his shovel. "Yer old mate's due back next month, ain't 'e?"

"Aye. Once I meet up with Sharkey, I'll be countin' on lots more blunt. With all that yeller hair and white skin, she'll bring quite a price from one o' them sheiks in the east." Clive pulled a flask from his pocket and raised it toward the coach. "That bit o' fluff is gonna make me rich."

He took a hefty swallow from the flask, then frowned at his cousin. "Hurry up, Andy. I don't wanna be out 'ere all night."

Victoria had little doubt Edward Damien was responsible for her kidnapping. It was obvious why he'd want her dead. Her only satisfaction came from the fact her uncle didn't know about the duplicate codicil and would never profit from her death.

Not that she was going to accept her plight easily.

Over the following weeks, Clive spent most of his time drinking in the local pubs, leaving his cousin to guard their captive. Victoria used these hours to gain Andy's trust, hoping he might be persuaded to help her escape.

Tall and thin, Andy was amazingly strong, but decidedly dimwitted. He'd been orphaned as a young boy and had spent his childhood living in the cruel poverty of London's slums with his only living relative, Clive. Victoria understood the feelings Andy had for his cousin and took this into consideration while making her plans.

On the first of December, she overheard Clive say that Sharkey's ship was due in Bristol in two days. As he rode away from the cottage, Victoria decided the time to put her plan into motion had arrived.

Andy came into the room carrying the old bucket she had been using as a necessary. "I've cleaned this good for you just like I promised, and there's a pot o' tea brewin' on the fire."

"That sounds wonderful, thank you. Andy, would you

please untie me for a while? My wrists are sore and my hands are like ice. I promise not to try anything stupid. You've freed my hands before, and I've never broken my word to you, have I?"

"No, you ain't never done that, Lady Toria." Andy bent down to where she was sitting on the bed and began unknotting the leather thongs on her wrists. "I told Clive he shouldn't truss you up tight like this, but there's no reasonin' wiff 'im. All this muckin' about wiff nuffin' to do but drink puts 'im in a foul mood. He's not really such a bad sort."

Victoria closed her eyes and fought the urge to shout the truth to the hapless man. *Not such a bad sort? Your wretched cousin is a beast! He's cruel and ruthless and takes pleasure in tormenting me every night with his vile descriptions of my being a slave in the Orient.*

She looked at her freed hands and sighed as she moved her fingers. "That feels better. Thank you. If I promise to behave, may I come out and sit beside the fire with you? I'm freezing."

"Awright, but don't forget your promise. Clive would kill me if anythin' 'appened to you." Andy helped her to a chair by the hearth and placed a cup of tea in her hands. "Drink this. It'll warm you some, Lady Toria."

Sipping the hot brew, Victoria watched Andy over the chipped rim of the cup. "You take good care of me, Andy, and I thank you for it. You take care of Clive, too, don't you?"

"Clive took care o' me when me ma died. 'Tis fittin' I do for him now." Andy knelt down in front of the fire. "Clive's the only kin I got. If anythin' befell him, I don't know what I'd do."

She reached over and patted his arm. "I'm so sorry, Andy. When the authorities find out what Clive's done to me, they'll hang him. You'll be truly alone then."

Andy frowned. "But Clive's always careful. Ain't never got caught afore."

"I'm afraid being careful won't be enough this time. My father is the Duke of Chatham. He'll never give up looking for me. He's a very powerful man and a personal friend of the king. By now all outbound ships are being searched before they leave the harbors. When Sharkey gets caught with me on his vessel, he'll save himself by turning your cousin in to the authorities. Don't you see the danger Clive is in?"

Andy chewed on his lip, pensively staring into the fire as she continued speaking to him in a soft, consoling voice.

"The man who hired Clive to kidnap me is my uncle, Edward Damien. It's only a matter of time before my father discovers his part in my abduction. Edward will show him my necklace and claim Clive was trying to get a ransom for me. Edward is an earl, a peer of the realm. Do you think the magistrate will believe him or your cousin?"

Andy frantically shook his head and ran his fingers through his hair. "Oh lord, Clive's gonna 'ang for sure. I gotta do somethin' to stop this. But Clive don't listen t'me."

Victoria touched his shoulder. "Maybe there's another way to help your cousin. If you get me back to my father, Clive won't be in trouble. I know the real villain is Edward. Papa would give you and your cousin a generous reward for rescuing me, and the earl would be punished. My goodness, Andy, you and Clive will be heroes!"

Andy wiped his eyes on his sleeve and looked at her. A hopeful smile lifted his drooping mouth. "Clive 'n' me would be 'eroes? We'd get rewards? Do ya mean it, Lady Toria?"

"I swear it, Andy. Have I ever broken my word to you?" When he shook his head, she smiled. "If you like, I'll ask Papa to give you a job with one of his companies or estates. You could earn honest wages and never have to worry about getting in trouble with the law again."

"Awright, I'll do it," he sighed a few moments later. "Clive's plannin' to take ya to Bristol in the mornin', so's we gotta leave tonight when he's sleepin'. He's gonna be mad as 'ell when he finds what I done, but I gotta do this for him."

Victoria sagged with relief. She was cold, filthy, and hungry, but also elated. If all went as planned, she'd be home in a day or so. Closing her eyes, she prayed silently.

Dear God, grant me the strength to face whatever's coming. Bless Papa and keep him safe. Let him know I'll be home as soon as I can . . .

Clive was in high spirits that night. Thanks to good tail winds, Sharkey's ship would dock in a matter of hours. Victoria sat on the old bed and heard him bragging about the large amount of money he was going to collect when he delivered her to his mate the next day.

"What's the matter, Andy? Ya ain't said a bloody word since I come in. Are ya ailin'?"

Andy shook his head as he cleaned up the remnants of their supper. "No, Clive. Jest tired is all."

"Toss all that stuff out, Andy. Tomorrow night we'll be eatin' in a fancy tavern on our way to London." Picking up his bottle of rum, he took a swallow, then wiped his hand across his mouth. "It'll be great gettin' back to town, won't it, Andy?"

"Yeah, Clive. I never liked dis place. It's awful lonely out 'ere," Andy mournfully replied.

"Don't be worryin', lad. I'll see you gets lots o' company from 'ere on." Clive corked his bottle and staggered to his pallet on the far side of the room. "I'm turnin' in. 'Night, Andy."

"G'night, Clive."

A few minutes later, when Clive's snoring echoed through the hut, Andy crept into the bedroom and whispered to Victoria. "Come on, we gotta get goin' while 'e's sleepin'. I'll saddle up the 'orses." Without stopping to untie her hands, Andy hurried from the cottage.

Victoria wrapped her cloak around her shoulders and followed him outside. She found him strapping the saddle on Clive's large dappled gray horse. The stallion was noisy and skittish from the unfamiliar hands tending him. She cautioned Andy in a low whisper, "You've got to keep that horse quiet or he'll wake Clive."

"Yeah, Andy, don't want old Clive t'hear you stealin' 'is 'orse, do you?" Clive's taunting voice rang out as he threw himself on top of his cousin.

"I was doin' it fer you, Clive," Andy cried as he fell to the ground trying to ward off the punishing blows of Clive's massive fists on his face and body. "Toria said you was gonna get in trouble and I dinna want ya t'hang. Please stop . . ."

Clive ignored Andy's pleas and struck him again and again. Suddenly, he got to his feet. "I'll catch up with you in London, ye silly fool. Now get on yer damn 'orse and get the 'ell outta my sight!"

Clive shoved Victoria into the hut after Andy rode away. He slammed the door and slapped her across the face. "Leave it to a cunnin' bitch like you to turn the lad's 'ead and cause trouble. Well, milady, you don't know what trouble is 'til you cross Clive Walters!" He struck her with his closed fist, knocking her to the floor.

Victoria screamed when he pulled her up by her hair. He wrapped his arms around her waist and leered into her tear-streaked face. "All dis time, I kept meself away from you. Virgins get a 'igher price, but I'll forgo a bit of profit if it means gettin' a piece o' you. So damned 'igh and mighty you are with yer snooty airs. I'll bet you ain't never been dirty like this afore. You looks like a filthy bitch. I seen dogs on the street what's got cleaner 'air than you.

But don't worry, darlin', I ain't gonna let a bit o' dirt come betwixt us."

Victoria tried pushing him away, but he was too strong. He grabbed the bodice of her soiled gown and tore it from her body. She screamed, kicking him ineffectively on his booted legs. Clive held her head and put his wet, gaping mouth across hers. As he pushed his tongue into her mouth, she gagged with revulsion and bit him. Roaring, he pulled back and slapped her several times across the face.

"So you wants it rough? Well, I can play that way, too!"

Shoving her down onto the table, he stood between her knees. Her screams filled the cottage when he bit her breasts, torturing her exposed flesh with his sharp teeth. He held her hands over her head as he struggled to get her tattered skirts out of his way. Releasing his grasp on her wrists, he shoved the dishes and utensils left from supper to the floor and failed to notice the strap binding her hands was coming loose.

Victoria tried to squirm away from him. As he threw up her skirts and touched her inner thighs, she felt something sharp poking into her back.

Clive opened his pants and grabbed his organ. "Look what I got fer you, m'lady."

While he was busy displaying himself, Victoria eased her hand under her back. Her fingers wrapped around the handle of the carving knife.

Misreading her silence as acceptance, he chuckled. "No need t' scream, darlin'. Jest lay there and enjoy it. I know I will." He grinned as he pushed toward her.

But before his manhood made contact with her flesh, Victoria raised her arm and plunged the knife deeply into his chest. She screamed and stabbed him countless times until he fell to the floor in a bloodied heap.

Victoria rolled off the table. Even in her dazed state of

mind, she knew he was dead. Wrapping her cape around her battered body, she stumbled out the door.

Clive's horse was tied outside the hut, still saddled. She approached the skittish gray stallion. When she reached to grab the saddle, she saw the knife dripping with blood clutched in her fingers. Dropping it, she pulled herself up onto the back of the large horse.

Without thinking of direction, Victoria let the stallion run along the deserted road. For the first time in weeks, she felt the exhilaration of freedom. She never saw the small carriage coming at her along the narrow road.

Justin Prescott was dozing while his carriage traveled across the dark countryside. He'd spent the entire day and evening delivering a baby at the Ross farm and was exhausted but elated. After years of being childless and six miscarriages, Joe and Mae Ross finally had a healthy baby boy. It made him proud to be a physician.

Suddenly, Justin heard his driver shout and felt the carriage veer off the road. He looked out the window as a gray horse reared up in front of his rig, throwing its rider to the ground before running off.

Justin ran to the injured person lying on the muddied ground. He turned the body carefully and realized the rider was a woman. From what he could see in the moonlight, she was covered in blood and dirt. He lifted the matted hair from her brow and found a large bleeding gash on her forehead. He gently lifted her into his arms.

"Sam, get me home immediately! Don't spare the horses."

Justin carried the unconscious woman into his house. "Mrs. MacWhorter, I need your help," he shouted. "Mrs. MacWhorter, where are you?"

"You dinna have to shout, Doctor. I can hear ye, verra

well." The tall, red-haired housekeeper came running from the kitchen, wiping her hands on her apron. She entered the treatment room as Justin carefully placed his charge on the bed.

"Bring me lots of hot water, soap and towels. Before I can treat this young woman, I'll have to get some of this dirt off of her." Justin opened his patient's cape and gasped.

Mrs. MacWhorter looked over his shoulder and clucked her tongue before she left the room. "Och, Doctor, what kind of hell has this puir lamb been put through, d'ye think?"

"What kind of hell, indeed!" he muttered through clenched teeth.

The once lovely gown had been torn away from her upper torso. Vicious bite marks and bruises covered her pale breasts. Dried blood was splattered over her chest and down her right arm. Her wrists were raw, her neck and jaw badly bruised and scraped. The right side of her face was swollen, and the blood on the gash along her hairline was clotting.

The woman's hair was so matted and filthy it was impossible to tell what color it was. He lifted her eyelid to examine the pupil's reaction to light. Her eyes were green.

Apprehensively, he pulled up her skirt and looked for other injuries. From her appearance, he feared she had been raped. But other than bruises and cuts on her legs, there was no bleeding or evidence of a forced entry.

When Mrs. MacWhorter returned, they removed their patient's ragged clothes. "Doctor, why don't ye go to the kitchen and have a bit of supper? Ye've been gone all day and ye must be famished. Leave the lass t' me. I'll bathe her and get some of that dirt out of her hair."

Justin returned a short time later to find Mrs. Mac-Whorter brushing their patient's hair.

She looked up at him and smiled. "Well, Doctor, ye'd ne'er believe what a pretty lass was under all the grime. I had quite a time with her hair. T'was so matted I had to cut off a bit so I could wash it. From the way it's beginnin' to dry, it appears to be the color o' gold."

Justin gathered his instruments from the supply cabinet and put them on a tray. "Thanks for your help, Mrs. Mac-Whorter. If you're finished, I'll see to that cut on her forehead. Why don't you go to bed? I'll probably need your assistance in the morning."

"Certainly, sir. Good night."

He watched her amble out the door and smiled. He was fortunate to have Mrs. MacWhorter in his employ. Besides being an excellent housekeeper, she had a rare gift of healing. In the past four years, he'd come to rely more and more on this special woman.

Justin walked to his patient's bed and set the tray on the side table. "Well, young lady, Mrs. Mac seems to think you're very pretty. Let's see how right she is."

He moved the lantern closer to the bed and turned up the wick. As the glowing light illuminated his patient's face, Justin gaped in disbelief. "Catherine, what are you doing here in England? You're supposed to be at home with your family."

Looking at her bruised face, Justin recalled the vile marks on her body and became a man possessed with rage. "Who did this to you, Catherine? So help me God, when I get my hands on the beast responsible for this, I'll kill him!"

Remembering the cut on her forehead, he pushed back her hair to examine it. She had a large bump, but the gash itself would not require stitches. Her skin was hot, though, and her cheeks were becoming flushed as well.

"God's blood, you're burning with fever, Cat."

Without delay, Justin sprang into action. Pouring cool water into a basin on the table, he dipped towels into it

and bathed her face and upper body. Placing a wet cloth
to her parched lips, he let drops of water slowly enter her
mouth.

Though she was wrapped in a blanket and a heavy quilt,
her body quaked with chills. He climbed onto the bed
and gathered her into his comforting embrace. Justin was
startled when, in her delirium, she started to talk.

"Please help me ... he shot Billy ... going to sell
me ... I'm frightened. Help me ..."

Justin cradled her against him. "I'm here for you, Cat."

She moaned. "No ... don't let him touch me like that.
He's hurting me ... make him stop."

She was reliving the attack. He listened as she thrashed
in his arms.

"Clive hit me ... I found a knife under me ... he's
going to ... no ... I can't let him! Grabbed the knife ...
stabbed him ... dead ..."

Justin's eyes filled with impotent tears. He kissed her
brow. "Don't worry, dear heart. He's gone and can't harm
you. I won't allow anyone to hurt you again—I swear, never
again."

As though she understood his pledge, Victoria's body
began to relax. She laid her head on his chest and drifted
off into a deep peaceful sleep.

Justin leaned back against the headboard. With her cuddled in his lap, he fell asleep.

Several hours later, Justin woke up to find sunshine
coming in the window next to the bed. His back was sore
and his arms ached, but he was a happy man. Catherine
was here, and when she was better, he was going to ask
her to be his wife. Smiling, he looked down at his sleeping
love and discovered she was awake and staring at him.

"Who are you?" she whispered.

"Come on, Cat." Justin frowned. "Don't tease me like this."

"Do I know you?"

"Of course you know me. I'm Justin Prescott, the man who's waited five years to have you back in his life. Behave yourself and stop teasing me." He smiled.

"If I promise to behave, will you tell me one thing more?"

Justin nodded and looked into her innocent gaze. In a soft, impassioned voice, she asked a single question that robbed him of his smile.

"Who am I?"

Chapter 16

After the meeting in the captain's cabin, things moved much too swiftly to suit Catherine. Miles gave orders for the ship to be readied for an immediate departure. Jamie was to sail the *Foxfire* to the Ryland coastal estate in Sheringham.

"When you dock in Sheringham, take several men and Rory O'Banyon to the main house. I'll give you a letter of introduction for my estate manager. Keep O'Banyon under lock and key at all times. It's imperative his presence there be kept secret."

"Ashamed to have an Irishman in the house, English?" she quipped.

"Not ashamed, merely cautious. I don't want the rest of your outlaw family to know where you are. That way there won't be any surprise attacks to rescue him or you." Miles turned away from her to give Jamie other orders.

Catherine was livid. This English lordling was egotistical, pompous, and a few other choice things! Her anger building, she searched the cabin for a distraction. She turned and found Garret staring at her. His smile was contagious, and she grinned back at him.

A plan began to form in her mind. *Getting to know the handsome rogue would be fun. Perhaps he could help her escape.*

"Garret, is that all right with you?" Miles looked over and found his friend gazing intently at Catherine. "Garret, if you can drag your attention back to the matter at hand, I'd appreciate your opinion," he snapped.

"Sorry, Miles. My thoughts were wandering a bit. What do you have in mind?"

"Jamie is taking the ship to Sheringham, so I'll need a place to prepare Cat for her appearance in London. Could we stay at your family's estate while we educate her?"

Garret grinned. "You want my help with Lady Cat?"

"Of course. I'll teach her all I know about Victoria while you groom her into a lady. She'll need to know about the social graces, table manners, dancing, and the like."

Catherine sniffed with indignation. "My entire life hasn't been spent on the bridge of a ship. My family has a large home with servants and gardens. I know how to act like a lady."

Miles cocked his brow. "From the way you dress, one could hardly tell. The ladies I know don't wear britches like men."

"Wearing britches makes good sense in my line of work. When I'm sailing my ship, skirts would hinder me from carrying out my duties. Climbing the rigging with billowing petticoats would prove most hazardous, English."

Miles chuckled. "Climb the rigging? You'd probably get yourself tangled in the lines. You may have assumed the title of captain, Cat, but no woman could truly understand the complexity of sailing vessels."

Catherine moved across the room and stood toe to toe with him. "I earned the title of captain, English. I've handled every job on the ship. I've swabbed decks, loaded cannons, mended sails, tied rigging, and helped repair a cracked mizzenmast. I'm also trained in navigation and can sail by charts, the stars, or instruments. So don't stand there on your elevated opinion of yourself and tell me what I do or don't know about my ship!''

"Knowing all that won't help you in the drawing room," he countered. "The society sharks will tear you apart. You'll have to work a lot harder to navigate around the likes of them. Torie was a lady in every sense of the word. You have a lot to learn to come remotely close to her refinement."

Before she could reply, Garret intervened. "My dear, dear lady, please don't think too harshly of my friend. The point he was trying to make wasn't meant to be inflammatory. In English society, people are too quickly judged by their manners. Everyone watches for errors in others' behavior and gossip runs rampant. For our plan to succeed, your impersonation of Victoria must be flawless. If you'll allow me, I'd be more than happy to assist you in any way I can." He took her hand and kissed it. "In *any* way I can."

Catherine was speechless as Garret tucked her hand in the crook of his arm and led her to the door. "Miles, we'll meet you in the coach," he called over his shoulder. "Jamie, have a safe voyage." Turning to Catherine, he smiled. "I think you'll like my home. My parents are traveling abroad, so we will have plenty of privacy . . ." His voice faded as they moved down the passage.

Miles frowned. "Jamie, what just happened?"

"Garret's glib tongue saved your neck. One more word from you, and she'd have spit in your face and sent you to the devil. Where would your plan be then?"

"You're probably right. That woman certainly knows how to goad me." Miles grabbed his seabag and packed it. When he finished, he turned to Jamie and shook his hand. "Take care. Get O'Banyon secured at my estate and meet us in London after the new year. I let Cat bid her brother farewell, so you shouldn't have trouble with him. If you do, remind him he's responsible for her safety."

Throwing his bag over his shoulder, he picked up his rapier and whip. When he moved toward the door, he saw Catherine's cape and mask on the bed.

"Can't let the lady catch cold." Miles draped her garment over his arm and stuffed her silk mask into his pocket. "Good-bye, Jamie. Watch your back."

As Miles hurried down the passage, Jamie chuckled. "I'll watch my back. But you'd better guard your heart, my friend."

The ride to the Morgan estate took less than an hour. During the trip, Garret continued his easy banter with Catherine. The more they talked, the more irritated Miles became.

"What is 'Cat' short for? Catlin—or Catrina, perhaps?"

"Probably wildcat," Miles mumbled, none too softly.

Catherine scowled at him before she smiled at Garret. "My given name is Catherine. My father began calling me Cat when I was little. A gentleman friend added Lady as a form of endearment."

Miles squirmed. "Gentleman friend, indeed." he muttered.

Garret took her hand and acted as if they were just being introduced. "Mistress Catherine O'Banyon, may I present myself to you? I'm Lord Garret Christopher Morgan, third son of the Duke of Cheswick—the black sheep of the Morgan family, but nonetheless a minor member of the aristocracy. I hope you won't hold that against me, my lady."

"Not as long as you don't mind my being a pirate!" They laughed. "By the time this escapade is completed, I have a feeling we're going to be good friends, Garret Morgan."

Garret brought her hand to his mouth and kissed it. "I'm counting on it, Catherine."

Miles continued to sulk as he stared out the carriage window.

After they arrived at the Morgans' home, Garret showed Catherine to a beautiful bedroom on the second floor. The large bed's canopy was covered in white lace which matched the spread. The sofa in front of the fireplace was done in the same pale blue brocade as the draperies, and a floral rug adorned the floor.

"This room belonged to my sister, Suzanne. She got married last spring and moved to Devonshire. Her husband, Freddy, gave her an entire new wardrobe, so feel free to use anything you find here. Good night, Catherine." Garret kissed her hand and left the room.

Catherine was awed by the richness of her surroundings. But curiosity soon outweighed her shyness, and she began exploring. Lace-trimmed nightrails, chemises, petticoats, and sheer stockings in a rainbow of colors filled the drawers. Other compartments contained handkerchiefs, hair ornaments, gloves, and every accessory a lady could ask for.

When a footman delivered a pitcher of hot water and built a fire in the hearth, Catherine noticed a door on the far side of the room. Carrying a lit taper, she investigated and found a large closet and dressing room. Gowns, skirts, blouses, robes, and coats hung in abundance. Shoes, hats, and slippers lined the shelves of one wall.

She examined the clothes. She and Suzanne were nearly the same size. Even the shoes looked as if they'd fit —but it would have to wait until tomorrow.

Stifling a yawn, Catherine watched the servant leave. She removed her clothes and washed with the warm water and scented soap. After pulling on a nightgown she had taken from the armoire, she stretched out on the bed.

In spite of being tired, Catherine was too nervous to

sleep. Her dagger was still hidden in the side of her boot, and she hurried to retrieve it. With it safely tucked beneath her pillow, Catherine smiled. She always felt more at ease with her "friend" nearby.

Moments later, she fell into a deep, dreamless sleep.

Sunlight was peeking through the drapes when Catherine woke up the next morning. It took her several seconds to remember where she was. As she sat up in bed, someone tapped on the door. A moment later it opened and a maid looked in.

"I'm sorry, my lady. Did I wake you? Lord Garret told me to take care of you, and I didn't know . . . I mean . . . forgive me—"

"I'm awake. Please come in and shut the door," Catherine instructed her.

The timid young woman inched nervously toward the bed. Her large brown eyes appeared to bulge out of her pale face.

"What's your name?" Catherine asked, hoping to ease the maid's obvious distress.

"Darcy," she whispered.

"Darcy, are you afraid of me?"

The mobcap covering Darcy's dark hair moved off center when she shook her head. "No, my lady. I'm just afraid I'll make a mistake and be discharged. Never been a lady's maid before."

Catherine winked. "I'll tell you a secret. I've never had a lady's maid before. Perhaps we can learn from each other. All right?"

Darcy smiled and nodded. As if a floodgate had opened, words flowed from her mouth. "Well first, I'll have your bath water prepared. 'Tis mid morning, but I can have Cook make you some tea and a muffin to hold you until dinner, unless you want something more. While you're

soaking in the tub, I'll have a dress freshened for you.
Then I'll wash your hair. You have lovely hair, my lady.
I'm very good with styling it, too, so I could try . . ."

Catherine rolled her eyes. *Now I've got her talking. How
do I get her to stop?*

Miles and Garret were talking and going over some
papers in the main salon when Catherine joined them two
hours later. Their conversation stopped as she entered the
room.

Catherine wore a gown of aquamarine velvet with long
sleeves and a sweetheart neckline. Her hair was arranged
in an elaborate style of intertwining braids pinned up on
the back of her head.

Garret rushed toward Catherine, complimenting her
appearance in his usual effusive way. Miles stood and stared
at her in shocked amazement.

Though she wore no jewels, Catherine looked like a
queen. Even the way she walked across the floor when
Garret led her to the sofa could be described as regal. Her
laughter was sweet, and the blush on her cheeks height-
ened her beauty. The sparkle in her eyes made them glow
like priceless emeralds. Her lips looked soft and inviting.
They invited him to—

Miles berated himself. *What in the hell am I doing? I can't
let this woman distract me. She's part of my plan to trap Edward.
I'm going to avenge Victoria's loss, not replace her.*

Catherine curtsied before him. "Good morning, my
lord," she offered, smiling. "I apologize for sleeping so
long. Garret informs me you've been up for hours."

Shaking off his malaise, Miles wasted no time getting
down to business. "I was anxious to get started, so I began
listing the names of Victoria's friends and employees."

He handed her several papers. "I've also given you their
physical descriptions and a brief bit about each person.

Once you learn the names, I'll give you additional information about them. Can you read my writing?"

Catherine looked at the pages and nodded. "Your hand seems to be quite legible, but what is this name? It's smudged."

Miles leaned over the page. Before he focused on the place she was pointing at, her scent, combined with the light fragrance of her perfume, assailed his senses. His insides fluttered, and he knew he had to put some space between them.

"Lucy Harper. The tip on the quill snapped while I was writing." He suddenly turned on his heel and began pacing the floor. "Every morning you and I will work together. I'll teach you everything I know about Victoria. In the afternoons, Garret will instruct you in fashion, etiquette, and dancing. He'll create the lady on the outside while I create Victoria from within. Any questions?"

"Yes, my lord. How long will I have to master this? Two or three months?"

Miles stopped at the door and turned to face her. "You'll make your debut at my parents' New Year's Eve ball."

"Are you insane?" Catherine gasped. "Today is the sixth of December! That's only twenty-five days away!"

He shrugged. "I know. We have a lot of work ahead of us. I'm going to the study to work on diagrams of Chatham Hall and Carlisle House so you can become familiar with Torie's homes. I'll take my dinner there. See you both this evening." Miles left the salon.

Catherine tried to follow him. When the door slammed shut across the foyer, she stopped in her tracks.

During their hours apart, Miles had shaved off his beard. He was even more attractive than she'd imagined. After all the primping and care she'd taken that morning, his lack of interest in her stung her pride. She'd hoped he'd approve of how she looked, but he'd said nothing about it.

Why should she care about him anyway? But she did, and that made her angry.

"Of all the arrogant, domineering, self-serving autocrats, he takes the prize!" Catherine stomped her foot, and a sharp pain exploded in her ankle. "Ow!" she cried out. "Look what he made me do. If I stay around him too long, I'll end up a cripple."

"Allow me to help, Catherine." Garret swept her up into his arms and held her. "I think I could get used to this. Would you like to be carried through all your lessons, my lady?"

Catherine wrapped her arms around his neck. "It might prove difficult learning to waltz in this position."

"But think of the fun we'll have trying." As he held her in his arms, he began singing and dancing her around the room. After a few minutes, Garret dropped down on the sofa, holding Catherine on his lap. They were flushed from laughing and fighting to catch their breath when she leaned forward to hug him.

"Oh, Garret, you do know how to make me laugh." Catherine kissed his cheek and giggled. "Even kissing you tickles!"

"I'd be happy to show you just how well my whiskers can tickle you, Catherine." Garret lowered his mouth toward hers.

"What in the hell is going on here?" Miles stood in the doorway with his hands braced on his hips. "This isn't the kind of lesson I asked you to provide, Garret!"

Garret set Catherine on the sofa beside him and signaled her to remain quiet. "Forgive me, Miles. Catherine hurt her foot, and I was trying to take her mind off the pain. In the future, I swear we'll keep strictly to our lesson plans."

At that moment, a maid came in to announce dinner. Garret stood up and offered Catherine his arm. "Come along, my lady. Let us adjourn to the dining room. Perhaps we can learn something from our meal. Maybe cook has prepared escargot or some other exotic creation." Passing Miles at the doorway, he nodded to him. "See you later, my lord."

Miles watched Garret and Catherine walk down the hall. He'd left the salon to get away from her. But when he heard the singing and laughter, he was drawn back again.

She looked so beautiful and happy as Garret swung her around. When they dropped to the sofa, Miles imagined himself in his friend's place, with Catherine sitting on his lap, hugging him. Then he realized Garret was going to kiss her and had been compelled to stop him.

Miles shook his head. Why was he acting like a jealous suitor? He cared for Victoria, but felt nothing for Cat. Somehow he must be confusing the two women. But not anymore. He would stick to the task and not allow his thoughts to wander in that direction again.

Over the next two weeks. Catherine became more and more like Victoria Carlisle. With Miles' assistance, she learned the names, descriptions, and family histories of Victoria's business associates, staff, and friends. She memorized the location of all the rooms at the offices and her homes.

Under Garret's tutelage, Catherine mastered the art of dancing, could play all the popular card games, and was able to ride sidesaddle. He also taught her about the *ton,* the cream of London society. Thanks to him, she could spout off their rules of conduct and name all the social leaders and give their descriptions, family histories, and approximate net worth.

Garret also helped her select a new wardrobe. A dressmaker newly arrived from France was brought to the house. Miles paid the woman generously for her labors.

The hardest thing Catherine faced was cutting her hair.

"No one said I had to cut my hair, Garret. I can't do it."

Garret followed her as she stormed out of the salon. "We don't have to cut off all your hair. Victoria wore some of hers curled around her face. The wispy tendrils would frame the perfection of your countenance, sweetheart."

"Don't flatter me with fancy words, Garret. I'm very nervous about scissors near my hair." She stopped in front of a wall mirror and studied her reflection. "Just around my face?" she asked warily.

"Well, we'd have to take a few inches off the back—"

Catherine spun around to face him. "Oh, no, you won't. The next thing you'll say is it's the wrong color. Tell English our deal is off!" With that, she bolted up the stairs.

Garret went to the study to inform Miles of their newest problem. "I don't know what to do. We're so close to our goal. It'd be a waste not to see it through."

"You're talking in riddles, Garret. What's happened now?"

Garret went to the cabinet and poured himself a glass of wine. "Cat's been doing very well. She could set the *ton* on its ear, but she won't do it as Victoria Carlisle. She absolutely refuses to cut her hair."

"Why does she have to be so stubborn about it? Hair grows back." Miles hit his fist on the desk. "She can't stop now. I won't let her." He stood up and walked toward the door.

"Miles, leave her alone for a while. Cat was very upset when she went upstairs," Garret warned him as he sipped his wine.

"But I can't drop this plan now. I wrote to my parents a few days ago and told them I'd found Victoria."

Garret choked on his drink. "You told them what?"

"Don't look at me like I've lost my mind, Garret, I told them she'd gone away for a while because of all the pressure she'd been under. I asked them not to tell anyone about her coming to their New Year's ball. My father is sending his traveling coach for us right after Christmas."

"You're going to lie to your own parents?"

"I want to bring Catherine home and see their reaction to her. Once they accept her as Victoria, I'll tell them the truth, but I need to be sure her portrayal is perfect before we expose her to Edward Damien."

Garret shook his head. "Perhaps you can change her mind, but don't force her. For some reason I think she's afraid of cutting her hair." He set down his glass and walked to the door. "Well, you deal with it. I have to ride into town this afternoon. Catherine's present should be ready."

Miles scowled. "Why are you giving her a present? A special bribe for the lady?"

"Why are you so hostile? Have you forgotten Christmas is five days away? I had something made for Catherine, and it should be ready today. See you this evening." Garret left Miles staring at his back.

After the terse way he'd treated his friend, Miles couldn't lie to himself any longer about his growing attraction to Catherine O'Banyon. Aside from her beauty, she was intelligent and possessed a delightful wit. Her ability to recall names, dates, and facts was phenomenal. She could speak on politics, religion, and history. The usual female pastimes didn't concern her. She had an uncanny mind for battle strategy and was unbeatable at chess.

This lovely, vivacious woman had totally captivated him. Out of loyalty to Victoria, he'd fought to put Catherine out of his mind. Between that struggle and his plot to trap Edward, he'd completely forgotten about Christmas.

He sat behind the desk and searched his mind for the perfect gift for Catherine. An idea came to him just as the courier from Ryland Shipping arrived with his packet of

correspondence. Miles hastily wrote a letter to his father
and sent it to London with the messenger.

Knowing he couldn't delay any longer, Miles walked up
the stairs to see Catherine. When he knocked on her door
a third time without getting a response, he entered the
room.

"If she's run off, I'll have to . . ." His words faded when
he saw her lying on the sofa near the fireplace, fast asleep.
Her hair was loose, hanging over the arm of the sofa. He
moved to her side and gently stroked the golden tresses
with his fingers. They felt like silk.

At the sound of his voice, Catherine awoke. She pulled
away from him and stood up, knocking her hairbrush to
the floor. A dagger was clutched in her hand. "Go away.
You can't make me cut my hair. I won't let you."

Miles held up his hands in surrender. "I didn't come
up here to force you into cutting your hair, Cat, but I don't
understand why you're so upset. It would grow back in
time."

Catherine shook her head, sending her unbound hair
swirling around her. "No, you don't understand. You don't
know me. You're so concerned with Victoria you never
took the time to learn about me." Tears ran down her
cheeks.

"When I was a little girl, I was fascinated by fairy tales,
mythology, and Bible stories. During my lessons, I learned
about the Norse warrior maidens, the Valkyrie. There was
a picture of one in the book. She was tall and strong, with
long, blond hair. She wore armor and held a sword in her
hand."

A sad smile curved her lips. "My brother, Colin, told
me I looked like her. That's when I decided I'd be a warrior
maiden, too. I worked hard till I mastered all types of
weapons, and I did it all without fear. I was invincible, you
see—the warrior maiden reborn. Though I had no armor,
I imagined my long hair protected me from harm."

"Like a good luck charm?" Miles offered.

"Call it what you will, a talisman, a charm, or the silly superstition of a young girl. I don't care. It gave me the confidence to succeed, to be what I am." Catherine shook her head and backed away from him. Her eyes welled with tears. "I'm sorry, Miles, I won't cut my hair. I can't let you destroy me."

Catherine stepped on the hairbrush and lost her balance. As she fell toward the blazing hearth, Miles moved quickly and pulled her from the fire's reach. The shock of her near accident caused her to drop the dagger and grab him around the neck.

Miles held her and murmured words of comfort as she sobbed against his shoulder. Conflicting thoughts assailed his mind.

Catherine needed solace, not passion, yet he couldn't ignore how perfectly she fit in his arms. Her bosom was crushed to his chest, her breath moist and warm along his neck. He cursed his body when he hardened with need, but he refused to release her.

As if sensing his torment, Catherine looked up into his face. Their eyes met, and Miles lost the battle in his soul. He lowered his lips to hers, sealing his fate with a kiss.

He explored her mouth with his tongue and shivered when she gently drew on it. His hand stroked her back, bringing her hips closer to him as they shared kiss after fiery kiss. When Catherine arched against him, he gathered her in his arms and carried her to the bed.

Lying beside her, he continued his assault of demanding kisses. His hand closed over her breast and kneaded her yielding flesh. All too soon, it wasn't enough.

He dragged his lips from hers and tenderly kissed the side of her neck, his fingers trembling as he managed to undo the buttons on the front of her gown. Gently, he pulled the fabric aside and freed the ribbons that held her camisole in place. Her breasts were pale in the fading daylight. He lovingly cradled one in his hand, then closed his mouth over her pink nipple and suckled on it. At her moan, Miles gazed up into her face.

Her tears were gone. Passion glowed in her eyes, and her lips beckoned to be kissed. Before he returned to the sweetness of her mouth, he caught sight of something on her exposed breast—a birthmark shaped like a quarter moon. He placed his lips on the mark and kissed it.

Catherine trembled with delight when Miles caressed her. Though she had little experience with men, her body instinctively responded to him. She greedily sought his lips and returned his kisses as she tried to quell the strange yearning inside her.

The tension of heated desire filled the room until a loud knocking came at the door.

"Catherine," Garret called, "are you still in there? I pray you aren't angry with me." When she didn't respond, he knocked again. "Catherine, are you all right?"

"Yes, Garret." She struggled to reply. "I'm fine, just resting a bit. I'll see you at dinner."

After Garret left her doorway, Catherine closed her eyes and turned away from Miles. She wasn't a coward, but she simply couldn't face him. The reality of what had gone on between them left her burning with embarrassment. She needed time alone to sort out her tattered emotions.

"My lord, forgive the shameful way I behaved. I guess I'm weary and confused. Please leave me for a while."

Had Catherine been looking at Miles, she would have seen the same warring emotions on his face. He was a man who prided himself on his ability to curb his base needs, but one kiss had destroyed his control. Catherine was a special woman, and he'd come to care for her far more than he ever imagined. She didn't deserve to be taken advantage of while she was hurt and vulnerable. Cursing his lack of restraint, he knew he couldn't leave before he apologized to her.

"I'll go, Catherine, but hear me out. You've done nothing that requires forgiveness. I'm totally to blame. I bullied you into helping me with my plan and then I practically forced myself on you. If you decide you don't want to be a part of this plot any longer, just say the word. I won't turn you or Rory into the authorities. Both of you will be returned to Ireland immediately, if that is your wish."

Sitting up on the bed, he spoke to her back. "Before you make your decision, I want to tell you about my relationship with Victoria. She was more than my best friend. We were engaged to be married. Now Torie is gone, and it's all my fault.

"When she needed me most, I was off seeking my revenge on your brother. Perhaps if I had stayed in England, she'd still be all right, but now it's too late. With or without your help, I'll see Edward is punished for what he did to Torie. I know he was responsible for her disappearance, and I won't rest easy until I can prove it."

Miles stood up. "Thank you for everything you did to help me, Catherine. I'll never forget you. My biggest regret is not telling you sooner how special you have become to me."

He quietly left her room and closed the door.

Alone with her thoughts, Catherine considered all he had said and made a decision. That night before dinner, she'd give him her answer.

"Better yet," she sighed, "I'll show him."

"You must be insane," Garret chided Miles in the study that evening. "If you told Catherine she didn't have to go through with your plan, she'll be on the first boat to Ireland."

Standing at the fireplace, Miles shrugged. "The lady may surprise us yet."

"Or you're praying she will." Garret filled two glasses

with wine and handed him one. "You'd better drink this. It might help you deal with the disappointment when . . . oh!"

Miles set his glass on the mantel and looked up to see what had garnered his friend's attention. Catherine stood in the doorway. Her gown was a deep blue velvet with puffed sleeves and an Empire waist, the latest fashion. A ribbon was tied around her throat.

She looked beautiful, but her golden hair was her crowning glory. It was swept up on the top of her head. A mass of curls cascaded down the back. Her lovely face was artfully framed by delicate blond ringlets.

Miles was so stunned by her appearance he could say only one word. "Catherine?"

"Of course it's Catherine." Garret rushed to her side. "You look incredible, my lady."

Catherine raised a brow at him. "Incredible because of the way I look, or because I look so much like Victoria?"

Bringing her hand to his lips, he grinned. "Both, my lady."

"Why, Garret," she replied, her smile coy, "you could be a diplomat, giving answers like that." Catherine crossed the room and dropped into a deep curtsy in front of Miles. "What say you, my lord? Do you think I can fool Edward Damien?"

Relief rushed through Miles. He let out the breath that had been imprisoned in his lungs. "Then you're going through with it? After our, ah, talk this afternoon, I wasn't sure."

Catherine's fingertips pressed against his lips. "We can discuss all that later. For now, just rest assured I'm going to help you trap that man and make him pay for his crime."

Miles lifted her hand from his mouth and kissed her palm. As he tried to find the words to thank her, he noticed a deep indentation across the width of her palm.

"Where did you get this scar, Cat? Were you injured in battle?"

She shook her head and pulled her hand away from him. "No. Surprisingly enough, I've always come through battles unscathed." Catherine traced the straight ridge of scarred flesh with her finger. "Da said I got this cut when I was a baby. According to him, if there was mischief to be found back then, I was the one to find it."

The clock on the mantel struck the hour of nine and Garret grumbled. "Having a late dinner is fine for the city, but this is the country and I'm famished. If you two will excuse me, I'll see what's holding up our meal."

With Garret off on his errand, Miles asked Catherine the question that had plagued him since she entered the room. "I offered you freedom, but you decided to stay and help me. Why?"

Avoiding his gaze, Catherine shrugged and sat on the sofa. "That's a silly question. Because you needed me."

Miles sat beside her. "So you cut your hair and agreed to go through with this plan to trap Edward Damien just for me?"

Catherine frowned at him. "Being smug doesn't become you, English. In the beginning I agreed to help so I could buy myself time. At the first opportunity, I planned to escape. I'm going through with this charade for you *and* for Victoria."

"But you don't know Victoria," Miles pointed out, trying to mask his disappointment.

"Thanks to you, I know her very well now. As I listened to you talk about her, I cried for her pain, cheered her successes, and understood the love she had for her father. I came to admire Victoria Carlisle. I can't let the man responsible for her disappearance go unpunished."

Miles took her hand. "And what of me, Cat? What have you learned about me?"

Catherine gazed into his eyes. "You're a very noble man,

Miles Grayson. Honor means a great deal to you, loyalty even more. You may be a titled lord, but your spirit yearns to be free. You're happiest on the sea, where you thrive on adventure, but because your family needs you, you've accepted the yoke of your inheritance and will be what is expected of you. I pray you won't sacrifice your soul for someone else's dreams."

The accuracy of her words stunned him. "How can you possibly know these things about me? I've never admitted any of this to a living soul. Are my feelings so transparent that you can see straight through them?"

Catherine shook her head and smiled. "No. During the past two weeks, you've kept your distance and wouldn't let me close to you. Today, all that changed, not by the physical things that passed between us, but by your honesty. You let me into your soul and allowed me to witness your pain. You offered me freedom but hoped I wouldn't go. You were willing to take a chance. So am I."

"What about your hair? Aren't you afraid cutting it is going to bring you bad luck?" he teased, trying to lighten their serious conversation.

Her eyes glistening, Catherine tentatively touched the curls resting against her cheek. "A nice gentleman told me it would grow back. Besides, we make our own luck, English."

"And the luckiest day of my life was finding you."

Filled with the need to kiss Catherine, Miles leaned toward her. Before his lips touched hers, Garret's voice called out to them from the corridor. They jumped apart as their boisterous host entered the study.

"Catherine, Miles, dinner is ready. Cook has prepared a crown roast of lamb that's been done to perfection." Garret stood before the sofa and bent into a courtly bow. "My lady, may I escort you to the table?"

As Miles followed them from the room, he realized the

lovely lady outlaw had succeeded once again. The infamous Lady Cat had stolen his heart.

Hours later, Catherine stared up at the canopy over her bed and tried to sleep, but failed. Even the dreams that usually filled her slumbering mind had deserted her in the past few days. Her nightly visions had been replaced by shadows and darkness.

She faulted her worries over the upcoming trip to London and its consequences for her restlessness. In ten days, she would make her debut as Victoria Carlisle. Thanks to Garret's help, she could walk, talk, dance, and ride like the missing heiress.

Her new wardrobe was of the latest fashions. Expensive gowns, shoes, coats, and accessories were ready for her use. With her hair cut and styled with its waves and curls, the metamorphosis was nearly complete.

Miles had schooled her on being Victoria, the dedicated daughter and businesswoman. She had a talent for memorizing things, but her lessons were far easier than she would have imagined. Sometimes she felt as though she knew all the names and information before she read it on the paper.

Her only shortcoming was not being able to match Victoria's ability to converse in five languages. Catherine could speak and read English and Gaelic and had studied Latin at the parish school, but that wouldn't help her now. Miles assured her he or Garret would be with her at all times when they got to London. Between them, they wouldn't allow her to be drawn into any situations that could expose her ignorance.

"If I'm to convince Edward Damien that I'm his niece, my portrayal of Victoria must be perfect. Miles needs my help."

Catherine turned over and hugged her pillow. Since she'd met him, Miles Grayson had filled her thoughts. At first, she'd thought he was cold and unfeeling. But after what had transpired between them that day, she knew he was a man of deep emotions. She had witnessed his pain, had tasted his passion. It would be very easy to fall in love with him.

The guilt Miles felt over Victoria's loss would have destroyed a lesser man. By the way he talked about her, Catherine knew they had been very close—engaged to be married. He must miss her . . .

Catherine suddenly sat up and punched the bed with her fist. Miles hadn't been kissing her. He'd been making love to his Torie. She might be a copy of the original, but Catherine wouldn't take her place in his bed. When a man made love to her, it would be to *her*, not some ghost from his past.

Scowling, she fell back on the bed. He could use her mind and face for this charade, but naught else.

Miles would never want her anyway. She was an outlaw with a price on her head. When he looked for a lady to take Victoria's place, he'd choose among his own kind. When this charade is over, she'd get on with her life and find her own happiness. She would . . .

Catherine shook her head and sighed. "Do what? Remain in England and see Justin? What if he isn't interested in a future with me? Perhaps I could find someone else to love."

Garret's smiling face flashed into her mind and she laughed. There was no denying Garret was a very attractive man. He constantly flirted with her. Tomorrow he was taking her to the village so she could purchase some Christmas presents. Maybe she should give Garret a chance to win her heart.

As she fell asleep, Catherine was thinking about Garret. Perhaps with his help and attention, she'd be able to forget about Miles Grayson once and for all.

Chapter 17

Christmas Eve had come to Morgan Manor. Pine boughs and holly adorned with bright red bows decorated the tables and mantels throughout the house. A Yule log had been brought into the salon's large fireplace and a wassail bowl was prepared in the kitchen.

Miles and Catherine were in the salon when Garret came in carrying a fluffy pine tree taller than he was. A wooden platform was nailed to the base of the trunk so it could stand freely on its own in the corner of the room.

"To celebrate Christmas, people in Bavaria bring a tree into their homes and decorate it with nuts, ribbons, and ornaments that they make—angels, animals, and stars. An unusual custom, but I rather like it," Garret said.

"Of course you would," Catherine pointed out. "You enjoy dressing up, so why not do the same thing for your home? But I don't see what a tree has to do with Christmas."

"It goes back to the mystery plays that told the stories of the Bible by reenacting important Christian events,"

Miles explained. "It was originally called a Paradise Tree, symbolizing Eden. I like to believe the tree represents new life and hope for us all. During the dull days of winter, we seldom see nature's green. By bringing the living tree into our homes, we're reminded of the bounty God has surrounded us with."

Catherine was moved by his sincerity. "I never realized how much of a philosopher you are, Miles. You sound Irish."

"I should. My maternal grandmother, Mary Margaret O'Malley, was a lovely lass from Kinsale on the east coast of Ireland. She had raven hair, a complexion like cream, and azure eyes." He smiled wistfully. "My grandfather called her his *cuillin*. When I asked her what it meant, she said in Gaelic it meant a pretty dark-haired girl. That piqued my interest, so she taught me the language and told me about Ireland. If I remind you of an Irish scholar, you have only her to blame."

Catherine tried to hide her surprise. "I, ah, don't suppose you remember much Gaelic?"

"Yes, I do. I can read and write the language, as well." He chuckled. "I knew every name and curse you shouted at me the night I captured you."

She scowled at him. "Then you must have understood what I said to Rory on your ship before we left. Were you hoping to catch me passing along some kind of secret code or plan of escape to my brother?"

"To be honest, Cat, I thought you might. But you gave words of encouragement and concern to Rory, and I felt foolish for being suspicious. I feared risking your anger to admit my knowledge before now. Forgive me?"

Before she could reply, Garret called them over to help with the tree. With the aid of Darcy and several servants, strings of berries were arranged on the spiny boughs, along with bows and ornaments cut from colored paper.

A while later, Garret stepped back to survey their work.

"Perhaps we could tie small candles to the branches and light up our creation."

"No fire! It's too dangerous!" Catherine exclaimed.

Miles put his arm around her. "You're trembling like a leaf. What's the matter?"

"I'm deathly afraid of fire. I have no fear of water, heights, or anything else. But for some reason I cannot fathom, fire terrifies me."

Miles squeezed her shoulder. "In India, people believe a soul must endure many lifetimes before going to heaven. Perhaps they're right and in a previous life you died in a fire."

"Now I know you're Irish." Catherine smiled at him. "Only a Celt would give credence to such a possibility."

"Keep doing that." He stroked her cheek with his hand.

His remark puzzled her. "Keep doing what?"

"Smiling. It makes the whole room light up. Then Garret won't need any candles for his creation." Miles gave her a reassuring hug. "Come on, Cat. Let's get this tree finished, or he'll have us up all night."

Catherine watched Miles walk away. In the past few days, she'd tried to stop herself from getting close to him. He was vulnerable, a man who had lost the woman he loved. She refused to be used to salve his wounds, yet she ached to be held in his arms.

Trying to put him out of her mind, she'd been more attentive to Garret. He treated her like a queen and openly courted her. His kisses were pleasant, but they didn't spark the fiery passion Miles' had instilled in her. She sighed with sad acceptance. Garret was a wonderful man, but he wasn't the man for her. He wasn't Miles.

Adding to her misery, it was Christmas Eve. She missed her family. With her parents, brothers, and Uncle Padraic, the holidays were always special. But this year she and Rory were in England. The rest of her family were probably at home, worrying about them. Tears filled her eyes.

Garret was standing on a chair placing a gold paper star on the top of the tree when Miles saw Catherine rush from the room. He followed her into the study and shut the door.

Catherine was facing the hearth, crying. He crossed the room and pulled her into his arms. She sobbed against his shoulder as he consoled her.

"Why the tears, Catherine? It's Christmas, a time for celebration, not sorrow."

She looked up at him. Tears glistened on the ends of her dark lashes. "How much is my family celebrating this year? Because of me, my entire family has been torn apart."

Miles put his mouth to hers and tenderly kissed her. "No, sweetheart. The blame for that belongs to me. I'm sorry I've caused you such pain."

At that moment, Darcy knocked on the study door. "My lady, are you in there? Lord Garret sent me to find you and Viscount Ryland."

Catherine moved to the door and opened it. "We're both here, Darcy. Come in and tell me what the problem is."

Darcy stepped in and curtsied. "No real problem, my lady. Lord Garret had me carry down your presents from your room so he could place them under his tree."

"Garret put my gifts under his tree?"

The maid nodded. "He said something about starting another tradition. Don't worry, I got all your packages there safely. I even remembered the velvet box you had on the dresser."

"But I didn't want that box—" Catherine stopped talking when she saw Miles looking at her. "Well, that's fine, Darcy. Why don't we all go back to the salon and help Lord Garret finish the decorating?" As she moved to follow her maid, Catherine turned to Miles. "Are you coming?"

"I'll join you as soon as I go upstairs and fetch my gifts. I don't want to dampen Garret's holiday spirits."

Darcy poked her head back into the room. "Lord Garret already put your things under the tree, my lord."

"He did what? I wish Garret would mind his own—" Catching the questioning look in Catherine's eye, Miles forced a smile and joined her at the door. "Let's see what else our host has planned for this celebration of his."

Garret was dismissing the housekeeper when they entered the salon. "There are only a few servants in residence, so I've asked them to join us for the festivities this evening. After we have a buffet supper, everyone will retire to the music room to sing Christmas songs. My father purchased one of those Viennese pianofortes, and I'm anxious to hear it played. We're in luck! Our housekeeper, Mrs. Cox, can play the instrument. Then we'll come back here, drink a toast to the holiday, and pass out the presents."

Miles and Catherine spoke at the same time. "No!"

After casting a startled glance at Miles, Catherine turned to Garret. "If you don't mind, could we give presents to the staff only and wait until morning to exchange our gifts? It's the way it's done in my family."

"Yes, that's the way it's done in my family, as well," Miles added. "The anticipation makes getting up on Christmas morning very special."

Garret shrugged. "Well, I'm all for tradition. We can do it that way, if you like. But no more talk," he declared, rubbing his hands together. "It's time for this party to begin."

The evening went as Garret planned. The dinner—roast goose, plum pudding, various vegetables, freshly baked breads, and six kinds of dessert—was enjoyed by everyone. Afterward, music and singing filled the Morgan house. Noble and commoner alike raised their voices in song, praising God and the miracle birth of the Christ child, Jesus.

With prodding from Garret, Catherine sang an old

Gaelic carol while she played the harp in the music room. She was surprised when Miles began singing with her. Their voices blended in perfect harmony. At the final refrain, their eyes met in silent communion across the room.

Following the singing, the entire group returned to the salon. Garret passed out the gifts to the servants, while Miles and Catherine filled glasses with spiced ale. Several toasts were made, and the party came to an end.

As everyone began to leave, Darcy hurried over to Catherine. "My lady, thank you so much for the wonderful presents. I've never had such a fine pair of boots, and the brush and comb set is the most exquisite thing I've ever owned."

"You've been a big help to me while I was here, Darcy. You've never asked questions or made any unseemly observations. I'll always treasure your loyalty."

Darcy pulled a small wrapped package from beneath her apron and handed it to Catherine. "This isn't anywhere near as grand as the beautiful things you gave me, but I made it myself."

Catherine removed the paper to find a soft white wool scarf with fringed edges.

"I knitted it just for you, my lady."

"Thank you, Darcy. I'll make good use of your lovely gift. Perhaps next year you can make me a shawl just like it."

Darcy nodded. "Certainly, my lady. It would be no trouble at all—" The maid suddenly gasped. "Next year? Did I hear right, my lady? Did you say next year?"

Catherine smiled at Darcy's look of surprise. "The position is yours, if you don't mind traveling a bit. Have you ever been on a ship, Darcy?"

"Oh, no, my lady, but I've always wanted to." Darcy gave her mistress an eager hug. "I promise I'll work hard and be the best lady's maid in the whole world."

Catherine laughed at her exuberance and patted her

on the back. "Run on to bed now, Darcy. I'll take care of myself tonight. Merry Christmas."

Darcy dipped into a perfect curtsy. "Thank you, my lady, and good night."

As Darcy hurried off, Garret tapped Catherine on the shoulder. "Excuse me, Cat, but it's my pleasure to inform you you're standing under the mistletoe."

Looking up, she saw the sprigs of green leaves and tiny white berries held together with a red ribbon hanging in the archway over her head. "Am I expected to pay a forfeit or be punished severely for this infraction, good sir?"

"Not unless you think kissing is a form of torture." Miles was standing on her other side.

Catherine responded to his grin with a smile of her own. "To whom do I owe this kiss?"

"Me!" Miles and Garret answered in unison.

First she turned to Garret. He gently pressed his lips to hers and embraced her for a moment. "Merry Christmas, Catherine. I'll see you in the morning and finally get you to open your presents. If you and Miles will excuse me, I forgot to give Mrs. Cox her orders for breakfast." Kissing her forehead, Garret went off to find the housekeeper.

"Cat, you still owe me your forfeit."

Turning to Miles, Catherine found herself encompassed in his arms. His mouth took hers in a passionate kiss that left them both wanting more. They reluctantly pulled apart as the servants came in to remove the glasses and punch bowl from the salon.

"Good night, Miles."

"Good night to you, my lady."

Catherine grabbed her skirt and ran up the stairs. She didn't stop running until she was in her room with the door closed behind her. Her heart pounded. She knew it had nothing to do with her exertion and everything to do with Miles Grayson.

"I am such a fool! Miles doesn't want *me*. I merely look

like the woman he really loves." Crossing the bedroom, she shook her head. She couldn't let him see the present she'd originally planned for him. But thanks to Garret, it was already under the tree!

On the afternoon she had been with Miles in this room, she'd felt very close to him. During that brief interlude, they had shared more than intoxicating kisses. Pain, anger, and truth had flowed freely between them.

When Darcy cut twelve inches off her hair that day, Catherine wove the shorn locks into a golden plait. She secured the ends with yellow ribbons and wrote a note to Miles. At the bottom of the page she added a few words in Gaelic that she'd intended to tell him was an ancient blessing. She'd put the braid and note into a velvet gift box, attached a name tag to it, and set it on the dresser.

Later that night, she'd realized how foolish she'd been to think that Miles genuinely cared for her and had decided to concentrate on Garret. But she forgot about the velvet box.

"Catherine O'Banyon, you're a blithering idiot," she chided herself as she undressed for bed. "In Gaelic, English, or Greek, it means the same thing! Unless I want to be embarrassed in the morning when Miles reads that note, I'll have to go downstairs and get it."

Wearing a robe over her sleeping gown, Catherine crept into the salon an hour later carrying a lit candelabrum. She sat on the floor in front of the tree. When she found the box, she set the brace of candles next to her and started to open it.

"Couldn't wait until morning, Cat?"

Miles' voice in the darkness startled Catherine, and she dropped the box. He stepped out of the shadows and sat beside her on the floor.

Picking up the box, he noticed his name on the tag.

"Did you change your mind about giving this to me?" Her silence made him smile. "I came down here after everyone had gone to bed so I could add something to one of the presents I'm giving you."

Miles set the box on the floor and gave her the wrapped package he was holding under his arm. "I want you to have this, Cat. It belonged to my grandmother, Mary Margaret. I think it will have a special meaning for you. Please open it."

Catherine's hands trembled as she removed the colored paper. It was an old book, written in Gaelic, entitled *Tain Bo Cuailgne.* "The Raid of the Cattle of Cooley? What does a book about cattle have to do with me, Miles?"

"It's the ancient story of the Irish hero Cuchulainn and his battle against the warrior queen Medb of Connacht. She was a beautiful, courageous woman who led an army into Ulster to capture the Brown Bull of Cooley."

"Did Medb succeed?" Catherine asked.

"Not at first. Rather than fight an all-out war, Cuchulainn made an agreement with Medb that each would send a single soldier out to duel every day. Her army was single-handedly defeated by Cuchulainn himself. One by one, her men fell."

Catherine sniffed. "She was stupid to trust him. A well-planned battle would have been far more expedient."

"Don't be quick to condemn Medb," Miles warned. "The queen wouldn't rest until she bettered the mighty warrior. With her help, all the other forces in the land rose up in opposition to him and he was badly injured in battle. Because of his great ego, Cuchulainn tied himself to a pillar in order to die standing up. All of his enemies, with the exception of Medb, were afraid to approach him, and his death went unnoticed until a raven sat on his head and plucked his eyes out.

"The renowned warrior Cuchulainn, heralded for his great strength, was conquered by a woman." Miles reached over and stroked her cheek with his hand. "You're not

like a Valkyrie, Catherine. You're the rebirth of Queen
Medb of Connacht—an incredibly beautiful woman whose
courage, guile, and intelligence are more than a match
for any man.''

Catherine held the book tightly to her chest. "I'm honored you see a bit of Medb in me. Most men are intimidated
by who I am, but you're not. Others tell me to change.
You accept my abilities and don't condemn me. I thank
you for that, Miles.'' She picked up the velvet box and
gave it to him. "I hope you won't laugh.''

Removing the ribbon, Miles lifted the lid. He picked up
the golden plait and removed the piece of parchment lying
beneath it. He held the paper to the candlelight so he
could read it.

> *When I cut my hair, I decided not to lose my luck, but
> to share it with you. May these golden strands shield you
> from harm and guide you to never-ending victories.*

Tha gaol agam ort, *Miles.*

Always yours,
Catherine

Miles looked at her and nodded toward the book she
held in her hand. "Read the inscription I wrote to you on
the front leaf of the book.''

Catherine opened the cover and read it aloud.

> *To my dear darling, Cat.*
> Tha gaol agam ort.

Forever,
Miles

She looked up at him. "Miles, you wrote I love you in
Gaelic.''

"Yes, I know. And you did, too."

She shook her head. "But you don't love me. You're in love with Victoria. You love what you created, and that's not me."

"You're wrong. It's you I love." Miles took hold of her hands and gazed into her eyes. "The other day you were right when you said I gave up my freedom because of duty. Adam's death made me my father's heir. I was determined to prove to my family that I was worthy of his title, so I took on all the responsibilities that entailed, including my betrothal to Victoria.

"She and I had been friends for years. When I learned she was marrying Adam, I felt betrayed and hurt. My brother had always lorded it over me that he was my father's heir. The thought of his taking Victoria from me was more than I could accept."

Miles sighed. "I intended to stop her from marrying Adam, but when I saw how happy she was, I couldn't interfere. Adam's death nearly destroyed Victoria. In her pain, she turned to me. We built a company together. A few months later, I asked her to be my wife. I knew Torie didn't love me, but I didn't care. Everything that had belonged to Adam now belonged to me."

Catherine squeezed his hand. "But you must have loved her."

"Of course I loved Victoria, but I was never *in* love with her. Even after we were engaged, I never pressed her into furthering our relationship. A few kisses and embraces were all we shared. I told myself I didn't want to rush her. In reality, I was doing it for myself."

Catherine frowned. "I don't understand what you're saying."

"A man can feel desire for a woman, a purely physical need. I wanted more," he explained. "I wanted to feel passion for her, as well, but it never came. I kept seeing her as Torie, my sweet, gentle friend, not the woman who could set my soul aflame with passion."

"Do you feel passion for me?"

Miles brought her hands to his lips. "Passion and so much more. I've never met anyone like you, Cat. We're kindred souls. The things I value most in myself I find in you. You're a part of me. I love you, Catherine."

For a moment, she couldn't speak. Tears filled her eyes. "I love you, too, Miles. But love isn't enough. It could never work out between us."

He cradled her face in his hands. "You said you love me. What's to stand in our way if we love one another, Catherine?"

"That's a silly question. You're a titled lord. I'm an outlaw, an enemy of your country. If my identity is revealed, you could be charged with treason, and both of us would be sent to prison. I love you far too much to see you hurt because of me."

Miles shook his head. "Stop talking of what might happen. Answer one question. Do you love me?"

"I love you with all my heart, but—"

"That's all I need to know. The world can go straight to hell, for all I care. From this moment on, I'll live for me and for what I want. No one can keep me from loving you, Catherine. Not now, not ever."

Miles pulled Catherine into his arms and kissed her without restraint. Their passion quickly flared into need, and he carried her up the marble staircase.

After entering her room, he locked the door and set her down beside the bed. Illuminated by the candlelight, Catherine was resplendent in a robe of pale pink satin trimmed with lace. Her hair fell in shimmering curls across her shoulders and down her back. The only deviation from her perfection was the slight trembling of her chin and the hint of panic in her eyes.

Miles touched her face with his fingertips. "What's the matter, Cat? Don't you want to make love with me?"

Catherine nodded. "Of course I do, but I, ah . . ." Her gaze left his and stole to the bed before she looked at the floor. "Well, I've never . . . done anything like this before."

He was stunned. Miles had thought Catherine was worldly, experienced in all things. How could she have been raised among thieves and renegades and still maintained her innocence? The thought made him smile. "You've never been with a man?"

Catherine's face flushed red as she scowled at him. "With my Da, brothers, and Uncle Paddy ready to kill the first man to lay hands on me, how could I be aught else? If you dare laugh at my ignorance, English, I'll never forgive you."

Shaking his head, Miles took her into his arms. "My dearest love, your innocence is the greatest gift you could offer me. But if you aren't ready to go through with this, I can wait. When we make love, I want you to be as prepared for it as I am. Do you understand?"

"I understand I ache with wanting you, Miles. Please make love to me now. Show me how to be a woman. Make me *your* woman, Miles."

Miles needed no further encouragement. He untied the sash on Catherine's robe, then pushed it off her shoulders. It fell to the floor. He unfastened the buttons on her nightrail, and the garment soon pooled at her feet. Slowly, he raised his eyes, surveying her naked loveliness.

Catherine was like a work of art. Her feminine form was the most perfect he'd ever seen. He longed to run his hands over her smooth white skin, but knew he had to be patient and guide Catherine slowly through their first passionate encounter.

He kissed her hands. "Have you ever seen a man's body?"

"On ship I saw the men going about without shirts, but

I've never seen the rest. Even at home, my brothers were always careful not to go around unclothed—though I'm not without some knowledge," she explained. "Mam told me about men's bodies and how they work, but the closest I ever got to seeing one was looking at statues in a museum."

Miles laughed. "Statues are cold marble and stone. When I'm near you, Cat, I'm anything but that." He put her hands on the fastenings of his shirt. "Undress me, love. See for yourself I'm not made of stone."

Catherine's hands shook as she removed his shirt and touched his bared chest. She was intrigued by the sparse matting of dark hair and his soft, warm skin. Her fingertips grazed his flat nipples, causing Miles to groan deep in his throat.

The sound seemed to be fraught with pain. When she tried to pull away from him, Miles grabbed her hands and brought them to the waistband of his britches. With his guidance, she soon had his remaining clothes lying on the floor with her own.

Now it was Catherine's turn to look at him. Miles was a large man, with a well-developed physique. His broad shoulders and defined muscles were evidence of his exceptional conditioning. Evidently sitting behind a desk hadn't softened the taut flesh of his buttocks, either. His long legs were powerful and strong, and led her examination to the part of him that was truly a mystery to her.

Topped by a nest of fine black curls, the object of her scrutiny was rigid and throbbing. She touched it and was surprised to discover the shaft felt like satin. Running her fingers along its length, she stroked it lightly.

"How can something be so hard, yet feel so silky?"

Miles sucked in a deep breath and grabbed her hand. "Much more of that and it will be all over for me." He eased her toward the bed and lowered her onto the cool white sheets beside him. "I want it to be perfect for you, Cat. Trust me to make it right for us both."

He captured her mouth in a hungry, heart-stopping kiss. Their tongues met and caressed each other, tasting and probing, heightening her growing desire.

Minutes later, she moaned in disappointment when he broke away from her lips to nuzzle her neck. But regret was forgotten as his nips and sucking kisses brought his mouth to her breasts.

He surrounded her breasts with his hands. Gently kneading her pliant flesh, he laved one nipple, then drew on it till the nub was hard and stiff in his mouth. Catherine's fingers entwined in his hair as he abandoned one breast and assailed the other. Sharp tremors of need coursed through her. She was shocked to learn the strange moans in the room were her own.

As Miles suckled on her breasts, his hand lowered slowly to her hip. She gasped and jerked away from him when he touched the curls at the apex of her thighs.

"No, Cat. Don't cower from me now," he whispered against her lips. "Kiss me, love. I know what you want, what you need. Pleasure will be yours, I promise."

Eagerly accepting his kisses, Catherine willed herself to relax. Her thighs parted, allowing him to explore her with his fingertips. When he touched the sensitive pearl hidden there, she cried out into his opened mouth.

"Easy, Cat, easy. Don't fight the feeling. Let me do it all. Enjoy my touch," Miles murmured huskily into her ear. He applied more pressure to the source of her arousal, and her hips rolled toward him. "It feels good, doesn't it, love? Yes, that's it. Let me teach you how to savor the sweetness. I'll not disappoint you."

Catherine felt a burning sensation building in her secret woman's place, and it frightened her with its intensity. "Miles, please help me. I want . . . I want . . ." Not knowing how to describe her craving, she shook her head in frustration.

Miles pushed a finger into her tight passage. He stroked

her gently till he wrenched a sigh from her lips. Increasing the momentum, he added another finger and continued to probe her depths. Catherine felt as if she was climbing higher and higher, reaching for some unknown place on top of the world.

He began kissing her again. The thrusts of his tongue matched the movement of his fingers. She gasped and arched against him. Her body began to tremble.

"Yes, my love. That's the way of it," he encouraged in a throaty purr. "You're so wet and tight around my fingers. Come for me, my love. Come for me now."

Catherine cried out his name as she soared to a height that enveloped her being in golden warmth. Sated and content, she closed her eyes and luxuriated in the pure elation of the moment.

When she opened her eyes, Miles was smiling at her. "Welcome back, my love."

"Oh, Miles, I've never felt anything like that before. It was as though I were flying."

"You only reached the sky, my love. Together, we'll make it all the way to heaven."

"Take me where you wish, my lord, but please don't make me wait any longer. I know there might be some pain, but not having you with me is far more agonizing." Catherine pulled his head down and kissed him with all of her newborn desire. "Please, Miles, do it now."

Miles moved easily over her, parting her thighs with his knees. Kissing her face and shoulders, he pressed his hardened manhood against her feminine core. He leaned on his elbows and cradled her face in his hands as he gazed into her eyes.

"I'm not confusing you with anyone else. Never doubt my word. You're the woman I love, Catherine."

He pressed his mouth to hers a second before he breached the membrane in her tight passage. Her soft cry of surprise and discomfort was muffled by his ardent kiss.

Miles began to slowly flex his hips, to fill her and recede. His strokes became quicker, more forceful. Catherine met his building passion with equal force. Her tongue played with his and their kisses mirrored the growing frenzy of their movements.

Miles felt her release as he heard her impassioned cry. His body relished the tremors of her climax clenching around his rigid staff. With a final thrust, he found his own escape. Groaning with pure male satisfaction, he rolled to his side and drew Catherine into his arms.

"You're my heart, Cat. I love you."

Drowsy and yawning, Catherine burrowed against his shoulder. "That's wonderful. I love you, too, Miles."

"Then forgive me for being a lowly *Sassenach* and marry me."

Catherine was suddenly wide awake. She leaned up to look into his eyes. "But what of your family and friends? What will they say when you bring home an outlaw for your bride?"

"No one will ever know the Viscountess Ryland was once the infamous Lady Cat. And if by chance your old identity comes to light, I'd gladly leave England and spend the rest of my days sailing the seas with you at my side." He stroked her cheek with his fingertips. "The world is filled with amazing places, Catherine. I want to show them all to you. Please say you'll marry me."

"I do love you, Miles. That you're willing to sacrifice so much for me moves my heart. I pray you'll never have to make that choice." A smile curved her lips. "Yes, Miles, I'll be your wife."

Pulling her into his embrace, Miles kissed her. *"Tha gaol agam ort,* Catherine." He pressed her head against his shoulder and stroked her hair. "As soon as I can obtain a special license, we'll be married."

Bracing her elbows on his chest, Catherine scowled at him. "But I want my family in attendance when we're married. My Mam would never forgive me if she weren't at my wedding. We'll just have to wait until our plans to trap Edward are completed. Then you can take me and Rory home for the wedding.''

"Can't your mother come to England for the ceremony, or does she hate the English as much as your brother does?"

"Mam doesn't hate anyone. She simply cannot abide sea voyages. If Mam can't reach her destination by horse or cart, she'd sooner stay home."

Miles laughed. "All right, love. When this is over, we'll fetch Rory and sail to Ireland. I just hope your father has a forgiving nature, or I could be in for quite a fight."

"Ye've naught to fear, English," Catherine assured him in an affected brogue. "Even if you weren't Trelane the Fox, with me at your side, we can't lose."

"Aye, love. Lady Cat and the Fox are an unbeatable pair."

Snuffing out the candle on the bedside table, Miles drew the quilt over them both. In a matter of minutes, they fell asleep, happy and replete in each other's arms.

Chapter 18

Justin Prescott paced his drawing room, waiting for his guest to join him for a late supper to celebrate Christmas Eve. As he stopped to rearrange the bouquet of hothouse roses that sat on the small dining table near the fireplace for the third time, his housekeeper pushed in a teacart laden with a vast array of prepared foods.

"Everythin' is ready, Doctor. The pheasant in wine sauce and mushrooms is in the large silver chafin' dish. Wild rice, yams, and peas are in the smaller ones." Mrs. MacWhorter placed the basket of rolls on the table set for two. "The apple cobbler your lady's partial to is settin' on the sideboard in the kitchen."

"My lady." Justin smiled wistfully. "I like the sound of that, Mrs. Mac. If all goes well tonight, perhaps I can make it a fact."

Straightening the napkins beside the plates, the old woman sighed. "She's healed right nice in the past weeks. Even the bruises are faded away. 'Tis a sin her memory still hasna returned. Is there naught ye can do to remedy that?"

Justin shook his head. "I treated the outward signs of her injuries, but there's nothing I can do to restore her memory. I believe the shock of her abduction is keeping the reality of what she suffered hidden away from her. Catherine may never regain her memory."

"Och, such a sin. And still no word from her kin."

"I sent a letter to her father through his contact in Bristol three weeks ago. I informed him of her injuries and asked him not to come just yet." Justin pulled the chair out from beside the table and sat down. "With everything else Cat's had to deal with, I don't know how she'd react to an entire family she can't remember."

Mrs. MacWhorter gave his shoulder a reassuring pat. "Well, ye've done a fine job tendin' to her. Wearin' all those lovely new clothes the Widow Sparkes done up for her and that smile o' hers, your Catherine hardly resembles the poor tortured dear that woke up in the treatment room that first day. I best go up and see how she's gettin' on."

Alone in the salon, Justin recalled that morning and the softly spoken question that had nearly robbed him of his joy.

Who am I?

The pain and confusion he'd seen in her eyes told him it wasn't a jest. The woman he'd considered spending the rest of his life with didn't recognize him. Worse yet, she had no idea who she was. It took every bit of his control not to let her see how upset he was.

"Your name is Catherine O'Banyon. You were thrown from a horse last night and struck your head. Can you remember anything about yourself or what happened?"

She touched the bandage on her brow and frowned. "No. My mind seems to be blank, devoid of everything. Does this usually happen to people who suffer this kind of injury?"

"It's been known to happen. Given time to heal, most people recover fully, with their memories intact."

Tears glistened in her eyes. "But what if I'm not like most people? What if I never regain my memory?"

Justin grabbed her quaking hands and gently rubbed them. "Then you'll have to rely on me to help you. Besides being a capable physician, I've been your friend for five years. While I treat your wounds, I can teach you all about the wonderful young woman you are, Catherine."

"You seem to know me very well, Doctor . . . ah . . ." She caught her lower lip with her teeth and concentrated. A moment later, she smiled up at him. "Prescott. You said your name was Justin Prescott. At least I'm not totally addled by my injuries. No doubt it's a credit to your marvelous care, Dr. Prescott."

Her happiness at recalling his name made Justin smile in return. "Marvelous care or not, you stopped calling me Dr. Prescott long ago. Please call me Justin."

Unable to stop himself, he placed a soft kiss on her lips. When he sat back, she reached up and touched his cheek. There was an odd look on her face when she spoke.

"You kissed me once on the deck of a large sailing ship. I thought you were so handsome in the moonlight. The color of your eyes reminded me of topaz."

Hope filled his heart. "My God, Cat! You're beginning to remember. Can you recall anything else?"

She shook her head. "No. The recollection is fuzzy, like a dream that lingers in your mind as you wake from a deep sleep." A question creased her brow. "Whose ship were we on?"

"Back then the ship belonged to your father, but he gave you the *Cat's Cradle* as a present several years ago."

"I own a ship? This *Cat's Cradle* belongs to me?"

He nodded. "Yes. You're a very accomplished captain."

"But I'm a woman. Women don't captain their own ships!"

Her disbelief made him laugh. "Oh, Cat, when I tell you about all you've accomplished, you'll probably call me a liar. But I can prove it with your own words. I have more than fifty letters you sent me during the past few years. In those letters you told me about your family, your adventures, and your dreams. Maybe reading them will help you remember."

In spite of the countless hours she spent studying the letters and listening to him talk about the time they had been together five years before, Catherine was still without her memory. Sensing her frustration, he suggested they become acquainted all over again—start from the beginning, as though they had just met.

Justin quickly learned Cat was still stubborn and restless. Rather than stay in bed healing from her injuries, she insisted on helping him with his work. As soon as he arranged for the local seamstress to make her some new clothes, she was at his side, treating patients in his clinic or visiting them in their homes. Her compassionate nature soon won her the admiration and respect of the people of Windell.

Gazing into the fire, Justin sighed. Part of him missed the hot-tempered Cat who had captivated him years before, but the lovely, soft-spoken woman she had become was a treasure beyond price. He was more determined than ever to make her his wife.

Mrs. MacWhorter smiled. "You look quite fetching in your new gown. The golden color is perfect for you, dearling."

Victoria plucked nervously at the skirt of her gown. "Do you think Justin will like it?"

"Of course he will. The lad's not daft! He'll likely fall all over himself complimentin' your beauty." The elderly woman snickered. "And if he doesna, he'll have to answer to me."

Turning to the housekeeper, Victoria smiled. "You can't fool me. I know how much you care for Justin. There's no way you can mask that maternal pride, Emma."

Mrs. MacWhorter chuckled. "I always hated my given name, but hearin' you say it gives me pause."

"Emma is a marvelous name. It comes from the Teutonic word for grandmother or ancestress. The German definition is healer. I think your name suits you perfectly."

"Well, if that be the case, I'll be insistin' everyone use it. Where did you learn about my name?"

Victoria shook her head and frowned. "I don't know. It was just there in my mind."

"Don't look so crestfallen, dearlin'. Mayhap your memory's returnin' after all. T'would be a verra lovely Christmas miracle indeed." She patted Victoria's cheek. "Finish your primpin', but don't be too long. Justin is waitin' on you in the salon."

As the door closed behind Emma, Victoria turned toward the mirror and smiled. Not being able to recall her past or even her own name was difficult, but, thanks to Justin, she had learned to accept it. She had no idea what their relationship had been before her accident, but there was no way to deny how she felt about this incredible man now. She was in love with him.

Arranging the curls to hide the scar on her forehead, Victoria sighed. "It's foolish for me to build up my hopes. Justin probably feels sorry for me."

A few minutes later, she entered the salon and found Justin standing beside the mantel alone. "Where are Emma and your new assistant? Won't they be joining us?"

Justin hurried to her side and led her to the table. "Emma and Simon have gone to spend the night with the vicar and his family. They'll attend services and return in the morning. The other servants have been dismissed for the night. This is a private Christmas celebration just for us.''

Victoria smiled as she plucked a rose from the vase and brought it to her nose to savor its perfume. "Roses in December? I love them, but these must have cost you a fortune, Justin."

"No expense is too great if it pleases you." He pulled out her chair. "Let's enjoy our meal, sweetheart. Emma prepared all your favorites."

While they were eating, Justin filled their glasses with wine. He set the bottle down and lifted his glass in a toast. "To you, darling. May this be the first of many Christmases we spend together."

Victoria's heartbeat quickened. "Many Christmases?"

"No less than fifty would please me." Reaching across the table, he took her hand. "I love you. I want you to marry me."

She felt her cheeks flush. "B-but I'm not the girl you met five years ago, and I have no recollection of who I am. Perhaps your feelings for me are confused with the need to protect me while I'm without my memory. Maybe—"

Justin stood up and pulled her into his arms. "I'm not confused. What I feel for you is real. I was fascinated by the girl I met back then and intrigued by the legend she became. But it's the woman here in my arms that I've fallen in love with."

After dropping a quick kiss on her lips, he led her to the sofa. When they were seated, he removed a ring from his coat pocket and slipped it on the third finger of her left hand. "Will you marry me?"

For a moment, Victoria could not respond. She nervously gazed down at the large oval diamond that sparkled like rainbow fire on her hand. "I love you, too, Justin. I want to say yes, but I'm afraid you're being cheated by my not having my memory."

Justin lifted her chin with his hand and made her look

at him. "We'll make our own memories. Please say you'll be my wife."

The love shining so openly in his eyes removed all of Victoria's doubts. She nodded. "Yes, Justin, I will marry you."

She put her arms around his neck and kissed him. Within seconds, the kiss grew into a passionate meeting of two starving souls.

A male voice thundered, "Get your hands off my little girl, Prescott!"

Justin looked up into the menacing visage of the Hawk. "Sean O'Banyon."

Victoria was frightened by the powerfully built man walking toward her. With his red beard and the rapier at his side, Sean O'Banyon looked every inch the pirate she'd heard about.

"My father?" She turned to Justin for confirmation. "Is this man my father?"

Sean stopped as he heard her question. "By God, 'tis true. You don't even recognize your Da. My poor Cat." He knelt in front of her and cupped her cheek with his hand. "T'was my fault you were hurt, little girl. I should have gone with you."

The concern Victoria saw in his face calmed her fears. "If what Justin told me is true, I probably never gave you a chance to stop me. He said I was a bit stubborn."

Sean chuckled. "A bit stubborn? That's like saying the ocean is an oversized pond."

Smiling tremulously, Victoria touched his whiskered face. "I don't remember you yet, but I like you. Can you accept me like this?"

Sean sat beside her and hugged her. "Little girl, having you alive and well is enough for me." Kissing her forehead, he nodded toward Justin. "Prescott, it appears I owe you my thanks again. If there's anything I can do to repay you, just say the word."

"The only thing I want is your blessing, Sean. I love your daughter. This evening she honored me by accepting my proposal of marriage."

Sean stroked her hair. "Is this what you want? Do you love this man?"

Victoria nodded. "Oh, yes, with all my heart. Even if I never remember my past, with Justin I can look to the future."

"Then so be it." Sean stood up. "But the wedding will be at home in Corbin's Cove with your Mam and all the rest in attendance. You'd best get packing. We sail on the morning tide."

"Why so soon?" Justin asked.

The Hawk shrugged. "There are arrangements to be made, and my daughter's been away too long to suit me. If you can't leave just yet, Prescott, I'll send a ship for you next month—"

"Next month? No, you don't, O'Banyon! If Cat leaves this house, I'm going with her." Justin kissed Victoria's cheek and stood up. "It will take me an hour to pack and write letters to Emma and Simon regarding my patients. While I'm doing that, why don't you gather your things, sweetheart?" He pointed at Sean. "Don't let your father whisk you out of here before I get back."

As Justin rushed off to carry out his plans, Sean chuckled. "I know 'tis wrong to bait the man like that, but Prescott is up to the task. Justin will make you a fine husband." He offered Victoria his hand. "Are you ready to go home, little girl?"

After a slight hesitation, Victoria smiled and nodded. "Yes, sir, I believe I am."

Several hours later, Victoria entered the captain's cabin on the *Cat's Cradle* with Justin and Sean. After two crewmen delivered her trunk and departed, the Hawk kissed her cheek.

"G'night, lass. If you need anything, Justin and I will be next door."

As the door closed behind Sean, Victoria surveyed the richly appointed cabin. The large bed was built on a raised platform. It was covered with a red spread that matched the curtains on the windows. There were cabinets on either side of the bed, and crowded bookshelves lined one section of the paneled walls. Four chairs and a table sat in the corner of the room. A pulled-back drape revealed an alcove where a washstand and the necessary were located.

Justin put his arm around her. "Don't be upset if nothing seems familiar yet. It takes time."

Victoria turned into his embrace and pressed her face against his shoulder. "I don't recall my father, so why should I remember this cabin? Oh, Justin. It's times like this that make me wonder if I'll ever recover my memory."

"You mustn't worry. Whatever happens, sweetheart, we'll deal with it together."

Kissing her good night, Justin left to find his own bed. He wasn't surprised to find Sean and Colin waiting up for him.

"Prescott, I need to know how you found Cat. According to the note she sent through Donovan, she and Rory were together and doing fine. They were going to return to Ireland in a month or so. Then she shows up alone and you find her."

Justin told them about the night she'd been thrown from the horse on the country road. He described the bruises, cuts, and abrasions that covered her body. Sean flew into a rage, swearing to kill the man who had defiled his daughter.

"You won't get the chance. Apparently, Cat dispatched the bastard herself with a knife when he tried to assault her." Justin related how she relived the attack while she was delirious with fever. "Although her legs were bruised, there was no evidence that the cur raped her."

Colin frowned. "She saved herself and escaped. But what has taken her memory away?"

"The human brain is a fragile thing. Sometimes a blow to the head can effect a person's memory or body functions. I personally feel her loss might have been caused by something in her mind that has little to do with her physical injury."

"Are you saying my daughter is daft?"

"No, not at all," Justin assured Sean. "I think Cat is suffering from a rare form of hysteria called amnesia. After suffering a painful experience, some people lose their memories or even the ability to see or speak. It's the brain's way of handling a reality too horrible to accept."

"Is there no way it can be fixed?" Colin asked.

"In the few cases I've read of regarding this form of amnesia, some patients recover on their own. Others never regain their memories at all."

Colin sighed. "And Cat's not remembering anything."

"But she has. Catherine recalled a bit of a conversation we had on the deck of this ship five years ago. She said the memory was fuzzy, like a dream, but she remembered it on her own."

"Saints be praised!" Smiling broadly, Sean sank onto his bed with relief. "Then all's not lost. My girl's going to recover."

"It certainly appears that way, but I must caution you not to pressure Cat. Her inability to recall the past is extremely difficult for her to handle. I never told Cat about her fevered rantings or the attack she was subjected to. It must come from within herself," Justin cautioned them.

Colin nodded. "All right, Justin. It will be as you wish. I blame myself for my sister's condition. I need to see she's well, but I won't if you think it will harm her."

"By all means, visit your sister in the morning. Your love and support are the best medicine for what ails her, Colin."

Sunshine was coming through the small cabin windows as Victoria became aware of the rocking of the ship. She enjoyed the subtle motion until someone knocked on the door. Pulling the quilt up to her chin, she called out for her visitor to come in.

The door opened, and a young man entered carrying a tray of food. He was handsome, with dark brown hair and blue eyes. A smile spread across his face when he saw her.

"Good morning, Miss Sleepyhead! I brought breakfast so we can spend some time together before Da and Justin are about."

Victoria heard the brogue in his speech. "You're my brother Colin, aren't you?"

Colin's smile faded for a moment but quickly returned. "Who else would know what you like for breakfast? Aye 'tis me, Colin Padraic Sean O'Banyon at your service, Lady Cat!" he announced, sweeping low into a courtly bow.

When Victoria laughed at his comical display, Colin sat on the edge of the bed. " 'Tis good to hear you laugh. I've missed you, little sister." He touched the curls around her face. "I like the new way you're doing your hair."

"I was told my hair was badly matted in the accident and had to be cut. The wave in the front covers the scar."

Colin lifted the hair to see the puckered line on her forehead. "How in the blazes did you do that?"

"I fell off a horse and struck my head on a rock."

He scowled. "You fell from a horse? Catherine O'Banyon, you can outride anyone! When you were small, Rory would howl because you always bested him on horseback. I've never understood how you got Rory to teach you about sword fighting."

A long forgotten vision entered Victoria's mind. In a

soft voice, she began to relate the event. "I taunted Rory and he ignored me. Then I called him Roderick and he became angry, but I got his attention. Only then was I able to charm him into teaching me."

Colin laughed and pulled her into a hug. "Oh, Cat, you're remembering! Rory hates his name, and you always knew how to use it against him."

Easing back, Victoria gazed into Colin's eager face. "Maybe I am getting better. I really hope so." Unexpectedly, her stomach rumbled and she giggled. "Suddenly, I'm starving. Let's eat. Then we'll tell Justin and Da about this."

Colin brought her a robe from the wardrobe. "While we're having breakfast, I'd like to tell you about something that's been on my mind. Smuggling is too dangerous and the days of pirates have passed. How do you think the family would react if I suggested we become a legitimate business? We could build our own shipping company. What do you think?"

During the next hour, Victoria and Colin discussed his idea of starting a shipping firm. He was amazed by her knowledge.

"I always knew you were clever, Cat, but I'm astounded by your grasp of business."

Victoria shrugged off the compliment. "Basically, good sense and hard work can make any business succeed. It's up to you to convince the rest of the family, Colin. You already have my vote."

"Thanks for your support." Colin picked up the tray and moved toward the door. "Mam had your sailing clothes put in the cabinet there. I'll see you topside, little sister."

After completing her toilette, Victoria ignored her trunk and opened the wardrobe Colin referred to. She removed a pair of black britches and a long-sleeved white wool blouse and put them on. A suede vest and a wide belt from the chest and woolen socks and a pair of tall leather boots completed her ensemble.

Brushing her hair, Victoria walked to the mirror that hung on the alcove wall and studied her reflection. "Well, Lady Cat, as the legendary phoenix arose from the ashes, you will live again. I don't know how long it will take, but I will do it!"

Armed with determination, Victoria left the cabin and found her way to the deck. When she spotted Colin standing on the bridge talking to a big, muscular man, she joined him.

Colin greeted her with a quick hug. "Now that's the Lady Cat I know. 'Tis good to have you back."

"There's not much I can do to help. I can't recall anything about sailing, but I can tell this is a beautiful ship." She looked up at the billowing white sails. "It's December, yet here in the sun, I don't feel the cold."

Colin nodded. "Aye, 'tis warm. Padraic was just saying—"

"Padraic!" Victoria turned to the big man at the wheel. A smile creased his fierce-looking face. "I read about you in the letters I sent to Justin. You're the first mate of this ship and my very dear friend."

"Aye, Cat, and I always will be. I was also one of the people who taught you how to sail this ship. If you like, I can teach you again."

Victoria smiled and happily accepted his offer.

A short time later, Justin and Sean came up on deck looking for her. The sight that met their eyes left them speechless.

Victoria was standing at the wheel, talking to Padraic. She was dressed in sailing clothes and steering the huge ship. Her gold hair glistened in the sunlight.

Sean put his arm around Justin's shoulder. "Just look at that, Prescott. Is that not the most beautiful sight that you've ever seen? Our Lady Cat has returned at last!"

Chapter 19

The day after Christmas, Garret departed for London. With his family's status, he could gain entrance to many of the *ton's* festivities and check out the latest rumors regarding Victoria's disappearance, as well as news of Edward's activities.

The Earl of Foxwood's traveling coach arrived at the Morgan estate two days later with six outriders. As soon as the large conveyance was loaded, Miles, Catherine, and Darcy began their own three-day journey into town.

Sitting on the upholstered seat with Miles, Catherine looked at her maid and noticed how tense she was. "Stop worrying, Darcy. If you simply remember to call me Lady Victoria, we won't have any problems."

Miles put his arm around Catherine and drew her closer to his side. "This is going to be a big adventure for all of us, Darcy. You'd better get used to traveling. Once this plan is completed, we'll be going to Ireland."

"Don't worry about me, my lord. I know how to keep busy." Darcy opened her satchel and pulled out skeins of

white yarn. "I'm going to start knitting that shawl I promised you, my lady. I see you're wearing the scarf I made
you for Christmas."

"I'm wearing several of my gifts today. Your scarf, the
lovely string of pearls Garret gave me, and this new fur
cloak from Miles." Catherine stroked the dark sable with
her fingers. "I've never felt anything as soft as this."

Darcy sighed. "You look just like a queen, my lady."

Miles leaned over and kissed Catherine's cheek. "She
should. Her Majesty's own furrier created this cape. I
wanted my lady to have the best, so I had my father purchase it for me."

Smiling at him, Catherine raised her brow. "You're trying to spoil me, English."

"Get accustomed to it, love. Once this charade is over,
we'll be married and I'll spend the rest of my life spoiling
you."

Catherine nodded. "I look forward to it, English."

"So do I," he whispered, nuzzling her ear. "So do I."

They arrived in London around midday on December
thirty-first. Through Garret, Miles had sent a message to
Carlisle House to prepare for guests. Cosgrove, the head
of the household staff, was aware of the viscount's status
with the family and didn't question the orders.

As the coach bearing the Foxwood crest pulled up to
Carlisle House, the carved entry doors swung open.

Miles stepped from the coach and turned to find Catherine staring at the large stately house. "Everything will be
fine, my love. If you need to ask me a question, use Gaelic.
No one will know what we are saying. Remember, *tha gaol
agam ort.*"

Catherine smiled and took strength from the knowledge
that she loved him, too. She was no longer intimidated by
his former fiancée. After spending the past week sleeping

in his loving arms, she was confident of her place in his heart.

Pulling Catherine's hood over her face, Miles lifted her to the ground. He escorted her into the foyer, where Cosgrove and the servants were assembled to greet their arrival.

Cosgrove bowed. "Good afternoon, Lord Ryland. You and your guest are most welcome at Carlisle House."

Catherine pushed the hood away from her face. "I would certainly hope so, Cosgrove. This is my home, is it not?"

"Lady Victoria, you're alive! Thank God! We've all been so worried . . ." The elderly butler's face grew red with embarrassment. "Beg pardon, my lady. I did not mean to babble."

Catherine patted his arm. "No need to apologize, Cosgrove. I'm sorry I caused everyone such distress by my absence."

Miles came to her side to address the staff. "Lady Victoria has just returned from a much deserved rest. Her arrival here is to be kept secret. Anyone who speaks of her return outside of this household will be discharged without reference."

Miles handed his coat and Catherine's cape to a footman as she issued orders to Cosgrove. "See that my things are sent up immediately and have Lord Ryland's trunks taken to the duke's suite. My new maid, Darcy, is to be given the small pink bedroom adjacent to my suite. His lordship and I will have lunch in the library as soon as it can be arranged."

Cosgrove bowed. "As you wish, Lady Victoria."

Remembering the diagram of the house, Catherine led the way into the library. As Miles closed the door, she turned into his arms and kissed him.

"They really believe I'm Victoria! Oh, Miles, I wasn't sure I could do it."

"I've told you before, your resemblance to Torie is

uncanny. If you doubt my word, turn around and judge for yourself."

Catherine turned to find a large oil painting of Victoria Carlisle hanging on the far wall. She stepped up to the portrait and touched it with her fingers.

"Oh, my! This could be a painting of me. Is it a good likeness of Victoria?"

Miles put his arms around Catherine's waist and studied the painting. "It's an excellent one. The duke commissioned the finest portrait artist in Europe to paint it last year."

A wave of uncertainty flooded over Catherine. "Miles, are you absolutely sure about your feelings for me? Could you still be in love with—"

Miles spun her about and into his arms. "We've been through all this before. I love you, my sweet Irish rebel, and no one else. You're not a substitute for anyone. The only thing you and Torie have in common is your looks. I fell in love with all of you, not just your face."

Lowering his mouth to hers, Miles soothed away her fears with a deep, passion-filled kiss. A knock on the door and Cosgrove's request to enter broke the heated moment.

Miles leaned his forehead against Catherine's and sighed. "I think our meal has arrived, my love. Personally, I'd prefer to do without lunch and go directly to dessert, but servants do talk." Stealing a quick kiss, he escorted her to a chair and called out to Cosgrove to bring in their meal. "I'm meeting Garret at my office at three o'clock this afternoon. Why don't you try to rest while I'm gone?"

Catherine whispered to avoid being heard by the servants who were delivering their food. "But I thought we could spend time alone this afternoon, Miles. After three days of traveling by coach with Darcy's constant prattle, I'm starving for a bit of solitude with you."

Miles patted her hand. "Sorry, love. Besides seeing Garret, I have several matters to attend to before the ball tonight. Be patient. We'll have plenty of time to be together when this is over."

An hour later, Catherine bid him farewell, dismissed Darcy, and went upstairs to Victoria's suite. Upon entering the lovely yellow and white rooms, she was struck by a strange feeling that she'd been in this suite before.

Going from one piece of furniture to another, she ran her hands along each familiar surface. She felt at home among these things. Without thinking, she pulled open a drawer, knowing it would hold lace-trimmed handkerchiefs. Catherine took one of the dainty linen squares out and held it to her flushed cheek.

"Perhaps I've worked so hard at becoming Victoria that I'm starting to believe it myself."

Suddenly tired, Catherine removed her gown and pulled back the quilt on the wide bed. She crawled beneath the cool, crisp sheets and closed her eyes.

"If I'm not careful, I'll imagine Victoria's spirit is haunting me. Seeing ghosts is the last thing I need to deal with right now." Within moments, she was fast asleep.

Miles was going through his correspondence when Garret entered his office and dropped into a chair in front of his desk.

"I'm totally exhausted, Miles. I've attended more than four dozen teas, parties, and receptions in the past few days."

"What have you learned about Edward Damien?"

Garret shrugged. "As the grieving widower, Edward has been receiving a good share of sympathy from everyone. He rarely goes out. The few times he's been seen, he speaks of his fears regarding the fate of his beloved niece, Victoria. He's offered an enormous reward for her return. Big of him, don't you agree?"

"Edward's a real hero," Miles snorted in disgust. "What

do the authorities have to say about Torie's disappearance?''

"Without a body or evidence that a crime has been
committed, they're limited as to what they can do. On the
night Victoria vanished, she left Chatham with her driver,
Billy Fletcher, a coach, and two horses. None of them have
been seen since.''

Garret looked at his pocket watch and stood up. "I have
to stop at my tailor to pick up a new coat he made for me.
Since he gossips like an old woman and outfits most of
the *ton*, I may be able to glean some information from
him. I'll see you later.''

Miles used his time alone to finish his paperwork. After
clearing his desk, he opened the office safe and removed
the small box that contained the Ryland betrothal ring.
Because their engagement hadn't been formally
announced, Victoria had refused to wear it. He put the
ring in his coat pocket and took a large flat leather case
from the bottom of the safe.

It was nearly seven o'clock when he returned to Carlisle
House. Eager to see Catherine, he went directly to her
room. Darcy greeted him with the news that her lady was
asleep. He told her to have bath water and a light supper
tray prepared for Catherine as soon as possible. When the
maid ran off to carry out her duties, Miles stole quickly
into the room and locked the door.

Catherine awoke as he sat on the bed and picked up
her hand. "I've brought you a surprise, my love. I hope it
pleases you.''

With a gasp, she sat up and gaped at the emerald and
diamond ring he slipped on her finger. "By the saints, I
never expected to wear jewelry as grand as this. Who does
it belong to?''

"This is the betrothal ring my grandfather gave to his
beautiful *cullen* from Ireland. As my intended bride, Cat,
it now belongs to you.'' He leaned over and gave her a

swift kiss. "As much as I wish it otherwise, I must go now. Your bath water will be delivered soon, and I shouldn't be here when it arrives."

Miles was nearly out the door when he remembered the other gifts he'd retrieved from his safe. "The items in the leather case on the vanity also belonged to my grandmother. I know she would have wanted you to have them. I'll see you downstairs by ten-thirty."

As soon as he left, Catherine ran to the vanity table. Her fingers shook when she released the brass catch on the end of the box. Viewing its contents left her breathless.

An elaborate necklace of gold, emeralds, and diamonds was displayed in the center of the velvet-lined case. Earbobs, a bracelet, and studded hairpins completed the set. The gems were of varied sizes and the colors were perfectly matched.

Darcy hurried into the room toting a dinner tray. "My lady, I've brought you some food to nibble on while I'm getting you ready for the ball."

Catherine closed the case. "Set that tray aside, Darcy. What I need now is your help to make me into the most elegant lady Miles has ever had at his side. I want him to be proud of me tonight, so let's get on with it."

By half past ten, Miles was nervously prowling the foyer. After seeing her reaction to the ring, he'd been too embarrassed to openly give her the jewels in the case.

Maybe Catherine would think he was flaunting his wealth in her face. Only weeks ago, she'd been wearing britches and boots. Perhaps she wouldn't feel comfortable wearing such gems.

His doubts vanished the instant he saw Catherine coming down the stairs. The former outlaw looked every inch a queen. Her Empire gown was metallic gold silk, with a scooped neckline and puffed sleeves worn off the shoulders. She wore long white gloves and carried a small reticule.

The emerald and diamond jewelry appeared to have been made for her. The lacy gold setting of the necklace caressed her pale skin. Sparkling gems twinkled in her hair, which was swept up into a cluster of curls, with thick ringlets hanging down the back.

She curtsied before him. "Do I please you, my lord?"

Miles brought her hand to his lips and kissed it. "You are truly magnificent, Torie. I shall be the envy of every man at the ball."

He took the ermine cape from the maid standing at the foot of the stairs and draped it over Catherine's shoulders. Leaning down to nuzzle her neck, he whispered, "We must be mindful of what we say. Edward may have spies in this house."

Catherine followed his lead and playfully pushed him away. "Behave yourself, sir. We have no time for such things now," she scolded as she looked around the foyer. Cosgrove and a young footman were stationed at the front door, while the parlor maid, Theresa, stepped forward to hand Miles his evening cloak. "Since we're the guests of honor at your parents' gala party, it would be ill mannered of us to arrive late."

Taking his cloak from Theresa, Miles guided Catherine toward the door. "As always, you're correct, Victoria. Our coach is waiting, so let's be off."

As the coach pulled into the drive of the Graysons' home, Catherine looked out the window and inhaled sharply. "Miles, you said this was your family's smaller house. Do they live in a castle when they're in the country?"

He gave her hand a reassuring squeeze. "Don't let the house put you ill at ease. My parents are very nice people. Even when they find out tomorrow how we fooled them with your charade as Victoria, they will understand and come to care for you as much as I do."

Catherine continued to stare at the brightly lit mansion and the richly attired guests getting out of the carriages ahead of them. "All the people attending this party are titled or very wealthy. Do you really think this Irish outlaw can fool them into believing she's a lady?"

Miles cupped her face with his hand and made her look at him. "In spite of where you were born or how you grew up, you are a lady. Never doubt that, Cat. Hold your head high and smile with confidence, my love. The titled you meet tonight cannot begin to touch your nobility."

Catherine and Miles approached the ballroom a short while later. Despite her confident stride, her insides were quaking with fear. The orchestra was playing a melodious waltz, but it did little to soothe her wildly beating heart.

Miles stopped at the door and kissed her cheek. "Well, my love, now the game begins."

"Viscount Ryland and Lady Victoria Carlisle," the major-domo announced.

As they paused at the top of the staircase, all eyes in the room were drawn to them. Talking ceased and the dancers stopped in the middle of the floor. Catherine and Miles descended the steps. When they reached the foot of the stairs, Mark and Vanessa were there to greet them. The earl turned to the orchestra conductor and signaled him to stop the music.

"Dear friends, I beg your indulgence. My son has requested the opportunity to make an important announcement. Miles, the floor is yours." Mark stepped back to stand beside his wife.

"Many of you know Lady Victoria has been away from London for nearly two months. After the stress-filled year she's endured, I convinced her to take a holiday so she could rest and gain a better prospect of her life. We are heartily sorry if her absence alarmed anyone, but her decision to leave was rather spontaneous." Miles put his arm around Catherine's shoulders. "We beg your indulgence and hope our good news will encourage your forgiveness. You see, this lovely lady, Victoria Carlisle, has graciously consented to be my wife."

The crowd applauded when Miles kissed Catherine. The orchestra began another waltz, and he led her out onto the dance floor. As they moved to the music, Catherine laughed, giddy with excitement. "Everyone thinks I'm Victoria. I really think we're going to succeed with this charade."

"Of course we are," he said, squeezing her waist. "I never doubted it for a minute."

Catherine raised her brow. "Not even when I refused to cut my hair?"

"Well, maybe for a moment or two," he admitted with a wry grin. "But, thank God, I fell in love with a very reasonable woman."

The amusement left Catherine's face when she saw Mark and Vanessa watching them from across the room. "Reasonable, yes, but I still feel bad about lying to your parents."

"You know it's necessary, love. Before you meet Edward, we have to be sure your guise is flawless. If my mother and father believe you're Victoria, everyone else will, too."

When the music ended, Miles led her back to his parents.

Vanessa embraced Catherine. "It's so good having you back, Victoria. We were overjoyed when Miles sent word you were all right."

Catherine fought back the guilt that assailed her and offered the caring woman an apologetic smile. "Forgive me for causing you such concern. After everything that happened, I was at my wit's end. Going to Miles for help seemed the only solution."

Mark patted her hand. "The important thing is you've

returned safely, my dear." He turned to Miles. "I still
don't understand why you wanted us to keep Victoria's
whereabouts a secret. Protecting your lady's reputation is
valid concern, but not being able to tell everyone she was
alive was quite unnerving."

"I know, sir, and I apologize for putting you in such an
awful position. Tomorrow, I'll come home for lunch and
explain it to you and mother. In the interim, we should
celebrate and enjoy this wonderful party."

"Our son is right," Vanessa agreed. "This is a celebration. Your questions can wait until tomorrow." She smiled
up at her husband. "The orchestra will play a gavotte next.
I believe this is our dance, my lord."

Mark placed a hand on his son's shoulder. "Why don't
you dance with your mother, Miles? My blasted rheumatism
is acting up, and I hate to disappoint her."

Miles cast a wary look at Catherine and shook his head.
"This is Torie's first public appearance in months. I really
shouldn't leave her side."

"Nonsense. Victoria will be safe with me. Go on with
your mother. The music is starting, and she hates to miss
a single set."

When Miles and his mother stepped onto the floor,
Mark laughed. "After facing the possibility of losing you,
he's apt to be overly protective for a while. Don't be upset
with him, Victoria. Men are like that when they're in love."

Catherine's anxiety faded and she found herself
enjoying her chat with the Earl of Foxwood. "I know. I'm
lucky to have a wonderful man like Miles in my life."

Mark smiled. "Vanessa and I pray you two will be as
happy as we are."

"We'll do our best to live up to your fine example, my
lord."

Their conversation was cut short by a voice Catherine
quickly recognized.

"Excuse me, my lord. May I interrupt?"

"Why Garret Morgan, where have you been hiding yourself this evening? You know Miles's fiancée, Victoria, don't you?"

Garret stepped forward. "Yes, my lord. Lady Victoria and I are acquainted." He bowed and kissed Catherine's hand. "Good evening, my lady."

"It's good to see you again, my lord," she replied.

Mark looked across the crowded room and scowled. "More late arrivals. If you two will excuse me, I must greet my guests."

Garret visibly relaxed when Mark walked away. "Everything seems to be going well. With the spectacular entrance the two of you made, all of London will soon be buzzing about the return of the Golden Girl."

"I hope Edward Damien finds out soon so we can get on with this plot and I can be myself again." Catherine sighed. "I've worked so hard at being Victoria that playing her is becoming second nature to me. Don't laugh, Garret, but I almost feel she's guiding me in some way."

Looking around, Garret lowered his voice. "You mean like a ghost haunting you?"

"It's more than ghosts," she replied. "When I was little, I had dreams about being rich and living in a big house. A few years ago, I dreamed about a lovely bedroom. It was yellow and white and lavishly furnished with everything a young lady could want. Garret, I found that room today. It's Victoria's bedroom at Carlisle House."

"Did you tell Miles about any of this?"

"No, he has enough things on his mind without my adding to his burden." Catherine frowned. "Please don't mention this to Miles."

"If that's what you want, I won't tell him." Garret tucked her hand in the crook of his arm and turned toward the dance floor. "Stop worrying. Let's find Miles and have a drink together."

Catherine smiled at his enthusiasm. "But what shall we drink to, Garret?"

"It's New Year's Eve, and we all have reason to celebrate. Victoria Carlisle is alive, Miles Grayson has secured the hand of the woman he loves, and Garret Morgan has returned to win the hearts of the young ladies of the *ton* once more."

Chapter 20

While one sister made her London debut, the other prepared for a very special occasion, as well.

Erin O'Banyon smiled as she fastened the last button on the yellow gown Victoria was wearing. " 'Tis hard to believe twenty-eight years have passed since your Da and I were wed. I pray your marriage grants you the same joy I've found in my own, Catherine."

"Justin loves me. In spite of my lost memory, I know we're going to be happy." Victoria hugged Erin. "Who knows? Maybe someday soon I'll wake up and be me again."

"If it doesn't happen, it won't be from lack of prayin'. I've made more novenas in the past month than I have in my entire life." Patting Victoria's cheek, she smiled through her tears. "Part of my prayers were answered when you came home, my own."

Tears of frustration burned Victoria's eyes. "Mam, I'm sorry I don't know where Rory is. If for no other reason,

I want my memory back so we can find him and bring him home, too."

"There'll be no more cryin', do you hear?" Erin gently chided her. "If your brother Rory wasn't such a scrapper, he'd never have gotten into trouble. Colin's right. The old ways are far too dangerous. 'Tis time our family got into a legitimate profession."

Erin pinned a wreath of flowers in Victoria's hair. "I'm sorry your pendant wasn't ready in time for the wedding. Old Mick was making a new chain for it when he took a tumble and broke his hand. Mick swears you'll have it back before you sail for England."

A firm knock sounded on the bedroom door. "Can the father of the bride come in? If I'm forced to remain here, I might—"

Erin opened the door and admitted the anxious man. "Stop your blustering, Sean, and come greet your daughter properly."

His smile rivaled the sun with its brilliance. "Erin, love, our daughter looks as pretty as you did when you wore that gown for our wedding."

"Sean, you've no need to flatter me, though 'tis nice to hear you say so." Erin hugged him. "Has everyone gone to the church?"

"Aye. Our carriage is waiting at the door."

Erin kissed his whiskered cheek. "I know you're near to burstin' with the need to talk to Catherine alone. I'll meet you both downstairs."

As the door closed behind Erin, Victoria smiled at Sean. "She knows you very well. I hope Justin and I will be as close as you and Mam are, Da."

Sean embraced her. "If you love him, then half the battle is won. Remember, girl, that I'll always be here if you need me. Justin may be your husband, but I'm your Da forever."

Hugging him, Victoria was sad because she couldn't

recall her past with this man. "Thank you, Da. No girl
could have a better father than you."

Sean kissed her forehead. He picked up her cloak from
the bed and led her to the door. "Come on, Cat. If we
keep your Mam waitin' on us, we'll have the devil to pay."

The pews of St. Ambrose Church were filled to overflowing with friends, crew members, and their families, all
gathered together to witness the wedding of Hawk's only
daughter. Hundreds of candles illuminated the village
church with a warm golden glow.

Walking down the aisle on Sean's arm, Victoria saw Justin
standing beside the priest at the altar. She could hardly
believe how much she loved him. Though she was plagued
with a condition that might have destroyed her spirit, Justin
gave her the strength and assurance to carry on with her
life.

When they reached the altar, Sean put her hand into
Justin's. "You take good care of her, do you hear me,
Prescott?"

Justin nodded. "Always, Hawk. I swear it."

A short while later, the ceremony was completed and
the priest declared them husband and wife. Justin kissed
Victoria and a cheer rose from the congregation.

At the O'Banyon house that night, wine, whiskey, and
ale flowed freely. Fine food had been prepared and served.
Musicians provided tunes for dancing. At midnight, wishes
for the new year were exchanged and the guests began
leaving for their homes.

Erin insisted on helping her daughter get ready for bed.
After tying the satin shoulder straps on Victoria's white
silk nightgown, she offered her some motherly advice.

"I know you're concerned about what's going to happen
tonight, but you've naught to fear, darlin'. Justin loves you.

Put your trust in him and he will lead the way. Be happy, my daughter." Kissing Victoria's cheek, Erin left the room.

Victoria sat at the dressing table to brush her hair. Her hands trembled so badly, she dropped the brush. "What's the matter with me? I can't stop shaking."

She couldn't understand why she was so nervous. Justin was a gentle man who loved her. Their relationship had never gone beyond warm kisses and embraces. Part of her wanted more. The rest of her was terrified.

Justin entered the room, wearing a brown wool robe. He came up behind her and put his hands on her shoulders. Their gazes met in the mirror. "I thought you'd appreciate some privacy, so I undressed in Colin's room." He caressed her hair with his fingertips. "You're so beautiful. I can't believe you're finally my wife."

Victoria stood and turned to face her husband. When he drew her into his arms, she couldn't control the quaking that coursed through her body.

Justin gave her an understanding smile as he led her to the upholstered chair near the hearth. Sitting down, he eased her onto his lap. "Can you tell me what's troubling you?"

Victoria shook her head. Her voice was barely a whisper. "I don't know. I want to be your wife in every way, but I'm frightened. The thought of . . ." She looked at the bed and a sob tightened in her throat. "Oh, Justin, am I going crazy? Why am I so afraid?"

Pulling her against him, Justin kissed her brow. "I want you to listen carefully to what I'm about to tell you. Don't become upset. You're safe in my arms, and no one is going to hurt you. All right?"

She nodded and cuddled into his embrace as he told her about the night he'd found her.

"While I was treating you, you became delirious with fever and began talking about a man who'd beaten and abused you. He tried to rape you, but you fought him off and escaped. You were running from him when you were thrown from your horse and struck your head."

Victoria sighed. "I don t recall any of this."

He gave her a reassuring hug. "Somewhere in the recesses of your mind, you do. That's why you're so nervous tonight. You aren't afraid of me. More likely than not, you're reliving the horror that man subjected you to."

She lifted her head to gaze into his eyes. "I can't remember the attack, but I did manage to escape. I refuse to let that man come between us any longer." Armed with new courage, she wrapped her arms around his neck and kissed him.

Justin responded to the seduction of her sweet, pliant mouth. He caressed her breast through the silken fabric of her nightgown and tenderly kneaded the supple flesh with his hand. Pushing down the straps that held the gown in place, he exposed her bosom and let his mouth adore her pink nipples.

Victoria ran her fingers through his hair and rubbed his neck as he suckled on her. Trickles of pleasure warmed her, making her yearn for more. When his hand touched her leg, fear threatened to assail her. She willed the terror from her mind and concentrated totally on Justin and the passion he was building inside her.

Her tension ebbed and she pulled his mouth up to her own. Their lips joined in a rapturous union, and he began to stroke the delicate skin of her inner thighs. When his fingertips gently parted her nether lips, he caressed the pearl of her desire and she moaned into his mouth. Victoria parted her legs, opening herself more fully to his intimate massage.

When Justin pressed a finger deep inside her, she raised her hips to meet the probings of his hand. Her breathing quickened as her body sought its peak. As the warm rushing sensation filled her, Victoria trembled with its force and cried out.

Holding her close, Justin kissed her cheek. "Are you still afraid, sweetheart?"

Victoria sighed happily. "No, not at all. I've never felt so . . . glorious." She looked up at him. "I want to make love to you now."

He smiled. "We'll make love together, sweetheart. Are you ready to go to bed now?"

"Let someone try to stop me." Victoria stood up and pulled on his hand until he stood beside her. Entwining her arms around his neck, she kissed him until they were both quaking with need. "Oh, my," she panted against his lips a few moments later. "I might become a bit wanton, Justin."

"I hope so, sweetheart. I certainly hope so." Pressing his mouth to hers again, Justin swept her up in his arms and carried her to bed.

Chapter 21

On the first day of the new year, Catherine awoke to the questioning eyes of her maid. Darcy wasn't content until her mistress had related every detail about the Graysons' ball over breakfast.

Darcy sighed. "It sounds like a fairy tale, my lady."

Catherine set her empty teacup on the tray. "So how was your evening, Darcy? Has anyone on the staff questioned you about me or his lordship?"

"Everyone's nice to me, but that parlor maid Theresa has been a mite *too* sweet—if you know what I mean." Darcy picked up the tray and put it on the bedside table. "After you left for the ball, Theresa invited me to her room to share some candy. She asked me how I got my position and lots of other things, but I told her only what you wanted me to say, my lady."

Recalling Miles' concern about a possible spy in the house piqued Catherine's interest in Theresa. "Exactly what did you tell her?"

Darcy placed a dressing gown on the foot of the bed. "That I was hired by Viscount Ryland to be your maid while we stayed at a large estate that belonged to a friend of the family."

"Where's Theresa this morning?"

"Theresa had the day off, my lady. I saw her leave the house over an hour ago." Darcy picked up the tray. "I'll take this to the kitchen and be back in just a bit."

Alone with her thoughts, Catherine fell back against her pillow and recalled the events of the previous night. It wasn't the elegant party that garnered her thoughts, but what had transpired when she and Miles returned to Carlisle House.

Because of the late hour, they didn't wake Darcy. Miles acted as Catherine's maid and helped her undress. He even removed the pins and brushed out her hair. She blushed with the memory of wearing nothing but the emerald and diamond jewelry while Miles made love to her. Recalling the dazzling heights they attained in each other's arms left her yearning for more.

Looking at the small brass clock on the bedside table, she frowned. "Miles went to see his parents this morning and won't be back until late this afternoon. What can I do until then?"

At that moment, Darcy came rushing into her room. "My lady, Lord Garret is downstairs asking to see you. He's with a big man with flaxen hair."

"That's Jamie. Maybe he has news for me about Rory. Help me get dressed, Darcy. I don't want to keep them waiting."

Darcy was pinning up her hair when a thought occurred to Catherine. "While I'm in the library with my guests, I want you to keep an eye on the door for me. Bring your knitting and sit in the salon across the hall. If anyone is lurking about, come tell me at once."

* * *

Five minutes later, Catherine joined her guests in the library. Garret recounted their stay at his family's estate and Jamie told them about Rory.

"That brother of yours isn't a bad sort, my lady. Once he was assured you were fine, he stopped ranting and accepted his lot."

Catherine was relieved. "I'm glad he hasn't done anything foolish, but I *am* surprised he hasn't tried to escape."

"Why should he? Rory's been given full run of the estate. You'd think he was lord of the manor the way he carries on. New clothes, his choice of fine food and spirits—he has it all." Jamie chuckled. "His guards have become his friends. They play cards, hunt, and ride horses across the grounds everyday. If that's not enough, Rory fancies himself in love with the estate manager's daughter, Louise."

Shaking her head, Catherine laughed. "To think I worried about him. Rory is making it a regular holiday! I don't think I'll ever worry about my brother again."

Garret put his arm around her shoulder and gave her a quick hug. "Well, we're rather glad you cared enough to come to his rescue last month. If you hadn't, we never would have met—or been able to help Miles expose Edward."

Catherine sighed. "Until Edward Damien makes his first move, we won't know if the plan is working. The waiting will drive me insane. Only God knows how long this is going to take."

"Be patient, Cat, and enjoy your leisure," Garret advised her. "Once Edward gets news of Victoria's return, there won't be a moment to spare for any of us."

Shortly before noon, the Earl of Sedwick received a female caller in his study. After the butler closed the door, the young woman removed her cape and joined him by the fireplace.

Edward sat in the leather armchair staring into the blazing hearth. "It's about time you finally arrived. When were you going to tell me my niece was back? After her wedding to that damned Grayson?"

Theresa fell to her knees beside his chair, resting her cheek on his hand. "Oh, Edward, I got here as soon as I could. Cosgrove was watching over the staff like a hawk. I couldn't get away until this morning."

His eyes never left the fire as he pushed her away. "I can't count on you, so leave me!"

Theresa grabbed his hand and kissed it. "Please, Edward, don't send me away. Without you, I'm nothing."

He looked at the desperate girl at his feet. Theresa was twenty years old, with pale auburn hair, rather pretty, and possessed of a good figure. During his stay at Carlisle House after Lorelei's death, he'd seduced the girl and had enjoyed her charms in his bed ever since. When he moved back to Sedwick Manor, she came to him several times a week. He used her to sate his lust and to spy on Victoria's household.

"Talk is cheap. If you truly cared for me, you would have found a way of getting word to me. Do you know how I found out about Victoria? The Graysons' driver is a cousin of my butler, Wilson. It was quite disconcerting to receive information from a stranger while you're living in the same bloody house with her!"

"Viscount Ryland ordered the staff to secrecy regarding Lady Victoria's return. When they arrived yesterday, six outriders accompanied them. The men guarded the house all night, so none of us could leave." Theresa put her hand on his thigh. "Please don't be angry. I swear I'll make it up to you."

Edward grabbed her hand and cruelly twisted it, causing her to cry out in pain. "Don't ever presume to touch me again. If I want your hands on me, I will tell you. Am I making myself clear, or must I give you another lesson in obedience?''

Tears ran down her face. "I'm sorry, my lord. I'll do anything you say, but please don't send me away." Her pained voice was barely a whisper.

Releasing her injured hand, Edward stroked her hair. "That's much better, pet. Now run upstairs to my room and prepare yourself for me. We shall spend the afternoon together. This evening, I'll go to Carlisle House and pay my respects to Victoria. In the meantime, I shall think of a way you can prove your love for me." He raised his brow at the trembling young woman. Theresa quietly got to her feet and left the room.

Edward removed the gold chain and heart-shaped pendant from his pocket and let it dangle from his fingers. "Clive brought this to me and swore Victoria was dead. Did the chit escape? Surely if my niece were alive, she would have come after me by now."

Edward went to his desk and opened the bottom drawer. He pushed its false bottom open and removed the documents he'd secreted there. He studied one paper in particular.

Was there another copy of the damned codicil? Did Miles Grayson know that on Geoffrey's death, he'd be a very wealthy young man if Victoria was dead? Placing the codicil and pendant with the other papers, he slammed the drawer shut.

"Damn you to hell, Geoffrey." No one had seen the duke outside his room for two months. Either he was dead or would be soon. At the meeting Edward called his brother's business associates, he would have been given the authority to run the company and could have petitioned the courts to be named administrator of Geoffrey's estate, as well. Now he had to change his plans.

Edward locked his desk and stuck the key in his waistcoat

pocket. This evening he'd go to Carlisle House and see if his niece was alive or if this Victoria was a clever replica Grayson had created.

Passing a mirror as he left his study, Edward admired his reflection. His silver wings of hair and dark piercing eyes gave him an almost demonic appearance, and he was pleased. His lips curled in a cruel smile.

"They'll soon learn I cannot be defeated. I'll do away with anyone who stands in my way. Success will be mine!"

"No, Miles! I won't do it." Catherine stormed past Jamie and Garret and dropped onto the sofa. "Fooling Victoria's uncle and friends is one thing. I'll never be able to convince the duke that I'm his daughter."

Crossing the library, Miles sat beside her. "I know we hadn't planned on this, Cat, but you have to try. Geoffrey's life may depend on it."

"No! You're asking too much of me, Miles."

Jamie was burning with curiosity. "What's happened?"

"This morning I went to see my parents. I told them of our plan to expose Edward and the truth about Catherine. Needless to say, they were caught completely by surprise. They never suspected she wasn't Victoria."

Garret smiled with pride. "I guess all our lessons paid off."

Miles sighed. "So it seems. But if I'd told my parents the truth in the beginning, we wouldn't be in this mess now."

"How so?" Garret asked.

"When my parents received my letter telling them Victoria was safe, they agreed to keep the information a secret. But the next day, they got an urgent summons from Lucy Harper, Geoffrey's companion in Chatham. The duke's health was deteriorating rapidly, and she begged them to come at once."

"Did he have another seizure?" Jamie inquired.

Miles shook his head. "No. It seems Geoffrey was aware Victoria hadn't returned from her trip and was worried about her. He stopped eating and refused to be consoled. His will to live has disappeared. Dr. Loudon told Lucy that unless something could be done, Geoffrey wouldn't be alive to see the new year. That's why she contacted my mother and father.

"My parents went to Chatham and discovered their old friend in grave condition. Sullen and despondent, Geoffrey wouldn't respond to anyone. In desperation, my father told him of my letter, read it to him, and set the pages before him as proof. When the duke finally looked up, there were tears in his eyes. My parents promised him Victoria would be home on New Year's Day, and that's what Geoffrey's been counting on."

Miles brushed away the moisture that welled in his eyes. "The duke's been improving since then, but the doctor's still pessimistic about his recovery. If Victoria comes home today, he has a chance. If she doesn't, Geoffrey will surely die."

Catherine turned to face Miles. "But would it be right, trying to fool him like this? Won't he know I'm not Victoria and resent the sham we tried to play on him all the more?"

"But he *won't* know, love. I'm positive we can convince him you are Victoria—for a little while, at least. When he's strong enough, we can tell him the truth." Miles took her hand. "Please, Catherine, I implore you. Geoffrey Carlisle is like a father to me. I cannot let the man destroy himself."

Catherine looked away from him and contemplated her decision. Without warning, a few moments later she stood up and headed toward the door. "I shall have Darcy pack straightaway. We'll be ready to leave within the hour." Never looking back, she left the library.

Miles expelled an audible sigh of relief. "My darling Cat, coming to the rescue again."

"This changes our plan." Garret took her place beside Miles. "What do you want Jamie and me to do while you're in Chatham?"

"Uncover everything you can on Edward Damien. Spare no expense. Bribe, barter, or steal any kind of information you can get a hold of—school records, bank files, the like. If his name is on a document, I want it. Seek details on his wife's murder. Although Edward has a sound alibi, I want to be sure he wasn't involved in that crime, as well."

Jamie went to the desk and made a list of what Miles wanted to know about Edward. An idea suddenly occurred to him. "In Victoria's last letter, didn't she say her house-keeper was acting strangely?"

"Yes, that's right. Torie suspected Mrs. Oliver was aiding her uncle. I believe her first name is Jessica. She's a widow who's worked for the Carlisle family for many years."

Garret joined Jamie at the desk. "Put down marriage records, her late husband's death certificate, family ties, and background under her name."

Miles stood up and went to his friends. "I'd also like you both to stay here at the town house. I have a feeling Edward has someone here reporting to him. Cosgrove will see to your needs."

Jamie offered a suggestion. "Our crews are anxious to help. Why don't we use some of the men to watch the servants of both households? They can report directly to your father at the Ryland offices with no one the wiser."

"Excellent! But keep me informed. I want a courier dispatched to Chatham daily with a report."

The Earl of Foxwood's coach and outriders arrived at Chatham Hall after eight o'clock that night. Miles was grateful it was well after dark when they got there. He feared Catherine would bolt if she saw the splendor of the

Carlisles' palatial estate. Its opulence dwarfed that of his family's London house.

The massive brass-trimmed doors opened and Miles led Catherine inside. For a moment, she was clearly stunned by her surroundings. The entrance hall was enormous, with a high vaulted ceiling, marble floors, and a pair of majestic staircases. Crystal chandeliers were lit with hundreds of candles. The sound of Miles' voice snapped her back into character.

"Mrs. Oliver, I trust all has been made ready for Lady Victoria."

"Yes, my lord. I followed your orders to the letter. May I take this opportunity to welcome you home, my lady?"

Catherine's gaze turned to the stern but attractive face of Mrs. Oliver as she rose from her curtsy. The woman was attired in a somber gray gown adorned with a pristine white collar and cuffs. Though she was apparently in her fifties, her hair was surprisingly dark and worn in a neat chignon on the back of her head.

"Thank you, Mrs. Oliver." Catherine took hold of Miles' arm. "Please carry on with whatever orders Viscount Ryland has issued. I'm leaving everything in his very capable hands."

The housekeeper nodded and turned to Miles.

"Mrs. Oliver. I'll be using the green guest room across from Lady Victoria's suite. See that her maid, Darcy, is provided for, as well as the guards who accompanied us. They are to be quartered in the guest wing."

"As you wish, my lord," she replied. "Will there be anything else?"

"Yes. Please have supper served to us in Lady Victoria's sitting room in thirty minutes."

Miles escorted Catherine up the stairs while Mrs. Oliver hurried away to carry out his orders. As they walked down the corridor on the second floor, a door opened and Lucy ran toward them.

"Victoria, I'm so glad you're safe! I told your father our prayers would be answered."

Catherine knew instantly the young woman with the bright auburn curls who pulled her into a vigorous hug was Lucy Harper. Casting a quick glance at Miles, she smiled at Lucy.

"I am sorry I caused you such concern, Lucy. I was so confused. I needed help to sort it all out."

Miles interrupted her. "What she needed was me! How do you do, Lucy? I'm Miles Grayson, Victoria's betrothed."

Lucy grinned at him. "Victoria never told me how handsome you were, though she did say your friendship was very important."

Miles laughed at her candor.

Lucy rolled her eyes. "Oh dear, I do tend to run off with my mouth, don't I? I didn't mean she doesn't find you attractive, but Victoria never said . . . I mean . . . oh, goodness, I'm doing it again." She stopped talking, took a deep breath, and began speaking in a calm voice. "I am very happy to meet you, my lord."

Taking her hand, Miles kissed it. "Please call me Miles, Lucy. You've been a good friend to Torie, and we don't require such formalities between us. Tell us about Geoffrey."

"Why don't we retire to your sitting room, Victoria? We can talk there without being disturbed." Lucy turned and led the way. "No one has used the room since you left, Victoria. I let the maids in to clean this evening when we received word of your impending arrival."

The small sitting room adjacent to Victoria's bedroom was decorated in peach and cream. There was a chintz loveseat and a matching chair, a lady's writing desk, and two carved chairs. A floral rug covered the floor in front of the fireplace.

After sitting down, Lucy confirmed everything Mark Grayson had said about the duke. "His Grace has been a changed man since the earl showed him your letter. Once he knew Victoria was coming home, he began eating and has been far more alert. He's even gotten some movement back in his hands and arms. The doctor warns his chances for a full recovery are tenuous at best, but now that you're here, Victoria, I know he'll be fine.''

"Can we see Geoffrey?" Miles asked.

"He's sleeping right now. Why don't you rest a while. I'll let you know when he's awake." Lucy got up and kissed Catherine's cheek. "It's good having you home, Victoria."

When Lucy left the room, Catherine sought the comfort of Miles' embrace. "How am I ever going to face him? I'm already torn with guilt because of Lucy. I hate lying to her."

"It can't be helped. Lucy has to think you're Victoria so she can convince Geoffrey. Once the duke is out of danger, we'll tell them the truth." Miles tenderly kissed her lips. "I want to be done with all this as well, my love."

Catherine sighed. "Don't worry, Miles, I won't let you down. I'll see it through to the end, no matter what."

Their meal arrived a few minutes later. For a little while there was no plan, no devious uncle, and no lies, just a couple very much in love enjoying an intimate supper together.

After the servants removed the dishes, Miles went off to see that all the men he'd brought along to Chatham had been taken care of. Catherine decided to explore Victoria's suite. As she was about to enter the bedchamber, Lucy ran into the sitting room.

"Victoria, your father is awake. I told him you were here and he tried to smile. He hasn't been able to do that since his seizure. Come on, he's waiting to see you."

Before Catherine could reply, she found herself being pulled down the hall and into the master bedroom. She nervously fussed with her hair and prayed it looked enough like Victoria's style as she stepped up toward the bed.

Geoffrey Carlisle was propped up with pillows, nearly in a sitting position at the head of the bed. His complexion was pale. His lean cheeks hardly detracted from his handsome face. He was clean shaven, attired in a crisp white nightshirt. A beige satin comforter covered his lap.

And he was looking directly at her.

Catherine thought his hazel eyes, flecked with green and gold, were the most vivid color she'd ever seen. They seemed to sparkle with a life all their own when she came closer to him. As she watched, his mouth curved up into a tremulous smile. She sat on the edge of the bed at Geoffrey's side. Her entire being quaked with anticipation when his unsteady right hand reached out for her. She took his hand and held it tightly. A mysterious aura of peace flowed over her.

"Forgive me, Papa. I'm sorry I took so long coming back to you."

His eyes filled with tears as she leaned forward and kissed him. Following some unknown direction, Catherine rested her head on his shoulder and spoke quietly to him.

"I love you, Papa."

She snuggled against him. Geoffrey's left hand slowly stroked her back as tears flowed from her eyes.

The rest of the world ceased to exist for them as they found comfort in one another. No one knew Geoffrey Carlisle's oldest daughter had finally come home.

Chapter 22

During the following week, Catherine spent nearly every waking hour with Geoffrey. Each day she helped him exercise his limbs and encouraged him to extend himself. He was soon able to bring a fork or spoon to his mouth, but lacked the dexterity to use a pen or a knife. Although frustrated by his inability to speak or write, the duke grew steadily stronger, and his mind was very alert.

Catherine wanted to give him mobility as well. She hired a local woodcrafter to build a chair on wheels for the duke. It was constructed like a piece of fine furniture and delivered to Chatham Hall within two days of being ordered. Geoffrey was pleased by her thoughtful gift and used the chair often.

Late one night. Miles and Catherine were cuddling in front of the fireplace on the sitting room rug. Because Lucy was sharing Victoria's bedroom with Catherine, the lovers had been forced to sleep apart. Their moments alone were treasured and far too few to suit either of them.

Miles kissed her and drew her close. "You're performing

miracles with Geoffrey, but I miss you, Cat. I don't know how much longer I can survive without making love to you."

"Stop complaining, English. Postponing our happiness for a bit surely isn't lethal."

"La belle dame sans merci!" he replied.

Catherine frowned. "That's not fair. You know I don't speak French. What did you just say to me, Miles Grayson?"

"I simply said the beautiful lady is without mercy. Don't you feel any compassion for this lonely man, my love?"

"Omnia vincit amor. Fata viam invenient," she responded.

"Now I'm in trouble. I never studied Latin." His brow arched in query. "Have you just insulted me?"

"Absolutely not. I said love conquers all and fate will find a way. How could you think I was being cruel to you?"

He kissed her on her pouting lips. *"Je regret, ma cherie. Tu êtes ma coeur, ma vie. Je t'aime."*

Catherine shivered from the intensity she heard in his words. "Saints above, I do wish I understood French."

Caressing her cheek with his hand, Miles gazed deeply into her eyes. "I said I was sorry, darling. You are my heart, my life. I love you."

He pressed his mouth to hers and hungrily feasted on her soft lips and velvety tongue. Their breathing became labored as one passionate kiss led to another. He possessively cupped one breast, kneading it through the various layers of her clothing.

Their intimate moment was shattered when Lucy stubbed her foot in the adjoining room and cried out in pain.

Miles groaned and pulled himself away from Catherine to lay flat on the floor. "God give me strength. I hope I can live through the rest of our plan." He shook his head as she reached over to console him. "Unless you want me to take you here on the floor, with the entire staff for an audience, please don't touch me for the next few minutes."

He closed his eyes and sighed. "Better yet, talk to me about something else."

Catherine shrugged. "Well, I was thinking about the meeting Edward called at Carlisle Enterprises on the fifteenth. The duke won't be up to traveling to London. Would it be possible to move the meeting here to Chatham Hall?"

Miles didn't respond, so Catherine explained her reasoning. "Edward has no idea how ill his brother is. For all he knows, Geoffrey is close to death. If we can get the business partners here, we can stop Edward from gaining control of the company. The meeting could be held in the library. The duke could sit in his chair and be present for it. Acting as Victoria, I would assure the associates we'd soon be back in our offices in full force. You could make a speech and tell them—"

"No, the speech must come from Victoria," Miles interrupted as he sat up. "By God, this could be the answer to everything. According to Jamie's last report, Edward is furious because he hasn't been able to see his niece since her return. If the meeting is here, he'll get his reunion with Victoria, but it will be in front of thirty important and influential people." He took Catherine into his arms. "Cat, my love, you are brilliant." He claimed her lips in a searing kiss.

Catherine tapped the side of his face with her hand to distract him from his ardor. When he looked at her, she gave him a wry smile. "My lord, it grieves me to admit this, but if we're going to move that meeting, we have a great deal of work ahead of us."

Frowning, Miles took several deep, calming breaths. "You're correct, of course, but once this bloody plan is completed, I won't be kept away from you any longer. If I have to take you to a deserted island to have you all to myself, then so be it."

He stood up and helped Catherine to her feet. "Come

along, Cat. Let's go down to the library and begin writing
those cursed invitations. The sooner we have this meeting,
the quicker we can expose Edward Damien and get on
with our lives.''

On the day of the meeting, Catherine was up before
dawn. To the unenlightened, this would be a business
gathering. To her, it was a battle. Using her intelligence,
accumulated knowledge, and courage, she was counting
on a total, all-out victory.

Thirty-one invitations had been delivered by couriers to
the company's shareholders. Each gentleman was asked
to spend two days at the Carlisle estate. After the meeting
was concluded, they'd be free to enjoy the duke's famous
hospitality. They were all coming—most out of loyalty to
Geoffrey; others couldn't deny their curiosity.

According to Jamie's reports, rumors were flying wildly
in London. The gossipmongers claimed the Duke of Chatham was near death. Other stories had surfaced that Victoria had been killed. Even more intriguing was her sudden
reappearance at the Graysons' ball. Everyone wanted to
know if Victoria was well. Was she still capable of working
in her father's stead?

In preparation for the expected guests, Miles sent his
men to his family's neighboring estate. The nurses were
returned to their homes with letters of reference and generous salaries. The duke's care was to be handled by Lucy
and Geoffrey's old valet, Quigley.

Although bedroom space was at a premium, Jamie, Garret, and Mark Grayson were also staying in Chatham Hall
during the event. They would mix with the guests and
keep Miles informed of the guests' reactions to Catherine's
portrayal of Victoria.

That morning, Catherine and Miles joined Mark in his
bedroom, which overlooked the entry of the house. As

each guest arrived and was identified, Catherine recited all she knew about him. Mark was astounded by her accuracy.

"My word, Catherine, you've done your lessons well. I point out a face, give it a name, and you're able to tell me the life story that goes with it." Turning to his son, he asked, "Where did you find her? Her ability of recall is phenomenal."

Catherine leaned against Miles and sighed pensively. "I've always had a talent for learning quickly, but this is different. It's as if I have met all these people before. Even being in this house with Geoffrey feels very familiar to me."

Miles gave her a reassuring hug. "Let's not question how you're able to do it. I'm grateful you can do it at all."

Suddenly, Catherine was drawn to the window. A shiny black coach drawn by a team of gray geldings was coming up the drive. A shiver rushed through her. She knew who was inside.

"Edward Damien," she whispered in a soft voice. "He's finally come to face me."

Mark looked out and watched the coach pull up to the house. "You're correct, my dear. But how did you know it was Damien? He doesn't have the Sedwick coat of arms on his coach."

Catherine didn't reply. Her eyes were fixed on the man who alighted from the vehicle. She was stunned by Edward's attractive face and polished demeanor. He wore no hat, so the sun reflected on his silver-winged temples and the rest of his thick dark hair. He was dressed entirely in black.

Edward's eyes turned to the window where she stood. His dark piercing gaze held her to the spot. With the sun in his eyes, she knew he couldn't see her, but he seemed to sense someone was watching him.

Catherine shuddered. "He looks like the devil incarnate." She gratefully accepted the comfort Miles offered as he pulled her into his arms. When she looked outside a few moments later, Edward was gone.

Mark's voice broke the silence of the room. "According to the list, everyone has arrived."

"Now we can proceed." Miles kissed Catherine's cheek. "Get ready for the meeting, love. When everything is set, I'll come for you. Father, in thirty minutes, Garret and Jamie will assist Geoffrey downstairs. In the interim, I want you to join the gentlemen in the gold drawing room for tea and polite conversation—test the waters, so to speak. I'll be in the library. I have a hunch Edward might be looking for me, and I don't want to disappoint him."

Catherine went to Victoria's room and prepared for her performance. Her Empire gown was of emerald silk. A short, fitted jacket with long tailored sleeves completed the ensemble. The only jewelry she wore was her engagement ring and the pearl necklace Garret had given her for Christmas. Her appearance was to be simple and elegant.

Even her hair was arranged with that in mind. Darcy pinned her long blond locks up into a smooth chignon. The only loose curls were a few wispy tendrils around her face.

When Darcy left the room, Catherine studied her image in the mirror on the dressing room wall. "Well, Lady Victoria, I certainly hope you're ready. The success of this plan depends entirely on you."

Miles went to the library and, as expected, was soon joined by Edward Damien. Sitting behind Geoffrey's desk, he bade the earl to enter.

"Good morning, my lord. Welcome to Chatham Hall. I hope your room is satisfactory."

Edward sniffed. "It's rather presumptuous of you, Grayson, to sit there and welcome me to my family's home. Have you forgotten I lived in this house?"

Miles shook his head and smiled. "On the contrary. I'd never forget anything about you, my lord. In a very short time, you'll be my uncle. It would be most impolite to neglect my new relatives."

Edward walked around the room that had been arranged for the meeting. The upholstered pieces of furniture had been removed. Three dozen chairs had been brought from the ballroom and were arranged to face the desk.

He turned to face Miles. "Will you be conducting the meeting, Viscount Ryland?"

"Whyever would you think that, my lord earl? The company belongs to Geoffrey and Victoria. She'll be the one to address the shareholders."

Edward's brow rose in surprise before he quickly governed his features. "If you'll excuse me, I think I'll take a short stroll about the grounds before the meeting begins."

"Don't be late, my lord. You wouldn't want to miss a word of Torie's speech. You'll be surprised, I promise you."

Edward stormed out and never saw the grin on Miles' face.

Walking through the gardens, Edward's mind was crowded with thoughts. Grayson must think he was a gullible fool. If this chit was Victoria, she'd be coming after him with blood in her eye. Having the meeting here was a ploy to distract the others while the imposter took Victoria's place. Obviously, Geoffrey wasn't expected to recover. By having this chit accepted as Victoria, Grayson could marry her and inherit Victoria's portion of the estate.

A sudden thought halted his angry tirade. If Grayson was going through with this charade, then he didn't know about the codicil. Everything would come to Edward when Geoffrey died if the earl could expose this charlatan for what she was. Tearing this bitch to shreds would be interesting.

Edward turned toward the house and chuckled. "You're right, Grayson. I wouldn't want to miss this meeting for anything!"

The library was already crowded with the associates of Carlisle Enterprises when Mark stepped forward and greeted him at the door. "You're to be seated up front at Victoria's right, as your position with the family and company dictates, Edward."

After Mark ushered him to his designated place beside the desk, Edward looked at the assembled men. Suddenly uneasy, he turned to his left to find the source of his discomfort.

Geoffrey sat in a large armchair by the desk, directly across from him. He was elegantly attired and appeared to be in good health. Edward shivered with dread as his brother's hazel eyes stared directly back at him.

Before he could move, the room came alive with excitement. All the guests were on their feet, greeting the new arrival. As a few returned to their seats, Edward finally saw the object of all the attention. She was a vision in green and gold. Her voice was low and musical. But it was her familiar face that caused Edward to stop breathing. His mind raced in confusion.

Evangeline? No, she's dead. Victoria? No, that isn't possible. Who is she?

She looked directly at him and smiled. "There you are, Edward."

As he stood up, the young woman rushed toward him and threw herself into his arms. He felt her soft lips kiss his cheek. A moment later, she looked into his face and smiled. "I'm sorry I gave you such a fright. Please say you'll forgive me."

Edward was thoroughly entranced by the golden-haired beauty he held in his arms. His eyes devoured her loveliness, and he was soon smiling back at her.

She kissed his cheek again. "Good. You're not frowning any longer, so you must have forgiven me, Uncle Edward."

Hearing her address him as uncle brought Edward's mind rushing back to reality. He gathered his composure and kissed her cheek. "Welcome home, Victoria."

"Thank you, Uncle Edward. I'm certainly glad to be back."

Edward sat down and watched her walk behind the desk. He intended to keep a wary eye on this mysterious young woman.

Catherine looked around the room. Jamie stood near the windows; Garret sat next to the door. Mark was in the center of the first row and Miles stood at the back of the room, directly opposite of her. Their positions were part of the plan. If during her oration she became nervous, she would look to one of them. It would appear she'd spanned the room with a confident gaze when in reality she was speaking to friends.

Catherine went to Geoffrey and whispered in his ear. "This is for you, Papa. Wish me luck!" She kissed his cheek and was rewarded when he smiled and winked at her. With this added bit of encouragement, she stood behind the desk and pushed her chair to the wall.

"I hope you gentlemen will forgive me, but I'm going to remain standing while I speak. I know it's not what proper etiquette dictates, but since when has Victoria Carlisle ever done what was expected?" A soft rumble of laughter emanated from the assembled men.

The image of poised confidence, Catherine began her speech. "Good afternoon. My father and I welcome you to Chatham Hall. Our requesting this meeting in our home serves several purposes. First, we wanted you to see that in spite of rumors currently being bandied about, the Carlisles are alive and well."

She nodded toward Geoffrey. "It's true my father suffered a seizure that a lesser man would not have survived. Some say his recovery is miraculous, but we who know him expected nothing less. He is Geoffrey Carlisle, a man who has continually succeeded where others have failed. Although my father hasn't been at the helm of Carlisle Enterprises, his skills at organizing a strong company have been proven true. Every division of our firm has continued to show profits.

"I've recently returned from a two-month tour of this country of ours. The information I've acquired while I was away will only strengthen this company. So, as you can see, the Carlisles are back, and God help the fools who get in their way."

Rousing applause from the audience showed their approval of her words.

"I'd like to take this opportunity to thank my wonderful Uncle Edward for all his help and the unselfish devotion he's shown during the past few months. I promise he'll be richly rewarded for his efforts and will get everything he deserves."

Facing Edward, she offered him her hand and a gracious smile. He kissed her hand. Catherine didn't allow herself to flinch as she met and then turned away from his searching gaze.

"While you gentlemen are here, Papa and I invite you to enjoy our hospitality. Following this meeting, there will be a buffet luncheon served in the dining room. This afternoon, we hope some of you will make use of our horses and tour the area. After dinner this evening, there will be an excellent musical program provided for your entertainment. A pheasant hunt and trout fishing have been planned for early tomorrow morning. So eat, drink, and be merry, good sirs! Come Monday, it's back to work for us all."

The assembled gentlemen applauded the end of her

speech and honored her with a standing ovation. During their resounding show of confidence, Catherine stood at Geoffrey's side, her hand on his shoulder.

"Uncle Edward," she called across the desk. "Would you please show our guests the way to the dining room? I have a few things to attend to, but I'll join you presently."

Without a word, Edward nodded and led the others from the library. When the last guest filed out, Garret closed the door and locked it. Mark and Jamie patted each other on the back as Miles picked Catherine up in his arms and kissed her.

Her cheeks were blushing when her feet touched the floor. She knelt in front of Geoffrey and held his hands.

"I know you don't understand all that went on here today. Just know that we did this to keep Edward from hurting you or taking over the company. In a few days, you and I are going to have a special talk, and I'll explain everything, I promise."

Geoffrey smiled and squeezed her hands.

Mark touched Geoffrey's shoulder. "We'd best get you upstairs, my friend, or Lucy will be down here giving us grief for not taking better care of you. That's one lady I'd rather not cross."

Five minutes later, Geoffrey was safely back in his room. Mark, Garret, and Jamie were in the dining room mingling with the guests while they watched Edward.

And for the first time in more than a week, Miles and Catherine were alone.

With his back pressed against the library door, Miles held Catherine in his arms. "I do believe I'll go insane if I'm not able to make love to you soon." He began nibbling on the side of her neck. "Can't we find some other room for Lucy to sleep in tonight?"

She shivered from his tender ministrations, but shook her head. "That won't be necessary."

Miles pulled away from her to look into her eyes. "Why? Are you saying you don't want to—"

Catherine kissed him and halted his words. A few moments later, she eased away from his lips. "You weren't listening to me. I said it wasn't necessary to find Lucy a room. With the nurses gone, the chamber next to the duke's suite is available. Lucy wanted to be closer to him, so she moved into that room during the meeting. I've been left all alone."

Miles chuckled. "Not if I have anything to say about it, my love."

Luncheon was over and the guests had retired to the drawing room for coffee and dessert by the time Catherine and Miles joined them. The next phase of their plan began.

Catherine walked toward Edward. Miles pretended to be engrossed in a conversation with Jamie as he watched her. Edward was talking to *Comte* Jean Claude Beauchamps, a former French ambassador who was now living in England. He was a close friend of the duke's and owned several businesses with him.

"Uncle Edward, thank you for playing host in my absence." She turned to the richly attired elderly gentleman at his side. *"Monsieur le comte,* I'm so happy to see you again!"

"As I you, *ma petite belle.* It has been too long between visits. Tell me, how is your *cher papa* really doing, Victoria?"

She could see the interest in Edward's eyes as she spoke to Jean Claude. "Papa's making strides in his convalescence, but still has a long way to go. With the possible exception of not being able to recall the seizure itself or the day or so preceding it, Papa should be fully recovered in a few months' time."

The Frenchman gave her an encouraging smile. "Geoffrey looked very well today, though he was quiet and a little pale. I was hoping for a chance to visit my old friend this afternoon."

"Papa would probably enjoy seeing you, but I should make you aware of his condition first." Catherine moved closer to Jean Claude and Edward before she spoke to them in secretive tones. "My father has yet to regain his ability to speak, nor can he use his hand to write. I'd prefer if no one else knew about this. Papa is a very proud man. He abhors being pitied."

Jean Claude gave Catherine a hug. "You are a good daughter, Victoria. Geoffrey should be very proud of you." He turned to Edward. "Did you know Victoria saved your brother and *Herr* Mueller a sizeable fortune by using her wits and talent?"

Edward frowned. "What occasion was this, Jean Claude?"

Hiding her confusion, Catherine listened to Jean Claude recount the event.

"A few years ago, Geoffrey held a meeting for business-men from various European countries. Two men from Spain were discussing a way to cheat your brother and Mueller with a spurious investment when they realized Victoria had heard their discussion and suspected she understood their language. They began speaking in Italian, so she feigned ignorance and appeared disinterested. When the pair approached Geoffrey about the wonderful investment, Victoria interrupted and told her father in German what she'd overheard."

Jean Claude chuckled. "Geoffrey never blinked an eye at the scoundrels. He thanked them, but declined their offer. I do not know who I admired more—Geoffrey for his great diplomacy, or Victoria for her ability to speak so many languages."

Edward turned to Catherine. A mysterious smile curved his lips. *"Ma Victoria, est une dame belle et savante! La femme ne craignant rien, n'est pas?"*

Catherine looked at him and was silent for a few seconds before she answered his question. *"Ce que je crains ce sont mes pretendus amis, mon oncle."*

Edward replied, *"C'est ne pas moi; je suis votre ami le plus fidele."*

Raising her brow, Catherine smiled at him. *"Gardez-vous. Qui s'excuse, s'accuse."*

Before Edward could respond, Catherine looked at Jean Claude. "Why don't you and I go up to visit Papa? I know he'll be pleased to see you." She took the older man's arm, and they left the drawing room.

During her conversation with Edward and Jean Claude, Catherine had never realized Garret was standing only a few feet away from her, listening to everything that was being said. As soon as she was out of sight, Miles motioned Garret to follow him to the library.

"Garret, what went on there? Was Edward harassing Cat?"

"Catherine handled herself very well. That lady never ceases to amaze me. I do believe her intelligence is just as remarkable as her beauty."

Miles was quickly losing patience with his awestruck friend. "Tell me what was said and forget the flowery phrases."

Garret sighed. "All right. The old gent was telling Edward how Victoria's talent for languages saved Geoffrey a great deal of money."

"What did Edward say to that?"

"He started speaking to Catherine in French. He said—"

Miles grabbed Garret by his coat. "I told you to keep a close watch on them! Bloody hell! You weren't supposed to let her face that kind of scrutiny alone."

Garret pulled himself free from Miles and scowled at him. "I know that. I was about to intercede when Catherine answered Damien all on her own."

"She fooled him? Tell me exactly what happened."

Perched on the edge of the desk, Garret carefully recited the conversation he had witnessed. "Damien said, 'My niece Victoria is a beautiful and learned lady who fears nothing. Is that not so?' Her response was, 'What I fear is my would-be friends.' Edward said, 'Not I. I am your most faithful friend.' Catherine smiled and replied, 'Be careful, my uncle. He who excuses himself, accuses himself.' Then she went upstairs with the *comte.*"

"Is that why Edward appeared so miffed?" Miles asked.

Garret shrugged. "Perhaps, but I think the way she said it annoyed him even more. She spoke French like a Parisian. Her dialect and pronunciation were perfect."

Miles shook his head. "That's impossible. Cat doesn't speak French."

"Whether it was a hidden talent or divine intervention, I know what I heard. What's more, Edward did, too. Her statement will certainly give him plenty to think about."

Miles turned from his friend. "Her statement's given me something to think about, as well."

At that moment, Catherine rushed into the drawing room searching for Miles. Her nerves were as taut as a bowstring. She had to tell him about the strange things that had happened to her while she was speaking to Edward. Maybe he could explain why she suddenly was able to—

"Victoria, my dear, how is my brother?"

Catherine turned to find Edward Damien standing beside her. It took every ounce of her control not to reveal how upset she was by his presence. "Papa is fine. Jean Claude will be a good diversion for him this afternoon." Hoping to disarm him, she asked a question she knew he'd avoid. "Would you like to visit Papa next?"

Edward simply shook his head. "There will be plenty of time for me to visit Geoffrey after the other guests have departed.'' An enigmatic smile curved his lips as he looked at her. "That's a lovely pearl necklace. But where is that lovely gold heart pendant you usually wear? I've always admired the filigreed edge and your scrolled initial on it. You still have that necklace, don't you?''

Catherine was startled by Edward's description of Victoria's pendant. Back in Corbin's Cove, she had a necklace that matched the design he had described. She'd worn it all her life. If the chain hadn't broken, she would have been wearing it when she was captured.

She suddenly realized Edward was waiting for her reply. Giving him what she hoped was a demure smile, Catherine sighed. "During my trip, I misplaced it. Perhaps I can purchase another if I don't find it.'' Looking up, she spotted Miles at the drawing room door watching her. "Will you excuse me, Uncle Edward? I have an important matter to discuss with Miles.''

Watching as she hurried away, Edward grinned. *Your tutors haven't told you everything about Victoria. You will never find that pendant. It is mine—just as you will be, my little actress. Yes, my darling, you will be mine.*

Chapter 23

It was past midnight when Catherine stood alone on the balcony outside of her room, tearfully recalling what should have been a glorious day.

Their plan had been going fine. Her speech had been well received and everyone believed she was Victoria. She'd felt so confident, so happy. But things began to change when Edward Damien started speaking to her in French. It frightened her when she miraculously understood what he was saying and answered him in the strange language. She'd hoped Miles could help her sort it all out when she'd rushed toward him in the drawing room.

But before she could utter a word, Miles had pulled her across the foyer into the library. Locking the door, he shoved her against the wall. "I thought you didn't speak French, Catherine."

"I don't."

"Then tell me how you were able to speak with Edward in perfect French. Not only did you converse with him, you even managed to insult him. How can you explain this?"

Catherine shook her head. "I can't, Miles. At first, I had no idea what Edward was saying. Then a strange feeling came over me and I suddenly understood what he said and heard myself answer him. I don't know how it happened. Please, Miles, you must believe me."

He stepped back to glare at her. "Maybe that's my problem. I have believed you. I believed you wanted to help me avenge Victoria's death. I believed you wanted to aid Geoffrey. What hurts the most is I believed you loved me."

"But I do love you." When she reached out to touch him, Miles retreated, avoiding her touch. "Please, Miles, you must listen to me. I don't speak French, and I've never lied to you."

He smirked. "I can't blame you for lying. You did what you had to in order to survive. I was a fool to think you could be anything more than the outlaw you were brought up to be." His brow rose in a cynical arch. "Tell me, Lady Cat, once this sham was over, did you have a means of escape devised for yourself? Perhaps you were going to seduce Garret into doing your bidding. God knows you've courted his affections from the very beginning."

Catherine slapped him across the face. "How dare you accuse me of such things? I fell in love with you, but you won't have to worry about that anymore. Maybe you're the one looking for an escape. Being involved with an Irish rebel is too great a risk for your lordship, so you changed your mind. I'll not trouble you a moment longer with my presence, English."

As she touched the doorknob, Miles called out a warning that stopped her. "Have you forgotten about Rory, Lady Cat? If you try to escape or foul up my plan in any way, you will never see your brother again—and I'll have you sent to prison, as well."

She slowly turned to face Miles. His eyes, once filled with love for her, now held icy contempt.

"If I help you expose Edward, will you keep your end of the bargain, or have you changed your mind about that, too?"

"As an honorable gentleman, I could do no less."

"Fine. Our original deal stands." Swallowing the tightness in her throat, she hid her pain behind a thin smile. "I don't care if you believe me, but I'm not a liar. I have no idea how I was able to converse in French with Edward. Nor do I understand why I feel so close to Geoffrey or find such comfort in this house. It's as if someone else is guiding me and showing me the way."

"Next you'll tell me that fairy tales come true and ghosts are real. Sorry, Cat. I'm not Irish enough to believe in such nonsense."

Catherine was nearly out the door when she looked back at him. "Just believe this, Miles Grayson. *Tha gaol agam ort.*"

As she ran up the stairs, Garret followed her. Before she could close the door to the sitting room of her suite, he pushed his way inside and locked it.

"What in the devil is going on, Cat? You came out of the library as if someone had attacked you. Catherine, look at me."

When she didn't respond, Garret lifted her face with his hand. "You're crying. God's blood! I'll kill whoever has caused you such pain."

She shook her head. "I can't let you hurt him. Promise me you won't interfere."

Garret frowned. "I won't promise anything until I know the truth. Come sit on the sofa with me and tell me what happened."

Catherine wiped her eyes with a handkerchief as she sat next to Garret. She told him of her confrontation with Miles, his accusations and threats, but carefully deleted what he'd said about her seducing his friend in order to escape.

Garret gave her a reassuring hug. "Things will work out. You love Miles, and he loves you, too."

"Miles doesn't love me. He thinks I lied to him."

"The two of you just had a misunderstanding. Miles will come to his senses soon, and you'll be together again."

Catherine shook her head. "You didn't see him. Miles was furious. He's convinced I've been using him all along. He even accused me of trying to . . ." Her voice faded to silence.

"What did he accuse you of? Tell me, Catherine."

New tears welled in her eyes. "Miles said I'd probably seduce you and that I'd been courting your affections from the start. Dear lord, I love that man with all my heart. How can he suggest such things?"

Garret sighed with disgust. "My old friend is, without a doubt, the biggest fool on the face of the earth. Perhaps if I talk to him, I could make him see reason."

"Don't waste the effort, Garret. Miles and I were doomed from the start. We're from two different worlds. The only place dreams come true is in fairy tales, and Miles doesn't believe in them. Maybe he's right."

Garret put his arm around Catherine as she walked him to the door. They were startled to find Miles standing at the threshold, preparing to knock.

Miles sneered at them. "Sorry to interrupt, but I wanted to remind Mistress O'Banyon that I will escort her down to dinner at eight o'clock. By the by, Garret, you really should take care when playing with cats," he warned. "They have a nasty habit of turning on you."

"Why, you dirty—" Garret punched Miles in the jaw, knocking him to the floor. "You are the most addlepated jackass I have ever known. If I didn't pity your blind arrogance, I'd teach you the meaning of the word *trust*. Obviously it's not in your vocabulary." Turning away from where Miles was sitting on the floor rubbing his jaw, Garret blew a kiss to Catherine. "Until this evening, my lady." Making a courtly bow, he strolled down the corridor.

Catherine went into the suite and closed the door. She didn't see Miles again until he arrived to escort her to dinner.

His demeanor matched the clothes he wore: black, formal, and very proper. Throughout the evening, he played the role of a gentleman and made polite conversation whenever necessary with the guests. But there was no feeling behind his cool smile, no warmth in his words when he spoke to her. During the musical program in the ballroom, he sat by her side, but he seemed to ignore the entire performance.

Catherine was mulling over his foul mood when Edward stood to make an announcement.

"Many of you were here several years ago and were fortunate to hear my lovely niece, Victoria, sing in this very room. If we ask her, maybe she'll do us the honor of performing for us tonight." Edward began applauding, urging the others to join his entreaty.

Catherine looked around the room and found everyone waiting for her reply. *Oh no, Edward, you won't scare me off this way!* She smiled at the earl. "As always, dear uncle, I shall do my best to please you."

Miles reacted with a look of surprise when she got up and borrowed a harp from one of the musicians. Sitting on a chair on the raised dais, she plucked the strings of the instrument and began to sing. The song she chose was "Greensleeves."

> *"Alas my love, ye do me wrong*
> *To cast me off discurteously,*
> *And I have loved you so long,*
> *Delighting in your companie."*

The audience appeared impressed by her rendition of the moving love song. They had no way of knowing how the beautiful old tune reminded her of Miles, nor could they see the pain it caused her as she sang it. At the final strains, they rose to their feet and applauded her wildly. But the praise Catherine yearned for never came.

Miles was gone.

Shortly before eleven, Catherine bid the guests good night and went to her room alone. She sighed with relief when Darcy completed her duties and left. Knowing sleep would evade her, she stepped out onto the balcony, where she stood for more than an hour recalling the events of the day.

The night air was cool and damp, but she relished how it felt on her burning skin. Even the wetness from her tears failed to douse the heat in her cheeks. She leaned against the stone rail and gazed up at the moon and stars.

"If you're making a wish on a star, Catherine, please make one for me."

The deep timbre of Miles' voice behind her caused Catherine to close her eyes and pray she wasn't dreaming.

His strong arms wrapped around her waist. "Catherine, my love, I have been such a bloody fool. Garret was right to hit me. God knows I deserve far worse for the hell I put you through today." Miles kissed her tousled curls and hugged her closer to him. "I'm begging you to forgive me."

Though she longed to accept, doubts over the things he'd said earlier plagued her heart and kept her from answering him.

"As you sang tonight, my love for you flooded my soul. I wanted to run up to that platform and implore you to forgive me. But I couldn't do it. After hurting you so badly, how could I ask you to pardon my doubts? I fled to the gardens to walk and think of what I should do next. It wasn't long before I found Jamie and Garret standing in my path.

"They listened as I ranted about my stupidity and the disgraceful way I had treated you. Then they assailed me. Garret told me about your dreams, the way you were affected by Victoria's room, and how you've felt haunted since we arrived in London. He even threatened to beat me senseless if I didn't get on my knees and beg you to forgive me."

His lips lightly grazed the side of her neck. "Jamie convinced me to face you. He reminded me some people never find true love in their lives, and if I was fool enough to let you go without a fight, then I didn't deserve you. So here I am, Catherine, my heart in my hand, beseeching you to accept my humble apology. I am sorry beyond reason that I hurt you. I love you. Please give me another chance to prove it to you."

Catherine turned to face him. In the moonlight, she could see his handsome features. His eyes were pools of despair. "If you love me, Miles, then you have to trust me, as well. Without trust, our love is an empty shell, something so fragile it can be crushed by the slightest bump. And life is filled with bumps, bruises, and pitfalls. I cannot accept your love if your trust doesn't come with it."

Miles stroked her windblown hair from her face. "A lack of confidence in myself caused me to doubt you, Cat. I admire your courage and talents, your zest for living. I feared my love wouldn't be enough to hold you. That's why I thought you lied to me. Forgive me. I love you with every fiber of my being, and I don't want to lose you."

He captured her lips in a deep, ravenous kiss. Pulling her into his arms, he caressed her through the silky fabric of her nightgown. Suddenly, he lifted his mouth from hers.

"By God, Catherine, your skin is like ice. How long have you been standing out here?" He swept her into his arms and carried her inside. Kicking the door shut, he brought her to the bed and carefully set her down on it.

He unbuttoned the top of her sleeping gown and massaged her skin, trying to bring the warmth back to it. When he leaned over the bed to rub her arm, Catherine grabbed his hand.

"I know of an easier way to warm me, Miles, that will please us both." Sitting up, she pushed his robe off his shoulders and put her arms around his neck. She took his mouth in a searing kiss and drew him down beside her.

Miles moaned with pleasure, all but devouring her with a hunger that could not be denied. Her nipples, cold and pebble hard, rubbed against his chest. He gently cupped her womanly flesh, and his mouth joined his fingertips as he squeezed, suckled, and adored her breasts. But soon this wasn't enough.

He took hold of her gown, pushing it down and off her legs. His mouth followed the path of her nightrail. His dark head moved down her body to the gold mound of her womanhood.

Miles nuzzled the pale curls, pressing open kisses against her soft, fragrant warmth. His mouth went lower, exploring the moist center of her desire. The first penetration of his tongue caused Catherine to jump.

She scrambled to escape the onslaught of his mouth, but Miles grabbed her hips and pressed himself against her. He looked up into her frightened eyes. "Catherine, let me love you. I need to have you completely, to feast on the taste of you. Nothing else will sate me."

"But, Miles, this can't be right. Surely you shouldn't touch me like that."

He smiled. "Why not, my love? Don't you like the way it feels?" He ran his tongue along her sensitive slit and hummed with satisfaction. "You are so warm, so pink, and so very sweet. I love the way you taste, Catherine. Don't deny me this pleasure. Give in and allow me to make love to you in this very special way."

His gaze held hers for a moment. Then he grabbed a pillow and tucked it beneath her buttocks. The tilt of her hips helped accommodate his loving quest. Spreading the petals of her sex with his fingers, he found her pearl of desire with his tongue. He captured the small jewel and gently suckled on it, loving it with his mouth. As he felt it swell to life and throb under his touch, he parted her legs and thrust his tongue inside her, consuming the feminine essence there.

Catherine abandoned herself to his intimate probings. She arched her back and raised herself to meet his mouth. Soon a quaking began to course through her. His penetrating kisses and relentless caresses sent her over the edge of a tumultuous climax. She was tossed and spent by the powerful surge that enveloped her.

Miles drank deeply of her and waited until the last shudder wracked her body. Then he knelt between her thighs and removed the pillow from under her hips.

She opened her eyes to find him watching her, then smiled and held her arms out to him. His eyes held her captive as he brought himself over her. The hard length of his manhood pressed against her, seeking entrance into her yielding warmth. Groaning, he slid inside her. Her hot, moist passage closed tightly around him, bringing him the greatest of all pleasures. Smoothly, lovingly, he moved deep within her, his eyes intent on her radiant face.

Catherine met his impetus with equal fervor. Her body rose, crushing against his until he could wait no longer. Grasping her shoulders, he plunged deeper and harder, building up to his last surging thrust. At her passionate cry of release, Miles found his own. His seed flooded her womb.

After a few minutes, he fell back onto the bed and pulled

her into his arms. "Catherine, have you decided whether or not you'll forgive me?" he asked in a husky whisper.

Catherine chuckled and snuggled closer to him. "You won my forgiveness the moment you carried me in from the cold. My feet were frozen. Here, see for yourself." She ran an icy foot along his leg, causing him to jerk in reaction. They were both laughing when he playfully swatted her behind.

"Be serious, Catherine. I need to know if you believe me. I'm truly sorry for all the things I said—"

She put her hand across his mouth. "Miles Grayson, you pick the worst times to talk." Replacing her hand with her mouth, she kissed away his fears. After a few seconds, she leaned back and smiled. "Now that I have your attention, Miles, I'll set your mind at ease. I love you and, yes, I will marry you. As long as we love and trust each other, we can deal with anything life may throw our way."

The cold night winds continued to blow as Catherine and Miles fell asleep in a room warmed by their love.

Not everyone slept as well. Edward spent most of the long hours pacing his room, planning a way to have his brother's wealth and the beauty who was portraying his niece.

Her performance was nearly flawless, but he knew she wasn't Victoria. She looked and sounded like her, but she lacked his niece's cool reserve. He sensed an inner heat in this impostor, as though she was trying to control a fiery spirit. The thought made him grin, and he wondered if her passions ran as hot.

Since Evangeline's death, Edward hadn't loved another woman. He'd used women, satisfied his lusts when the need arose, but never cared about any of them. Victoria's resemblance to her mother often confused him, making him resent the burning she evoked inside him. He was taunted by her looks and lusted for her, but because she was his niece, Victoria had been forbidden to him.

This fascinating young lady was not.

She was as beautiful as Evangeline and Victoria, but without the complications. Somehow, he would make her his own. It would be different this time, he promised himself. He wouldn't make the mistakes he'd made before.

Reclining on his bed, Edward spoke out loud to the object of his thoughts. "Though I don't know your name, your bright green eyes and silky hair remind me of a cuddly kitten. But, no, you're too much of a woman for such a childish comparison. You're more like a soft golden cat. Golden cat?" He smiled. "Yes, that is a perfect pet name for you. Until I know who you really are, you shall be my Golden Cat."

He closed his eyes and pictured her image in his mind. Yes, the Golden Cat would be his. He wouldn't force her to love him. He'd take great joy in taming her by trimming her sharpened claws with kindness and winning her affection with gentle loving care. It might take time, but he wouldn't be denied.

Tomorrow, he'd play his part with her in this little drama, the doting uncle to her Victoria. No one would learn from him that she was an impostor. When he returned to London, he'd make arrangements for a special holiday for the two of them. Once he had her at his side, he'd return and do away with Geoffrey once and for all.

Edward Damien fell asleep with a smile on his face. After a lifetime denied of happiness, even slumber couldn't diminish his joy and anticipation of things to come.

Chapter 24

By noon of the following day, Catherine was totally disconcerted.

"I don't understand, Miles. No matter what I say to Edward, I cannot provoke him. Yesterday he challenged me at every turn. I thought he was trying to prove I wasn't Victoria. Today he's been warm, witty, and extremely charming."

Miles hugged her. "To openly attack you would expose his involvement in Torie's disappearance, but I was counting on him showing his hand by defying us in some way."

"Perhaps my portrayal has been too good and he thinks I *am* Victoria." Crossing the sitting room, Catherine sat on the sofa and sighed. "Could we be wrong about him? Maybe he had nothing to do with his niece's disappearance."

"No, I'm positive Edward is responsible. Besides the codicil and the argument he had with Geoffrey, our investigation has uncovered other things about him."

Miles sat beside Catherine and told her about Lorelei's

will and the paltry sum she'd bequeathed to Edward. "Besides not getting her money, imagine Edward's surprise when he found out his wife had mortgaged the Sedwick properties to the hilt. He has one year to raise the funds if he wants to retain his estate."

"Why would she do such a cruel thing to her husband?"

"Evidently their marriage wasn't all it was supposed to be. Though Edward appeared to be devoted to his wife, Lorelei openly had affairs with many men. Jamie interviewed one young gent she was supporting. It seems the countess kept lovers like wealthy men keep mistresses."

Catherine frowned. "Do you think one of them killed her?"

"Who knows? The authorities haven't been very cooperative with my agents. I may have to go to London and see a few people I know in the government to gain access to the information that's been gathered on the case."

Leaning against Miles' shoulder, Catherine sighed. "What a despicable woman Lorelei must have been. Poor Edward."

"Poor Edward, indeed!" Miles scoffed. "I'm sure Edward knew exactly what he was getting when he married Lorelei eighteen years ago. According to the marriage contract I purchased from a clerk who works for the countess's solicitor, Edward gained her dead husband's title, a vast estate, and thirty thousand pounds in cash."

"That's quite a price to pay for a husband, even if Edward *was* handsome, educated, and charming."

"Need I remind you of the adjectives Torie used to describe her uncle: lying, envious, deceitful, untrustworthy, and so on. Don't let his facade fool you, my love. Beneath his fine trappings, Edward Damien is a very dangerous man."

A memory from the previous day caused Catherine to shiver. "When I first saw Edward standing in front of the house, I had a terrible foreboding."

"Follow your instincts and never take chances with him. I won't always be around to protect you." As she scowled at him, he laughed. "I know you're capable of defending yourself, Cat, but you can hardly go about the house with a rapier strapped to the waist of your gown."

"You really don't know me at all, English. I always have a weapon close at hand." She stood up and raised her skirts, revealing a sheathed dagger held against her leg by a lace-trimmed garter. "I'm proficient in all kinds of weapons."

Miles removed the dagger from its sheath. It had a six-inch blade and a handle inlaid with sapphires. "This is the toy you tried to skewer me with when I asked you to cut your hair. Another present from Garret?"

"That toy, as you call it, was a gift from Rory several years ago. My brother said it reminded him of me: small, pretty, and deadly. It's saved my life on three separate occasions, so don't take it for granted."

"But how did you get hold of this knife? Your rapier was left on the *Foxfire,* and I don't remember your having a dagger when I captured you that night."

Slipping the dagger back into its place, Catherine dropped her skirts and smiled at him. "Next time you capture a pirate, English, check her boots. You were so distracted by my britches, you forgot to look anyplace else."

Miles pulled her down onto his lap. "What red-blooded male wouldn't find you distracting in those tight black britches?" He playfully nibbled on her ear. "But I did look someplace else that night. I know for a fact you didn't have a thing under your blouse except—"

Catherine reared back and lightly smacked his cheek. "Why, you sneaky bounder!" Her eyes glittered with humor. "I never realized you'd taken such liberties with my person."

"Well, a man has to protect himself from the likes of an Irish outlaw, doesn't he?" Miles kissed her with undisguised passion. Gazing into her eyes a few minutes later, he sighed. "I never realized she'd conquer me with love— the greatest weapon of all."

As the guests were leaving Chatham Hall late that afternoon, Catherine made a final attempt to provoke Edward. He was bidding farewell to his associates and waiting for his own coach when she approached him in front of the house.

"Mrs. Oliver informs me you're returning to London. I thought you might spend a few days with us. Papa will be most disappointed that he never got to visit with you."

Catherine was startled when Edward put his arms around her and gave her an enthusiastic hug. "I am sorry, dearest. I wish it could be otherwise, but a matter of grave importance has come to light that requires my attention in town. Give Geoffrey my regrets and assure him I'll be in touch soon."

She eased back from his embrace to look at him. "If the matter has to do with the business, I'd like to help."

"I appreciate your concern, but the issue at hand is a personal one."

"Well, would you mind if I returned to work at the Carlisle offices? It's not that I doubt your abilities, Uncle Edward, but Papa is making great strides in his recovery and doesn't require my aid. The inactivity is driving me to distraction."

He smiled at her. "I'd welcome your company, my heart. Lord knows you're far too lovely and intelligent to languish here in the country." At that moment, his coach pulled up and the footman opened the door for him. Edward placed a quick kiss on Catherine's unsuspecting lips just before he stepped inside his coach. "*Adieu,* dear one. I'll see you soon." With a smile and a wink, he was gone.

Catherine was watching his coach pull away when Miles

came to her side and put his arm around her waist. "What's the matter, Cat? Did Edward say something to upset you?"

"I thought I'd goad Edward into revealing his true feelings by saying I wanted to return to work, but he said he'd welcome me." Catherine sighed. "What are we going to do, Miles? Just sit and wait for Edward to make the next move?"

"Not at all. Jamie and Garret are returning to London. I have men watching Edward, his home, and the staff at Carlisle House. We shall remain here. While you work with Geoffrey, I'll coordinate the information my people have gathered."

Catherine leaned against Miles as they entered the house. "We have to tell the duke the truth soon. It's not right to lie to him like this."

"I'd hoped for some word on Victoria by now. I have the finest investigators searching for her, but nothing's turned up. Geoffrey deserves to know what happened to his daughter."

Hearing the frustration in Miles' voice, Catherine kissed his cheek. "Why don't we go upstairs and visit with Geoffrey for a while? It will give Lucy a break, and I've missed him."

Over the following week, daily reports kept Miles informed of the comings and goings in London. Nothing much was discovered until one message gave him pause.

Theresa, the maid from Carlisle House, had been followed to Sedwick Manor. She'd hired a hackney and gone there late one afternoon and didn't leave until the next morning. When she returned to work, she had a large, colorful bruise on her face.

Cosgrove told Jamie Theresa often came back from seeing her family with similar bruises. He suspected she had a drunken father who beat her when she visited home.

The Carlisles' retainer didn't know Theresa was an orphan from Dorset.

If there was no family and no drunken father, whom did she visit at Sedwick House? There was a very small staff in Edward's home. Wilson, the butler, was married to the housekeeper, Sadie. The driver and footman were older men who'd worked at the manor for many years. The only other person in the house was Edward.

But why would Edward hit Theresa? Was he the kind of man who enjoyed hurting women?

A sudden realization caused him to drop the missive on the library desk. "If Edward liked inflicting pain, doing away with his wife would have been an easy task—especially if he believed her death would give him access to her fortune.

The description of Lorelei's death released by the authorities said the countess had been beaten and stabbed in her bedroom, but little else. When Garret and Jamie had tried to get more details about the crime, they'd been stonewalled by Nigel Bradford.

"Bradford won't ignore me. I'll go to London and call in favors owed to me to get the information I want."

Miles went to the master bedroom and found Catherine playing chess with Geoffrey. The duke was sitting in his wheelchair, smiling at his companion as she scolded him.

"You won again, Papa! You should be ashamed of yourself, taking advantage of a poor defenseless female like me. Everyone knows women are the weaker of the sexes—not to mention their lack of truly superior intelligence."

Miles chuckled as he recalled taunting Catherine with that belief. Suddenly, he realized Geoffrey was laughing along with him.

"Papa, you're laughing!" Catherine rushed to Geoffrey's side and hugged him. "I've never heard such a wonderful sound."

"What's all the commotion about?" Lucy asked as she ran into the room.

"Geoffrey was laughing about females having inferior intelligence," Miles explained.

Lucy sniffed. "Some men actually believe that pot of tripe! My brothers always teased me—" Her gaze whipped from Miles to Geoffrey and back again. "Did you say His Grace laughed? He laughed?" She ran to Geoffrey and knelt in front of his chair. "I knew you were getting better. Pretty soon, you'll be talking and singing. Just wait and see."

Miles motioned Catherine to follow him out to the hall. As the door closed, they heard Lucy reprimanding her employer.

"In the past few months, I've told you every humorous story I knew. But would you laugh? Oh no! Well, let me tell you . . ."

When they were in the sitting room of Victoria's suite, Miles told Catherine about the report he'd received. "So you see, I have to go to London immediately. If my suspicions are correct, Edward has gotten away with murder. Once I can prove that, perhaps the officials will conduct their own search for Victoria and solve that mystery as well."

"Of course you must go. The sooner the better. I'll stay here with Geoffrey."

Miles frowned. "My men have all returned to London. I have no one here to protect you and the duke." He pulled Catherine into his arms. "It's too much to risk. Maybe I'll wait until Garret can send some of our people back to Chatham."

Catherine poked him playfully in the ribs. "English, are you forgetting who I am? The only person who came close to defeating me was a rogue known as Trelane the Fox, and I'll not fall for his tricks again."

Miles wasn't smiling when he gazed into her eyes. "I'm serious about this. If Edward were to discover you and Geoffrey were alone, there's no telling what he might do."

She shook her head. "You're worrying too much. We'll be fine for a few days. By that time, either you'll be back or the guards you send will take care of us. Until then, I can bring some weapons up and stay with Geoffrey. His suite is virtually a fortress."

"But what about Mrs. Oliver? Victoria said her house-keeper was in league with Edward. I've yet to find the reason for that."

Catherine sighed with impatience. "For goodness sake, Miles, Mrs. Oliver doesn't frighten me. One false move from her, and I'll have the witch hanging from the rafters."

After a moment of deep thought. Miles reluctantly nodded. "All right, Cat, we'll do it your way. There are pistols and ammunition in the armoire in Geoffrey's room. I'll get a rapier from the cabinet downstairs. Promise me you won't leave this house while I'm gone."

Catherine rolled her eyes. "My God, you're talking as though we're at war."

"This is worse than war. On the battlefield you know who your enemies are. Here, we have no idea who can be trusted." Miles kissed her. "Please be careful, my love."

"I swear I'll do everything you ask. The only thing that will get me to leave this house will be an act of God," she assured him.

Within the hour, Miles was on his way to London.

After dinner that evening, Catherine announced her intention of spending the night in Geoffrey's room and sent Lucy to bed. With a rapier near the locked door and three pistols primed and ready, Catherine was prepared for any intruder foolish enough to enter the duke's suite.

Sitting in a chair beside Geoffrey, she passed the time reading to him from Shakespeare's *Midsummer Night's Dream*. He laughed as she took on the different voices of the characters in the play. Between the second and third act, Catherine set the book down on the seat of her chair and walked around the room to loosen the stiffness in her legs.

"My favorite play is *The Comedy Of Errors*. It's the story about twin boys separated when they were born. Perhaps I'll read that one to you tomorrow, Papa."

Geoffrey shook his head. His face was a mask of sadness.

Catherine smiled. "I understand. Two comedies in a row isn't such a good idea. Maybe I can try "Julius Caesar," though I'll have a devil of a time with all those male voices."

The duke's renewed smile made her happy. As Catherine moved back toward her chair, there was a knock at the door. It was Lucy.

"Victoria, since you're planning to stay near your father tonight, why don't you use the salon?" she asked, nodding toward the portal on the farside of the room. "You could leave the door open and sleep on the sofa. No one has been in there since you went away in November. I kept it locked, just as you ordered." Lucy handed Catherine the key and smiled at Geoffrey. "Good night, Your Grace. Good night, Victoria." With a wave to them both, she was gone.

Catherine secured the locks and looked at the door to the salon that Lucy had referred to. Shrugging her shoulders, she went back to her seat beside Geoffrey's wheelchair. She picked up the book and held it in her right hand as she sat down. In her other hand, she clutched the ornate brass key.

"Papa, will you hold this key for me? I haven't any pockets in my gown and I don't want to lose it." Opening her left hand, she offered him the key.

Geoffrey picked up the key and stared at her opened palm. Catherine saw him looking at her scar. She pulled her hand back, clenching it into a tight fist. He grabbed her hand and gently opened her fingers. He stared intently at her palm.

As she sought a way to explain the scar, Geoffrey looked into her face. His hazel eyes filled with tears. She watched while he strained to form a word and held her breath when he attempted to speak.

His voice was low and raspy. "Cath-erine."

She thought she'd misheard him. "What did you say?"

With a little more strength in his voice, he repeated the same word again. "Catherine."

She was stunned. "Who told you my name was Catherine?"

Geoffrey held up her scarred palm. His words were slow, but easy to discern. "Catherine. My Catherine."

Catherine shook her head in confusion. "Your Catherine? I don't know what you're trying to tell me."

Handing her the key, he pointed to the salon door.

"The salon? You want me to go into the salon?" Catherine asked. He shook his head and pointed to himself, and then to the door. "Oh! You want me to take you to the salon?"

Geoffrey nodded. "Y-yes."

"I don't understand any of this, but if that's what you want, then so be it." She handed him the candlestick and pushed his chair on wheels to the salon. Opening the door, she felt the chill of the closed room.

"Perhaps this isn't such a good idea. It's freezing in there." When she saw the pleading in Geoffrey's eyes, she knew he wouldn't be dissuaded. She pushed his chair into the room. Taking the burning candle from its holder, she lit the other candles in the pink and white salon.

Catherine rolled his chair beside the sofa while she looked around the feminine room. The sound of Geoffrey's voice brought her attention back to him.

"L-look th-there." He pointed to a large painting that was leaning against the wall directly in front of him.

Taking a candelabrum with her, she knelt next to the painting. It was a portrait of a blond woman and two baby girls. Catherine gasped. "Except for the blue eyes, she looks like me. Was she your wife, Evangeline?"

Geoffrey nodded. Raising his hand, he pointed to the painting again. "My Catherine."

She lifted the candles closer to the canvas to see what he was trying to show her. The baby was a pretty little girl with golden curls and green eyes. Seeing the necklace the child wore nearly caused Catherine to drop the heavy candle holder. "This baby is wearing a pendant that's identical to mine."

She studied the other child. The girls were obviously twins. The second one wore a pendant clearly marked with a letter "V." "This is Victoria, isn't it?"

"Yes," Geoffrey replied.

She set the candelabrum on the floor and turned around to face him. Tears pooled in her eyes. "I don't understand."

"My Catherine," he said again, stroking her cheek with his hand. "You are my Catherine."

In a soft whisper, she replied, "Papa? My papa?"

Geoffrey nodded. Tears trickled down his face. He gently pulled Catherine off her knees and lifted her onto his lap. Wrapping his arms around her, he held her close as she cried against his shoulder.

Suddenly, Catherine knew this was right. She didn't know how or why, but she was where she belonged. This was Papa, her papa, and she was finally at home.

Looking into his eyes, she kissed him. "I love you, Papa."

With clear determination, he spoke to her. "I love you,

Catherine." Kissing her forehead, he held her firmly against his chest. "Welcome home, my baby."

A while later, Catherine sat up and looked at her father's smiling face. "If I'm your daughter, why was I in Ireland?"

Geoffrey took the carved wood box from the table beside him and handed it to her. She ran her fingers over the small chest.

"Is this for me, Papa?"

He nodded. "F-from your mother."

Catherine opened the box. She removed the papers. Her hands trembled when she opened the folded parchment and read the top line of the page. "Dear Catherine . . ."

Geoffrey held her in his arms as she read the letter out loud and came to know the woman who'd given her life. When she finished reading Evangeline's missive, Catherine sighed.

"I've always felt that something was missing in my life. I was surrounded by people who loved me, but I was never content. I sought solace in my studies and training, yet there was no peace. What was lacking in my life was here. It was Mama, Victoria, and you, Papa. You all were the important part of me that was missing."

Geoffrey stroked her hair while she spoke to him.

"Since I was little, I've had the strangest dreams. I saw myself living in beautiful houses and wearing fine gowns. Once I dreamed . . ." An eerie feeling came over Catherine. She looked at Geoffrey. "Papa, did Victoria have a large black stallion that threw her and injured her leg?"

At his nod, Catherine shook with excitement. "Papa, I saw it happen in my dream! It was Victoria who fell, but I shared her pain and couldn't walk for days. All those times, I was watching my sister. That's why her rooms were so familiar to me. So many things make sense to me now. Even though we have been far away from each other, Victoria and I have never been apart. Did you ever tell Victoria about me?"

Seeing his sadness, she answered the question for him. "You never told her, Papa. You and Mama thought it would hurt Victoria if she knew she had lost a sister, especially a twin. I'm right, aren't I?"

Geoffrey sighed. "Yes. Too much pain."

"You never told Victoria the truth, but I think she found that painting and drew her own conclusions. That's why she locked the door to this salon and left the house that night. Only something as important as this would have made her leave your side."

Geoffrey then asked the question Catherine dreaded the most. "Where is Victoria?"

"I don't know, Papa. Miles believes Edward had her abducted because he feared she knew something that could ruin him. But according to Victoria's last missive to Miles, she was still looking for the proof she needed to go after Edward."

Catherine saw Geoffrey's gaze fix on the letter in her hand. "Edward knows about Mama's letter, doesn't he? That's why the two of you argued that day before you had your seizure."

There was no mistaking the pain she regarded in her father's eyes. "None of this is your fault, Papa. Edward is a vile, envious beast who has used everyone's guilt and love against them. Don't let him do this to you, Papa, or he has won!"

Geoffrey struggled to speak. "Is Victoria dead, Catherine?"

"The investigators Miles hired haven't found a trace of her and believe she's been dead for months. But after what I've learned tonight about Victoria and myself, I think they're wrong."

"You believe Victoria is alive?"

Catherine nodded. "She disappeared in the beginning

of November. If Victoria was dead, I wouldn't have dreamed about her. Though I cannot recall what the visions were exactly about, I remember feeling cold, hungry, and in pain. But most of all, I felt angry." She shook her head. "It wasn't me in those dreams, it was Victoria. My sister has to be alive to feel those things. After Miles captured me—"

"What?" Geoffrey gasped. "Miles captured you?"

Catherine gnawed on her lower lip. "Papa, I, ah, I'll explain all that later. I want you to know my dreams stopped early in December, but two nights ago, I had another one. It lasted only a few moments. Wherever she is, Victoria isn't alone. There's a man with her. I didn't see his face, but he has blond hair. She feels safe and very loved."

Geoffrey shrugged. "Perhaps it was only a dream, not her."

"I never have dreams like other people. They were always foreign to me and my way of living. Now I know why. The visions were Victoria's, not mine."

The clock in the hallway chimed twice.

"My goodness. Papa, it's two o'clock in the morning. We've been talking for hours. I have to get you to bed." Catherine tried to stand up.

Geoffrey surprised her with his strength when he wrapped his arms around her and stopped her from moving away from him. "No. I've waited too long to have you back. Talk to me, Catherine. Tell me about your life."

Catherine frowned. "But, Papa, that could take all night!"

"Fine," he replied, kissing her brow. "I have no other plans. Tell me about my Catherine."

She snuggled into his embrace. "If you insist. I'm a bit afraid you won't believe me, especially when I tell you about Lady Cat."

"Lady Cat, the pirate? Do you know her?"

Catherine took a deep breath. "Yes, I know her—but so do you, Papa."

Geoffrey was perplexed. "I do?"

"Before I begin, Papa, can you tell me if we have any Irish blood in our family?"

He nodded. "My mother's family were from Ireland. Why?"

Catherine swallowed hard. "Were there any rebels in our family tree?"

"None that I know of."

"Well . . . there is one now." She touched his chin with her finger. "Before you say anything, Papa, I want to tell you a story. 'Tis about the warrior Cuchulainn and how he met his defeat at the hand of Queen Medb of Connacht. It started when she led her army to capture the brown bull of Cooley."

"Bull?"

She patted his chest. "Now, Papa, don't interrupt. I'll get confused. Now where was I? Oh yes, now I remember," she announced, settling back against her father's shoulder. "The army was going to Cooley to steal that cow—"

Geoffrey smiled. "It was a bull, Catherine."

She nodded. "You're right, it was a bull. Have you heard this story before, Papa?"

Chapter 25

At nine o'clock the following morning, Lucy brought up the breakfast tray to the duke's suite. Using her key, she entered the bedroom, set the tray down on the table, and opened the drapes, as she did every day. Alarm quickened her pulse when she saw Geoffrey's bed hadn't been slept in and there was no sign of him or Victoria in the room.

Lucy was frantic until she noticed the door to the salon standing open. She ran across the floor, praying they'd be in there. The sight that met her eyes when she entered the salon would be etched in her memory forever.

Geoffrey was sitting in his chair with his daughter on his lap, cradled against his chest. Her long golden hair was loose, shimmering against the maroon velvet of her father's robe. His tawny head was bent down, leaning on hers. They were asleep.

As Lucy moved closer to them, Geoffrey looked up and smiled at her. "My baby is beautiful, is she not, Lucy?"

The rich sound of the duke's voice stunned Lucy. An

emotional lump gathered in her throat and stopped her response, so she nodded.

"My Catherine has come home to me. I couldn't let her go."

"Catherine? Who is Catherine, Geoffrey?" Lucy was so confused she never realized she'd used his given name.

Geoffrey gazed at his sleeping child. "This is my daughter, Catherine. We thought she died years ago. Victoria's still missing, but we'll find her. Catherine and I will bring her home."

Reading the bewilderment on Lucy's face, Geoffrey nodded to the loveseat beside him. "Sit with us, Lucy, and I'll tell you a fairy tale that actually came true."

For the better part of an hour, Lucy sat enthralled by his story of Catherine's life. By the time he finished, tears were running down her face. Her voice cracked with emotion.

"Oh, my, 'tis a miracle that you found each other at all."

Geoffrey reached over and brushed the tears from her cheeks. "Don't cry, sweet Lucy. Be happy for us."

Her bottom lip quivered. "I can't help it. I've always been rather high-strung at times like these, Your Grace."

His thumb brushed her lip. "Don't do that anymore, Lucy."

"Sorry, Your Grace. I'll try not to cry, I promise."

Smiling, he shook his head. "No, not that. A while ago, you called me by my name. I liked the way it sounded. My name is Geoffrey. Can you say it, Lucy?"

"O-of course I can, Geof-frey." Her mouth trembled.

He watched her lips. "Say it again, Lucy."

"Geoffrey."

He put his fingers through her auburn curls and gently pulled her face to his own. "I have longed to do this for months. I hope you don't mind, my dear."

Before Lucy could blink, Geoffrey brought her mouth

to his and kissed her. The kiss turned deep and tender. A moan came from his throat as he retreated from her lips.

Gazing at her, he smiled. "I knew you'd taste sweet."

Lucy could barely speak. "Sweet?"

He nodded and leaned toward her again. "Yes, very sweet, dear Lucy."

Catherine began to stir on Geoffrey's lap. Lucy fell back against the sofa agog as Catherine sat up and opened her eyes.

"Good morning. Papa, and to you, Lucy. If you'll excuse me, I have a few things to take care of." Standing up, she kissed Geoffrey's cheek and left the room.

Catherine closed the door behind her, smiling about what she had overheard. "Good for you, Papa. Lucy is a wonderful woman who cares for you, too. You both deserve happiness. If you can find it together, so much the better."

When she returned to her room, Catherine told Darcy about the revelations of the previous night. The maid was thrilled by the details of the story and relieved of some of her tension.

"I'm so glad someone else knows who you really are, my lady. It's been awful keeping your secret to myself."

Catherine was quick to caution her. "Remember, Darcy, I'm still Victoria to everyone else. Only Papa and Lucy know the truth. I want you to spend more time in my father's suite with us. You're a part of this intimate little group, and there's no reason why you shouldn't be involved in the celebration I have planned for today."

A festive atmosphere pervaded the master suite that afternoon. Lunch was more like a picnic, with sliced meats, rolls, vegetable salads, and fruit. A bottle of wine and a spice cake Darcy baked for the occasion rounded off the menu. A tablecloth was laid out on the floor in front of the fireplace in the pink salon for the meal.

Geoffrey smiled at the three women sitting on the floor around his wheelchair. "I'm a very lucky man. I've found my daughter Catherine and have high hopes Victoria will return to me, as well. I sit here surrounded by lovely ladies, eating good food, and looking forward to the future. Maybe I'm not as old and useless as I thought."

Catherine frowned. "Old and useless? I don't associate such words with you, Papa. Determined, handsome, and miraculous are far better descriptions."

"Miraculous?" He frowned. "I'm only a man, Catherine. Nothing special about that."

She waved her finger at him in a scolding manner. "Don't contradict me, Papa. When I arrived, you were quite helpless. In just a few weeks, you are up, using your hands, playing games, and enjoying life again. Need I remind you that until last night, you weren't even talking?"

"Perhaps until last night I had nothing important to say," Geoffrey teased. The expression on his face became serious as he took Catherine's hand and kissed her scarred palm. "This scar is the miracle. I damned that midwife for cutting you when you were born, but now I thank God she did." He kissed it again and closed her fingers over her palm.

Lucy shook her head. "I still can't believe you're Lady Cat. Can you really wield a blade and sail a ship like they say?"

While Catherine was telling Lucy and Darcy about her life as Lady Cat, Geoffrey began chuckling to himself.

"What's so funny, Papa?" Catherine asked.

"I was just picturing the old crones of the *ton* wielding a rapier or sailing a ship. If it ever came out that the next Duchess of Chatham had done all these things, every female of social standing would be competing with each other to do it, too. You'd start a new trend!"

"Papa, are people really so easily led in polite society?"

"They tend to be extremely jealous and competitive.

The *ton* has more than its share of backstabbers and scandal seekers.'' Geoffrey touched her cheek. "Don't be concerned, my baby. No one would dare accost you. I'm a very powerful man. With my influence and the stroke of a pen, I could destroy any of them, financially or otherwise.''

The mention of his wealth and authority brought a new fear to Catherine's mind. "Papa, you're not going to seek punishment for the O'Banyons, are you?''

"Quite the opposite, my dear. I'm looking forward to meeting your adopted family. I don't know how you came to be with them, but I owe the O'Banyons a huge debt for taking care of you. Once everything is resolved here in England, I'm going to Ireland so I can thank Sean O'Banyon personally for his efforts.''

When Darcy and Lucy took the remnants of their lunch down to the kitchen, Catherine sat on the sofa beside Geoffrey to talk. "Papa, I have something to tell you. It's about Miles. I want you to know that I, ah, that I . . .'' She shook her head and struggled for the right words.

Geoffrey took hold of her hand. "You're trying to tell me you and Miles have fallen in love, aren't you, Cat? You feel guilty because he was betrothed to your sister.''

She nodded, and he gave her hand a reassuring squeeze. "Miles and Victoria were good friends, but I never felt they were in love. When you came here posing as Victoria, I was confused by the changes I saw in the relationship. There was a passion between you that was lacking before. Now I know the truth, and I'm relieved. The right daughter is going to marry Miles Grayson.''

Catherine looked at her father with a shy smile on her face. "You're not just saying that to please me, are you?''

Geoffrey shook his head. "You and Miles will be good for each other. If Victoria was here, she'd think so, too.'' A cloud of uncertainty suddenly passed over his eyes. His smile dimmed, and Catherine knew the cause.

"Don't worry, Papa. Victoria is alive and well.'' She

leaned over and hugged him. "My instincts have never failed me, and they're telling me she'll be back soon."

After dinner, Geoffrey fell asleep and Lucy insisted Catherine return to her own suite to rest for the night.

As Darcy worked around the bedroom, Catherine brushed her hair and removed her betrothal ring. Putting it in the jewelry box on the vanity, she suddenly realized how much she missed Miles. The courier he'd promised to send with a message for her hadn't arrived that day, but she was confident one would be there in the morning. With that in mind, she went to the sitting room to write Miles a letter.

Besides wanting to share everything that had happened since his departure, Catherine wanted to tell him about the strange sense of foreboding that had haunted her for the past few hours. She'd experienced this kind of uneasiness before. On several occasions, the feeling had saved her ship from being captured. Another time, it warned her before she was ambushed by a rival captain during a raid.

Sitting at the writing desk, Catherine struggled to put her thoughts to paper. She started the letter four times, only to crumple it up and begin again. Darcy noticed her difficulties and made a suggestion.

"Perhaps you're trying to tell him too much, my lady. Why not tell him you have to see him? Doing it face to face could be easier."

Catherine sighed. "You know, Darcy, I think you're right. To tell Miles everything would take volumes. Explaining less would only confuse him."

"While you're writing your letter, my lady, I'll go down and make you a pot of tea and bring you some of those ginger cookies you like so much."

"Darcy, I believe you're trying to pamper me. The tea is a splendid idea, thank you."

As the young maid hurried to leave, Catherine stopped her. "Be sure to bring two cups with that pot of tea, Darcy. Can't have much of a tea party by myself, can I?"

Darcy was thrilled by her lady's invitation and was determined to make their refreshments very special. Upon entering the deserted kitchen, she saw Mrs. Oliver talking to someone by the door that led to the gardens. While she gathered the tray and tea things, the housekeeper came to offer her help.

"If you're making tea for Lady Victoria, the water is already boiling in the kettle, Darcy."

"Thank you, Mrs. Oliver." Darcy carefully put the measured tea leaves into the pot. "I want everything to be perfect for my lady. Are there any ginger cookies in the pantry?"

Mrs. Oliver nodded. "There s some fudge and a few fresh apple tarts in the larder as well—they're Lady Victoria's favorites. The cookies are in the crock right beside them."

Taking a plate into the cool pantry, Darcy selected two tarts from the tray. She took four large cookies from the crock and added them to the plate. As she reached for the fudge, she shook her head.

"I near forgot. My lady doesn't eat chocolate."

Darcy returned to the kitchen as Mrs. Oliver was pouring the steaming water into the teapot. "There you go, Darcy. The cream pitcher and the sugar bowl are on the tray. Is there anything else Lady Victoria requires this evening?"

Darcy looked at the tray. The housekeeper had put only a single cup and saucer on it beside a linen napkin and a spoon.

"Perhaps another napkin for the tarts. They're a bit sticky," the young maid explained. "My lady is writing letters in her sitting room, and she wouldn't want to get them soiled."

While Mrs. Oliver went to get another napkin, Darcy took a cup from the cabinet and hid it inside her apron pocket. *'Tis none of her affair if my lady wants to share her tea with me.*

A few minutes later, Darcy returned to her mistress with the well-stocked tray. "Have I got a surprise for you, my lady!"

Catherine saw the apple tarts and the expectant look on Darcy's face. "I'm not very hungry tonight but those pastries certainly smell good. Maybe I'll try half of one."

"Oh, my lady, I didn't bring a knife. I'll go down and fetch one right away."

"Don't bother, Darcy. I have something that will suffice." Catherine raised her skirts and removed the jeweled dagger from her garter.

Darcy gaped at the knife. "Do you always carry that with you, my lady?"

Catherine nodded. "Always. It has come to my rescue many times." After cutting the tart, she wiped the blade on her napkin and slipped the weapon into the pocket of her gown.

Darcy poured the tea and prepared a cup for both of them. "I see you haven't finished with your letter. While you're doing that, I'll turn down your bed and see to the hearth. I'll take my tea with me and give you some privacy."

Catherine watched Darcy close the door and she sighed out loud. Writing a letter to someone she loved wasn't an easy chore. Besides wanting to tell Miles how much she missed him, she also wanted to warn him. The fear of someone else reading her message gave her pause. An idea suddenly came to her.

She could write to him in Gaelic. Even if someone intercepted the letter, there was little chance they'd understand it.

As she wrote in the ancient language, Catherine concentrated on her spelling. It was important that the letter be perfect. Distracted by her chore, she ignored the slightly bitter taste of her tea. She prepared a second cup with extra sugar and cream, and drank it as well.

Within minutes, Catherine was yawning. Rubbing her eyes, she fought to focus on the paper before her. She must be more tired than she thought. Perhaps she'd rest her eyes and wait for Darcy to return.

Catherine was soon fast asleep with her head on the desk. She never heard the door to the hall open or saw the tall figure in black enter the room. The man in the greatcoat carefully lifted her up into his arms. Cradling her unconscious body, he carried her down the back stairs, through the kitchens, and out of the garden door to a large coach hidden behind the stables.

Leaning back against the leather seat, he wrapped the sable cape around Catherine and held her securely in his embrace.

"You have nothing to fear, my sleeping darling. I'll take good care of you. I've waited years for you, and now you're mine. My beautiful golden cat, I will never let you go."

Edward kissed Catherine's brow. Hugging her tightly, he settled back to rest as the coach sped off into the night.

Chapter 26

The early morning light found Miles racing back to Chatham with a dozen of his best fighting men. He'd been away from Catherine less than two days, but he needed to get back to her immediately.

Edward Damien had vanished. The men assigned to watch his house never saw him leave. No one knew anything was amiss until he failed to show up at the Carlisle offices for two days. When Mark went to Sedwick House, the butler told him the earl would be away on personal business for an undetermined amount of time.

It was soon learned Edward's fancy coach had been sold and replaced with a plain black one. He'd also exchanged his gray horses for a team of chestnut geldings. They were strong, serviceable horses, but not as distinctive as the grays had been.

Miles would have returned the night before, but Victoria's maid, Theresa, was missing. At first he assumed she'd fled with Edward, but a search of her room showed she'd taken nothing with her.

Garret and Jamie stayed in London to continue searching for the maid and Edward.

Miles and his men arrived at the Hall shortly before eight o'clock. Passing servants already busy with their duties, Miles ran up the stairs to Catherine's suite. He quietly entered the room, hoping to catch her in bed.

The room was dark and cool. There was no wood burning in the fireplace. Opening the draperies for light, Miles discovered the bed empty and not slept in. He opened the door to the sitting room and found no one in there, either.

Returning to the bedroom, he saw Darcy lying on the floor near the closet. He rushed over and lifted her onto the bed.

"Darcy, wake up! Where is your mistress?" Miles rubbed her cold hands. "Darcy, talk to me! Where's Catherine?"

The maid's words were slurred. "Writing letter . . . so sleepy . . ."

"Darcy, you must stay awake," Miles shouted. "I need to know where Catherine is. Wake up!"

Lucy came running into the room. "Miles, I heard you all the way down the hall. What's the matter?"

"Catherine's gone. I mean, Victoria is . . ."

Shaking her head, Lucy touched his shoulder. "I know she's Catherine. You don't have to pretend any longer."

"But how do you know? Did Catherine tell you?"

"Yes, Geoffrey and I know who she is. But that's not the issue now. We have to find her. I'll fetch a towel and some water to wash Darcy's face. That will help wake her up."

Darcy was soon awake, but drowsy as she spoke to Miles. "My lady was writing you a letter when I went to the kitchen to get our tea and dessert. When I returned, she hadn't finished it, so I came in here to stoke the fire. I recall going to the closet for Lady Catherine's robe, but nothing after that."

"Were the two of you up here alone?" Miles asked.

"Oh, yes. It was late. We were going to have a tea party and chat a bit. Too bad the tea was so bitter. It would've—"

Lucy interrupted her. "Darcy, did you say the tea was bitter? Where's the teapot?"

Darcy frowned. "It was on the desk next to Lady Catherine."

Miles brought the tray in from the sitting room. "The pot and Catherine's cup are empty. Where's your cup, Darcy? Did you drink it all?"

She shook her head. "I needed more sugar, so I left it on the dressing table while I finished my chores."

Lucy found the half-filled cup and smelled its contents. Dipping her finger into the brew, she touched it to the tip of her tongue. "I think it's laced with laudanum. I've taken care of many sick people, so I know the smell of it. The patients always complained about the bitterness. Who would do such a terrible deed?"

"Someone who wanted to capture a cat without getting scratched," Miles replied, starting toward the door. "Lucy, I want you and Darcy to check out these two rooms and see if any of Catherine's things are missing. I'll have the servants search the rest of the house and the grounds."

Within the hour, the house, barns, and outbuildings had been searched from top to bottom. Not a trace of Catherine was found. Miles ordered the stable hands and his men to mount up and explore the areas around Chatham. Being too anxious to stand about with nothing to do, he cut through the kitchens and rushed to the stables to fetch his own horse.

As he neared the stable, sunlight reflected off a shiny object that was partially hidden in the grass. Miles bent down and picked up Catherine's jeweled dagger. Holding it in his hand, he realized she was truly defenseless. She'd been drugged, carried off, and had no weapons to protect herself with.

From his position near the ground, he noted the deep

ruts in the soft earth. A large coach had recently parked there. He knew who the sizeable conveyance belonged to.

"Damn you, Edward Damien! When I get my hands on you, I'll send your worthless soul straight to hell!"

Miles returned to the house and found the duke in the pink salon. Although Lucy had said Catherine had told them the truth about herself, he dreaded facing his father's closest friend to admit his part in the deception. Before he could find the words to begin, Geoffrey spoke to him.

"You've no need to explain your actions, Miles." Geoffrey smiled. "By the look on your face, I can see that you didn't know about my miraculous recovery. The source of this miracle was my daughter."

Miles shook his head. "But she's not your daughter."

Geoffrey held up his hand. "Before you say another word, uncover the painting that's leaning against the wall in front of me. Then I will tell you a very interesting story."

Following his instructions, Miles lifted the sheet off the painting. In stunned amazement, he sat on the sofa beside the duke's wheelchair and stared at the portrait as Geoffrey told him about the twins, Evangeline, and the part Edward had played in their lives.

Miles sighed. "By God, Geoffrey, this is all so incredible. Catherine is your missing daughter. She and Victoria are twins. And if that's not enough, they've been sharing dreams of one another all their lives. Can it really be true?"

"Occurrences like these defy logic, but I've heard of such things before. According to Ella McKay, the nurse who raised me, my maternal grandmother, Ona, had an identical twin sister named Bridget. Ona and Bridget shared a bond that was almost magical. They communicated without words between them. When one was hurt, the other felt the pain. I thought Ella's stories of them were exaggerated, but after listening to Catherine, I'm more convinced than ever such things are possible."

"But none of this is going to help us find Catherine." Miles got up and paced the length of the salon. "She was drugged and carried away from this house. God only knows where Edward has taken her."

"How is Edward gaining access to my home? Is someone in this household helping him?"

Miles nodded. "Victoria suspected Mrs. Oliver was supplying Edward with information and was the one who stole the copy of the codicil to your will from the desk. Victoria also intercepted a letter your housekeeper sent to Edward. My people are checking into Mrs. Oliver's background. So far, we haven't found a motive for her actions."

"Mrs. Oliver has been in my employ for eighteen years. My solicitor hired her while I was in Ireland. It's hard to believe she'd do anything to hurt my family."

Miles shrugged. "According to Darcy, Mrs. Oliver was the only one in the kitchen with her last evening. That gave her the opportunity to put the laudanum in the teapot. If Darcy hadn't taken a cup of her own, we might not have known how Catherine was drugged. I'm surprised your daughter wasn't put off by the bitterness of the tainted brew Darcy complained of."

Geoffrey's brow arched. "You say the tea was bitter?"

"Yes. Laudanum has a vile taste that's difficult to mask. Cat was either too distracted to notice or simply added more sugar to her cup when she drank it."

The duke balled his fists angrily in his lap. "By the rood, it all makes sense! How could I have been so gullible?"

"What are you talking about, Geoffrey?"

"I believe my brother has used this drug on me as well. If I'm right, Edward killed his wife and employed me as his alibi."

Miles sat beside him. "I've had my own thoughts on

Edward's involvement in her death. Tell me what happened."

"Around eleven o'clock on the night of Lorelei's murder, Edward served me tea as a forfeit for losing the game. I remarked on its bitterness, but he blamed it on the blend. I fell asleep in my chair. Something woke me and I noticed the clock on the mantel said one-thirty. I nudged Edward, who was napping beside me and we went up to bed."

"That's less than three hours, hardly enough time for him to commit the deed and return to Chatham," Miles pointed out.

"Plenty of time—if he changed the clocks to fool me and used a good strong horse to ride cross-country. Victoria's stallion Black Magic was bred for such strength and endurance. He could make the trip without building up a lather." Geoffrey frowned. "As a matter of fact, I'd bragged to Edward about that horse earlier that day. What a fool I was!"

Miles patted Geoffrey's arm. "Don't deride yourself for being a caring brother. It may interest you to know that in the case of Lorelei's murder, Edward was the biggest fool of all."

He told Geoffrey what his investigation of Lorelei and Edward had uncovered. In a matter of minutes, the duke knew of their marriage contract, the thirty thousand pounds, and the details of the countess's last will and testament.

The duke shook his head in disbelief. "Her estate would have been worth millions. Did she give it all away?"

"Apparently. She also mortgaged all the Sedwick-entailed properties. Edward inherited that paltry trust fund, a title, and an estate that will be claimed by creditors if he cannot redeem it in one year. Lorelei must have hated him to do that."

"They deserved one another, and I think—" Geoffrey stopped talking as Lucy entered the salon.

"I know the two of you are concerned over Catherine's whereabouts, but you must take time to eat. If you like, I can have dinner served in here." Lucy touched the duke's cheek. "You're a bit pale. I hope you're not overtaxing yourself."

"Lucy, I'm fine, though I'm near to starving. Are you trying to weaken me with hunger?" he teased.

Waving a finger, Lucy scowled at him. "Geoffrey Carlisle, I'll not take the blame because you're hungry. I told you to eat breakfast, but you refused."

Geoffrey grabbed her offending finger and kissed it. "I usually don't like being scolded like a little boy, but I'll forgive you in this instance."

"As long as you act like a youngster, I'm going to treat you like one," she retorted, trying to suppress a smile.

"I hope that's a promise, sweet Lucy," Geoffrey called as she turned to leave.

Lucy looked over her shoulder as she went through the door and grinned. "You can bet your last farthing on it, Your Grace!"

The friendly banter between Geoffrey and Lucy reminded Miles how badly he missed Catherine. In a short time, she'd become the most important person in his life. Not knowing where she was or how to find her was more than he could bear. Telling the duke he needed to clean up before dinner, he headed down the corridor toward his room—but that wasn't his destination.

Miles went into the sitting room, where he and Catherine had shared many happy hours since they arrived at Chatham. Darcy had left a fire burning in the hearth and lit the candlesticks on the desk as though she expected her mistress to return at any moment. He sat in the chair beside the writing desk.

The familiar scent of her perfume, combined with Catherine's essence, soothed him. He looked down at the desk and found the letter she'd been writing the night before.

Picking up the sheets of parchment, he read her last message to him.

At first, he was shocked to see Catherine had written in Gaelic, but soon understood her need for its use. The ancient language provided her the privacy she needed as she bared her heart to him with her words. Miles was nearly overwhelmed by the intensity of the love that emanated from the paper in his hand. Her thoughts and emotions clearly mirrored his own.

On the second page, she hinted at news and asked him to come home immediately. As he continued reading, he discovered a far more important reason for his return.

Catherine explained something was going to happen to her. She didn't know exactly when or how, but she sensed it would be soon.

At this point in the letter, Catherine must have begun feeling the effects of the drug, Miles decided, because her handwriting became slack. He then realized she'd started writing in English. Her final sentence made absolutely no sense to him at all.

It read: *The guardian of the property is close at hand.*

At dinner, Miles told Geoffrey and Lucy about Catherine's letter. He read aloud the parts pertaining to her fear that something was going to happen and the advice she'd given him. He also read the last sentence to them, hoping they could make sense of it.

"Cat knew she was in danger, but had no idea what she was going to face," Miles told them.

Lucy frowned. "She may have known more than you think. Could you repeat that last line for me?"

"The guardian of the property is close at hand." Miles shook his head and turned to Lucy. "Perhaps Cat was groggy when she wrote that. It doesn't fit with the rest of her message."

Lucy nodded. "I think it does. The answer, I believe, is in Victoria's name book. I'll fetch it straightaway from her suite."

Watching her leave, Miles was puzzled. "Name book? What's she referring to, Geoffrey?"

"Victoria became fascinated with name origins and their meanings when she was a child. She keeps a journal of them. For example, my given name, Geoffrey Derek, means 'God's peaceful ruler of the people.' Last year she told me your name, Miles Trelane, means 'soldier of the evening star,' while Grayson is 'the judge's son.' Her own name, Victoria Roxanne, means 'victory at dawn.' Quite interesting. isn't it?"

Miles smiled. "Knowing how analytical and curious Torie is, I can see why the topic would hold her attention."

Lucy rushed in with the large leather bound journal. "I knew I'd heard that term before." Placing the opened book on the table, she pointed to the page. "It says here 'guardian of the property' is the Anglo-Saxon definition for Edward."

Geoffrey was astonished. "That means Catherine was somehow aware Edward was coming here last night."

"It's not the first time, either. On the day of the meeting, Cat saw a coach approaching the house. She knew it was Edward without seeing him."

"The more I learn about my daughter, Catherine, the easier it is for me to believe she's right about Victoria's coming home," Geoffrey admitted, his voice filled with awe. "But I won't take chances, Miles. We must continue looking for them, as well as for my brother. I'm counting on your help."

The unconcealed emotions Miles saw in Geoffrey's eyes tore at his own heart. It instilled in him a need to give this man the justice and the peace of mind he craved.

Miles nodded. "Since the search locally hasn't shown any results in finding Catherine, I'm leaving for London without further delay. From there I'll spearhead an all-out hunt to find Edward. He's taken my best friend and the woman I love." Miles took hold of Geoffrey's hand. "I swear to you, sir, even if it costs me my final breath, I'll see Edward pay for the turmoil he has caused."

Chapter 27

Justin Prescott thought himself the happiest of men. Though married less than a month, he couldn't imagine life without his beautiful wife. She was his reason to get up each morning, just as her passion drew him eagerly to her bed every night. The five years he'd waited were a small price to pay for the treasure that was his.

His musings were interrupted when Erin sat beside him on the parlor sofa with her embroidery basket. "Now that dinner is over, I can get started on sorting out these threads. It will keep me busy so I don't have to think about you and my girl leaving in the morning. I suppose you're anxious to get back to your patients in England."

"Well, I have been away five weeks. My assistant, Simon, is a fine doctor, but he probably thinks I've deserted him."

A bark of male laughter drew Justin's attention across the room to where his wife was playing chess with her father. Colin and Padraic stood near the table, watching.

She looked happy sitting there talking to them, but Justin knew how concerned she was about not regaining any more of her memory. Her inability to tell them about Rory was weighing heavily on her mind.

After taking them back to England, Sean O'Banyon was going to begin an extensive search for Rory. With a generous bounty still being offered for the death or capture of the Irish Hawk, Justin prayed the once notorious outlaw wouldn't need to sacrifice his own life to find his son.

Sean's laughter filled the room. "Come along, Cat. Admit it. I've got you in check. Your king cannot escape."

"Don't rush me, Da." Victoria stared at the chessboard, propping her chin up with her right hand. "You haven't got me in checkmate yet. There must be a way out of this."

"By the by, while you and Justin were out today, old Mick delivered your necklace. He said the new chain is thicker and shouldn't break like the last one." Sean took it from his coat pocket and held it out to her. "Mick takes a long time to get things done, but he's an excellent goldsmith."

"You'll not distract me now, Da. Just give me the necklace and I'll look at it after I have won this game."

Victoria's eyes never left the board as she put her hand out to him and took the necklace. Suddenly, Sean grabbed her hand and looked closely at her palm.

"Where is it? Where's that bloody scar?"

Frightened by the harsh tone of his words, Victoria jerked her arm back. She held her hand to the light to search for the scar he was asking about, but her gaze fixed on the pendant. A moment later she spoke in a hushed voice.

"This isn't my pendant."

Sean bolted to his feet. "And you aren't my daughter! Who the devil are you, and where is Catherine?"

Justin rushed to his wife's side. "Stop shouting at her, O'Banyon!" Kneeling beside her, he found her pale, her eyes glazed and unseeing. "My God, she's in shock! What in the hell did you do to her?"

"She isn't Catherine," Sean explained, pointing at Victoria. "Cat has a nasty scar across the palm of her left hand, and it's not there. When I handed her Cat's necklace, she admitted it wasn't hers. If she's not my daughter, who is she?"

"Shouting isn't going to help matters. Be quiet! Better yet, leave the room," Justin ordered.

Erin took hold of Sean's arm and tried to steer him out of the parlor, but he refused to go. "I'll not be leaving until I get some answers."

She nodded. "Fine. But you will sit on the sofa with me. With that temper of yours, you'll be scaring the poor child."

Grumbling, Sean sat beside Erin. Colin and Padraic stepped back to watch.

Justin pulled out a chair and sat in front of Victoria. In a calm voice he began to question her. "You've recovered your memory, haven't you?" At her nod, he asked, "Are you Catherine O'Banyon?"

Still staring at the pendant, she shook her head. "No. I'm Lady Victoria Roxanne Carlisle. My father is Geoffrey Carlisle, the Duke of Chatham."

"Chatham is quite a distance from where I found you, Victoria. How did you get so far away from home?"

"A few months ago, my father and his brother, Edward, got into a terrible row. My uncle did something to hurt our family and Papa disinherited him. Before I could discover what Edward had done, my father suffered a brain seizure and nearly died."

At her silence, Justin took her right hand in his. "What happened after that?"

"I discovered Edward was conspiring against my father, so I took measures to protect Papa. I never realized my uncle would come after me."

Victoria closed her eyes. Tears flowed down her cheeks. "One night, my coach was attacked by two men. They murdered my driver and abducted me. My pendant was torn from my neck to prove to my uncle I was dead, and he paid them. But the men had a different plan. I was going to be sold as a slave in the far east so they could double their profits."

Her fingers clenched around Justin's hand. "They imprisoned me in a hovel near Bristol. Clive was a massive brute who tied me up and tormented me about the vile things that were going to happen to me. I eventually convinced the other man, Andy, that my father would reward him for returning me home. But Clive caught us escaping and began hitting Andy. He sent him away, threatening to kill him if he came back."

Justin could see her struggling to swallow the tightness in her throat. "I'm listening. What happened next?"

"Clive started hurting me. He tore at my clothes and beat me. I was so scared . . . in such pain . . . he bit my breasts and forced me down onto the table. He was going to . . ." Blinking the tears from her eyes, she shook her head. "But I had to stop him. There was a knife under my back. I got the knife in my hand and I stabbed him again and again until he stopped hurting me. There was blood everywhere . . . all over me."

Justin took Victoria in his arms when she was overcome by her recollections. Over the top of her head, he saw Sean comforting his wife as she cried for Victoria's pain. Even Colin and Padraic seemed moved by the things they'd heard.

"You're safe with me, darling," Justin assured her. "No one will ever hurt you again."

Victoria shook her head against his shoulder. "But I killed that man. I've never hurt anyone in my life, but I killed him."

"He was a cruel beast who deserved to die. My biggest regret is that I wasn't there to kill him for you." Tilting her chin with his hand, Justin kissed her quivering lips.

"When we get back to Windell, I'll make arrangements to take you to Chatham to see your father. We can send a courier to him first so your family and friends will know you're all right. Is there anyone else we should notify?"

Suddenly, Victoria gasped and pulled away from him. "Miles must be out of his mind worrying about me!"

"Who is Miles?" Justin asked. "Your brother?"

Her gaze dropped to the floor. "No. Miles Trelane Grayson, Viscount Ryland, is my betrothed. We're engaged to be married."

Justin was stunned. "Engaged to be married?"

Padraic yelled, "That's the man who owns the *Foxfire!* He'll know where to find Catherine and Rory."

Victoria was quickly surrounded by Sean, Padraic, and Colin asking her questions. She answered what she could. "Miles and I own a shipping firm based in London. Several months ago, Rory attacked one of our ships. Miles took the *Foxfire* to Ireland to find him. Other than that, I don't know anything else. Until I reach Chatham, I won't be able to help you find Catherine or Rory."

Sean moved toward the door. "Tomorrow we leave as planned, but our destination is Chatham. Padraic, let's get to the ship and go over the charts. Colin, come along and take notes for our journey." The three men left the house.

Erin hugged Victoria. "I somehow feel God had a special purpose for bringing you here. You will always be welcome in our home."

"I don't believe your husband will agree with you. He seems to be quite angry with me," Victoria admitted sadly.

"Angry?" Erin smiled and shook her head. "Not at all. Sean is naught but eager to find our children. Your da and mam are probably just as concerned about you."

"My mother died five years ago, and I don't even know if my father's still alive. I'm liable to go home and discover I really am alone."

Putting her arms around Victoria, Erin hugged her.

"You won't be alone, dearling. I'm going to England with you. Maybe 'tis what the Lord intended. My girl is missing, so He brought you to us to care for. I'll not desert you."

Victoria looked around the room. "Where's Justin? Is he mad at me as well?"

"Not mad, but perhaps a bit shocked. 'Tis not every day a man discovers his wife is betrothed to marry someone else."

Victoria sighed. "Or that his wife isn't the woman he thought she was."

A few minutes later, Victoria entered their bedroom and found Justin sitting in the chair near the fireplace. As he stared into the flames, she quietly walked to his side.

"Justin, we need to talk."

"I know. I've been sitting here trying to find the right words to say. I've always been a man of honor, but I simply cannot do it this time, and that is final!"

Justin's terse words made Victoria flinch. She fought to keep her response soft and calm. "I'm sorry. When you find Catherine, I won't stand in the way. Because of my memory loss, we can have our marriage annulled and you can marry her."

Without warning, Justin stood up and grabbed her shoulders. "I don't care what your name is or how bloody important your father or this Miles is. You're my wife, Victoria, and I will not let you go!" Pulling her to him, he kissed her.

Victoria gazed up into Justin's determined face. "I don't want to leave you. I thought you and Catherine—"

His mouth claimed hers in another passionate kiss. When he eased back, he caressed her cheek with his hand. "You are my wife, and I love you very much."

"Oh, Justin, I love you, too. I was so afraid you wouldn't want me." Victoria put her arms around his neck and rested her head on his shoulder. "Miles and I have been friends for many years. We never had the love I've found with you. I agreed to his proposal because it seemed to be the right thing to do. Our families were happy and it was safe."

"You were going to marry a man because it was safe?"

She nodded. "For a long time, I thought my love was jinxed. Everyone I loved was taken away from me. First I lost my mother. Then I fell in love with Miles' brother, Adam, only to lose him in a duel two days before our wedding. Even my love for Papa wasn't safe. He nearly died from a seizure. But Miles was never harmed by my jinx. As long as I cared for him only as a friend, I thought he'd be fine." Shaking her head, she sighed. "Thinking back now, it seems so silly."

"Your pain at losing those you cared for caused the fear, but our love will banish it forever." Putting his arm around Victoria, Justin guided her to the bed and sat down beside her. "I'm sorry you had to relive that terrible attack. What spurred your memory?"

She opened her hand and showed him the heart-shaped pendant. "All my life, I've worn a pendant like this one, only mine is engraved with the letter 'V.' My father had it made for me when I was a baby, and I believed it was one of a kind. But on the night I was abducted, I made a startling discovery, and this pendant is a part of it."

Victoria told Justin how she'd found the portrait in her mother's salon and her suspicions that the other child was a twin sister her parents had never told her about.

"Papa was too ill to answer my questions, so I decided to visit Miles' mother and father. They'd been my parents' closest friends. If I'd had a twin, they would have known about her. I was so hurt and confused I took no precautions when I left home that night. My coach was attacked, and you know what happened."

Justin hugged her. "If Catherine is your sister, how on

earth did she come to be with the O'Banyons? Sean doesn't strike me as a man who would steal babies. He loves all his children, and Cat has always been his favorite.''

"I'm positive the Hawk isn't guilty of kidnapping," Victoria admitted. "My intuition tells me he's a very caring, protective person who's concerned with her well being. That's why I agreed to help him. Once we get to Chatham, I'm sure we'll be able to find out what became of Rory and Catherine.''

Justin laughed. "I hope your friend Miles is careful around Cat. She can handle a rapier like no one I've ever seen and would skin him alive if he crossed her.''

"Don't worry about Miles. Knowing him as I do, I'm sure he'll find a way to disarm her—or perhaps charm her.''

"For your sake, Victoria. I hope you're right. It wouldn't do having your sister and your best friend at odds with each other.'' Justin kissed her brow. "You and Catherine are sisters. Is it true, or are we just trying to rationalize the situation?''

She shrugged. "It's the only thing that makes sense. We look alike—so much so that you and the O'Banyons thought I was Cat. Then there are the pendants and the portrait of my mother and the twin babies. I wish there was another way of . . .'' Victoria's lips curved in a knowing smile. "The birthmark. Every child born in the Carlisle family during the past hundred years has one. If Catherine has one, it proves she's my sister.''

"We'll have to wait until morning to find out," Justin told her. "It's a bit late to go knocking on the Hawk's door.''

"Sean went to the ship to go over his charts for our voyage to Chatham and Erin's busy packing because she's coming with us, too.'' Victoria's eyes burned slightly. "Erin doesn't want me to go home alone.''

"As long as I live, you'll never be alone, Victoria.

Together we can face whatever the future holds." As Justin bent to kiss her, someone tapped on the bedroom door.

They were surprised to find Sean waiting on the other side. "Victoria, I'd be obliged if you'd come to the parlor for a few minutes. There are a few matters I want to discuss with you that won't wait until morning."

Telling Justin she'd return soon, Victoria followed Sean downstairs. They sat in the same chairs they'd used earlier and stared intently at one another.

Sean cleared his throat and began to speak. "First, I want to apologize for the wretched way I treated you tonight. I don't rightly know what came over me."

"You don't have to explain. You love Catherine, and when you discovered I wasn't her, you felt betrayed and hurt. I'm sorry. I never meant to cause you such pain."

Reaching over, Sean stroked her cheek. "No, little one. I'll not have you apologizing to me. You didn't know who you were. We told you you were Cat, so we were the ones at fault. I knew something was amiss, but I thought it was the memory loss that caused me to have doubts about you."

He cupped her face in his large calloused hand and held it toward the flickering light from the fireplace. "My gut's telling me you and Cat are more than a coincidence. I know her face and I'm looking at it now. You're identical, right down to the stubborn lower lip and those flashing green eyes."

"Does Catherine have a birthmark?"

Sean smiled. "Aye, she does. 'Tis the cutest thing you can imagine. On the left side of her chest, Cat has a crescent-shaped mark that looks like a quarter moon."

Victoria pulled aside the bodice of her gown and the trim of her camisole to expose the top portion of her left breast. "Her mark looks like this, doesn't it?" Sean nodded silently as she straightened her bodice. "I was born with this mark, just like my twin sister Catherine was."

After telling Sean about the portrait, the pendants, and the rest of the information she'd put together her last night at Chatham, she asked him the inevitable next question.

"How did you get Catherine? You're not a man who steals babies, but you *would* rescue one. Is that how it happened?"

Leaning back in his chair, Sean nodded. " 'Twas a stormy night. My crew and I were delivering goods up the coast. An old woman came running toward me bearing a precious gift, a baby girl whose family had been murdered. Frightened and in great pain, the old woman knew she was dying, but her only concern was for the child she called Catherine. Before she passed on, I swore I'd keep the babe safe from harm and I did. Cat became my daughter. Erin and I raised her as our own. Colin and Rory thought she was their blood kin."

For almost an hour, Sean told Victoria about the sister she had never known. As he spoke, she was very aware of how much this man and his family loved Catherine. She was an important part of their lives, and Victoria found herself a little envious of her sister.

Neither realized they were no longer alone. Erin and Justin had been quietly watching them talk about Catherine. As Sean began a new story, his wife walked to his side and decided to interrupt.

"Hawk, if you start on how Cat got you to give her that ship, you two will be up all night," Erin chided him. "If we're to leave at first light, I suggest you delay this conversation for another time."

"Aw, Erin, I was only . . ." Sean's brow furrowed with doubt. "Are my ears deceiving me, or did I hear you say *we*, madam?"

"That's what I said, Hawk. I'll not sit at home while the rest of my family's running about doing God knows what."

"But, Erin, you don't know about Catherine."

"Yes, I do. Justin told me everything. I may not have

given birth to these girls, but that doesn't change a thing. I care too much for them not to go along." Erin playfully tugged on his beard. "Time to find your bed, Sean. I'll not have my first voyage in twenty-five years begin with a captain sleeping on duty." She turned to Victoria and kissed her forehead.

"Don't worry, darlin'. With the O'Banyons on your side, you're sure to win. 'Tis the luck of the Irish, I think." Bidding Justin good night, she started up the stairs. "Sean Michael O'Banyon, you have two minutes to say your piece. Then I expect you up where you belong."

"Aye, aye, sir!" Sean teased as he stood up and watched her ascend the steps. "That woman can issue orders like an admiral!"

Sean drew Victoria out of her seat and enveloped her in his embrace. "I'll do all I can to get you and your sister back together again. It may take me a while to remember she isn't my daughter, so I hope you can be patient with this old man, Victoria."

She kissed his whiskered cheek. "Although my sister was separated from our family, I'm very glad she was part of yours. I know my father will be grateful to you and your wife for all you've done for Catherine. Good night, Hawk."

"Sweet dreams, little one." Kissing her forehead, he nodded to Justin as he walked out of the room. "See you in the morning, Prescott."

Justin put his arm around Victoria and led her back to their room. "You're exhausted, sweetheart. Let me help you undress and get you into bed."

Yawning, Victoria nodded silently, accepting his aid as he removed her clothes. When he tied the ribbons on her nightgown, he smiled at her sleepy face.

"Well, wife, I must admit that since the night I found you on the road, my life has never been dull. Nor have I ever been so happy."

With her eyes half closed, she patted his arm. "That's

nice of you to say, Justin. But we have a problem regarding our marriage. Because I signed Catherine's name on the church documents, they're not legal. Would you consider marrying me again?" Before she could say more, she yawned.

"Rest assured, sweetheart, I'd gladly marry you ten times if I were guaranteed the same kind of wedding night after each ceremony." Justin gently pushed her back onto the bed and covered her with a quilt. "If you stop talking and go to sleep, I might even propose to you all over again in the morning."

When he joined her in bed a few minutes later, Victoria snuggled close to him and heaved a contented sigh. "Don't forget, Justin, you owe me a proposal in the morning."

"Whatever it takes, darling, whatever it takes." Kissing her brow, he quickly fell asleep with Victoria in his arms.

As the *Cat's Cradle* made its way toward the channel and the east coast of England, Victoria adopted several of her sister's likes and habits. She enjoyed the freedom of wearing britches and loose blouses. Even her lifelong battle with seasickness disappeared, and Victoria discovered how much she liked sailing. She also came to appreciate Catherine's relationship with Colin.

Though Colin had been upset when he learned the truth about Catherine, he swore his love for her would never change. In his heart of hearts, she would always be his little sister. His loyalty only confirmed Victoria's earlier assessment of his fine character. She saw a great deal to admire in Colin. While they stood on deck watching the sunset on the third day of their voyage, Victoria made him an offer.

"We once spoke about your family starting a legitimate business. Until they're ready to do it, would you be interested in coming to work for me? You could learn a lot about shipping.''

"I'd love working for you, Victoria. Will I have to move to England?''

"Perhaps for a year or so, but I've been thinking about opening an office and docking facilities in Ireland—providing, of course, I'm able to find someone who can run the operation for me. Are you interested?''

He smiled broadly. "Of course I am. Thank you for the offer. I swear I won't let you down.''

When Colin hurried off to tell his parents of his new employment, Justin joined Victoria at the rail.

"The joy on Colin's face tells me he's accepted the position with your company, but it doesn't surprise me. From what Catherine wrote to me, Colin was never overly fond of being an outlaw."

Victoria put her arms around Justin's waist and leaned into his embrace. "Colin's a very clever young man. With the proper clothes and introductions, he should do very well as a gentleman in commerce.''

Justin chuckled. "I wonder how long it will take me to become accustomed to the fact that my wife is a businesswoman. I suppose it's far easier than being married to a former pirate.''

She playfully poked his midriff with her fingers. "You should be pleased I followed my father's path and not my night musings. All my life I've had the most bizarre dreams where I sailed ships, dueled with swords, rode horses astride, and . . .'' A thought suddenly left Victoria silent.

Justin pulled back from her to see her face. "What's the matter? Are you having another memory lapse?''

After a second, her gaze focused on him. "Justin, I had a dream about you. I told you I remembered kissing you several years ago. You teased me because my eyes were open. But you never said that to me, you said it to Catherine. All those times, I wasn't dreaming. I was watching my sister's life."

A feeling of dread swept over Victoria. "I had a dreadful nightmare last night. But it wasn't a dream at all. It was Catherine." She put her hands over her face. "Dear God, please don't let it be true!"

"What did you see, Victoria?"

Lowering her hands, she shook her head. "It's too late. Edward has Catherine. My uncle was holding her in his arms, telling her about the plans he had for their future together. Cat wants to escape, but she hasn't the strength to fight him. She can't even speak. What has Edward done to her?"

Justin put his arms around Victoria and tried to console her. "Maybe it was only a dream. You've had a great deal on your mind in the past few days, sweetheart."

"But I never dream about me. Only those crazy visions of sailing, fighting, and such. I only see Catherine's life, never my own." Resting against his shoulder, she shivered. "Oh, Justin, what should we do?"

He stroked her back with his hand in a comforting motion. "We can't tell the others about this just yet. If you're wrong, it could cause a panic. When we get to Chatham, we can decide what to do next. In the interim, we'll write down any dreams you have. If you're correct, the visions might help us find Catherine."

As the fiery sun set on the horizon, Justin held Victoria in his arms and let her cry.

Chapter 28

"Geoffrey, I don't want to leave you alone with that vile woman," Lucy protested. "You know as well as I do Mrs. Oliver cannot be trusted."

The duke set the latest message from Miles on his desk. "You're worrying for naught, Lucy. She's not likely to accost me here in my own library. Besides having a houseful of servants about, Miles sent John and Tom back here to see to my safety."

Crossing her arms over her chest, Lucy perched on the chair beside his desk and sighed. "I see my argument is falling on deaf ears. Why should I bother being concerned over your well being if you're not?"

"Stop pouting. I feel wonderful, stronger than ever. As a matter of fact, I have a little surprise for you. Stay right there."

Lucy watched Geoffrey push his wheelchair back from his desk. Placing his feet on the floor, he pulled himself up onto his feet. With a concerted effort, he took several labored steps toward her. When she saw he was wobbling, she leaped from her seat and caught him in her arms.

Resting her cheek on his chest, she braced herself so he wouldn't fall. "This is a marvelous surprise, Geoffrey, but you mustn't rush yourself. I won't have you getting hurt."

Lucy then realized he wasn't wavering. He was standing perfectly still. She looked up into his smiling face as his arms encircled her and held her tightly against him.

"My sweet Lucy, you are such a petite minx! I've waited a long time to hold you like this. It was well worth the effort, I assure you." Bending his head, he placed a gentle kiss on her lips. "You really are a tiny little beauty," he teased.

She scowled at him. "I'm big enough to handle the likes of you, Geoffrey Carlisle! How dare you frighten me in this manner? I thought you were going to fall!"

"I have, sweet Lucy. I've fallen for you." He caught her lips in a lingering kiss. When he began to sway on his feet, Lucy knew he wasn't joking any longer.

Carefully, she helped him into his chair. "Promise me you won't try walking again when you're alone. It's going to take time to rebuild your strength, and I won't have you injured because you lack patience." She saw him smiling. "Why are you grinning? I'm very serious about this."

"Lucy, you're a treasure! I admit you're right to scold me, but I promise you within a week I'll be out of this chair for good."

Brushing back a lock of tawny hair from his face, Lucy sighed. "With your determination, I'm sure you will, Geoffrey." She kissed his cheek. "All right, let's get on with your plan. I'm to send Mrs. Oliver in here on the pretext of going over the household accounts with you."

Geoffrey nodded. "And while I keep her occupied, you and Tom will search her room. John will stand guard at the library door. If you find anything, have him alert me, and I'll send Mrs. Oliver on an errand while you bring it in here."

Once Mrs. Oliver entered the library, Lucy and Tom went to her room and began hunting through her possessions. The search of her closet, dressers, and writing desk was fruitless. As Tom looked under the bed and turned the mattress, Lucy gazed around the room. It was large and airy, with several windows. The furniture was dark and polished. But something about the chamber wasn't right. Suddenly, she knew what it was.

There were no mirrors or personal items in the room, no keepsakes or souvenirs on the tables, no correspondence in the desk—nothing to let anyone know about the inhabitant of this room. There were no combs or toilet articles on the dresser, and even the Bible Mrs. Oliver carried to church every Sunday was nowhere to be seen.

Lucy pushed back the drapes and sat on the cushioned window seat while she perused the chamber again, looking for a hiding place she may have missed. The window seat was built high, and her short legs didn't quite touch the floor.

Their hunt was proving a failure. In frustration, she swung her foot back in anger and hit the panel of the window seat with her heel. A loud echo resounded all over the room.

Tom jerked up from beneath the bed. "What was that?"

"Sorry, Tom. My temper got the best of me and I accidentally kicked the . . ." Lucy forgot her embarrassment as she recognized the discovery she had just made. "Beneath this seat it's hollow. That's why it echoed. I wonder if Mrs. Oliver is clever enough to make use of this. Give me a hand with this cushion and see if the top can be raised, Tom."

A moment later, they found a cache of items inside. The

red leather-bound Bible came out first. Next they removed two wooden boxes. One contained letters and documents. The other held combs, hairpins, brushes, a bottle of dark liquid, and an expensive gold hand mirror.

As per their arrangements, Lucy and Tom carried the boxes down to the library after Geoffrey sent Mrs. Oliver to retrieve a list of household repairs she kept in the kitchen. With the two men guarding their privacy, Geoffrey began going through the papers first.

"There are several official documents. Here's a marriage certificate and two deeds for property in Dorset and Surrey. According to this baptismal record, her given name is Jessica Christine Chamberlain and she's fifty-seven years old."

Lucy's brow rose with surprise. "She has very little gray hair. I thought she was younger than that."

Geoffrey showed her the paper in his hand. "This marriage certificate shows she married her husband when she was thirty years old. He died a year later. Rather sad to think she waited so long for marriage only to lose him that quickly."

Lucy began searching the other box. "Why does she keep her toilet articles hidden?" Picking up the brush, she examined the dark bristles. "It looks like this brush is coated with some sort of oily substance." She rubbed her fingers on the bristles.

"Look, Geoffrey, it's coming off on my fingers. It's brown and sticky, and smells like tea and something else. Vinegar, I think. Mrs. Oliver must use this on her hair to keep it dark. But she never struck me as being a vain woman. She doesn't use lip rouge or color on her face. Even her hairstyle is rather dowdy, pulled back into that big bun."

Geoffrey shook his head. "The more I learn about the woman, the less I know. She's such an enigma."

"How can a woman be so vain that she colors her hair but lives in a room totally devoid of mirrors? The only one

I found was this beautiful hand mirror." Lucy gave the expensive looking glass to Geoffrey.

Taking it from her, he turned it over and studied the ornate scroll work engraved on the back of it.

"How can this be?" he gasped. "I haven't seen this mirror since I was a little boy. It was part of a set my father gave to my mother when they were wed. See, Lucy, the engraving matches the brush, comb, and tray on Victoria's dressing table."

"Perhaps Mrs. Oliver found it somewhere in the house."

"No, I lost it when I went to London to visit my father. The set was one of the few things I had from my mother. When I traveled to town, I always packed one piece of it with my clothes. My father never spent time with me, and I tended to be afraid of him. Having something that belonged to my mother gave me comfort."

"How old were you when you lost it?"

Placing the mirror on the desk, Geoffrey thought for a moment. "I was seven years old. Ella had taken me to London to see my father for my birthday. I was there a week, but he never spoke to me. Ella explained that my father was a lonesome man who couldn't help being so miserable. One night, I awoke to the sound of drunken laughter coming from his suite. I peeked into his room and saw him in bed with a woman."

Lucy raised a cynical brow. "He wasn't so miserable then."

Geoffrey sighed. "The next morning I begged Ella to take me home. I was too ashamed to face my father. That's the only time I recall hearing him laugh."

His painful recollections ceased when a knock sounded on the door. Lucy placed the boxes on the floor behind the desk before she let the housekeeper into the library.

Mrs. Oliver moved to the desk to present the paper she was carrying to the duke. "Here's the list you requested. Do you require anything else, Your Grace?"

He nodded toward the chair. "Have a seat, Mrs. Oliver. I have a few other matters to discuss with you."

"Could we delay this until after lunch, Your Grace? Cook is having a problem with . . ." Mrs. Oliver's voice faded to a whisper when she saw the gold mirror under the duke's hand on the desk. The list she was holding fell to the floor.

Geoffrey picked up the mirror and used it to point at the chair. "Sit down, madam. As I said before, we have a few other matters to discuss."

Taking her seat, Mrs. Oliver stared coldly at Geoffrey. Her head was held high as he began his interrogation.

"Why are you helping my brother Edward? I know you stole the codicil and gave it to him. You sent him letters warning him of Victoria's visit and my seizure. I also suspect you were the one who drugged my daughter the other night."

The housekeeper didn't open her mouth to confirm or deny his accusations.

"How long have you been in my brother's employ? Does he pay you well for your services? How can you work for a man who was responsible for my wife's death and the abductions of both of my daughters?"

Mrs. Oliver's stoic expression changed when he mentioned his daughters. "You have only one daughter, Your Grace."

"No, I have two daughters, Mrs. Oliver. One was cruelly taken from me years ago, because of Edward's first plan to steal my wealth. When Victoria disappeared in November, someone found my other daughter and brought her back to me. Catherine is Victoria's identical twin sister. She's the one Edward abducted from this house the other night."

"But he didn't know she was your daughter. Edward thought—" Realizing she'd said too much, Mrs. Oliver shook her head.

"Edward thought what? What aren't you telling me?" Geoffrey slammed his fist on the desk. "Damn you, woman, tell me what I want to know, or I'll beat it out of you! Why did that bloody bastard take Catherine?"

Mrs. Oliver's chin rose defiantly. "He thinks she's an actress young Grayson brought here to fool everyone. Edward would never hurt her. He says he's in love with her."

"So that makes it right? Edward fancied himself in love with my wife, and look what he did to her. He raped her and got her with child. My brother was responsible for her death. He's a bloody murderer!" Geoffrey stood up. His voice reverberated through the room. "Catherine is his niece, not some stranger! Damn your eyes, woman, where has he taken her?"

Mrs. Oliver turned away from him. "Do what you will. I'm not telling you anything else."

Lucy touched Geoffrey's arm. "Please calm down, Geoffrey. She's already condemned herself by coming to Edward's defense."

Taking a deep breath, Geoffrey resumed his seat. "Mrs. Oliver, I'm sending you to your room. Guards will be posted at your door to prevent you from escaping. You'd best accustom yourself to confinement, madam, because when Edward goes to prison, you will go along as his accomplice. Just pray that I find both of my girls healthy, Mrs. Oliver. If I don't, you may never get to Newgate."

Lucy asked Tom and John to escort the housekeeper to her room. As Mrs. Oliver walked to the door, Geoffrey called to her.

"With or without your assistance, madam, we will locate Edward. I don't know what your connection to him is, but I will get to the truth."

Mrs. Oliver haughtily left the room without a reply.

Lucy closed the door and returned to Geoffrey's side. "Whatever hold Edward has on that woman must be a powerful one. Bribery, extortion, simple devotion—I don't know which, but she seems determined to say nothing more."

Geoffrey shrugged. "Let's get these documents together and make a list of the other items we found in Mrs. Oliver's room. Miles is sending a courier from London today, and I want this packet ready when he gets here. Once this is done, I mean to practice my walking a bit more."

"But, Geoffrey, that's impossible. You can't rush yourself like this."

The duke merely smiled at her objection. "Sweet Lucy, you are about to discover that I'm a man who enjoys doing impossible things. When I see my daughters again, I intend to greet them on my own two feet. I'd prefer doing it with you at my side. Can I depend on your assistance?"

Lucy nodded. "For as long as it takes, Geoffrey."

His eyebrows raised. "Then count on forever."

Miles Grayson was a man possessed with a purpose. Using the library at Carlisle House as his planning room, he met with his men, investigators, and anyone who might have news regarding the twins or Edward.

Several days before, handbills had been printed, offering a cash reward for any information on the whereabouts of Edward Damien and his niece. Detailed descriptions of both were included on the leaflets. Thousands were distributed throughout London and the surrounding areas, and couriers were dispatched to all major seaports.

One evening, as Miles was sitting at the desk going through the packet he'd received from Geoffrey, Garret rushed in.

"I stopped at the Ryland Offices and heard you've sent Jamie to Sheringham to fetch Rory O'Banyon."

Miles nodded. "Yes. I don't look forward to telling Rory Cat isn't his sister and that she's been abducted, but he has the right to know. If Rory doesn't want to help with the search, I'll arrange passage for him back to Ireland."

Garret warmed his hands by the fire. "Your father also told me you've given orders for my ship to be prepared for an immediate departure. Has there been any news?"

"No, but if we receive word that Edward's fled the country, I want to be ready to leave at a moment's notice."

"What do you have there? A pouch from the duke?"

Miles showed him the documents. "These arrived yesterday. I'm sending out letters of inquiry to Dorset and Surrey about the properties Mrs. Oliver has deeds to. Geoffrey insists all letters be signed and sealed with his name."

Garret dropped into a chair and chuckled. "That makes sense. No one would question a request from the Duke of Chatham, and it would receive top priority."

"Messengers are going out first thing in the morning with these letters. I'll instruct them to wait for a reply."

Garret suddenly sat up. "All this talk about ships and documents, and I nearly forgot to tell you what I discovered today. The records of Edward's birth and his placement into that boy's home where Geoffrey found him were all altered many years ago. No one can tell me why or by whom, but they've clearly been tampered with."

Shaking his head, Miles dragged his fingers through his hair. "Why on earth would someone do that?"

At that moment, Cosgrove came in and announced a visitor was asking to see the duke.

"The person is a bit scruffy, my lord. Rather soiled and unkempt," the old butler explained. "I never would have bothered you, but he has a handbill."

"Show him in, Cosgrove." Miles leaned back in his seat as the butler left the room. "I hope this isn't another dead end. I'd be grateful if we could get word on either of them right now. This all seems so futile."

"Don't start losing faith, Miles. Keep telling yourself we're going to find them, and we will."

"You're the perpetual optimist, Garret. For all our sakes, I pray you're right."

Cosgrove returned with a tall thin man. From his ragged appearance, it was obvious he was poor. In his right hand, he clutched a tattered handbill.

When Miles asked the stranger to sit down and offered him some refreshments, the man shook his head.

"Much obliged, your lordship, but I want to 'ave me say afore I lose the nerve. Me name is Andy. Are you the duke? You seem kinda' young to be her pa. She tole me about her pa. Said he was rich and 'portant."

"She told you?" Miles asked. "Who was *she*?"

"Lady Toria tole me afore we tried to escape."

Miles nearly jumped over the desk. "Escape! What are you talking about?"

Seeing Andy's alarm, Garret frowned at Miles and tried to allay the poor man's fears. "Andy, why don't you tell us about Lady Victoria? No one will harm you. We're simply anxious to hear what you have come to tell us."

Andy told them how his cousin had been hired to abduct Victoria. Though he'd never seen the man who employed his cousin, Clive had described him in great detail.

"Clive said 'is lordship looked like the devil 'isself, tall and dark, wiff silver streaks where 'is 'orns should'a been."

A shiver ran through Miles as he recalled Catherine saying Edward reminded her of Satan. His hands clenched the arms of his chair while he fought to control his reaction to Andy's words.

The slow-witted man explained how Victoria's coach was stopped on the road before Clive shot the young driver. Andy told them about the old cottage near Bristol where they stayed for a month and how his cousin was paid by the lord once he proved Victoria had been captured.

Garret asked. "What sort of proof did Clive have?"

"A necklace he took from Lady Toria, wiff a gold 'eart.

Pretty like she is. Clive gave it to 'is lordship to get the rest of 'is money and tole 'im she was dead like 'e ordered."

Garret continued the questioning. "Why did your cousin keep her in the cottage for so long? Was he going to ransom her back to her father?"

Andy shook his head. "No. Clive said 'is pal, Sharkey, was gonna take her to 'Stanbul and sell 'er for a lot o' gold. I didn't wanna do it, but 'e paid me no mind. One day, Lady Toria and me was settin' by the fire and she tole me about her pa. Said 'e'd pay lots o' money to get 'er back safe."

"Is that why you tried to help her escape? For the money?"

"Money's important, but t'was the rest o' what she said. Lady Toria knew the man what hired Clive. Said 'e'd turn us over to the law and put all the blame on Clive."

Slumping in the chair, Andy began rubbing his hands. "Clive was me only kin. Lady Toria said if I was to 'elp 'er get 'ome, she'd not let us get in trouble wiff the law. Promised to get me a real job, too.

"That night, when Clive fell asleep, we tried to get away, but 'e woke up and caught us. Beat me bloody, 'e did. 'Urt me real bad and tole me to go back to London. Then 'e watched me ride out on me horse."

Miles' temper exploded. "You left her with that animal! How could you—"

Andy cringed in his seat. "I did go back after a bit, I swear it, but Lady Toria was gone."

After giving Miles a signal to remain silent, Garret turned to Andy. "Did Clive take her away?"

"No." Andy's lips trembled and tears filled his eyes. "Clive musta beat on 'er, too, but Lady Toria didn't let 'im get away wiff it. She was gone, awright, but 'e was lying dead on the floor, stabbed in the chest wiff 'is own knife." He wiped his nose on the dirty sleeve of his coat.

"I buried Clive by the cottage and tried to find Lady

Toria so's I could 'elp 'er, but I didn't find 'er that night. I searched for days until I seen 'er in Windell. She looked real pretty, dressed up and all."

Miles felt a surge of relief. "Victoria is well, then? Was she alone?"

Andy nodded, then quickly shook his head. "She was fine, but not alone. The barkeep tole me the man she was wiff was the doctor. A nice lookin' gent he was, wiff yella 'air. Lady Toria looked happy, laughin' and 'uggin' him. I saw she was safe, so I come back to London."

Miles was speechless, remembering Catherine's description of her sister and the man in her dreams. It was just as she'd said: Victoria was happy and in the company of a man with blond hair.

Garret stood up and shook Andy's hand. "We want to thank you for bringing us this news. There were other handbills out last month. Why did you wait so long to come forward?"

The awkward man shrugged his drooping shoulders. "Ain't never seen no other bills. Can't read. But las' week I got a job at the printin' shop where these was done. I 'eard the others talkin', so I asked Pete to read it to me. When I 'eard how this earl looked and 'eard Lady Toria's name, I got scared 'is lordship had got 'er again." He turned to Miles. "Is that what happened? 'As 'is lordship snatched Toria again?"

Miles shook his head. "No, Andy. The earl doesn't have Lady Victoria. I have it on very good authority she's still with her young man." Opening the drawer, he removed a sack of coins and gave it to Andy. "Thank you for coming here this evening. Spend your reward wisely. If you decide you're not content working at the printer's, there will always be a job waiting for you at one of our companies. Just stop here and Cosgrove will send me word."

Andy stammered his thanks and accepted the reward.

Before he followed Cosgrove out, he stopped to ask Miles a favor.

"When you see Lady Toria, tell 'er Andy's right sorry for what 'appened. Tell 'er I 'ope she's 'appy now."

"Certainly, Andy. I'll give her your message."

As the door closed behind Andy, Miles leaned back into his chair. "I'm going to Chatham in the morning. Geoffrey deserves to hear this news in person."

"I'll go to Windell and see if I can find Victoria."

"No, Garret. Send two of our men to check out this story about Torie's being with the doctor. I need you here to keep track of all the other incoming information while I'm gone."

Garret stroked his beard. "All right, I'll stay in London, but I'm going to pay a little visit to Sedwick House and have a look around tonight."

Miles cast him a disparaging look. "Edward's butler will never let you in the front door."

"Who needs the front door? Have you been back in England so long you've forgotten the many ways to gaining access to something forbidden? Remember that time in Spain when Perez tried to keep us from the cargo that was promised to us? Or the night we had to deal with that thieving French captain—"

"I yield, Garret! No more stories, please. Let's finish our drinks and get over there. If Edward could get out of that house without being seen, then there's a way in, as well."

An hour later, the two of them were standing in Edward's study. Garret teased his friend about their dubious undertaking. "I'm glad to see you haven't forgotten how to pick a lock. I wonder what your titled friends and family would say if they knew about your many hidden talents."

Miles scowled at him in the dim candlelight. "I think you're having too much fun doing this. You go through those shelves over there while I search the desk."

Sitting on Edward's chair, Miles examined the contents

of each drawer. When he got to the bottom drawer, he noticed it was difficult to open. He knelt beside the desk to remove the drawer and found a compartment hidden beneath it. Using the pointed end of his dagger, he pried up the cover and made a discovery that filled him with elation.

"Garret, come here. I've found it." Miles held up Victoria's pendant.

"Is there anything else in there?" Garret bent down and ran his hand into the dark cavity under the drawer. He removed several pieces of parchment and held them up to the flickering candlelight so he could read them.

"Here's the codicil to Geoffrey's will." He handed it to Miles and unfolded the next sheet. A shocked expression came over his face as he read it. "I wish I could be with you when you show this to the duke in the morning."

Miles took the paper and held it to the light. "My God, we must have been blind not to have put this together long ago."

Garret shrugged. "Sometimes the most obvious answers are the hardest to find."

Placing the pendant and documents in his coat pocket, Miles moved toward the garden door. "Well, we have what we came for. Let's go back to Carlisle House and make our plans for tomorrow."

Chapter 29

Geoffrey and Lucy were in the library when Miles arrived early the following day. After greeting them, he sat down and told them about Andy and the story of Victoria's abduction and later appearance in Windell.

"My Catherine was right!" Geoffrey exclaimed. "Victoria is alive in spite of Edward's devious plot. How long will it take to confirm the man's story?"

"I sent two men to Windell this morning. But we already have proof on some of it." Miles handed him the codicil and Victoria's pendant.

The color drained from the duke's face. "I knew it was Edward all along. If only we could figure out how he manipulated my housekeeper into aiding him."

"I have the answer to that question, as well." Miles handed him the other document from Edward's desk.

Lucy looked over Geoffrey's shoulder as he read the yellowed parchment. "I can't believe it," he said. "How did they hide this from me all these years? I never suspected a thing."

A few minutes later, Mrs. Oliver was led into the library by her guards. The neatness of her starched gown was a contrast to the disheveled appearance of her hair, which hung loose around her shoulders. Miles directed her to a chair in front of the desk. Lucy stood beside Geoffrey, who simply stared at his housekeeper.

Miles approached the woman and frowned. "I don't think I've ever seen you so unkempt, Mrs. Oliver. Your hair is falling from its pins and I see streaks of gray showing at your temples. You never seemed to be a vain woman, but you color your hair. Why?"

She said nothing, but sat with her hands folded in her lap.

"For a servant, you're quite arrogant, Mrs. Oliver. But then again, you were born to a prosperous family. Your father was an Anglican bishop. From what I've learned, Reverend Bishop Chamberlain was a mighty tyrant of the church doctrines and extremely tightfisted with his money."

Mrs. Oliver ignored his taunts and averted her eyes. Miles sat on the edge of the desk next to her.

"A beautiful young girl forced to live such a confining existence would likely find a way to assert her independence. Is that why lovely Jessica Chamberlain rebelled against her upbringing and threw herself at a man she knew her father would object to? Why else would she pursue one of the wildest rogues in London?"

The verbal barb pricked Mrs. Oliver's ire. "Because she loved him, curse you!" Her hands clenched into fists. "It's easy to condemn me, but you have no idea what kind of brutal life I was forced to live in my father's house. My sainted father beat me for looking in a mirror. Vanity is a sin, and there was to be no sin in his house. When I met Malcolm Carlisle, he made me feel alive and free. I loved Malcolm with all my heart."

Her eyes filled with tears. "I was sixteen when I gave

myself to Malcolm. I loved him so. I hoped and prayed he'd learn to love me, too. But when I told him I was going to have a . . ." Her voice faded and she stared at the floor.

Geoffrey began speaking to her. "You were with child and Malcolm wouldn't marry you. My father was a cold man, so I understand your anger with him. But why did you hide the fact you were Edward's mother from me? I would have welcomed you into my home. Why the duplicity, Mrs. Oliver? What have I ever done to you?"

The woman fixed her wild gaze on Geoffrey. "You were Cathy's son! Malcolm said he couldn't marry me or have other children without endangering his beloved wife's only child! I was cast aside and my son declared a bastard with nothing because of your father's devotion to a dead woman!"

Incensed, Geoffrey stood up. "According to Malcolm's solicitors, money was sent for Edward's care. He was put in a home for orphans when you abandoned him. That's where I found Edward when he was ten, and I brought him to live in Chatham."

Mrs. Oliver sniffed with disdain. "You know nothing about what became of us, but your father and those fancy barristers did. In the beginning, Malcolm paid for Edward's keep because he was born with the Carlisle birthmark on his chest. But my father controlled my life. All of the payments were sent to him. Edward and I never saw a bit of it."

"Surely your father provided a home for you both."

"What my father provided was a marriage to a fifty-year-old man I'd never seen before. My husband, Nathan Graham, was a wealthy man from Dorset who cared little for me and even less for my son. But I served a purpose, warming his bed and keeping his house. And, like my father, Nathan enjoyed inflicting pain in the name of righteousness."

Mrs. Oliver stared down at the floor as she continued.

"Nathan tormented me with threats of hurting my son if I didn't do his bidding fast enough or without complaint. For five years I was beaten with fists, belts, and whatever else my husband could find. One day, he raised his whip to Edward. I went berserk. I picked up a knife and went after Nathan, but he forced the weapon from my hand, threw me down, and beat me. Then he tore my clothes, meaning to take me on the kitchen floor.

"I fought him and screamed. His hands went around my throat, and he began choking me. As I was losing consciousness, Nathan ceased his attack and fell to his side."

Tears streamed down Mrs. Oliver's face. "That's when I saw Edward standing beside me. My beautiful little boy was stroking my brow. There was blood on his small hands and down the front of his shirt. I sat up, pulled Edward into my arms, and found the courage to look at Nathan. My husband was dead. The knife I'd dropped was sticking out of his back. Edward patted my cheek. My angel smiled and said, 'He won't hurt you again, Mama.' Then he hugged me. Before I could do anything, one of my father's friends arrived at the house and found us on the floor."

In hushed tones, she told how her father tried to use his influence to squelch the scandal. When that didn't suffice, he blackmailed Malcolm into helping cover up the killing by threatening to tell everyone Malcolm's bastard son was a murderer.

But Malcolm demanded a price of his own. Edward had been taken away from his mother and sent away to school. His birth records were altered. By changing his mother's name and surname, the Chamberlains would never be able to find the child. The bishop received a final cash payment from the duke for the promise of keeping his daughter away from London and the Carlisle family.

"After Nathan's death, I was in shock and sedated. By the time I regained my senses, my son was gone and I was in my aunt's home in Yorkshire. When I asked where Edward was, my father told me my little boy had been sent away by Malcolm. He warned if I interfered, Edward would be punished for killing Nathan. Not wanting that to happen, I went on with my life."

Geoffrey held up Edward's baptismal record. "If what you said is true, how did my brother get this certificate? It shows your name as his mother."

"From my father. He saw Edward at Oxford when he was a student and realized this handsome young gentleman was his only grandchild."

Geoffrey interrupted her. "How did he recognize Edward?"

"Edward looks like a Chamberlain and resembled my father as a young man. Even the streaks in his hair were inherited from our family. My father befriended Edward and encouraged my son to seek revenge on the Carlisle family."

"He also told Edward about you."

She nodded. "While you were in Ireland, my father became quite ill. Before he died, he told Edward that he was his grandfather and where to find me. My new husband, Bram, had died of lung fever the year before, so I was widowed, living alone in a lovely home in Whitley. My joy at seeing my son was tempered with pain. He was a deeply troubled young man. On that day, I swore I'd do everything in my power to make it up to him, and I have."

"Madam, what you've done is criminal!" Geoffrey's voice was heavy with contempt. "For eighteen years you have acted as his spy and conspirator in this house. You sacrificed your own happiness to help Edward destroy my family."

Miles could be quiet no longer. "Mrs. Oliver, if you don't tell us where Edward has taken Catherine, I swear you'll pay for his crime as well."

Mrs. Oliver stood to face Miles. "Do what you will to

me. My son has been robbed of everything that should have been his. I'd give my life to insure his new found joy."

"But Catherine is his niece," Miles countered. "If Edward discovers the truth about her, he'll think he's been played for a fool and hurt her. You must tell us where he's taken her."

Glowering at him, Mrs. Oliver spat out her reply. "You can go Hades, my lord. I will never betray my son."

As Miles raised his hand to strike her and vent his rage, a familiar voice called out from behind him.

"Don't hit her, Miles. I know where Catherine is."

Miles spun around to face Victoria, who was standing in the doorway. She sounded like his old friend, but her appearance had changed. She was dressed in a flowing blouse, britches, and high leather boots.

He could muster only a single word. "Torie?"

Geoffrey was coming around the desk when Victoria ran into his arms. He kissed and hugged her. "Victoria, you're home! Catherine said you were coming, and I prayed she was right."

"Oh, Papa, I've missed you. You look wonderful. When I left, I was so afraid . . . Oh, let's not talk of that now. I have so much to tell you all, I hardly know where to begin."

"Before we do anything, I want that woman taken from my sight," Geoffrey ordered. "Lucy, please have John and Tom take her back to her room. Victoria, while we tend to Mrs. Oliver, will you please talk to Miles? I believe he's lost his ability to speak."

Victoria looked at the stunned expression on Miles' face and smiled. "I'm not a ghost, Miles. It's really me."

Miles grinned with embarrassment. "I know. I'm just glad to see you. Welcome home." He pulled her into his arms for an enthusiastic hug. "I'd nearly given up hope, but Catherine told us you were alive and well. She even said you'd found a—"

His unexpected silence caused Victoria to look up and follow the direction of his gaze. Justin stood in the doorway. "Come in, Justin." Going to his side, she took hold of his arm and led him into the room.

"Papa, Miles, I want you to meet my husband, Dr. Justin Prescott. Justin, this is my father, Geoffrey Carlisle, the Duke of Chatham, and the rather quiet gent to his right is my good friend Miles Grayson."

After the introductions were completed, Geoffrey's smile turned to a frown. "Victoria, I am sorry I never told you about Catherine. Can you forgive me for keeping such a secret?"

"You've done nothing that requires my forgiveness. The important thing now is to find Catherine and bring her home as soon as possible."

Geoffrey peered into his daughter's eyes. "You said you know where Catherine is. You can see her in your dreams, can't you?"

"Yes. Catherine is very weak. Edward has her, and she's alarmed by some of the things he's said to her."

Justin told them about the dreams Victoria had been having and how they wrote down everything she could remember. "From the way Catherine is feeling, I believe Edward's been dosing her with laudanum. Cat has never been one to sit back and let anyone get the best of her."

Miles turned to Justin. "What do you know about Cat?"

"I've known Cat for five years. When I found Victoria injured and suffering from amnesia, she had no memory of who she really was. I thought she was Catherine and told her so. I wrote to her family and told them I'd found their daughter."

Victoria gasped. "I nearly forgot to tell you, Papa. I've brought help to find Catherine. They're waiting in the parlor."

"The O'Banyons must think they've been abandoned."

He walked toward the door. "Hurry along, Victoria. Let's go and greet our guests."

"But, Papa, how did you know it was the O'Banyons?"

Smiling, Geoffrey stopped to face his daughter. "After what Catherine told me about them, I'd expect nothing less. They've loved and protected her all these years. The least I can do is see they're welcomed properly to my home." He smiled and offered her his arm. "Come, Victoria. Introduce me to Catherine's other family."

Erin laughed as she watched her husband pace back and forth across the parlor. "Hawk, if you don't stop walkin' to and fro like that, you're going to wear a hole in that very fancy rug. Whatever is the matter with you?"

Sean jerked to a halt to glare at her. "I can't believe you're asking me that! I'm about to meet one of the most powerful men in England. Added to that is the fact I've raised his daughter for eighteen years. He'll likely think I stole her!"

Standing beside his mother, Colin sighed. "Da, just tell the duke how Catherine came to be with us. I'm sure he'll believe you."

"I pray to the saints you're right, Colin, or I might spend the rest of my days here in England as a guest of His Majesty in some prison or other."

Geoffrey spoke from the arched entry of the room. "Never a prison. Everyone knows a hawk must always be free, especially an Irish Hawk."

Sean's apprehension died when the duke walked toward him and shook his hand. "It appears I owe you my undying gratitude, Captain O'Banyon. You and your family have taken good care of my daughter, and I'll never be able to thank you enough for that."

The smile on Sean's face mirrored Geoffrey's. "We thought Catherine had no kin, so we became her family and loved her as our own. She brought incredible joy to our household. Your Grace, may I present my wife, Erin, and our son Colin?"

Geoffrey bowed over Erin's hand and kissed it. "Thank you, dearest madam, for being such a good mother to my daughter. In spite of her britches and talent for sailing and combat, you've raised Catherine to be a fine lady."

Blushing, Erin timidly thanked him. Victoria, Justin, and Miles entered the parlor as the duke approached Colin.

"Well, Catherine certainly told me a great deal about you, Colin. She said you had a good head on your shoulders. Have you ever thought about going into business and giving up the sea? Your sister believes you'd be happier behind a desk than manning a sailing ship."

"Yes, I would. I've been thinking about—" Colin stopped speaking and regarded Geoffrey with uncertainty. "You just called Catherine my sister."

Geoffrey nodded. "I'm aware of that, Colin. Catherine has been a part of your family for most of her life. She was your sister and a daughter to your parents, I can hardly mind sharing her with people who love her as much as I do."

Lucy came into the parlor to announce lunch was ready. After he introduced her to the guests, he issued an invitation.

"Let's adjourn to the dining room. While we eat, we can discuss the situation and compare notes regarding Catherine's rescue." After tucking Lucy's hand into the crook of his arm, he led the way to the dining room.

Miles saw Victoria smiling at her father's actions. He leaned over and whispered, "Go away for a while and things can happen."

"You're right, Miles. It seems like I've been away forever. After lunch, I need to talk to you privately."

Miles nodded and frowned at Justin. "I guess we have a few things to discuss."

Victoria poked him with her elbow. "I have something to tell you about Catherine. When I do, you won't care a fig about Justin, me, or anyone else."

Giving him a wink, Victoria walked away with her husband.

During lunch, Sean told Geoffrey and the others how Catherine had been brought to him by Ella. After regaling them with stories about Catherine's childhood, the conversation turned to the events of the past few months that had brought them all together. Then Victoria told them about her recent dreams.

After describing the vision of Catherine and Edward in the coach she'd had the week before, Victoria related the newest dream from the previous night.

"Edward has taken Catherine to a large house in the country. I saw her standing at a window, looking out at the ruins of a castle, when he came up behind her. He told her the castle once belonged to a boy king, Aethelred the Unready. But before I could hear the rest of his tale, my dream came to an abrupt end. I woke up, and the only clue I had of their whereabouts was that stupid name and title."

Colin started laughing from his place across the table. "This morning Victoria was pacing the deck, grumbling about hating history. I questioned her, and she told me about the dreams and how they pertained to Catherine. She then mentioned Aethelred the Unready and cursed herself for not paying closer attention to her history lessons."

"Colin came to my rescue," Victoria admitted. "He likes history, even English history, and knew exactly to whom I was referring."

Colin explained. "In 978, Queen Elfrida murdered her stepson, so her son Aethelred could ascend to the throne. But he was only ten years old and so he was called the Unready. His home was a Saxon stronghold named Corfe Castle."

Impatiently, Miles pushed his chair away from the table. "History lesson be damned. Where is this Corfe Castle?"

"On the Isle of Purbeck in Dorsetshire," Colin replied.

Lucy, Geoffrey, and Miles looked at each other in amazement. Lucy ran to the library to retrieve the documents she had found in Mrs. Oliver's room. She returned and gave them to the duke.

Locating the right one, Geoffrey sighed with relief. "Edward has taken her to his mother's home in Dorset. According to the deed, the property is located between the town of Corfe and St. Aldhelm's Head on the Isle of Purbeck. With the weather we've had lately, the roads shouldn't be too difficult to use. We could be there in a week."

Sean smiled. "If we go by sea, we could be there in a few days. The *Cat's Cradle* is sitting here in the bay. What better way to bring her back than on her own ship? How about it, Your Grace? Are you up to a little seagoing adventure to rescue your daughter?"

"I'd sail to China on a raft if it meant rescuing *our* daughter, Captain O'Banyon," Geoffrey replied.

Sean grinned over the emphasis Geoffrey had placed on the word *our*. "If I have to share Cat with another father, I'm well pleased the man is you."

The duke nodded his thanks and stood up. "You and I will select the horses we'll take with us. Colin and Miles, you see about ordering the supplies we'll need to sail on the morning tide. Lucy, please see our guests are given rooms and made comfortable. Victoria and Justin, check your medical supplies. If you need anything, we can send to the village for it this afternoon."

Laughing, Sean stood beside Geoffrey and clapped him on the back. "I believe you've got the makings of a very fine ship's captain, Your Grace. You crack out orders even better than Cat, and I always thought she was the best . . . well, next to me, of course."

"Being captain of a ship is a lot like being head of a company. Orders are given to be carried out. Everyone has a task and does his job. If they didn't, the company, like the ship, would go under."

"Aye, 'tis true," Sean admitted. "But working in a company has its advantages. If you don't do your job, you're discharged and can go home. Neglect your duties on board a ship, and you could be flogged or thrown overboard."

Geoffrey laughed. "Since I don't relish flogging or tossing anyone in the ocean, I suppose I must be content with my place in business." He put his arm around Sean's shoulder. "Come along, Hawk. Our daughter is waiting for us."

Sean's booming voice could be heard as they moved down the hall. "Our Catherine never had an overabundance of patience, Geoffrey. One time, Cat decided she wanted to learn how . . ."

Erin turned to Miles. "I know everyone's concerned about Catherine, but may I ask how Rory is?"

"Rory is fine, Mrs. O'Banyon. He's been staying at my estate in Sheringham and will be here in a day or two." Miles took her hand. "From what I understand, Rory has enjoyed his confinement and claims to be in love with my estate manager's daughter."

Erin rolled her eyes. "Leave it to my Rory to make the best of things. As for being in love, 'tis not the first time I've heard that claim, but I pray it may be the last. None of my children are married yet. At the pace they're going, I'll never have a grandbaby to dandle on my knee."

Colin put his arm around her shoulder. "Mam, Miss Lucy is ready to show us to our rooms. We can talk of this later."

Erin scowled up at her tall son. "Colin O'Banyon, your da was a married man when he was your age. You're not even keeping steady company with a lass. I'll be old and withered before I get to dance at your wedding."

Hugging his mother, Colin led her out of the dining room. "It's your own fault, Mam. Before I can marry, I'll have to find a woman as wonderful as you."

As Miles watched them go up the stairs, Victoria touched his arm to gain his attention. "I sent Justin to the library to work on the list of medical supplies we'll be taking with us. Why don't we go to my sitting room to talk?"

A few minutes later, the two friends were sitting on the loveseat in the peach room. Victoria took his hand as she started speaking to him.

"A great deal has happened during the past few months. When I fell in love and married Justin, I had no idea who I was. Then my memory returned, and I was consumed with guilt over forgetting our betrothal. But I quickly realized you'd understand and be happy for me."

Staring down at their joined hands, Miles shook his head. "Your marriage to Justin isn't disturbing me, Torie. I'm glad you've found happiness with him. It's just that I feel awkward about all this."

She gave his hand a gentle squeeze. "You're feeling guilty because you thought I was dead and went on with your life. No one would fault you for that. You met Catherine and fell in love with her, didn't you?"

After a slight hesitation, he nodded. "Yes. I love Cat with all my heart. Not knowing where to find her is killing me." Miles turned to look at Victoria. "Earlier, you said you wanted to tell me something about Catherine. What is it?"

"When I told everyone about my visions of Catherine,

I left one out. I discussed it with Justin and he agreed you alone should be told about her condition.''

"Her condition? Is something wrong with Catherine? Has Edward hurt her?''

"No, Edward hasn't hurt her. Catherine's problem has nothing to do with him . . . well, not directly.''

Her reluctance goaded his impatience. "Get on with it, Torie! What has happened to her?''

Victoria's cheeks flushed pink. "For the past few days, Catherine's been suffering severe bouts of nausea. The smell of food makes her ill. Her breasts are tender and she's concerned about her flow—or should I say the lack of it?''

"Are you telling me Catherine's going to have a baby? Maybe you're wrong. Perhaps her symptoms are being caused by the laudanum.''

She shook her head. "No. I'm positive Catherine's with child, and she's convinced of it, as well. Justin thinks she's in her second month, but won't be able to confirm it until he can examine her.''

Miles was silent. His lack of response made Victoria anxious. "I know this is a shock to you, Miles, but surely you're not upset about Catherine's having your baby.''

The muscle in his jaw tensed. "What has me riled is the fact that I now have twice as many reasons to despise that uncle of yours. I've never hated anyone as much as I do Edward Damien.''

"I appreciate your pain and your hatred of Edward. He's a very disturbed man who's never been happy. I can almost understand what drove him to do all those awful things to my family.''

Miles turned his cold blue gaze on Victoria. "Good! You forgive him, but don't expect me to do the same. All I see is a vile, jealous beast who wants to punish everyone because of the actions of his father.''

Victoria shook her head. "I never said I forgave him. I

said I understood. There's a big difference between the two. Let's stop wasting time talking about him."

Standing up, she held out her hand to Miles. "Come along, my friend. There are supplies to order, a ship to prepare, and packing to be done. Catherine and your child are waiting for us, so we shouldn't disappoint them."

Chapter 30

As the inhabitants of Chatham Hall prepared for their rescue mission, the object of their quest stood at a window gazing at Corfe Castle, reviewing the events of the past two weeks.

Catherine remembered drinking tea as she wrote a letter to Miles on the evening of her abduction. Her last conscious thought was feeling extremely tired. She woke up in a moving coach. Though the wind blew outside, she felt protected and warm in a strong embrace.

When soft lips kissed her brow, Catherine sighed to herself. *How nice. Miles must have come to take me away with him.*

The rocking of the vehicle was lulling her back to sleep just as her companion's voice purred against her ear and alerted her to the grim reality of her situation.

"Sleep, my beautiful one," he whispered. "I'm going to take excellent care of you, my precious cat."

She recognized Edward's voice and heard him use her

nickname. *Edward knows who I am and means to do away with me, too. I have to escape before he kills me.*

Pure terror swept through Catherine when she realized she was unable to move or speak. A strange weakness pervaded her entire body. In spite of her struggle to remain alert, she soon fell into a deep, dreamless sleep.

When she woke again, Catherine felt sunlight on her face as the coach pulled to a halt. The door opened and she heard Edward speak to someone in hushed tones.

"I trust everything has been arranged?"

A young female voice replied, "Yes, my lord. Your rooms are at the top of the stairs. Can I help you with her?"

"No. Lead the way. I'll carry my niece to her chamber."

Catherine kept her eyes shut as Edward carried her upstairs. From the noises and the smell of cooked food, she guessed they had stopped at an inn. She was placed on a bed, and Edward stroked her hair while he issued orders to the maid.

"My niece is quite ill. Do not speak to her, just assist her with her toilette and see she's made comfortable. Don't be surprised if Victoria starts acting strangely. The doctor says in time she'll stop suffering the delusions of her troubled mind. I won't let my brother put her into an institution because of her illness."

"I'll do my best. I've brought her things from Carlisle House, as you ordered, along with the new items I purchased for her in London."

"Fine. See to Victoria while I order breakfast. We'll rest a few hours and be back on the road after lunch. I'll return in thirty minutes. Have her ready by then."

Catherine opened her eyes when she heard the door close. The first thing she saw was the face of the parlor maid from Carlisle House, Theresa. She tried to speak, but discovered she could not. Tears of bitter frustration gathered in her eyes.

Theresa spoke softly as she removed Catherine's clothes.

"You poor dear. Edward's been so worried about you. Don't be afraid. He won't let them take you away, my lady."

While the maid pulled off her gown and helped her sit up on the bed, Catherine felt some strength returning to her limbs. With Theresa's assistance, she moved laboriously around the small room as she completed her morning ablutions. Catherine was shamed by her inability to tend to her own needs, but had to let Theresa help her. After she was dressed in a nightgown, the young woman got her onto the bed.

Marshaling her concentration, Catherine fought to speak. "Please . . . help . . . me."

Theresa raised her eyes and looked at her. "I am, my lady. I'll do everything I can to help you, I promise."

Edward slammed the door behind him. "I told you not to talk to her, Theresa. Can't you follow my orders?" He slapped the maid across her face. "Now get out of here and see to our breakfast tray."

Theresa held back her sobs as she scurried from the room.

Edward looked at Catherine and smiled. "I see the concern in your eyes, my heart. Don't worry about Theresa. She's received far worse punishment for disobedience in the past. I will have my orders followed, or she'll continue to suffer the penalties of provoking my wrath." Leaning down, he caressed her cheek. "You are so important to me. I'll not let anyone come between us—ever."

He sat beside her on the bed with a brush in his hand. Holding her in his arms, he drew the bristles through her long, wavy hair.

"Your hair is like gold silk, so lovely and bright. I think that's what first attracted me to Evangeline. She was blond like you. In time I'll tell you all about her."

Catherine listened as he spoke, hoping to discover what he planned to do with her.

"I knew from the start you weren't Victoria," Edward

admitted. "Although you look like her, my niece never had your fire, my golden cat. My brother turned Victoria against me, and she became as manipulative as he. The two of them meant to cheat me out of what should have been mine."

Setting the brush on the bedside table, Edward eased her back against the pillows and cupped her cheek with his hand. "You'll be my salvation. I've made mistakes in the past and have paid for it with my loneliness. But never again." He pressed his lips to her forehead and kissed her.

When Theresa returned with the food, Edward had her put the tray on the table and sent her away. He prepared a cup of tea and poured honey into the bowl of steaming porridge. Sitting on the bed, he tucked a napkin under Catherine's chin.

"I know you feel weak, but until our journey is complete, I must have you docile. It will make the traveling easier for you while I outwit Grayson and his plan to entrap me. You have no need to fear. I won't let him coerce you into his charade any longer. No one will ever take you away, my golden cat."

As Edward fed her porridge, Catherine watched and listened to him. There was a glint of madness in his dark eyes. She knew how to protect herself in open combat, but was confused about how to counter his demented assault. When he brought the teacup to her lips, she refused to drink it. He smiled and sipped from the cup.

"See, my heart? There's nothing in the tea."

Suddenly, she felt dizzy. Sleep overtook her once more.

For the next few days, this routine continued in different inns along the way. Traveling by coach during the afternoons and late into the night, they would arrive at their lodgings and stay long enough to rest the horses, eat breakfast, and nap for a bit. Washed and refreshed, they'd be back on the road after lunch.

Edward was never far from her side. After that first day,

he seldom left her alone with Theresa. He always allowed her privacy while she tended her toilette and dressed, but Catherine could sense he was close by. Theresa never spoke to her again and averted her eyes from Catherine's. Her fear was evident by the way she constantly looked toward the doorway.

Catherine began to wonder if Edward ever slept. Whenever she was awake, she found him watching her. Under his constant scrutiny, she often feigned sleep and never let him see how unaffected she was becoming to the drugs she knew he was putting in her food every day.

She'd always had a high tolerance for whiskey and ale. Rory often teased her, saying it wasn't ladylike of her to drink a man under the table. She decided this might be why the drugs weren't weakening her as much.

After nearly a week of traveling, they arrived at their destination. Although it was late afternoon, Catherine could see the pretty whitewashed house in the setting sunlight. The weather was milder than in Chatham, and bushes and plants decorated the front of the home.

She had no idea where they were, but as Edward carried her toward the house, the breezes brought a familiar scent to her nose. The ocean's briny fragrance filled her senses. They weren't directly on the coast, but perhaps a short distance from it. Having the sea close by gave her comfort.

With great care, Edward conveyed her into a bedroom at the rear of the house. He held her in his arms while Theresa lit the candles in the room. When the task was completed, he sent the maid for firewood and placed Catherine on a large, canopied bed.

"This was my mother's room. I spent many happy hours here when I was a little boy. Mama would sit in her rocking chair and hold me in her arms while she told me stories."

As Edward lifted Catherine to tuck a pillow beneath her head, she looked around the beautifully appointed room. Its wood furniture was polished mahogany. The bedspread and canopy were made of delicate ecru lace. A rocking chair with crewel cushions done in burgundy and green stood near the fireplace.

She was suddenly aware of how clean everything was. The mystery of this was soon revealed by Edward.

"When I decided to bring you here, I sent word to have the house made ready for us. The larder is stocked and there's a pot of stew simmering on the stove. I hope you'll be happy in your new home, my heart." Kissing her cheek, he left the room.

Catherine shuddered with revulsion. *My new home? I think not. Somehow I must find a way out of this place.*

Within moments, Theresa came in to build a fire and unpack the clothes that had been brought for Catherine to wear. The maid remained silent while she worked. Theresa had just finished helping Catherine prepare for bed when Edward returned with a dinner tray and sent the maid from the room.

Although it galled her, Catherine allowed him to coddle her. When he fed her or brushed her hair, Edward would often let down his guard and speak freely. She used these opportunities to get to know her captor.

After feeding her stew and fruit compote, Edward kissed her cheek and left her alone. Before she could get out of bed to search her new surroundings, Catherine felt the effects of the laudanum taking hold on her. Rather than fight the drug, she allowed herself to fall asleep.

The next morning, Catherine awoke to find herself wracked with dizziness and nausea. Theresa came in as she struggled to get up and helped her to the chamber pot behind the screen in the corner of the room. The maid held Catherine over the porcelain container as she choked up the bile rising in her throat.

"I'm so sorry, my lady," Theresa cried. "I knew you were going to get sick from that drug. 'Tis why I put water in the bottles to dilute it. I guess it wasn't enough."

Wiping her mouth, Catherine looked up at Theresa's sad face. "Why did you do that for me? If Edward found out, he would punish you for it."

"I know, but I've seen what laudanum does to folks. My pa used it when he hurt his back in the mines. The need for the drug took over his life and it killed him. I didn't want that happening to you. Please don't tell Edward what I've done."

"I won't say a word, I promise." Catherine patted her hand. "It'll be our little secret."

Suddenly, Edward's voice rang out. "What's all the talking about? Theresa, are you ignoring my orders again?"

Catherine put her hand over the maid's mouth and answered him. "Oh, Edward, please help me," she called in a breathless voice. "I feel so sick. I need you."

Before she uttered the last word of her plea, Edward rushed behind the large screen. He swept her into his arms and carried her back to the bed. Theresa brought a bowl of warm water and cloths over to him. After sending the maid for tea, Edward dampened a cloth and washed Catherine's face.

"Oh, my dear one, what's the matter with you? Your face is so pale. Are you in pain?"

Catherine decided to use his concern to her advantage. "I was so sick to my stomach, Edward. I've felt this way ever since the night I drank the tea in the sitting room. Now it's gotten much worse. Please help me, Edward." Lifting a trembling hand, she touched his cheek before letting it drop to the bed.

Edward brought her hand to his lips. "Forgive me, my heart. I never meant to hurt you. I only used the drug because I wanted you to stay with me."

Catherine looked up at him, tears pooling in her eyes. "Have you so little faith in your charm, Edward? Must you use such devices to keep my attention?"

He shook his head. "No more drugs for you, I swear it, my golden cat. I won't risk your health any longer."

Theresa came in with the tea tray and prepared a cup with cream and sugar for Catherine. She brought it to Edward, who was sitting on the edge of the bed, then left the room.

He took a sip, proving to her that the tea wasn't tainted. Easing her up, he put it to her lips and encouraged her to drink. "Tea can sometimes soothe these kind of upsets. When you finish this, I'll have breakfast prepared for you. Would you like porridge or eggs? A sweet roll, perhaps?"

The mention of food caused Catherine's stomach to churn anew with nausea. She swallowed back the bile in her throat and shook her head. "No food yet. Just tea."

He smiled. "As you wish, my lovely cat."

Curiosity made her ask the question that had been plaguing her for days. "Who told you my name was Cat?"

Edward's brow rose in surprise. "I called you cat because that is what you remind me of with your bright green eyes and silky gold hair. Is Cat really your name?"

"Actually, my name is Cat . . ." Quickly catching herself, she adjusted her answer. "Catlin Mary O'Hara. Catlin is usually a boy's name back in Dublin, so I preferred being called Cat."

"So you're Irish. That must be where your quick wit comes from. I want you to tell me all about yourself, Cat."

Giving him a shy smile, she touched her neck. "My throat is burning too badly from spitting up to speak at the moment. Why don't you tell me about your life first?"

"But, Cat, I don't think . . ."

"Please, Edward. If we're to become friends, it's important we get to know one another."

Reluctantly at first, he began to tell her his life story. But the words came easier as he told her how his mother was seduced and abandoned by his father and then forced into marriage with a stranger. He smiled when he recounted the few pleasant memories he had of his early childhood and was close to breaking down as he talked of the miserable existence his mother had been subjected to while married to Nathan Graham.

"My stepfather was always beating my mother and me. He said I deserved to be punished, that bastards had to pay for the sins of their fathers and the whores who gave birth to them. When I was five, he took a whip to me. Mama grabbed a knife and tried to stop him, but he disarmed her and started choking her. I had to stop him. I found the knife she had dropped and ran up behind him. Holding it in both hands, I brought the knife down with all my might into his back. Blood poured from his wound and he fell over. I was scared, but when Mama opened her eyes, I forgot my fears. Mama was alive, and Nathan would never hurt us again."

Edward suddenly got to his feet and rushed from the room. Seconds later, Catherine heard the key turn in the lock. She stumbled to the door and banged on it with her fist.

"Why are you locking me in here?"

"You'll be afraid and want to get away from me now. I never should have told you what I did."

"Please, Edward, don't leave me locked up. I won't try to escape. I'm not afraid of you, I swear it." Catherine pressed her ear to the door and waited for his reply.

Edward's voice was tempered with remorse. "I need to be alone for a while. You'll be safe in there, Cat. No one will harm you." The sound of his footsteps faded as he walked away.

Catherine searched the room for a means of escape. She pulled back the heavy brocade drapes behind the round table in the alcove and discovered the windows had been nailed shut.

The breathtaking view beyond the glass garnered her attention. A vista of trees and foliage, still green despite the winter months, offered a lush setting for the ruins of an ancient castle on a not-too-distant hill. Always attracted to history, she became enthralled by the regal display in the morning sunshine.

But reality came crashing back when she noticed the iron bars on the outside of her window. She was truly a prisoner here. In order to escape, she'd have to come up with a very good plan.

Another wave of nausea hit and she moved quickly to find the chamber pot. Dizzy, she sank to the floor to relieve her stomach. When she felt strong enough, she made her way back to bed and fell asleep.

The sunlight was fading and evening was close at hand when Catherine woke up feeling more like her old self. Going to the basin, she washed in the cool water and prepared herself for Edward's next visit.

She dressed in a warm gold velvet gown and sat in the rocking chair to brush her hair. The fire in the hearth had burned itself out. The only light in the room came from two candles Catherine lit on the mantel.

Hearing the key in the lock, she turned to see Edward entering the room. "Oh, Edward, I'm so glad you came back. I've been so lonely locked in here." Catherine watched as he came toward her. "Are you all right, Edward?"

He knelt in front of her and stroked her cheek with his hand. "I'm fine. I've never told anyone about that day. Doing it brought all those bad feelings back. I didn't want to frighten you. Pray tell me you don't hate me."

"I don't hate you, Edward. I'm sorry I made you recall that dreadful event. Please forgive me."

Edward smiled. "Let's forget what happened today. I've ordered a special meal for us this evening. Are you hungry?"

Returning his smile, Catherine nodded. "Famished. My

sick stomach seems to have cured itself and I'm looking forward to dinner."

"Would you mind if we had dinner in here? I'm not overly comfortable with the rest of this house."

"If that will please you, we can bring the table and chairs from the alcove by the windows and eat right here in front of the hearth. But soon you must show me the rest of this house."

"I promise to you show you everything in a day or so. Right now, let me get some wood and build you a fire. I don't want you to catch a cold."

As he left the room, Catherine noticed he'd left the door open. She forced herself to remain seated. It would take time, but she would gain Edward's trust—and with it her means of escape.

He'd arranged a delicious dinner, complete with apple pie with clotted cream for dessert. He was charming and attentive, his manners exemplary. After the meal, they played cards and chatted as if they'd been friends for years. When the hour grew late, he kissed her hand and bid her good night. The click of the key in the lock reminded her of the precarious position she was in.

Catherine knew Edward was capable of great anger; she'd witnessed his cruelty the day he struck Theresa for speaking to her. It was just a matter of time before that side of his nature showed itself again.

She awoke the next day to discover her nausea had returned. For the better part of an hour, she had her face over the chamber pot. Theresa came in to help her dress and found her sitting on the rocking chair with a basin in her lap.

"Oh, my lady, you're sick again. Edward said he wasn't going to give you the drug anymore." Theresa removed the bowl from her trembling hands and helped her back into bed.

Once under the covers, Catherine found the strength

to reply. "He didn't give me any last night. I found it very difficult to fall asleep."

Theresa worried her lower lip with her teeth. "My granny was a healer and midwife. I used to help her treat the sick people in our village. Maybe I can mix up one of her herb remedies to ease your ailment. Have you any other symptoms beside the stomach upset and nausea?"

Catherine shrugged. "No pains, but last night when I tried to sleep on my stomach, my breasts were very sore and tender. Theresa, what can be wrong with me?"

"My lady, I'm not meaning to pry, but can you tell me when you last had your woman's time?" Theresa blushed and turned away. "Sorry, 'tis none of my business. I'll fetch you some tea and toasted bread to settle your stomach."

Alone with her thoughts, Catherine tried to recall how long it had been since her last flow. Since she was twelve, she'd been as regular as the calendar. During the past few months of preparing to trap Edward, she'd lost track of time. She recalled how Darcy had fussed over her, telling her to stay in bed because it was expected that all ladies should do so during their "time." That had been in early December while they were staying at Garret's family estate.

"That was three months ago. I've never missed before." At once, the answer to her ailment became obvious to her. "A baby? Could it be I'm going to have a baby?"

Closing her eyes, she envisioned the beautiful nights spent making love with Miles. Was it possible they'd conceived a child together?

Filled with mixed emotions, she touched her abdomen. She loved Miles and wanted to give him a child. Yet the fact that her mother and grandmother had died in childbirth couldn't be ignored. But she was healthy and strong. Erin said some women were made to birth babies and boasted that Catherine had been one of them, with her easy flows and well-endowed body. There was also some mention about her hips being wide enough, but Catherine couldn't remember it all. Having a babe had been the last thing on her mind back then. Now it was a priority.

"Oh, Miles, we're going to have a baby. I hope it's a boy. Every man wants a son. But having girls isn't so bad. Ask my father if you have any doubts." Her musings were forgotten as she opened her eyes and recalled where she was.

Edward had been sweet and attentive to her. If he discovered she was really his niece, he'd feel betrayed. If he learned she was expecting a child, only God knew what he'd do. He was jealous of Geoffrey and hateful of Miles. Should he find out Miles was the father of her baby, he'd see it destroyed.

"I can't let him know about this. I won't let him harm my child." She closed her eyes, and tears coursed down her cheeks.

At that moment, Theresa appeared at her side. She gave Catherine a handkerchief. "Don't cry, my lady. You're not to worry over the babe. Soon you can go home and marry that handsome man you're engaged to."

Catherine looked into the maid's trusting face. "You don't understand, Theresa. Edward will never let me go back to Miles."

"Of course he will. He said he was keeping you here because you were ill, Lady Victoria, because you were working too hard. When Edward knows about the babe, I'm sure he'll want to see you married as quickly as possible."

"Edward is lying to you. I'm not Victoria, and he knows that. I heard him tell you I was demented, but I'm not the crazy one. He is!"

The maid shook her head. "No, Edward said he was taking care of you because your father wanted to have you sent away."

"Listen to me. Edward has no idea I am Catherine Carlisle, Victoria's identical twin sister. He thinks I died eighteen years ago in a fire—a fire he arranged to kill my entire family. Someone carried me to safety and, by some miracle, my parents and sister escaped, too. Several months ago, my father learned of Edward's guilt in this and other things. My uncle was also the one responsible for Victoria's abduction. Can't you see Edward Damien is a very dangerous man?"

Crying, Theresa shook her head. "Edward loves me. He wouldn't lie to me." When she tried to turn away, Catherine grabbed her arms and Theresa gasped in pain.

Catherine pushed up the long sleeves of the maid's gray gown and revealed bruises and red slash marks across her arms. Around her wrists were welts, as though she'd been tied.

"My God, Theresa. Edward's done this to you, hasn't he? Is this the way he loves you? This is the act of a depraved man. Inflicting pain has nothing to do with making love."

Theresa's chin quivered. "Edward was quite gentle at first. I've never been with anyone but him. He said if I loved him, I should want to please him. He told me pain increased his pleasure, so there must be something wrong with me. Oh, my lady, I love him so much."

Catherine put her arms around Theresa. "I know you care for Edward, but he's a very troubled man. In this very house, he suffered cruel abuse by his stepfather. But he blames my papa for everything. Edward is resentful because he was born a bastard and will never become the Duke of Chatham."

Theresa nodded and wiped her eyes. "I know. Edward told me. He gets quite angry when he talks of it. I get frightened. But other times he treats me tenderly, and I forget the bad times and the pain. I don't even mind when he calls me by that other woman's name."

"What does he call you?"

"Evangeline. Sometimes he whispers that name in my ear as he makes love to me. He told me she was the first woman he ever loved and that she died. Do you know her?"

Catherine sighed. "Evangeline was my mother. She died five years ago. My sister and I look exactly like her. That's why Edward kidnapped me. He knows I'm not Victoria, but I am the mirror image of his lost love, Evangeline. He wants me to take Evangeline's place in his life."

"B-but if what you've said is true, you're Edward's niece," Theresa stammered.

"And that's precisely why he must not know who I really am. If Edward discovers I'm Geoffrey's daughter, he'll kill me, and you could be his next victim. Please, Theresa, you must believe me. I need your help to get away from him."

Theresa eased herself from Catherine's embrace and sat on the bed beside her. "I do believe you, my lady. But how can I help you? I don't even know where we are."

Catherine patted Theresa's hand. "You can leave that matter up to me. For the present, we must let Edward think he's fooled us. But please be very careful, Theresa. If he suspects what we're doing, there's no telling what he'll do. Where's Edward this morning?"

"He rode to the village, but left his new driver, Curtis, here to keep an eye on things. He's a big brute of a man Edward hired in London. I stay away from Curtis," Theresa added with a shiver. "He scares me."

"Well, first things first." Catherine sat up and swung her legs over the edge of the bed. "Knowing Edward, he won't be gone long. Help me get dressed. Edward mustn't know I was ill this morning. He might get suspicious. Remember not to speak to me when he's around. I'll ask for a bath this evening. We'll be able to talk then."

She was dressed and Theresa was brushing her hair when Edward entered the bedroom. His dark eyes darted toward Theresa, but Catherine quickly diverted his attention.

"Edward, I'm so glad you're back. Theresa is very help-ful, but far too quiet for my liking. Keep me company while she finishes pinning up my hair."

"Leave your hair down. I prefer it that way. You may go, Theresa." Taking the brush from her, he nodded his approval.

As the door shut, Edward walked behind Catherine's chair and began brushing her hair himself. "I could brush your hair for hours and never tire of the task. It's like the sun, so shiny and bright." His voice was almost reverent as he drew the bristles through her blond tresses.

"I've always kept my hair long. Until recently, it hung below my hips, but I thought I'd try a different style. I had some length removed and cut curls around my face."

Edward ran his fingers through the strands. "I don't want you to cut it anymore, Cat. It's far too lovely to be shorn."

"I wouldn't have to bother Theresa with doing my hair if I had a mirror. Why are there no mirrors in this room?"

"My mother was never overly fond of mirrors." Edward put down the brush and turned Catherine to face him. "But if you want a looking glass, my heart, I will have one brought in today. Every lady deserves the right to be vain occasionally, especially when she is as lovely as you."

From the heated passion in Edward's eyes, Catherine knew she had to defuse the situation and quickly changed the subject.

"Edward, I can see the ruins of an old castle on the hill. What do you know of it?" Getting up, she went to the window that faced the ancient structure. "I'm sure there's an abundance of history connected with that place."

He came up behind her and placed his hand on her shoulder. "That's Corfe Castle. Among its various owners was King Aethelred, who was given the dubious nickname the Unready. When he was ten years old, his loving mother murdered his older half brother so he could inherit the throne. Oh, the worth of a mother's love for her only son! Too bad my own mother wasn't inclined to do the same for me."

Edward continued his narration about the history of Corfe Castle, but his lesson was nearly ignored by his captive student.

He'd spoken about murdering her father as though it was a simple task that had been overlooked. His callous disregard for his brother's life repulsed her, but she hid her reaction beneath a veneer of smiles and nods.

His lecture ended when Theresa brought in their lunch. As they ate, Catherine asked Edward about his education and interests, keeping his attention focused on himself rather than on her.

"I went to the village this morning and purchased a chess set. Have you ever played, Cat?"

She shook her head. "No, but I've always wanted to learn. Do you think you can teach me?"

He smiled. "It will be a pleasure, my sweet. I'll get the board set up and we can play this afternoon."

Over the next few hours, he patiently told her about the pieces, the importance of each one, and the moves allowed in the game. Catherine made enough errors to let him think she was a novice. It was difficult for her to go against her natural instinct to win, but she did it. While they were putting the set in its carved box, Edward asked if she'd like to play again after dinner.

"Could we play tomorrow afternoon instead of this evening? My hair needs to be washed, and I'd love to take a long hot bath tonight. Would it be too difficult to arrange?"

He shook his head. "Not at all, my heart. I thought you might want a bath, so today I purchased some fine milled soap and rose oil. I hope that pleases you."

"Thank you for being so considerate." She beamed up

into his handsome face. He never suspected the plotting going on behind her innocent smile.

Edward surprised Catherine by having their evening meal served in the dining room. Though not as richly appointed as the dining rooms in the Carlisle households, it had a stately elegance all its own. The walls were a muted gold, the furnishings polished black walnut. Branches of silver candlesticks illuminated the table set for two.

While they were having dessert, a huge, hulking man entered the room. He was staring at Catherine when Edward spoke to him.

"Curtis, has everything been taken care of as I requested?"

Seeing Edward's driver, Catherine understood why Theresa was so fearful of the man. Curtis was tall, with broad shoulders and a barrel-like chest. His bushy hair was peppered with gray. He had a thick mustache and a long scar across his left cheek. His eyes seemed to leer at her.

Curtis nodded to Edward. " 'Tis all arranged, milord."

"Fine, you may go. I'll send for you when you're needed."

With a curt bow, Curtis took his leave.

Edward led Catherine back to her room and opened the door. "I hope you're pleased by my efforts to make you happy."

In front of the blazing fireplace sat a large bathing tub filled with steaming water that emitted the fragrance of roses. A tall mirror on a floor stand stood in the corner of the room beside the wardrobe cabinet.

"Edward, this is wonderful. Thank you for your kindness."

He was about to put his arm around her, when Catherine rushed to the tub and tested the hot water with her fingertips. Offering her a taut smile, he stepped back into the hall.

"Enjoy your bath, Cat. I'll send Theresa to assist you."

Within minutes, Theresa came in and locked the door from the inside. She ran to Catherine, speaking in frantic whispers.

"My lady, I don't know what happened in the dining room, but Edward warned Curtis to stay away from you. He told Curtis if he ever looked at you again, he'd find himself dead."

As Theresa helped her disrobe, Catherine asked what she knew about Curtis.

"Not much, I'm afraid. But I did hear him tell Edward that he'd been a sailor for many years. He got into some trouble a while back and could only work as a driver or guard."

Catherine entered the hot, sweet-smelling water and leaned back against the tub. "I think I've seen Curtis before, though I can't remember where or when. Perhaps it will come to me, but in the interim, I'll simply avoid him as much as I can."

After washing Catherine's hair, the two women talked in hushed tones about their plans. Theresa had found a cabinet in the study that held guns and ammunition. Catherine told her to bring a pistol to the bedroom with the powder and balls needed to load it. When Theresa reported the direction Edward had ridden that morning, Catherine was confident the village was west of the house. The information was limited, but Catherine would not be deterred.

"Theresa, search the house for a rapier for me to use." Noting the look on the maid's face, she explained. "A rapier is a sword."

"I know what a rapier is. I just don't know what you would do with one. Ladies don't use swords." She laughed.

"Have you never heard of Lady Cat? She can defeat anyone with a sword."

"Of course I've heard of Lady Cat, but everyone knows she's not real." Seeing the arch of Catherine's brow and her sly smile, Theresa frowned. Catherine nodded and confused Theresa even more. "But you couldn't be . . . she's Irish, a rebel supporter, an outlaw."

Catherine replied in her seasoned brogue, "To be sure, lass, you're not of a mind t' be callin' me a liar, are you? 'Tis not a way to see if I've a forgivin' nature, I assure you. I've brought men t'their knees for far less."

Theresa swallowed hard against the lump in her throat. "Oh, my goodness, you are her! Please forgive me, my lady . . I mean, Lady Cat . . . I never thought . . ."

Catherine put her arm around Theresa's trembling shoulder. "You have no need to fear me. I only wanted you to know I was capable of fighting our way out of here. All right?"

"Whatever you say, Lady Cat."

Catherine grimaced. "While I appreciate your acceptance, you must be careful not to call me that. Someday I'll tell you all about my other life. For now, we must concentrate on getting away from Edward. One mistake, and we may never escape his wrath."

Theresa nodded and grinned back at her.

"Get the bucket of fresh water that's standing near the fire and help me rinse my hair. Edward will wonder what's taking me so long."

Catherine was sitting on the rug in front of the hearth drying her hair when Edward came in and dismissed Theresa. After closing the door, he sat behind Catherine and brushed her damp tresses.

"I trust you enjoyed the bath."

"I did, Edward. Thank you. Soaking in a hot tub helps me to relax. I probably won't have any trouble sleeping tonight."

Edward turned her face toward him. Gazing into her

eyes, he kissed her cheek. "Then you shall have a bath every night, my heart. Anything to please you." As he leaned down to kiss her again, Curtis knocked at the door and announced himself.

Catherine used the driver's intrusion to get away from Edward. Standing in front of the mirror, she fussed with the belt on her robe as she watched the two men.

Edward was watching his servant fill buckets and take the water from the room. After several trips, Curtis removed the tub and Edward shut the door behind him.

"I'm going to lock your door tonight. Forgive me, but I don't think I can trust that man. Good night, my dear."

Catherine heard the key click in the lock and for once didn't mind the sound. Oddly reassured, she took off her robe and climbed beneath the quilt on her bed.

Sleep eluded her for quite awhile. Besides the misgivings Curtis provoked, she couldn't forget the growing desire she'd seen in Edward's eyes that evening.

Edward might not want to frighten her, but soon his lust would overtake his judgment. Somehow, she had to get away before that happened. Catherine sighed. "Maybe she could dream up a solution by morning."

The next day, Catherine opened the draperies and looked out at Corfe Castle, where she stood thinking about the events of the past weeks. The solution she'd hoped for never appeared in her dreams, but something just as important had.

She'd dreamed of Victoria.

Though she could recall only a small part of the vision, there'd been enough to give her hope. Victoria was alive and well and on her way home to Chatham.

If her sister could survive Edward Damien's devious plans to destroy her, Catherine was confident she could, too.

She had to be patient. In a few days, she would lull

Edward into thinking he was winning her heart. When he least suspected, she'd make her escape with Theresa and go home to Chatham, as well. What a celebration that would be!

Chapter 31

Over the next few days, life in the house in Corfe fell into a simple routine for its residents. After breakfast, Edward and Catherine discussed history, literature, and read books, then played chess following lunch. The time after dinner was reserved for Catherine's bath, and then Edward brushed her hair dry in front of the hearth.

Catherine's morning sickness continued with a vengeance. Every day before dawn, Theresa would wake her with a basin in one hand and a cup of tea in the other. By getting up early, Catherine knew she'd be over her nausea when Edward joined her for breakfast.

One morning, Catherine was already awake and sitting up in bed when Theresa came in with her tea, dragging her leg as if she had been injured. Her nausea was forgotten, Catherine became alarmed by the maid's condition.

"My God, did Edward hurt you again?"

"No, my lady, but this was the only way I could get this in here without being seen." Theresa lifted the skirt of her gown, exposing the length of her left leg. A rapier was tied to it with strips of cloth and prevented her from bending her knee. She untied the sword and placed it under the bed.

Handing Catherine her tea, Theresa gave her a sly smile. " 'Tis not the only thing I brought you." She removed a small pistol from her apron pocket and gave it to Catherine. "I'll bring the ammunition later, but I think it's loaded already."

Catherine checked the firearm and hid it beneath the pillow on her bed. "You've done well, Theresa. Now we can concentrate on planning our escape." Stomach spasms wracked her again. "But one thing is definite," she muttered, gasping for air, "we won't plan on an early morning departure."

Theresa quickly brought the basin to the bed for her. When the nausea subsided, Catherine asked her how Edward was acting.

"In the past few days, he's practically ignored me. When he isn't with you, Edward spends most of his time alone in his room. He's been drinking to excess every night."

"What about Curtis?"

Theresa shrugged. "Can't rightly say. Since the night Edward had words with him, Curtis has been keeping to himself. He only comes in the house to fetch your bath water."

Catherine came to a decision as she dressed. "Tonight we must leave this house. Edward's actions are like the calm before a storm, and I can't risk another day with him. Does Edward have any more laudanum in the house?"

"He has three bottles in his room. Why?"

"While I keep him busy this afternoon. I want you to take some of the laudanum, replace the liquid in the bottle and put the drug into the bottle of wine you'll be serving with dinner."

Theresa giggled. "Trapping Edward by his own means. 'Tis most fitting, my lady."

"Be sure it's that sweet port he likes so well. After Curtis brings in the water and Edward retires to his room, we'll leave. Tell Curtis he needn't return to drain the tub until morning." Catherine's lips curved in a wry grin. "Better yet, we'll reward him with some of our special vintage wine."

Theresa went off to prepare breakfast, leaving Catherine alone with her thoughts. As she brushed her hair, the familiar feeling of impending danger seeped into her being. In spite of her sudden misgivings, she refused to be dissuaded from her plans.

Edward arrived to find her pacing the room. "What's the matter, my heart? Are you feeling ill this morning?"

Covering her distress, Catherine smiled. "Not at all. If anything, I'm a bit restless. Could we take a walk after lunch? The exercise and fresh air will brighten my spirits."

Edward studied her face as though looking for deception. A few moments later, he nodded. "All right, my sweet. We'll take a walk, if that will please you. I pray sometime soon you'll repay me for my faith in you." Taking her hand, he pressed a kiss to her palm and gazed into her eyes. "Soon, my beloved Cat. Very soon."

Catherine forced herself not to shrink from Edward's touch. There was no mistaking the sensual message in his eyes. She hoped escaping that night would be soon enough.

After lunch, Edward placed her cape around her shoulders, and they left the house for their walk. She held his proffered arm as he talked about the region around them.

Edward liked to impress her with his knowledge. When he explained the Isle of Purbeck was actually a peninsula bordered on the north by Pool Bay and by the ocean on the east and south, Catherine pretended ignorance on the topic.

"I'm continually amazed by your wisdom, Edward. Geography was never my strong suit. What else can you tell me about the area?"

As he continued his educational monologue, Catherine mentally recalled her charts and maps of the English coastline. While his voice droned on, she thought to herself, *With my beloved sea close by I will not fail.*

Smiling with confidence, Catherine wasn't aware of the dark, menacing eyes that watched her from afar.

Catherine never got a chance to speak with Theresa before dinner, so she had no idea if the wine had been drugged. Edward was being overly attentive, and she wasn't able to catch the maid's attention until the main course had been served.

Theresa gave her a nod. Taking her lead, Catherine asked for wine. Edward surprised her by declining it for himself.

"No wine for me this evening. I've been indulging a little too much lately, and it has a tendency to give me a raging headache in the morning."

"But surely one glass won't hurt, Edward. It is your favorite port." He shook his head. She looked up and saw Theresa grinning.

Have I been wrong to trust this girl? Our plan has just fallen apart and she's smiling! Is Theresa trying to trick me instead of Edward?

Theresa put the dessert tray on the table and Edward smiled with pleasure. "Theresa, this is a wonderful treat! You've made my favorite custard with hot fudge sauce."

She curtsied. "I only hoped to please you, my lord."

"My heart, you must try this chocolate sauce. It is very good," Edward told Catherine as he poured the fudge over his baked custard and began devouring the rich dessert.

She shook her head. "None for me. I'll eat my custard the way it is. Chocolate gives me a rash."

Theresa frowned apologetically as she faced Catherine. "Sorry, my lady. I forgot." Suddenly, she winked.

It happened so swiftly, Catherine thought she had imagined it. "No harm done, Theresa. I prefer it plain."

A few minutes later, Edward started to yawn. "Forgive me. I guess our excursion this afternoon has left me a bit tired."

Catherine looked up to see Theresa standing behind Edward, nodding her head. Catherine followed her cue. "Edward, why don't you nap for a while? I can have my bath and wake you when I'm finished."

He came to his feet and stretched. "That's an excellent idea. I'll see you a little later." Edward kissed her cheek and went to his room.

Catherine dragged Theresa to her room. When the door was secured, she turned to face the giggling girl. "What happened? He never touched the wine."

The maid nodded. "Edward was complaining this morning about having head pains from the wine. He always does the unexpected, so I did, too. I knew you always refused chocolate, but Edward has a weakness for it. I laced the fudge sauce with laudanum. It contains so much sugar and cocoa, he never detected it. Did I do the right thing, Lady Cat?"

Catherine hugged her and laughed. "My dear Theresa, you were fantastic! If I were still sailing my ship, I'd ask you to join my crew."

Theresa's happy face became solemn. "Then at least I'd have a job. Once I leave here, I have no place to go."

"Yes, you do, Theresa. You were Edward's victim, just as my mother, Victoria, and I have been. I'll not desert you. How much do you know about babies? It seems I'm going to have one in a few months, and I'll be needing help. Would you like to work for me?"

Grinning, Theresa nodded. "Oh yes! I used to help my granny deliver babes all the time, and I tended children for folks in our village as well. I promise to work hard and make up for everything I did—"

Catherine shook her head. "We have no time for apologies, especially when they're not needed. Take the wine to Curtis now and tell him he needn't return for the water until morning. While you're gone, I'll check on Edward."

Quietly entering Edward's room, Catherine found him fast asleep on the bed. A single candle flickered on the night table. In the dim light, with his mussed hair falling over his forehead, he looked like an innocent child resting. She couldn't resist speaking to him.

"Just once in your life, Edward, I wish you'd do something unselfish and find the goodness inside you. But I fear that will never happen. In order to make such a sacrifice, there must be love, and I don't think you know how to love anyone like that, dear Uncle Edward."

Catherine closed the door and never heard Edward whisper, "Victoria?"

Theresa was waiting when Catherine got back to her room. "Curtis is nowhere to be found, my lady. I left the wine in his room. Perhaps he'll drink it when he returns."

Catherine retrieved the rapier from under the mattress and placed it on the bed. "While I'm getting ready, fetch your cloak. Be sure to dress warmly. We may be traveling for quite some time, and it could get very cold. Come back as soon as you can."

When Theresa left the room, Catherine noticed the filled tub in front of the hearth. Steam rose from its surface, meaning Curtis had not been gone very long. Without warning, a deep voice called from behind the privacy screen in the corner.

"Goin' somewhere, Lady Cat?" Curtis stepped out from behind the screen, a rapier in his hand.

Slowly, Catherine backed up to the bed, hoping to

retrieve her weapon. "How do you know who I am? Have we met before?"

His mouth pulled back in a vicious sneer. "In a manner o' speaking, we have. Though we ain't been formally introduced, Lady Cat, you should remember me. Hell, meeting up with you five years ago changed my life."

"Five years ago? I was barely more than a child. How could I have been responsible for changing your life?" She moved closer to the bed. "Where would I know you from?"

"I was a boatswain on a large merchant ship coming from the colonies. I worked hard to get my rank. Thanks to you, I lost it all." He kept walking toward her, brandishing the sword in front of him.

"If you wish me to remember, Curtis, you'll have to be a bit more precise. Was there anything special about you or your ship?" The back of her leg touched the bed and she ran her hand along the spread behind her, searching for her rapier.

Curtis snorted. "The only thing special about that day was you, Lady Cat. No one had seen the golden woman-child before. Not only was she beautiful, but she could fight like a man. I got the scar to prove it. Tell me, do you still have that fancy little knife of yours?"

Recognition hit Catherine full force. "You're the man who shot Da. You ignored your captain's order for a peaceful surrender and shot the Hawk."

"I would have killed him if you hadn't interfered. That dagger of yours hit its mark, all right, and crippled me. A boatswain can't work without two good arms. He's in charge of the rigging, the cables, and such."

Her fingers wrapped around the hilt of the rapier as she waited to make her move. "You needn't instruct me, Curtis. I have a ship and I know the duties of my crew. Even if you were hurt, there were other tasks you could have handled."

"Not with the ridicule I got from my mates. To be undone by a mere slip of a girl—they deemed me a fool! All the respect I'd earned after twenty years at sea was gone, thanks to you."

Curtis leaned forward and eyed her womanly form. "You sure have grown up, Lady Cat. Perhaps I'll clip your claws and have a sample of what his lordship's been getting."

His leering threat pushed Catherine into action. In the blink of an eye, she brought her sword toward his chest. "The only thing you're going to get is a taste of my blade, Curtis."

Theresa returned to find Catherine and Curtis fighting with rapiers. She edged her way to the bed as she watched them. Despite her untrained eye, she could see Catherine was the better of the two. The sound of their swords striking against each other reverberated in the air.

Curtis chuckled. " 'Tis amazing, Lady Cat. You fight well even though you're carrying a child. Most women would fear injuring the babe, but not you."

She continued her offensive attack and tried hard to ignore her opponent's taunts.

He shook his head. "Guess it don't matter. The babe's naught but a bastard anyway."

Catherine began losing her concentration. Hampered by long skirts and petticoats already, she found herself thinking about what Curtis had said. Was she taking too many risks fighting with this man? Why hadn't she tried to get the pistol that was under the pillow? It would have been easier, but she'd opted to fight him head on. What had she been thinking?

Catherine forgot about the bucket of water standing in front of the hearth, she bumped into it, splashing water onto the polished floor. She slipped on the wet surface and fell. The next thing she felt was cold steel pushing through her chest. Losing consciousness, she sank into a void of black.

Theresa was kneeling on the bed when Catherine fell. She pulled the pistol from beneath the pillow and turned to see Curtis plunge his blade into Catherine. Without a moment's forethought, the young maid cocked the hammer and shot him before he could stab his victim again. The sound boomed off the walls, and the big man collapsed to the floor.

Theresa rushed to Catherine's side as Edward crashed through the door, shouting, "What in the bloody hell was that noise?"

Surveying the room, he gasped. Curtis was on the floor near the tub with a wound on the side of his head. Theresa knelt in a puddle of water next to Catherine, whose yellow gown was crimson with blood.

Edward ran to Catherine and lifted her off the floor. Tears coursed down his face as he gently placed her on the bed. "My precious love, what has that animal done to you?" His hand trembled when he attempted to examine her wound.

Theresa bolstered her courage to stand across the bed from Edward. "My lord, I have experience nursing people. Why don't you allow me to do this?"

He nodded and asked what he could do. She told him to fill the basin with hot water and to bring the towels to the bed. After he did this, she sent him for sheets and a bottle of brandy. She removed Catherine's clothes, draped a towel over her breasts and covered her lower body with the quilt. Using towels, she applied pressure to the wound to stop the bleeding.

With great care, she washed the area around the wound and found the cut was several inches wide and very deep. The rapier had entered the lower left side of her chest beneath her breast, and appeared to have missed her heart and lung. Theresa used her fingers to probe the wound and discovered the blade had gone between Catherine's ribs. The bleeding had slowed, but the gash needed to be stitched closed.

Upon Edward's return, she sent him to get a needle and thread from her room. Then she had him hold Catherine's shoulders down on the bed while she poured brandy on the wound and sewed it closed. She applied a pad of cloth against the sutured gash and kept it in place with strips of sheets she'd torn for bandages. Theresa pulled the quilt up and covered her unconscious patient.

Edward stroked Catherine's hair. "This is all my fault. I knew that animal lusted for her. He couldn't keep his eyes off her. Tell me what happened."

"Curtis was hiding in here when my lady came to bathe," Theresa replied. "When he attacked her, I ran and got a pistol from the gun case. By the time I got back, Curtis had stabbed her with the sword. I couldn't let him do it again, so I shot him."

"I'll always be grateful to you. You've saved her life, and I shall never forget that. Please stay with her while I remove that bastard's body from this house."

A short time later, Edward returned to Catherine's side. "Go to bed, Theresa. I will stay with her tonight."

Theresa was afraid to leave Catherine alone with Edward, but realized she had no choice. "If she develops a fever, please wake me, my lord."

"I swear I'll come for you the instant there's any change in her condition. Get some rest."

When the door closed behind Theresa, Edward sat on the bed next to Catherine. As he brushed back the curls from her pale face, he prayed to the deity he thought had forsaken him.

"Please God, don't let my beloved Cat die. If one of us must die, let it be me. I cannot live without her. An eternity in hell would be preferable to remaining alone. Dear Lord, grant me your mercy this one time. Let Cat live."

Catherine slept on, unaware she'd been wrong. Edward

knew how to love and had offered to make the ultimate sacrifice to prove it.

Aboard the *Cat's Cradle* as it sailed a few miles off the English coast, Victoria sat up in bed screaming. "Oh, God, no!" Her eyes tightly closed, she clutched the left side of her chest and groaned in pain.

Justin pulled her into his arms. "Victoria, wake up. You're having a bad dream."

Miles rushed into their cabin, his britches not fully fastened and his shirt gaping open. "Justin, what's the matter? I heard Torie scream."

Before Justin could answer, Victoria began speaking.

"He hurt Catherine. She fell and he stabbed her with his sword." Victoria opened her eyes and saw Justin and Miles staring at her. The vision she had witnessed came rushing back to her, and her chin trembled.

"Catherine was trying to escape, but she didn't know he was hiding behind the screen."

Miles flinched. "Edward? What has he done to her?"

Victoria shook her head. "It wasn't Edward. He was a big man she called Curtis. He said Cat had ruined his life and he attacked her with a sword. She was defending herself very well with a rapier until he started taunting her about the baby."

"How did he learn of the child?" Justin asked.

"Curtis must have overheard my sister talking to Theresa. Cat was upset by his words. She slipped on the wet floor near the tub and fell. That's when he . . . he . . ." Victoria struggled to speak past the lump in her throat. "Catherine saw the blade plunge into her, but she didn't cry out. I felt the pain with her, but she never cried."

Justin pulled slightly away from her. "Victoria, show me where Cat was stabbed. Where did the blade strike her?"

With a trembling hand, she touched the tender spot on

her chest. "It was here. I can still feel the pain, though it's not as bad now."

Miles let out a tense sigh. "Then Cat is still alive?"

Victoria nodded. "Catherine is alive, Miles, but she's lost consciousness." At that moment Victoria decided not to tell him about the gunshot she had heard at the end of her vision. Until she knew the truth about the incident, she didn't want him to worry any more than he had to.

Justin tried to console Miles. "If the blade entered where Victoria's shown me, the wound may not be too serious. The one thing that concerns me is the possibility of an infection. A fever could weaken Cat and slow her recovery."

"Or kill her," Miles spat out. A look of grim determination crossed his face. "We'll arrive there by late afternoon. Edward may not have wielded the weapon that struck her, but he's responsible for her injury. God help that man when I find him."

Hearing the vehemence in his voice, Victoria cautioned her old friend. "We can't let the others know about my vision. My father mustn't be told Catherine is hurt until we know how bad she is. And if the Hawk even suspects something has happened to her, he'll be uncontrollable. Promise me this will remain our secret."

Miles thrust his fingers through his hair. "You have my word, but I'll guarantee nothing else. As far as your uncle is concerned, the minute I see him, he'll die." Miles left their cabin.

Victoria shivered. "Justin, I'm worried about Miles. I've never seen him like this."

"You've never seen him in love before." Holding Victoria in his arms, he hugged her. "If it were you in Cat's place, I'd be as angry as he is."

"I'm afraid Miles is underestimating my uncle. Edward is skilled in handling weapons and has a brilliant mind. He was obsessed by his love for my mother. Now he has

Catherine to take her place, and Edward would destroy her and himself before he'd willingly lose her."

"But Cat's his niece. Surely when he finds out the truth about her, he won't feel that way."

Shaking her head, Victoria trembled. "If Edward learns the truth, he'll kill her. He wants the entire Carlisle family to pay for the pain he has suffered. I pray we can get to him before he discovers who Catherine really is."

Justin kissed her and eased down beside her on the bed. "Let's get some sleep, Victoria. Stop worrying. In a few hours we'll land at the Isle of Purbeck and rescue Cat."

Resting in her husband's embrace, Victoria recalled the gunshot she'd heard in her dream. Curtis had no such weapon showing, so the gun must have been shot by someone else. But who had done it, and who was the target? Had someone been able to stop Curtis before he was able to hurt Catherine again? Was her sister dead?

A twinge of pain jolted her. Victoria touched the spot where Cat had been stabbed and found the area sore and warm. A smile curved her lips.

"You're alive, Catherine. As long as I feel your pain, I know you're alive. Be strong. We'll be together soon, my sister. Very soon."

Near dawn, Theresa entered Catherine's candlelit room carrying a bucket of hot water. She was surprised to find Edward sitting on the bed exactly as she'd left him hours before. He was watching Catherine sleep while his fingers caressed her hair. He didn't look up, but he knew Theresa was there. In a soft voice he spoke to her.

"You see, Theresa, she has no fever and seems to be resting peacefully. My Cat is so beautiful. Lying here, she looks like an angel. When Cat is well, I shall make her my wife. She'll be mine throughout eternity."

Listening to him, Theresa shuddered. Edward had used

Catherine's nickname and given up the ruse of calling her his niece. The facade of concerned uncle was replaced by that of devoted lover. His next statement convinced Theresa he was truly mad.

"This lovely lady is a gift to me from God. He's sent my love back to me. But this time, Evangeline will be mine. Won't you, my dearest?" He stroked Catherine's cheek. "Yes, my angel, my sweet Evangeline, you're mine."

Frightened, the young maid placed the bucket on the floor and moved toward the bed. She had to get Edward out of the room before Catherine woke up and heard him calling her by her dead mother's name.

"My lord, now that I'm here, why don't you go to your room and rest?"

Edward shook his head. "No. I must be here when she wakes."

"But, my lord, she'll probably sleep for several hours. By then you'll be too tired to remain awake. While you rest, I'll check her wound and see she's bathed and gowned in one of her nightrails. It would distress my lady if she awoke to find she wasn't properly attired."

"Very well, I'll go to my room. But if she wakes up, you must come for me straightaway." Edward leaned down and placed a kiss on Catherine's lips. "Be sure to brush her hair and see she's gowned in blue. My Evangeline has always been partial to blue." He rose from the bed and left the room.

Pouring the hot water into a basin, Theresa prepared to bathe Catherine. She carefully removed the bandages to check the wound. As she was covering it with a new dressing, a mark on Catherine's upper chest caught her attention.

"I never noticed that before." Looking closely at the crescent-shaped mark on Catherine's left breast, she gasped. "Oh, no! Edward has the same mark on his chest.

He called it the Carlisle family curse. If he sees this, he'll know for sure you're related to him.''

Theresa quickly wrapped the bandages and dressed Catherine in a white cotton nightgown. It had a high neckline that closed with a row of tiny pearl buttons.

"My lady, I wish you were awake. Edward's acting most peculiar, and I don't know what to do.'' Theresa pulled the quilt over Catherine and sat on the bed beside her. "You've got to get better soon, or he's going to find out who you are. Then we'll both be in trouble. Please, Lady Cat, wake up.''

But her entreaties went unanswered. As Theresa looked down at the sleeping woman, she admitted Edward was right.

Catherine did look like an angel.

Chapter 32

The *Cat's Cradle* docked near St. Aldhelm's Head at noon. While the horses were saddled and led off the ship, Miles went into town to gather information and Geoffrey met with the harbormaster regarding their use of the berth. It was agreed everyone would meet at a nearby pub in an hour.

At the appointed time, the group of seven gathered. Seated in a private dining room, they ordered food, but ate little as they discussed their plans.

Geoffrey chuckled. "Even flying an English flag didn't allay the harbormaster's fear we'd come to raid his town. I had to shove my ducal signet ring in the man's face so he could see I really was the Duke of Chatham." He gave Sean an apologetic smile. "It appears that you, the *Cat's Cradle*, and Lady Cat are well known in this area, and they're not overly fond of the Irish. To avert unwanted attention, your crew will have to remain on board, Sean."

"I thought as much. Colin, Padraic, and I will curb our tongues while we're about." Sean looked around the table.

"Between the lot of us, I know we'll be able to rescue Cat without much difficulty. What did you find out at the local constabulary, Miles?"

Taking a piece of parchment from his pocket, Miles showed them a hand-drawn map of Corfe, the location of the ruins, and the surrounding homes that had a view of the ancient castle. "The castle lies in the center with nine different houses having the view Victoria described. By using the ruins for the central meeting point and dividing into smaller groups, we can cover the area quickly. When a group locates Edward's home, one rider goes back to the castle to alert the others. No one should try to rescue Cat on his own."

Justin made a suggestion. "Perhaps we should select someone to remain at the ruins. When the rider is approaching, he could signal the others and save valuable time." He turned to look at Victoria but she shook her head.

Wearing her sister's britches, blouse, and boots, Victoria poked Justin's chest with her hand. "No you don't, Dr. Prescott! I may be a woman, but no one can ride faster than I on Black Magic. Papa would be a good choice for the position at the castle. The rest of us can divide into three units—Miles and Sean, Justin and Padraic, Colin and I. That way if we met any of the local people, they'd never know one of us was Irish."

Everyone agreed with her. Within minutes, they were on their way to Corfe Castle.

Edward returned to Catherine's room and sent Theresa to prepare his lunch. Taking his place on the edge of the bed, he touched Catherine's forehead.

"Theresa has taken good care of you, my angel. You don't have a fever, but you're still sleeping. Perhaps this is good. Rest, my angel and, I'll be close by if you need me. I won't leave you again."

Theresa heard his words from the corridor before she ran to the kitchen. Her hands trembled as she prepared the tea tray and sliced the bread and cold roasted meat for the meal.

What was she to do? If Edward didn't leave the room, she wouldn't be able to warn Catherine. She'd have no idea what she'd be waking up to. Dear God, what should she do?

Her hands shook so badly, she cut her finger on the knife she was using to carve the meat. Bringing the cut to her lips, she looked at its blade and wondered if she had the mettle to use it against Edward.

She'd shot Curtis to save her lady, but this was different. For months, she'd thought herself in love with Edward. How could she think of killing him?

While she worked, her memories, conscience, and sense of survival battled inside her. By the time she completed the lunch tray, her mind was made up. As long as Edward didn't know who Cat really was, she wouldn't interfere, but if he came close to the truth, she'd stop him. Cat was right. He'd kill them both.

Theresa tucked the knife into the deep side pocket of her skirt and fluffed her petticoats beneath it to disguise the slight bulge it caused. Picking up the tray, she went back to Catherine's room, silently praying heaven would help her when the time came to stop Edward.

Following the directions Miles obtained from the constable, the group of riders arrived at Corfe Castle. From their vantage point on the hill, they could see the nine surrounding homes. Before anyone could object, Victoria picked out the houses she wanted to investigate.

"Colin and I will take those three to the east."

No one realized Victoria was using her instincts to find her sister. She knew Catherine would be in that direction and was drawn toward the big white house across the valley.

As she turned to go, Geoffrey called to her. "Victoria, don't try anything on your own. If you find them, let Colin stay there and you come back so I can alert the others."

Pulling the hood of her cloak down to ward off the wind, she rode off with Colin. In a matter of minutes, they were riding through a glade of trees that stood beside the stately white house. They decided to explore the barn behind the house first. Using the woods for cover, they hid their horses and crept up to the neatly maintained building.

Four horses were stalled inside the barn, as was a large traveling coach. Looking in the last stall, Colin made a gruesome discovery.

"There's a dead man in here. He's been shot in the head."

Victoria recognized the corpse as the man who'd attacked Catherine in the vision, but kept the knowledge to herself.

"Come on, Colin. Let's go to the rear of the house. Perhaps we can peek in a window."

She and Colin cautiously approached the house. Crouching down, they came upon a window that had drapes firmly pulled across it. They proceeded to the next window. Even before she looked inside, Victoria knew who would be there.

On the side of the bed closest to the window, Edward sat holding the hand of a woman propped against the pillows. Victoria's heart jumped when she saw her mirror image lying there on the bed.

"Look, Colin, it's her! It's Catherine!"

Colin's head came up beside hers. "Cat doesn't look well. Is that your uncle?"

She nodded. "Yes, that's Edward Damien in the flesh."

"You better go tell the others. I'll stay here and see he doesn't leave."

"You go, Colin. I've waited all this time to see my sister. I can't leave her now. Take Black Magic and get the others."

He shook his head. "I don't think that's wise. What if—"

Victoria put her hand over his mouth. "No arguments, Colin. If you want to work for me, you must not question my orders."

Colin pulled her hand from his lips. "You're getting to sound more like Cat every day. All right, I'll go, but don't try any heroics." He shook his head. "Why do I feel I've been through this before?" Without another word, he ran to the woods, where their horses were hidden.

Victoria turned back to watch the occupants of the room. Being so close and yet so far away from her sister was agonizing for her. "Oh, Catherine, I want you to know I'm here. Miles, Papa, and the others will be along soon. Then we'll take you home."

Catherine began to stir on the bed. Victoria could see Edward's startled expression when her sister's lips moved, forming words. When Victoria leaned forward to see if she could make out what Catherine was saying, she saw Theresa moving toward the bed behind Edward.

Without knowing it, Victoria had roused Catherine with her softly spoken words. Though her ears hadn't heard the message, Catherine's heart and mind had.

"Victoria," she whispered. "That you, Victoria?"

Edward didn't understand her words, but Theresa did. Holding her hand against her pocket, she crept up behind him, listening to Catherine's labored speech.

"Miles . . . where is Miles? Must tell him . . ."

Edward jerked Catherine up by her shoulders. "Why are you calling him? You belong to me, Evangeline. Do you hear me? Damn it all, you are mine!"

Theresa tried to reason with him. "My lord, she's not herself. People often say crazy things while they're getting over such a severe injury."

Edward glared at Theresa. "Get the hell out of here and mind your own affairs. This has nothing to do with you. Remove the water from that tub and go back to the kitchen."

"But, my lord, I'm concerned for her well being. Please let me help you take care of her," she implored him.

"You're a sorry excuse for help, Theresa. I told you to dress Evangeline in a blue nightgown, and you couldn't even do that. If I want something done right, I'll have to do it myself. Bring me the gown I requested and get out of my sight!"

Catherine was struggling to wake up as Edward spoke to her in comforting tones and began to unfasten the tiny pearl buttons on the neckline of her nightgown.

"I'll take care of you, Evangeline. You've always liked to wear blue. It goes so well with your lovely blue eyes."

At that moment, Catherine looked up at him. Her emerald eyes caused Edward to falter. "Green? Evangeline has blue eyes."

Hearing his confusion, Theresa used the opportunity to sneak up behind him. The blue nightrail was hanging over her left arm as she held the knife in her right hand. She poised to strike him with the blade, not realizing the candles sitting on the table near the door had cast her shadow over the bed.

Seeing the image, Edward turned as Theresa brought the blade toward his back. He twisted away from her and grabbed the hand holding the weapon. Using his superior strength, he easily disarmed her. He imprisoned her slight wrist within his grasp and started beating her.

"You silly bitch!" he taunted. "You're so jealous of my beloved, you dared to attack me!"

For the first time, Theresa fought back. She slapped him

and screamed, then lashed out, scoring the side of his face with her nails. This infuriated Edward. Releasing his hold on her, he hit her with his fist and knocked her to the floor.

Victoria was momentarily shocked by the savagery of Edward's assault on Theresa. When he picked up the knife and moved toward the young woman lying on the floor, she ran to the front door of the house to stop him.

The sound of his vicious laughter could be heard throughout the house. "You're a fool, Theresa! Your ignorance never ceases to amaze me. Poor chit, so easily led. I shall miss the evenings of pleasure and pain we shared. I took the pleasure while you had the pain. But soon you won't feel anything, my pet."

Victoria arrived at the bedroom door to see him reaching for Theresa. "Don't touch her, Uncle Edward. It would be a fatal mistake, I assure you."

Forgetting his intended victim, he whirled around to face his visitor. Victoria stood in the opened doorway, a pistol aimed at him.

"Victoria? You're supposed to be dead. Clive swore he'd killed you."

"*Au contraire.* I wasn't partial to being kidnapped and raped, so I put him out of his existence when he attacked me. I see you doubt my word. Don't. It appears you're not the only member of this family capable of taking a life. Only our motives were different—I did it to survive. You did it out of greed."

Edward snarled at her. "It's easy for you to judge me. The world was handed to you on a gold tray by your father. Do you know what my sire gave me? Nothing! He took me from my mother and ignored me for the rest of his sorry life. The only thing that mattered to my father was his heir, my brother Geoffrey. Everything was for Geoffrey."

"My father didn't have an easy time of it, either." Victoria countered. "Malcolm blamed him for his wife's death and deserted him, as well. When Malcolm died, he left the family holdings in shambles. The lands were mortgaged, the money wasted on gambling and drinking. From what I've learned of your past. you have that in common with Malcolm, Uncle Edward. Tell me, what kind of debts did you pay off when Lorelei paid you to marry her?"

While Victoria kept her uncle busy talking, Theresa crawled to the doorway. Keeping the gun aimed at Edward, Victoria spoke to her. "Theresa, help will be arriving soon. Wait for them outside and tell them where I am."

The injured maid passed her and stumbled down the hall.

Edward stared at his niece. "Last night I dreamed you stood at my bed and talked to me. You actually sounded as though you cared for me. You called me dear Uncle Edward and looked so sincere. The dream was so real, I thought I could reach out and touch you."

"It was me," a soft voice answered from the bed.

Edward turned and found Catherine awake, looking at him. "But why would you say such things, my angel? Your charade at playing my niece has been over for quite some time. Why would you torment me by calling me uncle?"

"Because you *are* her uncle," Victoria retorted. "She's my sister, Catherine Elizabeth Carlisle. We're identical twins."

Shaking his head in disbelief, Edward moved toward the bed. "This cannot be. You're lying, Victoria. Your twin died in the fire. This is my precious angel, my darling. She loves me."

"Stay away from Catherine, Edward. I will not hesitate to shoot you, so don't tempt me."

His brooding gaze followed Victoria while she went to her sister's side. With the gun aimed at him, she never looked away from his face when she put out her hand to touch Catherine. Their two hands joined in a loving squeeze as the sisters united for the first time in eighteen years.

Catherine struggled to speak. "Sorry our reunion has to be like this."

"Don't worry, sister. We have years to catch up on and a wonderful future ahead of us."

Edward wasn't convinced. *This must be a trick. They're trying to take my love away from me again, but I won't allow it. No matter what they say, she's my Evangeline. Only mine.*

Miles and Sean were riding toward the third house in their assigned area when Black Magic ran out of the woods, Colin clinging to his back. Sean rode to his son while Miles headed to the house in the distance that Colin had come from. If Victoria had given up her treasured horse, he knew she'd found Catherine and had refused to leave her.

In the past few days, Victoria had been acting more and more like her twin, and that caused Miles to worry. Although they looked alike, Victoria wasn't the skilled fighter her sister was. He was concerned her false sense of bravado and stubbornness would get her into trouble. If Catherine couldn't successfully fight her way out of the situation with Edward, her untutored sister wouldn't stand a chance, either.

With this in mind, he raced toward the white house.

While the twins talked, Edward became more agitated. He looked about the room for a means of disarming Victoria. Lying at his feet was the blue nightgown Theresa had dropped. He bent down, picked it up, and rubbed the silky fabric with his fingers as he gazed at the gun in his niece's hand. The pistol was heavy, and her slight hand trembled from its weight. Without warning, he threw the garment into Victoria's face.

Startled by his actions, Victoria jerked, causing the gun to fire. The sound of the single shot was music to Edward's ears. He dashed to the bed and pulled her away from Catherine.

While Victoria fought to get out of his clutches, Catherine began striking him, too. With his arm firmly around Victoria's waist, he raised his other arm and backhanded Catherine across the face, throwing her back to the bed. In her weak condition, the blow was more than sufficient to knock her out. Seeing he'd injured her infuriated Edward.

"Look what you've made me do! Because of your interference, Victoria, I've hurt her. Your presence is poisoning my love, and I won't stand for it!" He dragged Victoria kicking and screaming toward the open door.

Using the heel of her right palm, Victoria placed a blow to the underside of his nose, causing him to lose his balance. He slammed into the table beside the door, sending it crashing to the floor. In his haste to get Victoria out of the room, he never saw the lighted candlesticks that had been on the table roll toward the draperies that covered the corner windows.

Closing the door behind him with one hand, he struggled to keep Victoria away from his face. Blood dripped from his nose as he carried her into the parlor. He dumped her onto the sofa and struck her jaw with his fist.

"You and that damned brother of mine are determined to destroy me, but I won't let you. I'll get rid of you myself this time and see it's done right," he screamed.

Miles rushed into the house as Edward was putting his hands around Victoria's throat. "Let her go, you cowardly bastard, and fight me!"

Edward spun around and Miles charged him. Victoria was too weak to raise herself from the sofa while the two men fought.

The parlor was soon in a shambles. Edward's face was bloody from Theresa's scratches and Victoria's blow to his nose. His left eye was badly bruised. Miles continued to pummel him, warding off his jabs as though they were of no consequence. The only blood on him was on his knuckles, and that belonged to his beleaguered opponent. His anger echoed in the words that accompanied his assault.

"You wretched snake! You murdered your wife and tried to do away with Victoria. You abducted Catherine, and I'll kill you for that."

Edward shoved himself away from Miles. "You're betrothed to Victoria. Why does Cat mean so much to you, Grayson?"

"Catherine and I are in love, and you are going to pay for endangering her and the life of our unborn child."

Edward was startled by his words. "Child? What are you talking about?"

Before Miles could reply, the odor of smoke permeated the room. A woman's scream met their ears. Instantly, he recognized the voice. "My God, that's Catherine!"

He turned toward the hall, which was filling with thick smoke. He'd barely taken a step when Edward picked up a chair and struck him with it, knocking him to the floor.

"You won't touch her, Grayson. She's mine! I'll not let you near her." His pain and injuries forgotten, Edward rushed to help Catherine.

Victoria struggled to stand up, but fell in front of the sofa. The smoke became more dense as the fire spread through the house.

When the other rescuers arrived, Theresa told them Edward, Miles, and the twins were inside. Without a second to spare, Sean, Padraic, and Justin ran into the burning house. Geoffrey and Colin ushered the horses and the injured maid into the relative safety of the barn.

Sean could barely make out Miles' tall figure staggering

through the thick smoke. He rushed to him and tried to lead him out of the house, but Miles pushed him away.

"Let me go! Edward's got Catherine in there."

Sean looked in the direction he had pointed and saw the flames totally engulfing the hall. "You'll not be able to get through there. Maybe we can find a window or door round back."

While Miles and Sean made their way through the heat and smoke, Padraic found Victoria lying on the parlor rug. He swept her into his arms and hurried outside. Justin took her from Padraic and carried her to the barn to check her injuries.

Dodging the flames in the hall, Edward kicked in the burning door of Catherine's room and rushed inside. Through the smoke he saw her cringing against the wall, staring at the fire. Before he reached her, Catherine slid to the floor. Her voice trembled, her eyes glazed with fear.

"I don't like fire. Please help me," she pleaded.

Kneeling beside her, Edward wrapped his arms around her. "Everything will be all right. I won't let it hurt you, my angel. I promise."

She pointed to the doorway. "The hall's totally engulfed in flames. We can't get out that way."

Edward pulled the quilt from the bed and dipped it into the water that was left in the tub. He draped the wet covering over Catherine and carried her to the window across from the bed. Sitting her against the wall, he tore the draperies down and tossed them aside. When the window failed to open, he picked up a small table and smashed it into the glass.

The sound of breaking glass drew Miles and Sean to the bedroom window. Even though the window itself was broken out. there were iron bars across the opening. As they pulled at the bars, Edward tried pushing from the inside. Then he got an idea.

"Get some rope and bring a horse back here. If it's tied properly, the animal could tug these bars out of place."

Scan returned moments later with Geoffrey and Black Magic. The ropes were secured to the bars and, after several tries, the horse pulled them from their secured position.

Edward lifted Catherine into his arms. "I told you I'd take care of you, my angel. I'd die before I let anything hurt you." He pushed the quilt back and gently kissed her lips. "I do love you, Cat."

Catherine looked into his battered face. His hair was singed and his eyes reddened by the smoke. Before she could thank him, Edward carried her to Miles and Geoffrey, who were standing outside the window. As Edward released her, a loud roar swept through the chamber and he fell back into the room. A ceiling beam crashed on top of Edward, trapping him under its immense weight.

"Please help him," Catherine screamed. "He saved my life. I don't want him to die in there."

Leaving her in Geoffrey's care, Miles and Sean threw off their coats and climbed into the opening. They lifted the beam and pulled Edward from under it. Sean loaded the unconscious man over his shoulder and carried him to the window, where Padraic was waiting. Swiftly, Padraic toted the injured man to the barn.

Catherine stood with Geoffrey and watched with bated breath as Miles and Sean emerged from the burning building. Once she saw they were safe, dizziness overwhelmed her, and she swayed on her feet. Miles moved quickly and caught her up in his arms before she fell to the ground.

"My poor darling, you're shivering with the cold." Taking his coat from Geoffrey, he tenderly enfolded her in its warmth. Her eyes opened and he kissed her. "I love you, Catherine. I've come too close to losing you, and I won't ever let that happen again.'' His mouth took hers in another kiss.

Geoffrey put his arm around Sean's shoulder as they watched the young lovers. ''Hawk, it appears our little girl won't be needing us anymore. There seems to be a new man in her life.''

''Now, Geoffrey, I'll not be counting us out just yet. Cat's quite a handful, even for the likes of young Grayson, I expect she'll be wanting to see us once in a while—or maybe Miles will,'' Sean said with a smirk, ''when he needs to track her down. For the life of me, I can't picture Cat staying home having babes.''

Laughing, the duke patted his new friend on the back. ''Besides, you and I are entirely too young to be grandfathers.''

Padraic came running toward them. ''The doc says you'd best come quickly. Edward's bad and doesn't have much time left.''

A few minutes later, they were all gathered in the barn. Justin explained the beam had fractured most of Edward's ribs and that he'd suffered massive internal injuries that would prove fatal.

Geoffrey knelt beside his brother. When Edward opened his pain-filled eyes and saw him, he struggled to speak.

''Is Cat all right, Geoffrey?''

The duke nodded. ''Yes, Edward. Thanks to you, she wasn't hurt in the fire.''

''May I see her?'' Edward gasped.

Wearing Miles' coat, Catherine sat at his side and took his hand. ''I'm here, Edward. As you can see, I am fine.''

He looked at her smudged face and tousled hair and smiled. ''You see, my angel, I promised I'd keep you safe. You were wrong about me.''

"About what?" she asked.

Laboring to breathe, Edward explained. "Last night you said I didn't know how to love, but I do. I loved Evangeline, but I made terrible mistakes and hurt her. When you were stabbed, I blamed myself. I was afraid you wouldn't survive. I made a pact with God. If He allowed you to live, He could take me in your place. Wasn't that love?"

Catherine nodded. "Yes, Edward, that was love. The very best kind, unselfish and giving. But you should rest now."

"No, I have to tell you one more thing," he wheezed. "I'm very sorry for everything I did. I don't expect you to forgive me. Just try to understand."

Tears burned her eyes as she nodded to his request.

Edward shuddered in pain. "Cat, may I beg you for one final indulgence? Would you kiss me farewell and stay with me till I am gone? I've never liked being alone. I've been alone most of my life. I don't want to die that way."

Catherine bent down and kissed him. "I won't leave you, Edward. I'll stay right by your side for as long as you need me. I promise."

His lips turned up in a smile. "Thank you, Catherine. I know now you are Evangeline's daughter. I can see her light shining in your eyes. I would gladly die for her child to make up for the pain I caused her. Do you think she'll know that?"

"Yes, Uncle Edward. I'm sure she'll know."

"Good, Catherine. That's very good." Closing his eyes, he squeezed her hand and sighed. "I'll never be alone again."

As Victoria stood nearby, crying against Justin's shoulder, she felt a sharp pain in her lower chest. She turned quickly to look at her sister. Catherine was holding Edward's hand. Her expression was placid as she comforted the dying man. Another pain shot through Victoria, but she bit down on her lips, so as not to cry out.

Within moments, Edward Damien passed away. His face relaxed and a smile remained on his lips. In death, he was finally free of his torment.

Catherine kissed his hand. "I pray God will understand, Edward. In His infinite mercy, may He grant you the peace you so desperately needed."

When Justin bent down to cover the body, he looked over at Catherine. Her color was ashen, her breathing labored.

"Cat, are you all right?"

Instead of replying, Catherine collapsed against him. Miles dropped quickly to her side and took her into his arms.

"Justin, what's wrong?" Miles asked.

The answer to his question came from Victoria. "It's her wound. Catherine's been in great pain for quite sometime, but she's been hiding it from everyone," she explained, rubbing her own sore midriff. "Check where she was wounded, Justin. I'm afraid something is terribly wrong."

Miles carried Catherine to an area of the barn where Justin could examine her. Removing the wool coat, they discovered the bodice of her nightgown was soaked with blood. After a few minutes, Justin announced they'd have to return to the ship immediately.

"Theresa did a fine job of suturing the wound, but I think there may be a nicked artery or a bone fragment causing the bleeding. My surgical tools are on the ship. Catherine's lost a great deal of blood, and we haven't time to spare. I suggest we use this coach and get her back to the *Cat's Cradle* as soon as possible."

Late that night, Victoria sat in the captain's cabin watching Justin tending her sister. He'd reopened Catherine's wound and repaired the damaged artery that had caused the bleeding. Theresa had aided him during the surgery while Victoria consoled her father and the others.

That had been hours ago. The ship had set sail, and Theresa had gone to bed after Victoria insisted she could take care of their patient. Secretly, she looked forward to spending time alone with Catherine. It was still hard to believe she had a twin sister, yet it felt very right. The missing part of her life was lying on the bed before her, and a feeling of contentment filled Victoria's being.

But her time alone with Catherine wasn't to be. First Miles came in to sit with her. After supper, Geoffrey and Sean dropped by and stayed, too. Colin and Padraic joined the vigil when they completed their watch.

Sitting on the bed next to Catherine, Victoria held her hand and spoke softly to her. "You'd best get well quickly, sister. Your visitors are overflowing the room. If love could guarantee your recovery, you'd be instantly cured."

Miles stood behind Victoria and put his hand on her shoulder. At that second, Catherine's eyes fluttered and slowly opened. She squinted to focus on the two people beside her. A smile spread across her face.

"I wasn't dreaming. You are both here." Catherine suddenly recalled the other events of the past two days and the smile left her face. "It was real—Curtis, the fire, and Edward dying after he rescued me?"

Victoria squeezed her hand. "Celebrate the good things and forget the bad, Cat. You're here and safe, and for that I'm truly thankful. At long last we're together again, sister. We have eighteen years of catching up to do, but that will have to wait." Lifting her hand, she directed Catherine's attention to the visitors who surrounded her bed. "There are a few others here who are glad to see you, as well."

Geoffrey came to her side and kissed her forehead. "I'm grateful we found you, my daughter. I was worried, but your sister wouldn't allow me to give up hope. Get some rest. I'll be back to see you in the morning."

424 *Susan Grace*

When her father stood up, Sean O'Banyon took his place. "Well, little girl, 'tis good to see your bright eyes twinkling at me. Your papa and I have come to an understanding. We've decided to share you." He stroked her cheek with his fingertips. "You may be a Carlisle, but you'll always be an O'Banyon, as well. Your mam is waiting in Chatham to see you. She thought you and Victoria were worth risking a voyage for. I imagine she's pledged enough novenas to keep her on her knees for quite some time." Bending down, he kissed her cheek. "I love you, little girl."

Catherine touched his beard. "I love you, too, Da."

As Sean stepped back, Colin leaned over to kiss her cheek. " 'Tis good seeing you, little sister. You gave us quite a turn. I'm glad you're back with us—though I must admit I never missed your bossing me about. Victoria did that for you."

Colin's smiling face was replaced by that of her serious protector, Padraic. "I'm not much for fancy words, Cat, but know how very glad I am to have you back. The crew send their best and wish you a speedy recovery, Captain."

"Why, Padraic, aren't you going to kiss me, too?" Catherine teased. "Before I became your captain, you were the best Uncle Paddy any girl could have."

His ruddy cheeks flushing, he kissed her brow. "Bless ye, Cat."

Then it was Justin's turn. Before he could speak, Catherine pointed at him and laughed softly. "I just realized you were the man in my dreams with Victoria. Oh, Justin, had I known Victoria was with you, I never would have worried. Thank you for making her so happy."

Justin kissed her hand. "Your sister has made me happy, Cat. We'll have plenty of time to talk later on. I want you to get some rest." He leaned down to kiss her cheek and whispered close to her ear, "The babe seems to be fine. If you take proper care of yourself, you'll deliver a healthy child before winter, Lady Cat."

Tears welled in her eyes. "Thank you, Justin, for everything, but especially for that."

Gazing up at Miles, Catherine wished she could find a gentle way of dismissing the rest of her well-meaning visitors so she could speak with him in private. Her sister came to her rescue.

Victoria turned to Sean, Colin, and Padraic. "Excuse me, gentlemen, but if you're all here, who's sailing this ship? I certainly hope you didn't leave Emmet at the wheel. He's a very nice young man, but he has the worst sense of direction I've ever encountered. Do you know he thought France was west of Ireland?"

Catherine laughed as Padraic and the O'Banyons suddenly said good night and hurried from the cabin.

Victoria put her arm around her father. "Papa, it's well after one in the morning. If Lucy ever found out, she'd take me to task. Kiss me and Catherine good night and we'll see you in the morning."

Geoffrey reluctantly did as she suggested and was walking toward the door when he seemed to figure out what she was doing. With a wry smile, he left the cabin.

"Well, Justin, how would you like to take your wife to bed? I swear I could sleep standing up." Victoria let out a dramatic yawn. "Good night, Miles. Very pleasant dreams, Catherine."

Justin put his arm around her and they took their leave.

When the door closed behind them, Miles sat on the bed and took hold of Catherine's hands. Bringing them to his lips, he kissed them. "Thanks to Victoria, I finally have you all to myself. One father is bad enough, but I had to fall in love with a lady who has two fathers, a brawny guardian, and two brothers. Not to mention my two best friends, who are also totally enamored of you. I'm just grateful they aren't here with Rory, or you and I would never be alone." Leaning forward, he put a soft kiss on her lips.

Catherine cradled his face with her hands. "Miles, I'm not made of spun glass, you know. Could you lie down beside me and hold me, please? I may have been wounded, but I need to be in your arms tonight."

"You've just had surgery. I don't want to hurt you."

"Then you'll be very careful," she countered.

His brow rose. "But what will your father and the others think?"

"I don't care. Our weeks apart have shown me how much I love you. I need to be with you tonight, Miles. Please don't refuse me this request."

"Never, my love." Miles removed his clothes, turned down the lanterns to a dim glow, and joined her on the bed. Propping himself up with pillows, he held her gently in his arms, cautiously avoiding her bandaged midriff. "Enough talk, my love. It's time for you to go to sleep."

With her head on his shoulder, Catherine sighed. "Miles, I need to tell you something first, but I'm not sure you're going to be happy about it." She timidly whispered her announcement. "I, ah, well . . . we're going to have a baby."

Miles tilted her chin with his hand and turned to face up to him. "How could I not be happy about that? This child was conceived in love, the love we have for one another. If they gauge the amount of love we share by the number of children we have, be prepared for a very large family, my darling. I love you very, very much."

"But what will your parents think? We're not married and—"

He put a quick kiss on her lips to stop her words. "We're going to be married as soon as it can be arranged. As a matter of fact, your father was hoping we might consider making it a double wedding with Victoria and Justin. We all talked about it while you were sleeping. Geoffrey thinks the *ton* would be so caught up in the excitement caused by such a spectacular event they wouldn't have time to question the sudden and mysterious arrival of his long-lost daughter. The final decision is up to you, my love. Will it be the social event of the season, or do I kidnap you for a trip to Gretna Green?''

Hearing the teasing tone in his voice, Catherine smiled. "A double wedding would be lovely. After missing out so many things with my sister during our time apart, sharing this special day with her seems the perfect thing to do. Poor Papa is going to spend a fortune."

"Your father can well afford it. He's even decided on our wedding gifts. Justin and Victoria are getting the Westlake Estate in Sussex, while you and I are receiving Fellsmere Manor in Ireland. I told Geoffrey he was being far too generous, but he refused to change his mind." Miles frowned. "With all this talk about gifts and the big wedding for us, I just recalled something else Geoffrey said. I wonder what he meant."

"Well, what did he say?"

"That a double wedding would get people's attention, but a triple ceremony would keep the old crones of the *ton* buzzing for years with excitement. Who'd be the third couple?"

Stifling a yawn, Catherine smiled. "Papa and Lucy. The two of them are crazy about each other. I'm glad my father has found someone to love. He deserves to be happy, too."

Miles kissed her brow and drew her down against him. "Enough talk for now. Close your eyes and go to sleep. I want you fully recovered and back on your feet in time for our wedding."

"All right." She rubbed her cheek on his chest and closed her eyes. "I forgot to tell you, Miles. Papa said twins run in the family. Do you think . . . we will . . . have . . . twins . . . too . . ."

Catherine's voice faded to a husky whisper. From the slow, even way she was breathing, Miles knew she was asleep. His reply would have to wait, but he didn't mind.

There would be plenty of time to talk. They had the rest of their lives ahead of them. And if God was just, He'd give them fifty or sixty years together.

Cuddling Catherine against him, Miles shut his eyes and, for the first time in weeks, fell into a peaceful sleep.

Dear Reader,

When I first wrote DESTINY'S LADY, everyone who read it asked me the same question: *"Did the lady outlaw and the nobleman really live happily ever after?"* To answer them, I wrote FOREVER AND BEYOND which will be released in October 2000 by Kensington Publishing as a Zebra historical romance.

Three years have passed and Catherine and Miles Grayson seem to have the perfect life. But when they're tragically separated by the treachery of others, Catherine is blackmailed with her notorious past to spy in France for the British War Department. Wanting to protect her family, she goes to Paris as Lady Cat and becomes the endangered pawn of Napoleon Bonaparte and his "spy master," Joseph Fouche. But thanks to the help of an orphan of the revolution and a love that is truly meant to last forever and beyond, Catherine learns that happy endings aren't confined to fairy tales.

I love hearing from my readers. If you'd like a bookmark and a copy of my latest newsletter, send an SASE to me at: P.O. Box 16434, West Palm Beach, FL 33409

Yours always
Susan Grace

LOVE STORIES YOU'LL NEVER FORGET . . .
IN ONE FABULOUSLY ROMANTIC NEW LINE

BALLAD ROMANCES

Each month, four new historical series by both beloved and brand-new authors will begin or continue. These linked stories will introduce proud families, reveal ancient promises, and take us down the path to true love. In Ballad, the romance doesn't end with just one book . . .

COMING IN JULY
EVERYWHERE BOOKS ARE SOLD

The Wishing Well Trilogy:
CATHERINE'S WISH, by Joy Reed.
When a woman looks into the wishing well at Honeywell House, she sees the face of the man she will marry.

Titled Texans:
NOBILITY RANCH, by Cynthia Sterling
The three sons of an English earl come to Texas in the 1880s to find their fortunes . . . and lose their hearts.

Irish Blessing:
REILLY'S LAW, by Elizabeth Keys
For an Irish family of shipbuilders, an ancient gift allows them to "see" their perfect mate.

The Acadians:
EMILIE, by Cherie Claire
The daughters of an Acadian exile struggle for new lives in 18th-century Louisiana.

Put a Little Romance in Your Life With
Constance O'Day-Flannery

__**Bewitched** $5.99US/$7.50CAN
    0-8217-6126-9

__**The Gift** $5.99US/$7.50CAN
    0-8217-5916-7

__**Once in a Lifetime** $5.99US/$7.50CAN
    0-8217-5918-3

__**Second Chances** $5.99US/$7.50CAN
    0-8217-5917-5

—**This Time Forever** $5.99US/$7.50CAN
    0-8217-5964-7

__**Time-Kept Promises** $5.99US/$7.50CAN
    0-8217-5963-9

__**Time-Kissed Destiny** $5.99US/$7.50CAN
    0-8217-5962-0

__**Timeless Passion** $5.99US/$7.50CAN
    0-8217-5959-0

Call toll free **1-888-345-BOOK** to order by phone, use this coupon to order by mail, or order online at **www.kensingtonbooks.com.**

Name _____

Address _____

City_____ State _____ Zip _____

Please send me the books I have checked above.

I am enclosing $_____

Plus postage and handling* $_____

Sales tax (in New York and Tennessee only) $_____

Total amount enclosed $_____

*Add $2.50 for the first book and $.50 for each additional book.

Send check or money order (no cash or CODs) to:

Kensington Publishing Corp., Dept C.O., 850 Third Avenue, 16th Floor, New York, NY 10022

Prices and numbers subject to change without notice.

All orders subject to availability.

Visit our website at **www.kensingtonbooks.com.**